COLD, DARK, AND SILENT

DAVID C. REED

Library of Congress Control Number: 2024919817

Publishing Coordinator – Sharon Kizziah-Holmes
Cover Design – Jaycee DeLorenzo

Paperback-Press
an imprint of A & S Publishing
Paperback Press, LLC
Springfield, Missouri

ISBN 978-1-964559-20-9 (Paperback)
ISBN 978-1-964559-21-6 (Hardback)
ISBN 978-1-964559-22-3 (eBook)

DEDICATION

This is for my children, Savannah and Caroline
~ who always listened as I spun my stories.
But mostly for my loving and patient wife, Audrey
~you give me wings and the clearance to fly.

CHAPTER 1

The world had stopped making sense and at every turn life was confusing. People didn't know what to do, what was open, or who to trust. Everything was on hold, so everybody was on hold. They locked down their lives like the people on TV told them to.

But in this early autumn, stores and some restaurants gradually began to reopen. Ashe was sitting in his car outside a locally popular café in his small hometown. He watched the windshield wipers work in the slow, steady drizzle as he considered whether to go inside. His desire for some hot coffee, human conversation, and fresh food made up his mind. Unsure of the new rules, he grabbed a face mask hanging from his rearview mirror and darted through the rain toward the café door, trying not to get wet. At his age, he didn't want to catch anything even resembling a cold, much less the virus.

It felt good but a little strange to be there after the lockdown. This was the first time in months he'd actually been inside a business. His groceries and take-out meals had been curbside and touchless.

The radio said that businesses in the small lakeshore town of Seacord could open on a trial basis, so he pushed open the big glass door and stepped in.

"Chig!" a familiar woman's voice shouted his childhood nickname.

"Tilly!" he answered. She'd waited tables there at Roger's Café since they were both in high school.

"How are you and how is your family? I hope you haven't been sick," he said through his medical mask.

"Oh, I'm good. Hey...you don't have to wear a mask now unless you want to."

Ashe removed it and breathed in the delicious smell of coffee, hamburgers, and all-day breakfast cooking.

"God, I don't mind admitting I've missed that smell," he said. Ashe took off his coat and looked over the café. It was a medium-sized storefront place with booths and counter seats that could hold maybe twenty-five people. There wasn't a corner here that didn't hold a memory for him.

"Please, come sit over here in my section. We only have every other table open this week." She smiled broadly at Ashe. There were only a couple of other customers seated and they were carefully spaced apart.

"So, everybody says you've moved back home now for good, at your daddy's place again, huh?" she said.

"It's my place now, Tilly. Coffee?"

"You bet," she said as she walked a bit briskly toward the counter. She looked back and smiled at him again.

Ashe watched her as she walked off and thought how good it felt to see her. She didn't seem to have changed much in forty years. She'd added a few pounds, perhaps there was a touch of gray here and there left un-tinted. Older of course, but still an attractive woman and obviously kept herself in shape.

He then caught his own reflection in a polished steel napkin holder as he sat and was surprised to see his own grandfather looking back at him.

I have possibly not kept myself up so well during the lockdown.

Ashe shook his head to himself. Time to go back to running, which had been his default workout since his Army days. At six foot and 175 pounds, he was used to looking trim, clean-shaven, and being in good shape. Now, according to this napkin holder, he'd shrunk and appeared to resemble someone somewhere between the Unabomber and a bridge troll.

She returned with the pot and an old heavy ceramic cup. "I was thinking of you the other day, boy," she said as she filled his cup. She leaned a knee into his side of his booth. "I was wondering when we'd get to catch up?"

"Well, it's been pretty…complex lately."

She nodded. "Amen. God awful is what it is. Well, I'm just happy to have you back here."

Ashe smiled as she filled his cup. "Me too, Tilly. You remarried

Tommy, right?"

"Oh…yep. I guess that was before your dad…you know."

"Died. Hey, I'm happy for you though. These are no times to be alone, Till."

Roger Clancy, the owner of the café, poked his head from around the kitchen door and waved at Ashe. He stripped off his apron and wiped his hands on a rag as he walked over. To Ashe, he never seemed to age, just slow down. He was shorter and a bit more rotund, it seemed, but Ashe had always heard that he'd been a boxer in the Army many years before. That kind of tough didn't just go away.

Tilly reached over and tugged at Ashe's ear. "I guess *you* were all alone though. In that big old house by yourself. I don't reckon your lawyer girlfriend was there."

Ashe looked up, a little surprised. "It's not that big…and just how do you know?"

"Huh! I work at Seacord Central here. I know everything. Oh, I guess Roger wants to talk to you," Tilly said.

"Then I better order quick," Ashe replied. "Two eggs…"

"Over hard, bacon, grits, and wheat toast," Tilly finished for him, grinning. "I've fixed that for you myself a time or two."

"I remember," Ashe said as Roger slid into the booth seat opposite him. Then to Roger, Ashe said, "There was an ambulance involved right after."

Tilly glared at Ashe as Roger chuckled. She popped Ashe on top of the head with the menu.

"Smart-assed as ever, boy!" she said and winked as she went to put in the order.

Roger stuck out his hand toward Ashe then seemed to think better of it and changed it to a fist bump, then paused at that. Ashe just reached out and took his hand and shook it, to Roger's obvious relief.

"Just got used to not doing that. Now we supposedly can, I forgot how," Roger said.

"I know, hopefully it'll come back to us all. Anyway, your waitress with minor anger management issues said you wanted to talk to me."

"Well," Roger started and then noticed Ashe's coffee cup. He popped up, went and got one for himself, and returned to the booth. "Retired now from Metro Detectives, right? Living at your dad's?"

Ashe raised his cup in a small salute. "In order, I'm divorced, retired from Metro, moved back here, and now living in what is *my* family house. And as of now, glad to have coffee other than my own."

"These days that's not nothing," Roger said. "You seen Stevie yet?" he asked. "She's been a good curbside customer."

"No. I have not." Ashe hadn't seen Stephanie Collins in over a month, and then only at a distance. Their breakup was four months ago just before the lockdowns.

"I guess we all figured she'd maybe stay with you during the Covid."

Ashe shifted some in his seat and sipped his coffee. "Roger, I offered. She preferred to stay on her own."

"Hey, sorry. None of my business, I guess. Just a lot of people didn't think she should be alone and locked down and all."

Just then, Tilly arrived with more coffee. "None of mine either but she was *way* too young for a man your age if you ask me, Chig."

"Well, nobody asked you, Till!" Roger said and jerked his thumb over his shoulder for her to get back behind the counter.

"Well, she is too young," Tilly added and glared at her boss.

"Was I supposed to feel bad about that?" Ashe said, smiling over the rim of his coffee cup.

"I know how damn old you are and I don't know her age but I bet she's at least thirty years…"

"Only twenty," Ashe interrupted.

"Oh, fried bull hockey," Till said.

"Speaking of *fried bull hockey*…my breakfast?"

"Hey!" Roger said defensively to Ashe then again motioned to Tilly. "I'm having a private conversation, here!"

Tilly spun and looked back at Ashe, rolling her eyes.

After she left, Roger shrugged and said, "Again, none of our business. But she shouldn't be alone."

Ashe knew what Roger was insinuating. It had been a poorly kept secret, only discussed in quiet tones around town for well over a year. Since her husband had left her, Stevie's drinking issues had become more obvious.

Ashe moved back to town to take care of his father and, not knowing any of this, he hired her to set up an estate and legal guardianship. They worked late one night and over drinks, a *lot* of drinks, their affair had started.

A month later, it ended badly.

"Hey, Chig," Roger said. "There is something else. Do you know our new sheriff?"

Tilly brought his breakfast then lingered at the table. Roger again motioned her away. Annoyed, she walked off.

"From here? No. He's a Jacobs, right? I don't guess I've ever met him." Ashe started in on his breakfast.

"Well, he knew your dad and he knows you by reputation. He's been wanting to talk to you, but this stuff with the Covid and all."

"What about?"

"What about? I'm not actually sure," Roger said. "But, hey. He's right over there."

Ashe shrugged. It was likely nothing. The sheriff probably just wanted to pay his respects since it seemed everyone in town knew his dad or had a story about him. Covid had shut down public funerals, especially right at the start of the closings, and a lot of Hurrt County that would have shown up simply couldn't.

"It's okay. Send Tilly out with some water and more coffee first please."

Roger nodded and went and spoke to a man in uniform that had just sat down. Ashe looked at himself in the reflective napkin holder again and huffed at his image. His beard was wilder, and longer than he thought. At least his hair was combed. Both were much grayer than just a short time ago.

Geez, Ashe, you could've at least straightened up a bit.

While Roger and the sheriff talked, Ashe looked around the restaurant and noticed a new face at another table. It was a man with longer, dark hair and a full beard. Both were styled well. This was a man Ashe didn't recognize, but given that not long after returning to Seacord the lockdowns had started, he didn't think that was unusual.

What was unusual was how the man stared at him then smiled. There was nothing friendly in the smile though, so Ashe thought perhaps he was contemptuous of his disheveled appearance.

Roger brought the sheriff over to his table, so Ashe stood up to shake his hand.

"Hey, Mr. Ashe, I'm Sheriff Jacobs," he said.

"Sheriff," Ashe said and took his hand. He had big calloused hands with a few age spots and his deeply creased face looked like worn leather.

"Hey, I appreciate you taking the time to meet with me," Jacobs said.

Ashe had worked with a dozen or so sheriffs and police chiefs in the towns and counties that had surrounded Metro. This Sheriff Jacobs was feeling him out.

"No problem, please have a seat. How can I help the HCSO?"

"Um, how have you been? You done all right? I know this shutdown's been rough on a lot of folks…on all of us."

Ashe realized the sheriff was looking at him and not seeing what he'd expected.

"I'm fine, really. Maybe a haircut when they open back up."

Jacobs smiled. "Yeah, me and you both. Uh, you go by Chig, or Chigger, don't you?"

Ashe held in the long sigh he wanted to release. "Chig was a childhood nickname and my dad…"

"Oh hey, I am so sorry. I knew your dad back in the day. Really, really good man."

"Thanks, and yes he was."

"I'm sorry if I brought up, well, if I made you think of your dad again."

"No problem. I think of him and Mom every day. Anyway, Sheriff, I prefer Ashe. It's what all my adult friends call me."

"Okay, Ashe."

Jacobs looked at his hands for a long beat as if he was figuring out how to say something. Maybe to stall, he turned and made a motion like sipping coffee in the air toward Tilly.

She snatched up a pot and all but jogged over to bring him a cup.

Seacord Central, Ashe thought.

As Jacobs fixed his coffee and they waited for the lingering Tilly to leave, Ashe took another look at him. He was older than Ashe expected.

Especially for such a newly elected official. An end-of-career job? Or maybe a last chance to do what he'd always wanted by being a sheriff.

After Tilly was out of earshot, Ashe spread his hands wide on the table.

"Sheriff?"

"Oh. Yeah, I guess so, sure. Down to the business at hand. There's an old case from here, but you weren't living here at the time. You remember a missing woman named Georgia Murphy?"

"No," Ashe said.

"Lived in the Calvary Hills area. Worked as some kind of secretary or clerk with Hurrt Land and Title. About two years ago, she just up and disappeared. No call, no note, no cell phone record."

"No, I can't say as I do recall that."

"Husband Murphy was a piece of work. Lived up in Metro. Had a little of jail time here and a lot in Metro. They tried hard to hang this as a murder on him... You sure none of this rings a bell?"

Ashe thought for a second longer then something popped up from the back of his mind.

"Tony Murphy?"

"Yeah. That's the husband. Anyway, Sheriff Laughton, the guy I replaced when he retired, always said it was a killing and it happened *here*. But the assistant DA at the time gave the case to Metro because the ADA *there* said he had evidence an actual murder happened up there."

"I was the Chief of Major Crimes in Metro. This would have come to me." But Ashe couldn't remember much about it.

"Yeah, well it did. A big detective came down and questioned everybody here. Took the case file and left."

"Two years ago, you say? It would have been Pat Keagan."

"Keagan," Jacobs said to himself.

"Big Irish guy. Little ears for his size. Fingers like sausages."

"That's the guy."

"I was his boss. Before that, we were partners."

"That's why I wanted to talk to you, Chi-uh, Ashe. I figured you ran this case up there in the city."

Ashe started thinking hard and he hated where his thoughts led him. Two years ago. His dad was doing poorly and his divorce, although messy, had been over almost a year by then.

"Remind me, then, what eventually happened?"

Jacobs scoffed and shook his head. "Nothing. Nada. Tony Murphy is in the state pen on an aggravated robbery charge out of Metro but nothing has happened with Georgia Murphy's disappearance."

"Keagan never made an arrest."

"Oh, 'insufficient evidence' is all we've ever gotten out of them. 'Case is still open,' they say."

Ashe sat back in the café booth hard. Was it possible he'd been so distracted? This would have happened at the worst possible time for him personally. But to have not been engaged properly in his job; he shook his head, angry at himself.

"So, what can I do now, Sheriff?"

"Well, I was hoping you could…"

Then Jacobs slowly looked Ashe up and down again. The look in his eyes told Ashe all he needed to know. He'd gone to seed. The answer to Ashe's question to the man was obvious.

Nothing. Jacobs doesn't think I can do anything now.

"Why here if it's in Metro's legal venue?" Ashe asked to keep Jacobs going. "Why Hurrt County S.O.?"

"Because I was around when this happened. I wasn't sheriff but I was around. I think this case ran a good man, Jack Laughton, to retire a little early. When I won the election, there was one case he wanted to talk to me about. Just one."

"This Georgia Murphy case."

"Yeah. Look, it ate at him. Sheriff Laughton never believed that bullshit from the ADA about Metro having jurisdiction. He was certain whatever happened, happened *here*. In Hurrt County."

"So with no corpse to say otherwise and the fact Metro Homicide never made a case, just fuels the idea there's nothing up *there* to prove her disappearance or death occurred up there."

"Well, I'm not accusing anybody of anything, but it sure seems like this was sent out of this county just for that reason. To die."

Ashe bristled a bit at that. He was from here but worked twenty-five years in Metro. If anything, he would be sure to take special care of a hometown-referred case.

Except I hadn't.

"Ok. So why discuss it with me now? I've been here since just before the shutdowns and you've been in office all that time."

Jacobs took a long drag from his coffee. "Because frankly, I figured if there was something fishy going on, maybe you must have had a part of it."

"Now hang on, Sheriff…"

"But," Jacobs interrupted. He held up his palms and said, "Everybody, and I mean everybody, tells me I'm crazy for thinking that."

Ashe was still a bit warm under the collar. "But I'm guessing you're out of options."

"Yeah. It's been a dead end. Look, I'm sorry for dragging all this up with you. You…look like you got enough on your plate without all this. I mean, uh, you're retired now and all."

"Yes. I am."

Jacobs stood and fished some change out of his pocket for a tip. "I'll be in touch, Ashe, if I have any specific questions. Again, sorry."

Ashe stood as well and caught his reflection again. Old. Disheveled.

He'd gotten a little pissed at the inference he'd either been incompetent or involved in covering up a woman's disappearance and possible murder until he realized, how else could local authorities see it? Had he been so emotionally distracted back then that he'd passed the case off and never looked back? Yes?

Yes.

"Sheriff?"

"Yeah?"

"Let me make some calls. Let me quietly poke around a bit."

"Look, you don't have to…"

"Yes, I do."

Jacobs looked at Ashe for a long beat.

"Okay. You go get that…uh, haircut and come see me tomorrow."

"And, Sheriff, *I'm* telling you, not *everybody* telling you, just me. I had nothing to do with burying this case."

CHAPTER 2

Five months ago

Ashe turned off the main highway and onto a tree-lined county road in a rented convertible with Stevie. He wanted to get her away from the legal papers and office work and have her all to himself today. With the top down, the smells of pine trees blended with burning leaves and fresh mowed hay. She smiled and laughed a lot which washed through him like the sun on his face and wind all around them, so he took the long way home from the restaurant.

"So, as my lawyer, should you be drinking that wine here in the car?" he teased.

"Just don't get pulled over," she answered and reclined her seat far back enough to lean back from behind her seat belt.

She wore a pair of dress shorts designed to look like a skirt, and a dressy white blouse as he'd picked her up from her office early to play hooky. Once they'd left the restaurant, she had slid out of her shoes and propped her tan and pretty feet out on the rearview mirror as the wind blew her hair across her face. She reached into her huge shoulder bag and pulled out an open bottle of wine.

"You?" she asked and gestured toward him with the bottle.

"Nuh-uh. Driving, honey," he said, smiling. They had already gone through two bottles at the restaurant but he'd only had a couple of glasses himself.

She shrugged and started to fill a red plastic cup sitting in the console, spilling a little as he went around a curve. She recapped the bottle and took out an apple to eat.

"You haven't said anything lately about your dad," she said and took a huge bite out of the apple.

"Not much to say, I guess. He's depressed, pretty much aware of his condition and his prognosis," Ashe said. "I need to call tonight or tomorrow."

"Have you told him about me?" she said and smiled, still munching on the apple.

"Not yet. He still thinks I'm going to get back with my ex. He refers to us as 'separated' still."

"You've been single almost two years! She's remarried, right?"

"Yeah, she is. So, I let Dad have that, I guess. At his age, it's easier not to aggravate or confuse him."

Ashe decided to not call but to drive over in the morning. Then he decided to change the subject to reclaim their happier mood.

He was driving a convertible sports car he'd rented for the occasion, had the top down and was with a gorgeous woman who liked to laugh and drink and have fun. It was precisely what he needed to bring some light back into his darkening life.

And it didn't hurt that her tan legs propped up on the car door brought back the wonder and the nervous excitement of his youth. A little electric vibration ran from his gut to his throat when he looked at her and listened to her. When she laughed, her whole body convulsed. And she laughed often, loudly, without reservation.

Sometime between the leaving the restaurant and where they were, she had unbuttoned the top two buttons on her blouse. Laying back in her reclined seat, he could see her chest and admire her neck and a little of her shoulder. The vibration became a longing inside him.

I'm going to make love to her.

She saw him watching and smiled mischievously. He hoped she was thinking the same thing.

Stevie sat up to down a good deal of her wine then casually tossed her apple core out the window.

"Litterbug," he said, grinning.

"It's not littering, it's only an apple core."

"Hey, Counselor, whatever you say, but if it's tossed from a car most say that's littering," he teased.

"Oh, come on. It's all natural. It's bio-degradable." She hadn't caught on he was messing with her.

"So, your napkin. You throwing that out too?"

"Don't be a pest! Of course not..." She suddenly seemed to

catch on. "But I could."

"Because it's bio-degradable?"

"Yes," she said.

Ashe drove on for a few minutes in silence, giving her time to let her guard down.

"So, say we had a dead dog in the car…"

"Oh my God, Ashe!" she yelled.

"Bio-degradable."

"You are such an ass! It was just an apple core!"

"Sacks of office paper, steel scrap. All will eventually…"

"Just shut up, *Chig*," she said, feigning irritation.

"You know I do not prefer you call me that."

"Chig! Chig! Chigger Bug, Chigger Bug!" she shouted and reached over to tickle him.

A smile spread across his face so broad it hurt. He couldn't stop it even if he wanted to. She tried unsuccessfully to smooth back her hair from her face as she pulled out the wine again to refill her cup. He saw that she couldn't help herself from smiling too.

Yes, I want to make love to her and see that smile a lot more.

Four months ago

The local stations and the internet said that businesses were closing and that only a few essential stores were remaining open. Schools and daycares, churches and public facilities were shutting down to stop the spread. Ashe was in town to get some final stuff he'd need and went to see his lawyer and girlfriend at her law office where he assumed she'd be at eleven a.m. He was coming to suggest what he thought was a great idea.

"Jesus! How can he be so cruel?" Stevie cried to him as he walked in. Her sudden outburst caught him off guard. He'd expected to see her receptionist but instead had run into a crisis of some sort.

Stevie, through jags of crying and broken sentences, explained a note she held that her ex had left for her at her daughter's school. Ashe took it and read it. It was short and blunt.

Her ex-husband was taking their daughter back with him to the city. Immediately. He wrote he was doing this so that the nine-year-old would be better taken care of and wouldn't be sheltering during the pandemic with a drunk. He had underlined *drunk*. He'd all but dared her to take him to court.

Ashe had never met the man. The divorce was final before he'd returned to Seacord. According to people, he had worked in Metro as a successful engineer and had initially been home most evenings despite the long commute. But fewer and fewer as time passed. Then the divorce.

"I...don't know," Ashe said to her as he walked into her inner office, looking around for the first time at the chaos in the room. It was barely the middle of the day and there was already the faint aura of alcohol about her.

She wailed openly and nonstop. Her pretty face red and sloppy as she walked around in circles in her office. She was stumbling and tripping over boxes of work papers and personal belongings. She was wearing a white, professional-looking but feminine blouse and a short black wool skirt. She was walking around the room barefooted. Her long hair had come undone.

Her once-classy green leather and brass-buttoned sofa was being used as a bed. A lot of her and her daughter's clothes were hanging from doorknobs and from hooks over the doors. A haphazard collection of boxes was scattered across the floor and on furniture. Clothes and personal belongings, hers and her daughter's, all mixed with piles of work papers and legal pads.

"Christ, you living here now, Stevie?"

It was worse than he'd known. Her drinking had been fun and sexy at first, but seeing this, her office, was shocking. He'd been busy the past couple of weeks after his dad's funeral, handling things, and hadn't had time to be with her.

"I -want-my-baby!" she cried, her voice hitching and mournful.

"Whoa, honey. Here, here," he said.

Ashe moved to her and took her in his arms then slowly moved her over to the sofa. He kicked a box of her stuff off one end of it with his foot, not wanting to let go of her, and sat her down.

"Let me get you a water. Just, stay still."

"I...want..." she started but didn't finish.

"I know, sweetheart. I know you do."

He went to the office's private bathroom. Makeup and curling irons were crowded on the small sink. Hose hung from the back of the door. He found a water glass and smelled it. Vodka. He rinsed it as best he could and took her the water.

She took a small sip and nodded.

"Try to sit back some and take deep breaths."

She closed her eyes and flopped over onto her blanket to cry more.

Ashe took the glass from her before she dumped it on the floor and looked around for a flat surface somewhere to set it that wasn't covered in clutter. He scooted some papers over on her desk to make room and a big pile fell to the floor.

He bent to pick them up and, having been a detective in Metro too long, couldn't stop himself from glancing at them.

A large manilla envelope from the State Board of Professional Responsibility had been torn open. It had been registered mail requiring her to sign for it.

He looked over at Stevie, feeling a little guilty, but her eyes were still tightly closed.

The cover letter said it all. She was to appear on a specified date to defend against allegations of professional misconduct and financial misappropriations. There were complaints that she had accepted funds from clients and not provided the services contracted for. She had not properly set up the required escrow accounts to hold then transfer monies for claims.

Other attorneys had also filed notices with the Board asking to investigate. Some were her friends. It ended with the admonition that she was constrained from taking new clients or filing any new actions until after the hearing.

His girlfriend was in bad trouble.

Ashe put the papers back on her desk. The TV in her office was on and the news was talking nonstop about the impact of the pandemic in Metro. He found the remote on the floor and switched it off.

"Stevie, honey, can you sit up?" He went and got a wet paper towel and sat beside her. He gently wiped her face with the towel.

She had stop crying and dug in her pockets for a tissue, wiping her nose.

"Better?" he asked. She nodded and looked into his eyes.

Ashe felt that hitch in his throat that he'd felt since first seeing her. Stephanie Collins was a young and intelligent woman. When she'd first opened her own small law office three years ago, she was the darling of the town. Older, more established firms threw work her way and treated her more like their little sister than a competitor.

It didn't hurt that she was stunningly beautiful as well. Her bright smile, big dark eyes, and chestnut hair had caught Ashe's attention on her one billboard in town. If he was honest with himself, it was why, lonely and divorced, he had made that first appointment. He hired her right away to navigate him through the myriads of legal entanglements an aging, departed parent and large financial estate mandated.

"You're a mess," he said to her, smiling. "You can't stay here by yourself. Just look at this place."

She seemed to obey him and looked around her office.

"They are calling for lockdowns to 'slow the spread' that will last three weeks. I'm guessing maybe more."

"I am going to get my daughter. I'm going to file for custody," she mumbled.

"You mean to live here? In your office?"

"With me!" she shouted.

"But, Stevie, you can't."

"I am going to," she said, straightening her hair with her hands. She popped up and went to the bathroom and closed the door behind her.

Ashe stepped over to the bathroom door. *Why is she living here instead of her apartment?* he wondered. But the answer became obvious. She had been putting up a brave front to him.

"Honey, I saw the papers," he said through the door. "The state says you can't do anything right now."

Silence.

"Plus, hell. You really shouldn't live here, with or without her."

There was no response from the bathroom.

"Look, I think I can help. I know a lot of people in Metro. Even quite a few lawyers. And, hey! I have a great plan!"

She slowly opened the door. She'd washed her face. Her eyes were clearer and focused on Ashe. *Is she pissed off at me?* he wondered by her look.

"Why don't you pack a few things and come stay with me, honey? It's a huge house, you could set up shop there. We could work on getting your daughter back together."

"Stay with you? Move in with you?"

"Yeah. How long is this lockdown stuff going to last, anyway?"

She stared at him and abruptly pushed past him, walking around the room as if looking for her cell phone. "Stay with you. Move in?" she repeated.

He turned and followed her with his eyes as she began more frantically to pick up, look under, then pitch aside whatever stuff was in her way.

"I could take care of you. We'd have each other."

She found what she was looking for. A small bottle of vodka.

Before he could even try to stop her, she'd opened the half-empty pint and swallowed half.

"Ah, dammit, Stevie!" He took a step and tried to grab it, but she jerked her arm back and glared furiously at him.

"No! You go home!"

"I'm just trying to…"

"I do not need any help!"

"C'mon, Stevie, please!" He kept trying to get the bottle out of her hand, but she waved it about out of reach.

"Get out!"

He caught her by the waist and wrestled a little as he tried to take the bottle.

"Let me take you with me to…just give me that!"

"Fuck off, you stupid old man!"

He stopped at that. It felt as if she'd slapped him dead in the face.

"You think I'd come live with you?" she shouted. "You think I'd pick living with you? Shit! I could've done that before I moved in here!"

"I am on your side! Christ help me, but I think, despite all this, I…"

"You think I give a shit what you think? I don't need some useless old man, some dusty, dried-up old…old…you! All the time following me around, all the time nagging at me, hovering over me…"

"Yes, you do! C'mon, you're a wreck!" he said angrily. He was starting to feel his back and neck tighten up.

"You go to hell, Ashe!" She lifted the bottle and took another drink. Slowly, defiantly.

He stepped over to her desk and picked up the legal papers off her desk and waved them at her.

"You first, Stevie! You think *this* is just going away?"

He picked up Michael's note. "Or *this*?"

She glared at him and pointed the bottle at him.

"Now," he interrupted whatever she was about to say, "before you say anything else nasty to me, you need to get it through your damn head that I want to help you. Your damn stupid drinking is what is causing all of this. Let me help you. Come stay with me!"

She drew in a deep breath, capped the bottle, straightened her skirt and blouse, then pulled her hair back.

"Please?" he said.

"You need to leave, Ashe. I've been thinking about this for a while anyway. We are definitely done. You are way too damn old for me. Everybody is laughing." She turned her head and would not meet his eyes.

"You're an alcoholic, Stephanie."

"You're a joke. Get out. Do not come back."

Ashe stepped toward her but she moved away.

"I'm your last friend, I can…"

"Ha!" she shouted.

Ashe moved to the outer office area and opened her office door. Before leaving he said, "Please, for your daughter, for yourself. Get some professional help."

"Fuck off," she answered.

He started out but paused halfway through the door.

"Oh, and, Ms. Collins. You're fired."

CHAPTER 3

Present day

Ashe pulled up to the barbershop and parked right outside the door. It was closed, but from the sign they'd reopen at 9:30 a.m., which left him with twenty minutes.

He figured this gave him some time to think. He poked around his old Jeep Cherokee for a pad and pen but didn't find anything useful. The pen over his visor had leaked out, causing a stain. Damn. He preferred to write things down because his memory wasn't what it used to be.

Note to self, get out your old leather portfolio and start wearing a pen again.

The rain made it a little cool, so he kept his engine running but shut off the wipers. He took a breath to relax and let his thoughts come.

In his past job, where so much static came at him from all corners, jet-propelled and tagged with "immediate action required," it was easy to get overwhelmed. Everything was a priority until thirty minutes later when new priorities arrived. Computers and smartphones compounded the overload.

Ashe had learned to close his office door, deep breathe, and just relax his head. Fifteen minutes of solitude would often allow him to hear his inner voice tell him what he needed to hear. So, he decided to try it while waiting on his barber.

At first, just random everyday trash surfaced, but he knew to relax past all that. Another breath. *Try not to think in words. Go for blank. Don't force it.*

Stevie's face, smiling at him. *Happier times.* He shook his head. No time for that.

Why had I not paid better attention to Georgia Murphy's case?

That popped his eyes open. His dad at the time was dying and he was trying to set up hospice care. Ashe was divorced and it had not been his idea, but it was likely a good deal his fault. Those thoughts brought up buried emotions.

Excuses. So why hadn't I dug into the case to occupy my mind?

As Chief of Major Crimes Unit, Ashe knew he didn't personally investigate many cases but managed the assignments. A fact his boss often reminded him of. He was to manage and oversee multiple investigations, not be over occupied as lead on any one case.

Keagan

He'd assigned his best investigator, Pat Keagan, who had been his partner for five years. He wouldn't bury a missing person case and certainly not a potential homicide. Pat lived for the hunt. He was a bit of a brute, huge and old-school tough, but way smarter than people's initial impression. The big Irishman had carried Ashe personally through more than one hard time, and he had returned the favor when Keagan's son had died in Iraq. They were partners.

More than that, we are brothers.

Ashe breathed deeply again and closed his eyes. The two years were an eternity ago. There must had been eight or so open homicides at the time, and sadly, dozens of missing person cases. But this came from here. Home.

He'd assigned Pat Keagan.

No. Keagan had *asked for it*. He had asked Ashe for the case.

"Hey, Chig," Keagan said. *"Maybe you want to work this yourself but you have evals to write, case reports, and the budget to get done. I know shit's gotten real for you lately. I'll have a look at this and let you know what I find."*

His eyes popped open. Ashe really wished for something to write with. A hundred questions flooded his mind.

"Hey!" the barber said, startling Ashe for a second. He was tapping on Ashe's driver's side window.

"We're reopening! Come on in, you'll be the first haircut in a couple of months."

"I'll be back!" Ashe said through the glass, and threw the old Jeep into reverse.

He had to get to a notepad and phone quick.

At home, he stripped off his raincoat and hat and hung them on the large, mirrored deacon's seat in the red-tile foyer. Kicking off his wet shoes, he walked sock-footed into the house. It was a little different to him from what he'd known his whole life growing up here, but the changes made to update the old place during the lockdown were his.

It's mine now. I have made it mine.

He moved to what had been his dad's—his—office. Along one wall of the big, high-ceilinged room were banker type boxes neatly stacked and marked. Ashe ignored those as they contained his dad's papers and documents. The opposite wall held a few of the same type boxes. This is what Ashe was looking for. *His* papers and notes from Metro.

He selected a box with the right date range and brought it to his desk. Then picked up the old wired phone on the desk, as cell service was sketchy here. The number he dialed he'd used a thousand times.

"Metro Homicide, this is Lois."

Ashe disguised his voice. "Excuse me, ma'am, I'm looking for a *real* detective."

She paused. She was falling for it. "I can connect you to the detective's office. What is this in reference to?"

"Oh, dear. It's a bad one. I need your *best* investigator."

She was calm as ever. "Sir, have you reported a crime already? Let me connect you with 911."

"But I need the *best* you have! Is Lieutenant Ashe available? He's the best…"

"Oh, for damn crying out loud, you piece of crap!" Lois shouted into the phone. "I cannot believe I fell for your stupid pranks after all this time…again!"

Ashe laughed and, from the sound of it, she dropped her headset on her desk.

"Hey, Lois…" he said, still laughing. "Lois? Hello?"

She came back on the line. "You don't even bother to text or come see me, then you pull this!"

"Sorry, lady. So, how are you?"

"Oh, do not ask me! I was a half second from starting a trace on this line, you rat!"

"When you collect yourself, I need a favor."

"I should tell you to jump sideways up my butt!" she said.

"But...you won't. It is really good to hear your voice again."

"Oh lordy-god, Ashe!" She was finally laughing. "First, tell me how is retirement?"

"I highly recommend it."

"I am still so sorry about Mr. Ashe."

"I got your card, thank you, that was nice. Retirement has had me renovating this old house while locked down. I completely tore out and put in a new kitchen. Redid the HVAC and floors in a lot of the rooms."

"I need to come see it. That is such a gorgeous place. Your granddaddy built it in the 1930's, didn't he?"

"Yeah. Then him and Dad re-did it in the 70's. But...about my favor."

"Oh, whatever! But okay."

"First, I need Pat to call me from his desk. Not out somewhere by cell. I need to ask him about an old case he worked, so I want him near his computer."

"Ok, sure. He's out now but I expect him in an hour or two."

"Good, now, this is the ticklish part. Do you still have access to my old computer calendar? Specifically, appointments."

Like all bosses and their admin people, they digitally shared computer calendars so she could keep him on time and insert appointments for him.

"Good question," Lois said. Ashe could hear her clicking away at her keyboard.

"Okay. Huh. So..." she whispered to herself.

Ashe opened his desk and took out his old brown leather portfolio. It had his initials embossed on the cover and had been a gift from his ex-wife in happier times.

"Let me see now," Lois continued to herself.

Opening the portfolio, Ashe went through the legal pad inside. He retrieved a pair of reading glasses from the top drawer. There were dozens of pages of old work notes and he flipped past them to get to a blank page. On the other side were notes stuffed into a fold, and in a pocket were his old Metro business cards.

"Got it. Yeah, I see some of your appointments because you

cc'ed me on them or included me or Pat in a meeting."

"Great!"

"What am I looking for?"

"Any mention of a Georgia Murphy case. It'd be about two years ago."

"Huh!" she said and stopped typing in the background.

"Why 'huh'?"

"Well, because Pat started asking about that case just yesterday. That's 'huh' for you."

Ashe felt a tingle run down his back, as if an icy finger traced a line along his spine.

"Yeah, okay. Well, good. He'll be up to speed for when he calls."

"Ashe. He never asked me about *your* calendar appointments though," she said.

He knew the tone. She wanted him to get what she was hinting at.

"I see."

"I have to be careful here, Ashe. This is listed as an open cold case."

"Yeah, well, Lois, I don't want you to compromise…"

She cut him off.

"But since you're just cleaning up your old calendar, I'll export *all of this* to a file and send it to you. You can look into it to see what you want."

Ashe made a mental note to hug her next time he saw her.

"Thank you," he said.

"I gotta go. The captain's here," she said and cut the connection.

Ashe hung up and sat at the desk a minute thinking. Hopefully there would be something in what Lois sent him that might explain what's what.

He wrote on the blank page in front of him.

One, search through the data Lois sends and isolate any mention of Hurrt County ADA, Georgia Murphy, or any missing woman going back two…no, three years.

He was assuming the two-year time frame that had been told to him by Sheriff Jacobs, but that could be off.

Two, anything to indicate I assigned Pat Keagan to the

investigation. Also, any follow-on appointments or updates from him. In other words, to verify his own recollection.

Even if the case was ongoing as he retired, he'd have had a "hot wash" meeting with all his sergeants and key investigators. If for no other reason than to set whoever was going to be his replacement up with a solid status on all pending cases.

Three, any calendar notes or anything that might explain why I'd not followed up with Pat on the case. Or if I had, what had been discussed.

Ashe couldn't think of anything else but left space on the page should he have a thought later.

Then he flipped to the next blank page.

Who was Georgia Murphy? He wrote. *Friends, family, co-workers, associates?*

Next, he wrote, *HCSO file/investigation.*

Then finally, *Tony Murphy = inmate. Robbery? When and how close to disappearance?*

He flipped the pages of the notepad back and started to close the portfolio then stopped.

He started paging through his old notes. It was his habit to write a date at the top of the page and a subject when taking notes, even for simple things, so he started looking through them for the date range this case might have come to Metro.

He found the page from about the time she had gone missing and looked for any mention of her. Nothing. Five pages back, five pages forward. He saw nothing obvious.

Then in a margin he saw a familiar name. *Portals.* A law firm from here in Seacord. There was a phone number below it and another name, *Crews, ADA.* Phillip Crews was the assistant DA for Hurrt County back then.

Ashe looked more carefully at this line on the page. There was no mention of Georgia Murphy, but he had jotted down, kind of skewed to one side, *Missing woman, suspected homicide.* Beside that small note was a second phone number. He thought he recognized it.

Ashe fired up his laptop and searched the first phone number through his personal contacts. Nothing. He next searched the internet, which was very slow this far out of town, so he waited.

Portals, Crews, and Fischer, Attorneys at Law finally popped up. This made sense to Ashe as the number was beside Portals' name in his notes. But did it have anything to do with Georgia Murphy's case?

He searched the other number but nothing came up on the internet. Still, it looked familiar so he searched his personal contacts. Again, nothing.

He looked at the box on his desk marked "Office/Metro" and a date range that went back two years and before he'd retired, and would cover the same date as was on his notepad.

There wouldn't be any case file documents in the box as the state's Official Records Act prohibited the removal of any official documents or evidence from the MCU, but he'd made a few copies of things he thought perhaps he could be subpoenaed to testify on after retirement. He rummaged through his papers inside looking for anything pertinent. It was a long shot, but he wanted to be thorough before Keagan called and before he met again with the sheriff.

All this makes a man thirsty. He took off his glasses and walked to his kitchen, opened the fridge to grab a beer, thought better of it, and replaced it with a can of diet soda instead.

The doorbell rang and Ashe jumped. He hadn't heard it in months.

Walking through the foyer and looking through the stained-glass window in the front door, he saw a refracted and multicolored silhouette he thought he recognized.

Opening the door, he saw he was right.

"Well," he said.

"Surprised?" Stevie asked.

CHAPTER 4

"**I** couldn't be more surprised if my dead grandmother were standing here," Ashe said, smiling.

Stevie smiled politely back and raised her hand as if to ask permission to enter, so Ashe held the door open wider and made a sweeping motion with his arm.

"By all means, please."

"I wasn't sure if you'd let me in or slam the door in my face."

"Well, the thought occurred to me."

She cut her eyes at him, still smiling.

She took off a red raincoat in the foyer and kicked off her light-purple running shoes that had a deeper purple swoosh, and walked sock-footed over to his kitchen island counter. She turned slowly all the way around, looking and obviously appreciating the renovations he'd made to the house in the past four months.

Ashe took in a long breath and looked at her. There was that feeling in his chest and throat he hadn't felt in a while. *Is she here to see me?*

Stevie wore gray workout pants and an athletic top that showed her newly toned midriff. She looked fit and had obviously been going to a tanning bed somewhere. All in all, Ashe thought, she looked fantastic. But that realization brought up another thought.

She's doing well now that I'm not with her. He pushed that one aside.

"I love what you've done with the house," she said. She walked from the kitchen toward the living room. "There used to be doors here, and a...another thing there."

"Yeah, I tore it all out and made it more open."

"You're selling?"

"Not on your life. Just kind of making it mine."

She nodded, and Ashe realized she seemed to notice he had not stopped staring at her.

"I bear gifts," she said and plopped a thick manilla envelope onto the counter.

Ashe slid the bundle closer to him.

"It's your estate. It's done. Signed, sealed, and now delivered."

"Oh," was all he could think to say.

"It took quite a bit. This house and property, the accounts, the lake place and boat, your dad's old Scout. You own it all. Final and complete."

"I thought..." he started and then stopped. "Thank you."

"You fired me," she said, attempting to complete his sentence.

"No! I meant... I thought you weren't able to."

"I've been clerking for retired Judge Harold Marsh's private firm while getting my act back together," she said.

"Oh, yeah. He had a business years ago with Dad and old Tyler Danner I think."

"A fact he mentioned to me about a hundred times. He's been asking me if I called you, about twice a week."

"Nice guy."

"He even caught me at the gym and made me bring this over to you instead of mailing it," she said.

Ashe looked down and turned the big envelope around on the counter but didn't open it.

"So, what's up with this?" she said.

"What?"

Stevie reached across the counter and grabbed a handful of his unkempt beard. "This!"

"Oh. Yeah, I haven't been out much and, I don't know, I've never really grown one past a couple weeks before."

"Good God, Ashe!" she laughed. "You have to cut this off."

"Today," he promised. "And a haircut."

They smiled at each other for a minute, then he looked away.

The silence was thick. "I should have tried more to talk to you, honey."

He noticed her stiffen a bit at the word "honey" and scolded himself for it.

"If you recall, you did call and leave me messages. Texts. Emails. A card with flowers. It was me who..."

"Hey," he started. He reached for her hand across the counter, but she slid it back away from him.

"Oh!" she interrupted. She'd discovered the stainless pop-up electrical outlets on the granite counter. She pressed on the little silver disk and a cylinder popped up with a pair of 110-watt outlets for appliances. Then she pushed down and they went back flush.

"This is so cool."

She doesn't want to talk about us, Ashe realized. He'd sent her at least a dozen apologies and offers to help her. What was obvious was, she hadn't needed him. She'd ignored every text, every phone call.

A hot bolt of a thought struck him.

Without saying anything, he jogged back through the house to the office and retrieved his portfolio.

"Ashe?" she called after him.

With his reading glasses low on his nose, he flipped back the page he'd dog-eared. The one with the strange but familiar phone number.

"Ashe?"

He reappeared in the kitchen. "Hey, sorry. Do you recognize this number?" He held the portfolio out to her with his thumb beside the note.

She squinted at the page. "Jeez, you write like shit."

He flipped it around and read it to her. "Ends in 7846."

Stevie straightened up and took a step back from the counter and looked away.

"Yes. That's my old private office number."

That was it. It was the number he'd had for her when first he needed help with his dad. Hospice. Power of attorney. The DNR. Once he'd gotten to actually know her, and particularly once he'd started dating her, he had only used her cell number. That was why it was familiar but he hadn't immediately recognized it.

"That phone got disconnected. Right before *that day*, you know," she said.

"That day?" Ashe was momentarily confused. How could Stevie know what day Georgia Murphy had disappeared? Then he realized what she'd meant.

The day they'd broken up.

He took off his glasses. "I'm sorry. I was trying hard not to bring old news up," he said.

"It's fine."

"No, I'm just kind of working on something and…"

"Georgia Murphy?"

Whatever aching in his heart Ashe had felt suddenly dropped to his stomach.

"You knew Georgia?"

"Of course. She worked as an assistant at the Hurrt Land and Title company. Small town. Every lawyer or real estate person in this town would at least know who she was."

"But you *knew her*, knew her. More than just by reputation," Ashe stated. It wasn't really a question.

Stevie turned to face Ashe across the counter and started tugging at her short top. She looked down at the counter and whatever fresh, tan, renewed appearance she'd had when arriving was marginally pushed aside and replaced with a look of hard concern and fear. It wasn't dissimilar to the look she'd had when Ashe had last seen her. That day.

"Why do you have my old private office line in those notes?" she asked.

"Because I've been asked to…you know why I'm asking?"

"The sheriff asked you for help."

"That was three hours ago! How the hell did you hear?"

She took in a breath, but Ashe took a guess first.

Seacord Central. Tilly.

"The old judge heard the sheriff wanted to relook at it and he recommended you. And then, mentioned it to me."

Oh. Sorry, Tilly.

"But you knew her other than just by reputation," Ashe repeated.

Stevie exhaled hard. "Yes. No shock here, I was her attorney."

Ashe set the portfolio on the counter, put his glasses back on, and flipped to a blank page. "I need to know what you know about her."

"She's just missing as of now. There's a limit to what I can say."

"Two years, Stevie. I think even Harold Marsh would agree you need to tell me anything that might help her."

"You're going to find her," she said. Not a question.

"I'm going to do my level best."

"I thought this was a Metro case."

She's avoiding the issue. Does she know something?

"The sheriff, and apparently Harold Marsh, don't think so. He sent you here to see me, knowing I would be looking into it. Besides, I've put in a call to Metro Homicide."

There was a long pause. She didn't meet his eyes but started nervously tapping her fingers against the granite.

"Surely you can describe your relationship without violating client confidentiality."

After another long pause, she said, "I was her lawyer. She hired me. That much is public record."

Ashe nodded. He didn't want to push her too hard or she'd just walk out. Plus, he knew a recovering alcoholic of only four months or so could be fragile.

"You were a family law attorney. So, she was either filing for bankruptcy or for a ..."

"Divorce," she said flatly. "She was divorcing Tony Murphy. Or at least starting to."

"Not finalized?"

"No. Christ, Ashe! I was a mess. I was going through my own troubles and she came to me for help and honestly, I think I lost the papers or filed them wrong and had to redo them and then she disappeared!"

A second hot bolt hit Ashe. Convict Tony Murphy would not have liked it that his wife wanted a divorce. People had gone "missing" for less.

"You told all this to the S.O. at the time?"

"Yes, through my attorney of course."

"Judge Marsh?"

"No, Mark Portals."

The other notation in my notepad.

Ashe started writing on the pad. "So, you were Georgia's attorney in a divorce suit that..." He paused and looked up at her. He didn't want to be cruel. "We are not sure ever got properly filed. When Georgia went missing, you came forward to the investigators after...um. How long after she went missing did you talk to the sheriff's office?"

"A week. Ten days maybe. I had to talk to Mark Portals first.

He agreed to go with me."

Lawyers. Damn, her associate and client go missing and she was worried about herself? As much as he cared for her, it was not his favorite color on her.

"I'm just going to lay this out here, Stevie. Ten days is a long time to wait and reveal that Tony Murphy had a very real motive for possibly killing her. I could see maybe a day, or two."

"I had to take care of a couple of things first. Mark made sure I was…ready."

Ashe nodded to himself. *Portals sobered her up. That explains her delay, but why wouldn't Portals notify the sheriff?*

Ashe made some notes and checked his phone. Still no call from Keagan.

"*You* didn't do anything either," she said.

"Huh?"

"This was sent to you in Metro where Tony Murphy lived. There was evidence there, I heard. You didn't do anything about it either."

Someone told her that. And recently, because it had never come up before.

"I assigned my best detective to the case. Pat Keagan. You met him once when I first hired you and you drove up to meet with me, remember?"

"Oh, okay, yeah," she said. "He spent time down here poking around too."

Ashe flipped back to the page where he'd listed the questions and answers he wanted to get from Metro and added one. *Did Pat ever interview Stevie?*

He finished making his notations and looked around for his soda he'd opened. Stevie was staring into his fridge. She took out an aluminum bottle of beer.

"Stevie, wait!"

"It's okay! It's just beer."

He walked around to take the beer from her and as he got close to her, she turned into him and embraced him.

"I do appreciate how much you have cared for me and tried to help me. I could never say this before, but…thank you, Ashe," she said. She slowly took off his glasses and kissed him gently.

Ashe was stunned. He had wanted this so badly. *Why right*

now?

"Oh, wow!" she shouted right into his face and pulled away from him abruptly.

"Go shave that god-awful beard right now!"

Ashe chuckled and rubbed his face. "Ok, but stay here. I'll be right back."

He started toward his bedroom as she opened the beer and took a long pull.

"Oh, shit! Dammit!" she cursed loudly.

"What?" he shouted back.

"Damn low-carb light beer!" she said and tossed the can into the sink.

CHAPTER 5

By the time Ashe had shaved and showered, Stevie had left, which he mostly expected. He checked his messages and there was still no call from Pat Keagan.

While in the shower, he'd replayed this morning in his head and realized that in his elation to see Stevie and to be on speaking terms with her again, she hadn't answered his toughest questions.

She knows more about Georgia Murphy than she's letting on. She must be in trouble again.

Which Ashe figured meant that the very best part of his day so far, her sudden embrace and kiss, wasn't real. Which next led him to figure when she thanked him, it was also not authentic. A decoy.

And that awareness brought forward something else; a darker thought.

How do I know she's not involved somehow?

That made him mad. Mad at himself mostly, but he reserved a little for her.

Ashe dressed in nicer jeans, tan boots, and a white oxford cloth dress shirt. He didn't put on a tie. *This is Hurrt County after all,* he thought, but did put on a dark-brown wool sport coat. He checked himself in a mirror and decided he no longer looked like the Unabomber.

He next reviewed the notes he'd taken while talking to Stevie. He was so mad at himself for being so damn easy for her to divert, and for stupidly mooning over her. The only new information he'd learned was that Georgia wanted a divorce from Tony, and Stevie had been her lawyer.

Assuming she hadn't lied to me about that.

Then when Georgia had disappeared, it took Stevie maybe ten days to come forward and tell the sheriff what she knew about the divorce. A potential motive for her disappearance.

And Mark Portals. What does he have to do with Georgia? Or for that matter, Stevie?

Ashe looked at his notes and decided he needed to know everything the sheriff's office knew.

"Time for that haircut," he said out loud to no one.

As he gathered his wallet, portfolio, raincoat, and keys, he wondered to himself, *Should I be carrying a gun?*

He knew that he was about to start picking at a scabbed-over wound. He also believed Georgia Murphy to be dead. *Or worse, murdered.*

As a retired cop in good standing, he had the authority to carry a gun but had given up the habit a little after moving here. The only concealed-carry-type gun he had anymore was a snub-nosed Smith & Wesson .38 that he kept by his bed. He paused for a beat then decided against it and headed out.

Once Ashe got closer to town and had better cell service, his phone beeped. There was a voicemail so he pulled over and listened to it.

He'd expected Pat, but it was Lois' voice.

"Ashe, this is Lois. I gave your message to Pat but he said he had a meeting with Captain Speakes and instead of calling would come down and see you in the morning."

Interesting. Why drive 75 miles to come see me here?

"Ashe," she continued, but in a lowered voice, "I have not said anything about our call or your calendar to anybody. That stuff you asked for is in your email, so you should have it by now."

Good job, Lois. He'd look at it when he got home.

"And, Ashe, be careful. I don't know anything specific, but people in the office have gotten…tense over this Georgia Murphy for some damn reason."

Also, interesting.

"Please delete this message for me, please. And watch yourself. I have a very bad feeling about this," she said, then the voice message was over.

Ashe sat in his Jeep where he'd pulled over at an old abandoned gas station at the edge of town and listened to the voice message one more time. He resisted his normal urge to make notes as he didn't want anyone to see them and know she'd spoken to him. He deleted the voicemail as she'd asked.

Lois, nervous? Hell, she's tough as woodpecker lips.

"Pat? What's going on, old partner?" he said out loud to no one.

He finished driving into town and pulled up near the barbershop, but it was obvious there was a line of ten to twelve people waiting. The only other barber in town, besides the beauty parlors, Ashe didn't like, as it was traditionally full of cigarette smoke. After a quick recheck in the rearview mirror, he decided again his freshly shaved face was change enough for one day and he'd go see the sheriff as is.

The Hurrt County Sheriff's Office and Jail was about what Ashe had expected, given he had worked with many of the county agencies that bordered Metro or those that had business with Metro. Mostly these small county offices got along with little to no resources and facilities that were only modernized as a result of a lawsuit. Hurrt County did not surprise.

As he parked in a diagonal slot near the front, he looked over the building. Old brick that was missing some mortar in places and had been inexpertly repaired in others and a glass-walled front entrance. It looked like a 1960's post office to him. A pair of marked sedans were parked in front, their overhead lights at least ten years older than the cars themselves. The light bars were also obviously designed to fit a larger car but had been forced onto these smaller ones.

No judgement. Have to get by with what you have.

The inside of the office was stuffy and there was the odor of cigarettes and perspiration. The tile floor was swept but hadn't seen a mop in a while. Old metal-framed double chairs with plastic cushions lined one wall with what looked like a yard sale end table. A plastic brochure stand held flyers for crime prevention tips and warnings against fentanyl and drunk driving. A couple of McGruff coloring books lay under a goodly amount of dust.

As Ashe walked in, there was a door to his right and a big tinted window that took up the whole rear wall of the entrance. He stepped up to it and could make out a woman at a desk talking to a deputy. He saw a speaker with a call button and pressed it.

"My name is Ashe, I'm here to see the sheriff."

"Okay," said the woman over the speaker. The door buzzed and Ashe pushed it open.

He stepped into a narrow hall which would take him beside the room he'd seen behind the glass. The woman who buzzed him in leaned out a Dutch door with the top open.

"Go down the hall and turn left again," she said with a cigarette in her mouth.

Ashe thanked her and walked by, and as he did, the deputy he'd seen stepped to where he could fix his stare on Ashe. He crossed his arms and all but seethed at Ashe.

No, may I ask who you are? No, may I see some ID? No, just what the hell do you want, buster?, or even, Are you carrying any explosives or fully automatic weapons?

But Deputy Dude here will intimidate me with his steely-eyed gaze that I'm sure he practices in the mirror.

The woman leaned out the upper part of the door again after he had passed and said, "Ashe? You any kin to the Ashe that was sheriff and then a county commissioner here?"

"Robert Ashe. He was my dad. He was the sheriff here for one term."

He continued to an open door with a placard mounted above it that simply said *Sheriff.* He tapped on the door.

"Hey, Chi-uh, Ashe," Sheriff Jacobs said.

"Just Ashe. You'll get used to it."

Jacobs stood and shook his hand then got up and walked over to a side door that connected to another office. He leaned on it to get it to close then excused himself and walked toward the front office.

"Gimme a second, Ashe."

So, alone for a minute, Ashe looked about the room. The sheriff had a huge wood desk that was set catty-cornered so both windows in the office were at his back. A long conference table with four comfortable-looking chairs took up the other side of the room. He went and sat at one.

There was nothing on the sheriff's desk but a laptop computer with no external monitor. A leather portfolio not unlike Ashe's was neatly on the center of a leather blotter. No loose notes, no files, Post-it notes, or even loose papers.

There were only a few photos of family and friends around the room, and of course the obligatory Hurrt County Sheriff's Office calendar hung near the door. He had only a few certificates, all in matching polished wood frames, showing he'd graduated the basic police academy and the state sheriff's course the year he'd been elected. He'd been a soldier and was honorably discharged. He also had a handgun training certificate from a company Ashe recognized: Tactical Analysis Group.

So, the old boy can shoot.

Jacobs returned to the room and closed his office door then went and leaned on the connecting door again. It was warped and didn't want to fully close, so Jacobs put his weight against it as it complained loudly until it would stay shut.

"Damn door. I just want us to talk privately," he said. "My detective is out."

Jacobs came to the table and sat close to Ashe with a file folder.

Ashe opened his portfolio to a blank page and put on his reading glasses, but Jacobs put his big hand on the pad.

"Just us talk, first," he said.

"Sure," Ashe replied and closed the pad and pulled his glasses down on his nose some to see over them.

"Like I said, I think there's a lot going on here with Georgia Murphy's disappearance."

"You said this morning you think she went missing here. Not Metro."

"Honestly, I can't prove it but I think she went *dead* here."

Ashe sat back and thought for a second. "Tell me why you think that."

"First, it's been two years. When I came into office and asked questions around town, everybody got really nervous. The former assistant DA, a couple of local lawyers, friends of hers. It was like to mention her name got everybody wired."

Ashe had experienced that himself. Stevie and Lois.

"The sheriff at the time was working the angle that she'd disappeared here, but there was that deal between the district attorneys to send it out of county. They shut him down."

"Sheriff Laughton," Ashe said.

"Yeah."

"He still around?"

"Nope, he's dead now."

"So, to be clear, you have nothing but a feeling, a gut instinct, that she disappeared or died here."

"A touch more than a feeling," he said and smiled. He handed Ashe what looked like a crime scene photo.

Ashe studied the photo. It was of two women's purses hanging from a plastic hook on the inside of a closet door. One was fancier, a bejeweled clutch with a tiny strap. The other purse looked more every day, a larger burgundy leather type with a gold-colored clasp made from a letter A. The A was partially broken off and the leather looked well-worn.

"Okay, two purses. Women can have a dozen or more from my small experience."

"Yeah, look beside the closet. On the floor."

At the very edge of the photo was a small cellular phone.

"Who leaves home and goes to Metro to disappear and leaves her everyday purse and phone behind?"

Ashe set the photo down. "This is damn thin, Sheriff. That could be an old phone. She could have another everyday purse."

"These pictures were taken by the deputy who took her missing person report the night we got the call."

"Okay."

Jacobs handed Ashe another photo.

It showed close to the same angle, the open closet door. But there was one purse, the fancy one, hanging there by itself. And no phone on the floor.

"This was taken..."

"Next day by my detective who went back in daylight to look around."

"Georgia Murphy's leather purse and phone are missing."

"Uh-huh."

"They weren't moved? Even by accident? Not in another photo?"

"You can look at all of the shots. That purse and phone are gone from her apartment the very next morning."

Ashe looked at the sheriff. "Huh."

"Huh, indeed," he said.

"Your detective see this? What does he think?"

"She. And no, I haven't shared this part with Detective Davis."

Ashe took off his glasses and set them on his portfolio. "You don't trust your own detective?"

Jacobs leaned over and looked at the warped connecting door again. Satisfied they were still alone, "She was there both times. The night we took the report and the next day. Deputy Clark took the first set of photos and she, the next morning, took the second set by herself."

"And the purse and phone went missing between those two times."

"Uh-huh. Maybe seven hours apart."

"They didn't lock down the crime scene?"

"Yep, taped the door and all. Landlord let them in both times as they didn't have Mrs. Murphy's key. Detective Davis and Deputy Clark are the only ones who were ever in there. Plus, the landlord swore no one had been in there overnight."

"Where did you get this first photo? With the leather purse and cell phone?"

"Sheriff Laughton had kept it. He handed it to me when he retired and asked me to keep at this case."

"So, again, straighten me out if I'm off course. Your Deputy Clark takes the initial set of photos of Georgia Murphy's apartment. He assumes at the time she's only missing, and takes a special photo to show the purses and the phone on the floor as well."

"Yep."

"They made an impression on him."

"Yes."

"Then seven hours or so later your Detective Daniel..."

"Davis. Tracy Davis."

"Detective Davis goes to the crime scene by herself. Landlord lets her in and she takes a second set of photos. But no purse, no phone."

"Right, you see my issue."

"So why didn't anyone notice this right away then? Especially Clark or Davis. Or the former sheriff."

"According to Sheriff Laughton, the reason she went back and rephotographed the scene was that the first batch wasn't clear enough. Too dark. She had all the photos, both sets, together by then in her office."

Ashe sat back and whistled softly. "You suspect she trashed the first set of photos, removed the purse and phone, then shot the second set so it'd look like Georgia Murphy had left on her own for Metro."

"Something like that. I'm not quite sure Davis did all that herself, but she took the second set of pictures and had the first set in her office for a while. She had to see the purse and phone were gone when she went back to the apartment."

"And Davis never said a word to anyone about the missing items."

"Not to Sheriff Laughton anyway."

"So…where did Laughton get this first photo if they don't exist anymore?" Ashe held up the photo that showed the leather purse and cell phone.

"Deputy Clark's digital camera."

"They didn't take the digital storage card from the camera as evidence?"

"Yes, but the photos were originally in his camera's inside storage or hard drive, or whatever you call it."

Ah-ha. Technology is a bitch.

"So, Detective Davis?"

Jacobs shrugged. "I don't know. I can't say for sure that she's done anything crooked with this. She's been a pretty good detective and employee since then. Doesn't seem right she'd conceal or destroy evidence. I mean, why would she?"

"Regardless, she knew there was a big damn difference in the crime scene the next morning. Assuming *she* didn't remove the purse and phone herself."

"She and Clark are the only ones who were in that crime scene. I pretty much trust Billy Clark. He could have deleted his photos at any point later but didn't. And I don't think he ever actually saw the second set."

Ashe put his glasses back on and started making notes. "Then this all got shipped to Metro and nobody's the wiser."

"Except Sheriff Laughton."

"Yeah, and he's dead. Who actually boxed up the crime scene?"

"Uh, Davis, I suppose. Still before I came into office."

"Have an inventory?"

"Yeah, and a hand receipt signed by your evidence guy in Metro."

Ashe opened his portfolio and made notes of new things to ask Pat when he saw him.

"Have you questioned Davis about this?"

"This all happened before I was sheriff. I started not to keep her on as a deputy, but she has a lot of friends and family here. Besides, like you say, there are a thousand other possible answers besides a longtime deputy and Hurrt County native tampering with evidence."

Ashe just lifted an eyebrow and looked over his glasses at Jacobs.

"Plus, I can't figure out why she'd do it. I don't want to start something without having a clue as to *why*. She didn't suddenly get rich, she's not kin to any of these people. Her kids and my grandkids play soccer together, for Christ's sake."

"Well, if there's a burgundy purse or cell phone in Metro, we'll know for sure."

"For sure?" Jacobs asked.

"That somebody wants this to be a Metro case and not a Hurrt County case. That somebody got the purse and cell phone out of the crime scene so it doesn't *look* like a crime scene. Just an empty apartment. That somebody must have ensured Davis kept quiet, or had her do it in the first place. Like you said at Roger's Diner this morning, send it to Metro to die."

"Yeah," he said, "but I still don't know why."

"You keep a copy of the case file from here?"

"In Davis's office."

Ashe stood and stretched. It'd been a busy day for the first time in months and he usually took a nap about this time of day.

"So, with all this stuff you've shown me, why me? Why not go straight to your ADA?"

Jacobs also stood and walked over and checked the connecting door again.

"The assistant district attorney back then is now a law partner of Mark Portals. Name's Phillip Crews."

"Okay. So?"

"We don't necessarily get the cream of the crop down here. We usually get a young rookie prosecutor or whoever the DA appoints. But Crews was sharp. Experienced."

"Okay."

"So, Mark Portals pushed his other nephew, John P. Price, right out of law school to the front of the political line and he's now our ADA."

"You think there's a conflict? Portals hires the former ADA who's sharp and has his nephew appointed behind him. Seems typical behavior to me for lawyers."

"Mark Portals controls a lot of things around here. He's so connected, he pressured the DA to take his nephew *and* he can call the governor on his private line. He's a big real estate lawyer and works with big companies and big business deals all over the state."

"Yeah, he has an office in Metro too," Ashe recalled.

"And for sure if Mark Portals does something, there's a reason. Usually to benefit him."

Ashe walked back to his pad and made a couple of more notes.

"I need you to look into this quietly for me, Ashe. Until we have a reason for all this, it can just be explained as sloppy local police work."

Ah-ha. "You need me in case you're wrong," Ashe said. "Everything you've shown me so far could have a different explanation."

"I don't know what to do, but I talked to old Judge Marsh and he said you might."

Ashe nodded. "I'm retired. And my poking around won't snap back against you politically."

"Um…yeah. Something like that. Marsh said he worked with your dad and knew you could be trusted."

"Why should I? No, seriously, Sheriff, why should I? I don't know you or Georgia Murphy or your deputies or Mark Portals or…"

"You know Stevie Collins," Jacobs interrupted. "She was Georgia's lawyer and I think somehow she knows something."

"Stevie?" Ashe felt the familiar ache deep in his throat. *Oh, dammit, honey, what are you into?*

"The judge said to trust you. So I do. He said he's worried about Stevie though and that you two dated."

"That…was a while ago."

"He said he cares about *her*. Nobody else really, and he says you care about Stevie too."

God help me, I do. "Somebody took her statement a few days after Georgia went missing."

"Yeah, well, Davis did. I wasn't sheriff yet. She said Stevie had Portals with her."

"As her attorney?"

"No, just a friend, she said."

"What did she say?"

"Basically, from what I read later, that Georgia wanted to divorce Tony because he was a thug and they were separated, yada, yada. Also, Georgia was afraid of him, she wanted an Order of Protection, he was violent, and so forth."

"Makes Tony a suspect. Plus, he lives in Metro."

"Yeah. Neat, huh?"

"Have you talked with Tony Murphy in prison?" Ashe asked.

"I tried a couple of times, but he refuses," Jacobs said.

"Any indication of how Stevie seemed at the time?"

Jacobs hesitated and rubbed his hands together nervously.

Ashe sighed. "I know she was a drunk. Even then."

"Oh, no. Detective Davis stated she was sober or she wouldn't have allowed her to give a statement."

"Right."

"But it reads to me like a scripted statement. You know, you've seen them. Especially when a lawyer won't allow their client to talk much. Like that."

"Huh."

"Of course, that's just my gut talking from reading this stuff. But even Davis's questions were just topical. I'd have asked more about their personal relationship, which everyone in town knew they were friends, but nothing. Just straight to the divorce thing. Nothing else."

And as of today, Stevie was still evasive about the whole topic.

"Ashe, I got a whole bunch of junk and all of it stinks, but I don't know what to make of it. I'm not sure I can trust anybody here in the S.O. or the ADA's office either."

Both men sat and looked at the table. Ashe sorted his thoughts.

"Did she say why she had waited so long to come tell the sheriff she had been hired to file for Georgia's divorce? It would seem that was important."

"Of course not to me. Sheriff Laughton told me she started out saying she wasn't sure she had filed the documents with the clerk, but it was Mark Portals who kind of hinted she wasn't, um, able to recall."

"Able?"

"He figured it out. By that time, they knew she was slipping some and Mark Portals was, ah, helping her out."

"But did Davis or Laughton follow up and check with the clerk?"

Jacobs paused and thought about that. "Not that I know of and you know what, neither have I. I think it all got shipped up to you, ah, I mean Metro, the next week and everybody moved on to the next thing they had to work."

Ashe raised his palms toward Jacobs. "Well, I guess I can't throw stones. I assigned a good detective to it but I didn't follow up either."

"I still say whatever happened to Georgia Murphy happened right here in Hurrt County," Jacobs said. "What I don't know is *why*. Why did she get killed or abducted at all? What's the motive? And why would Detective Davis possibly tamper with the crime scene to help make it look like a Metro case?"

"And also, why ship it to Metro?" Ashe added. "Assuming someone is actually orchestrating all this, they'd have to know we had more resources to bring to bear and…"

"And you were there," Jacobs added. "You are from *here* but were working up *there*. Now you get why maybe I hesitated in talking to you at all."

"And a false but convincing crime scene would stall the case and still keep it away from Hurrt County," Ashe finished.

"Like I said. You guys have a hundred cold cases and a new hundred cases opening every day. Somebody wanted Georgia Murphy's case to disappear. *In Metro.*"

Ashe realized a new enormity to his having been distracted and not following up on this case. He got mad again. Somehow somebody counted on him not following up on it. Betting it would stall on his watch and go into the back of a file cabinet in the bowels of Metro Police.

"Sheriff, I think as privately and quietly as possible, you better deputize me."

CHAPTER 6

Ashe drove back to the town square and parked back in front of the barbershop. Sheriff Jacobs had filled out something online that reactivated his state law enforcement status as a reserve Hurrt County deputy sheriff.

No pay, of course, Ashe noted to himself. Jacobs had handed him a badge on a leather belt clip and it sat in his coat pocket.

He wanted to talk to Detective Davis, but as Jacobs had admonished, without mentioning his new deputized status. That was good for Ashe as she might open up a bit more. If she was hiding evidence and wanting to be sure Georgia Murphy's case stayed in Metro, Ashe guessed she'd assume he would want that too.

On the other hand, if she wasn't involved in such a conspiracy, maybe he'd learn something new. Exactly what Ashe didn't know, but Jacobs said he'd call Ashe the minute she came back into the office.

Regardless, the sheriff had been crystal clear. Keep their association private for the time being. Ashe decided he could nose around and find out what he could but not cause a ruckus.

Yet. And one other thing Jacobs hadn't mentioned.

I need to know how Stevie is mixed up in all this.

But for right this minute, it was time to complete his transition from wild Covid man back to human. He got out of his old Jeep and stepped inside the barbershop.

Afterward, Ashe checked in with Jacobs on his cell, no Davis yet, so he decided to start with his dad's old business partner, retired Judge Harold Marsh. Marsh had sent Stevie to see him after all. He tried to start his Jeep, but it made a noise he'd become familiar with. The starter was going bad, or had gone bad, and it just whined at him.

Ashe knew how to hit it and get it to crank but didn't want to embarrass himself right in front of the old men in the barbershop, so he grabbed his portfolio and starting walking toward the far side of the town square to Third Street. One block up was Marsh's office.

Ashe figured Marsh had to be on the high side of eighty. He knew he only still acted as a judge when asked as a favor to one of the sitting judges, like when they were on vacation or needed to recuse themselves. He had been on the circuit bench for thirty years before retiring the first time.

When Ashe's dad had been mayor of Seacord, he had appointed the retired Marsh to several public service committees and planning panels. Once the elder Ashe retired, the two men and a third gentleman from Carson County named Danner had started a small local land investment company which later became the Hurrt County Land and Title company.

The general idea, it later seemed to the younger Ashe, was less of a way to make a profit than to have a way of finding, buying, and preserving good bird hunting properties so the three old coots could hide from the world. Of course, as the partners grew older and less able to live their outdoor life, they sold off the companies and most of the land.

But not all the land, Ashe thought as he approached Marsh's office. *Now a nice parcel of it is mine.*

As Ashe walked across the square, he noticed a man trying hard not to be seen watching him. The hair went up on his neck. He'd been a cop too long not to notice and his instincts went on high alert. The man was standing on a sidewalk across one corner from the courthouse, staring into a shop window. It was an old trick; pretend to be innocently looking in a window while using the reflection to watch someone.

Tall, Caucasian, longish but neat-looking hair, late thirties to early forties, beard. Jeans and a dark fleece jacket. Ashe wasn't sure, but it could have been the man from Roger's Café.

As Ashe walked, the man seemed to angle himself slightly to keep an eye on him until Ashe made Third Street and was out of sight. He waited to see if this dude reappeared or was following. He didn't, so after about five minutes, Ashe headed on toward the old judge's office.

Harold Marsh's office was a two-story narrow brick building that was attached to the single story Hurrt County Land and Title office, a block off the town square.

Ashe had forgotten the proximity of the title company to Marsh's office which, when he thought about it, made sense given Marsh and Ashe's dad had started it.

May as well knock out two birds this afternoon, he decided to himself as he stepped into the office. *After I'm through with the judge, I'll see if Georgia's former boss, Ms. Marlin, is available.*

The inside of the law office was warm and a tad stuffy. Ashe walked in on thick carpet that held a slightly old smell mixed with molded leather and a trace of cigar smoke. Large paintings of fox hunts and thoroughbred horses in big thick mahogany frames adorned the deep-green and burgundy-striped silk-covered walls.

Everything was sturdy and expensive-looking, doubtlessly by design. Matching wood end tables held old copies of law review and bird hunting magazines that nobody read anymore. Huge and heavy-looking old glass ashtrays were on each table. All of this had a layer of dust and seemed a decade or more out of time. Leather and mahogany wooden chairs were available for those who had to wait to see the old barrister.

Ashe supposed nobody had to wait much anymore.

An elderly woman Ashe didn't know had quickly dropped a crossword book and made herself busy at a computer as he'd entered. She sat behind a long professional-looking desk and sideboard and had doubtlessly been with the old judge for years.

"Good afternoon," she said in a well-used law-office monotone.

"My name is Ashe. I'd like to see if the judge can spare me a few minutes?"

She stared at him for a beat. "Are you Robert Ashe's son?"

"I am."

"You look a lot like him," she said, not a bit warmly.

She turned and picked up the phone and punched one button. She waited a few seconds and Ashe could hear a phone buzzing somewhere in another room behind her. She rolled her eyes and hung up.

"One minute, please have a seat," she said as she got up and walked back toward what was probably Marsh's office.

Ashe started to sit but then thought it might be more work to get back up than to just stay standing, a calculation he made more and more often these days.

"Judge," he heard the receptionist say in the back. "Judge! A Mr. Ashe wants to see you."

He heard the judge mumble something.

"No, silly, his son! From Metro Police, I think. Sit up!"

Another muted conversation, then she reappeared.

"The judge will see you when he gets off the call he's on," she said. Stiff, formal, ever-so-mildly annoyed. "I'm Katheryn, may I get you a cup of coffee?"

"Oh, no thank you," he said and gave her one of his 40-watt smiles. Nothing.

Big important judge. Big important receptionist. Sit and wait, enjoy a 1990's magazine, you interloper.

Ashe heard a toilet flush from the rear of the offices and Marsh clearing his throat then blowing his nose loudly. Katheryn heard it too and met Ashe's eyes.

"Ah…he's off his call. I'll walk you in."

She escorted Ashe down a wide hall, and to one side was an open door to a small office. The lights were off. At a glance it seemed feminine. A pair of red high heels were tucked under a chair.

Stevie's place while clerking here.

Marsh's office was decorated and furnished like the rest had been, only larger. There was a row of tall glass-doored bookcases filled with law books and references. A four-foot-wide globe took up a corner, and along one wall that held floor-to-ceiling windows was a well-made conference table fifteen feet long or more. Eight matching chairs with green leather and brass buttons were in place around it. The only modern-looking accessory was one of those triangular conference call speakers in the center of the table.

Harold Marsh had a tall shock of white hair over his cratered face. His skin seemed almost translucent. Deep-purple veins rose like ribbons on his face and hands, and cataracts blurred his eyes.

He was dressed in a pressed dark-gray three-piece suit with banker stripes. His shoes were brightly polished. He wore a pink-and-dove-gray striped tie over a white shirt and had a pocket handkerchief in his breast pocket that matched. A gold chain crossed his vest that suggested a pocket watch. Gold and onyx cufflinks completed his look. All of it seemed to have been sized years ago and for a man twenty pounds heavier. As it was, his excellent and well-chosen attire barely hung on him, so he looked like a child wearing his father's clothes.

All this, Ashe realized, the clothes and the office, was a product of his having carefully crafted an image many years ago to foster the deep impression of power and success.

But, Ashe thought, it was actually the reverse. It was all an anachronism; a moment of time, long since gone, that the old judge and Katheryn continued to relive.

Harold Marsh watched him enter. There was at first no recognition in his eyes. Then a spark.

"Well, *Chig*," the judge said, his voice thick and croupy. "I've been waiting for you to come see me."

"Judge Marsh. It's been too long." Ashe shook his hand.

Marsh's hand was bony but held Ashe's hand firmly without letting go.

"Oh, thirty or forty years, I guess. Call me Harold. You were just out of the Army and going to college, I think. Anyway, I see you got my message."

Ashe blinked. *Message?* "Oh, you mean Stevie."

Marsh held his hand a minute longer. "Precisely," he said. His voice growing clearer.

Ashe was shown to one of a pair of high-back leather chairs that faced the judge's desk. A small table sat between them, and Ashe opened his portfolio there.

"I want to talk to you about her, and a woman named Georgia Murphy."

"Before you start…" Marsh said, but then paused as Katheryn entered with a pitcher of ice water with lemons and two glasses. "Oh, Katheryn, please hold all my calls and no interruptions."

She poured the glasses full and nodded to him with a silent *as if*, but instead said, "Of course, Judge."

"Before you start with questions, I should tell you what, as an invisible old man, I have seen and heard about this town."

"Please," Ashe said.

"I agree with our former and our current sheriff. Georgia Murphy was abducted here in Hurrt County and probably is dead."

Ashe started making notes.

"I told him to speak with you about it, as he seemed unsure of his own ability to properly investigate the matter. I vouched for you. I knew your father so very well. He was my best friend and a solid one at that. He spoke often of your work in that great city to our North as a policeman and a successful criminal investigator. He followed your career closely, as such a proud father would. Therefore, as he and I talked every day, so did I!"

"I guess I never knew that. Thank you."

"I believe when you talked to Stevie this morning," Marsh continued, "she may have mentioned she was Mrs. Murphy's attorney back then."

"She did. She told me she was handling Georgia's divorce from Tony Murphy."

"I'm not sure that's true. At least there's no record of it."

That made Ashe stop writing. "You think she's lying?"

"Let me be clear. I think Stevie has had nothing to do with the disappearance of Mrs. Murphy. Not intentionally."

Accidentally, then?

"With her problems over the past couple of years, I have tried to take her under my wing, and I used my considerable abilities of persuasion and influence with the state bar to have her assigned to me as my clerk. To help her work off her law license suspension and eventually be reinstated."

"She sort of said that to me as well."

"I did so because, well, maybe I'm an old fool, but I have grown fond of her. She has a sharp and agile mind, and she displayed a wonderful and sympathetic passion for her clients in my court. With time, she can still be a very fine counselor."

"I...think so too."

"I also did this because she very much wants...no, *needs* to be reunited with her daughter. Something I'm making progress with on her behalf."

"I'm glad about that. I think losing custody was what drove her over the edge."

Marsh paused but held Ashe's eyes with his. "Or was she pushed?"

Ashe felt the darker focus. "I'm sorry?"

"Another local attorney has held sway with her during her

darker times. Mr. Mark Portals was beginning to have more and more influence over her."

Portals. Him again. "I'm not sure I get your meaning."

"Mr. Portals. You know this, I assume. From when you hired her."

"I hired her to represent me and my dad while I was still working in Metro. To help organize his affairs," Ashe said. "I didn't know about her…issues then. I've never met Mark Portals."

"By the time you hired her to handle Robert's, ah, *your father's* affairs, I believe Mr. Portals was deeply involved in her practice."

"I admit I hired her not knowing her. I saw a billboard with her face on it here during a trip to see Dad…"

"I know. I know all this," Marsh said. He waved his hand as if to wipe the air clean.

"I know you fell in love with her, she's told me. When you moved home to take care of my friend, your father, the two of you were already quite the item by then."

Ashe sighed. "Judge, I may not have exercised the best decision-making back then. I suppose, given the situation with Dad's declining health, I didn't see she was…"

"A drunk," Marsh said. "She was quite adept at concealing it until she couldn't."

"I guess I didn't help. She was an alcoholic and I was depressed. She was young and beautiful and seemed to, well…a woman like her pays attention to an older man like me, it was all very flattering, I guess. I fell for her, I'll admit that."

"Not your fault. And, more importantly, *not hers*," the old judge said, narrowing his eyes.

"I still don't follow," Ashe said.

"You will. Which brings me back to Georgia Murphy."

Ashe waited while the judge took a drink of water then wiped his face with his handkerchief. Ashe took the opportunity to down a glass himself.

"You know Mister Portals?" the judge asked.

"As I said, no. But I'm beginning to think I need to introduce myself." Ashe felt his face grow hot but remembered he was to tread lightly.

Marsh must have seen him flush a bit. "Have patience, he'll introduce himself to you. He is a well-connected and excellent attorney. I have seen him argue contract law with an amazing ability to capture every nuance and detail in such a way as to captivate a jury. He has brought to life and illustrated legal issues any lesser orator would bore a jury to tears with."

"You admire him?"

Marsh smiled and seem to weigh the word *admire* in his mind.

"I respect the man's abilities. He is probably the one lawyer I would hire to handle any legal issue I might need handled."

Ashe hadn't expected that.

"He is likely the finest real estate, contract, and trial lawyer in the state."

"Huh," is all Ashe could think to say.

"And I also believe, through my years of observation both in court and out, that he has the ethics of a hungry copperhead snake."

Ashe felt himself shifting back to disliking the guy. "You said Portals was into her business, meaning her law firm. Influencing Stevie, I take it not in a good way."

"Well first, Mrs. Murphy had a lot of business with Mr. Portals through the title company your father and I started next door. After we no longer owned it, of course. I do not know any facts as to their business, but she and Stevie were first introduced to each other by Mr. Portals, or perhaps one of his associates."

That was interesting, Ashe thought as he made a note. The sheriff had said something about Stevie and Georgia being friends too.

"Oh, Mr. Portals handled Stevie's divorce. Stevie has told me she and Portals and one or two of his associates, including Mrs. Murphy, used to stay in his office late at night and drink together."

"She wasn't a known alcoholic then?"

"No, not that anyone knew. I'd only seen her drink socially and never to excess. Local Bar Association meetings and what not. I suppose one never knows about such things. Certainly though, she was encouraged to it by her new associations."

Marsh continued, "Stevie and Georgia were by then seen together quite a bit. It's a small town and all, only a couple of places to order drinks. Both professional women, both attractive, well dressed, *and* both more and more seen in public somewhat inebriated. You could say they stood out a bit."

Ashe frowned to himself. He'd known none of this even after they were dating.

"It was about this time I noticed Stevie starting to slip. Small things but noticeable. Missed deadlines, documents with errors, and so on. Mark Portals was only too happy to step in and help."

Marsh drank some of his water. "And honestly, we here in this small-town legal community were glad he did. She was so well-liked, everyone figured she'd get straightened out."

"So, what does one lawyer get for basically mentoring or managing the practice in such a situation as this?"

"Well, you're right. Mark Portals wasn't being altogether altruistic. I'm sure he ensured he took a goodly percentage of her fees, if not all of them in some cases. Plus, access to her clients. It did not surprise me that many switched to his law firm even before she was suspended."

"And afterward?" Ashe asked.

"Good question! Yes, you were a detective. Normally when a law firm closes for whatever reason, clients go to other law firms in the area. But in this case? *All* of Stevie's former clients are now 100 percent Mark Portals' clients."

"Well I guess he's the largest firm in town, right?"

"Not relevant," the judge admonished. "You see, many people prefer the personal attention a one- or two-person firm gives them. These firms don't have the expenses a big firm have and their fees are often quite less. No, the kind of client Stevie had would not naturally just hop over to a large firm like Portals, Crews, and Fischer."

"Wasn't this Mr. Crews the assistant DA at that time?"

"Yes. Now a partner with Mr. Portals."

Ashe made more notes as Marsh waited. Finally Ashe held up a hand. "Harold, you said you didn't think Stevie had represented Georgia Murphy in her divorce? Hasn't anyone confirmed this?"

"Sir, I think the *whole topic* of Mrs. Murphy's filing for divorce came *after* she had gone missing."

Boom! That is a big accusation.

"So…wait. That means Stevie has lied about it. To us and worse, to the sheriff's office of all things," Ashe said.

"I think that she has been manipulated from the start. I cannot prove anything, but I cannot believe the things the state board has alleged. The misappropriated client funds, mishandled court filings. I can't argue the facts, they are documented and seem incontrovertible, but they *do not* match with what I know of our girl!"

The old judge had worked himself up and started coughing hard. His whole body shook and Ashe went around his desk to help him drink some water. Katheryn appeared at the door and glared at Ashe.

"I think your time is up today, Mr. Ashe. The judge should probably call you back."

Marsh took a long drink of water and waved Katheryn out of the room. She retreated but kept her eyes on Ashe. Once he had settled down, he said, "No, please, sir, continue."

"So, Harold, you believe someone, likely Mark Portals, used her drinking issues to sack her career? For what? Her clients? So why then would she lie about Georgia Murphy filing for a divorce after the disappearance?"

"The alleged divorce filing is interesting, isn't it," Marsh said.

"Yes. It might give her husband a motive for whatever happened to her."

"Hmm, Mister Ashe. Now take that thought a step further."

"It also could lead one to believe any crime concerning her was committed in Metro."

"And not here."

Especially considering the photos and her missing phone and purse. Ashe closed his portfolio and shook his head.

"Well, I still don't understand the motive, even from what all you've told me. Who wanted Georgia Murphy gone so badly to be worth all this?"

"Ah," is all Marsh said.

"And of special interest to me and you, Harold, what is Stevie's part?"

The old man sat back and set his substantial gaze directly into Ashe.

"Well. That, sir, is where you come in."

Katheryn was back at the door and her expression made it clear this time that Ashe was done. He stood and thanked Marsh for his time and insight.

This time, the old judge didn't stand but just nodded. Ashe

figured he must have mustered a good deal of his daily strength and focus just for this conversation.

Ashe stepped out of the office and walked next door to the Hurrt County Land and Title Company, but the door was locked and lights were off. He checked his watch; he'd spent longer with the judge than he'd thought as it was just after five.

Fifty feet away from the land office, a burgundy Chevrolet sedan sat parked, its windshield spattered with old rain. Inside sat a man looking at his phone.

Without staring Ashe couldn't be sure. *Was it the guy from the square before?*

Anyway, he decided to come back to the L&T for sure, and started looking around for where he'd parked. It started to drizzle rain again. He walked back up the sidewalk a ways looking for his car until he remembered.

"Damn," Ashe said out loud and started back down Third Street to the town square, where his Jeep still sat in front of the barbershop.

CHAPTER 7

Mark Portals sat at his desk in his law firm listening to an online video meeting with several potential clients participating. He had his staff set up an expensive and realistic facade behind him to make it appear he was seated at a window with a beautiful lake scene just outside. To complete the image he wanted them to see, he wore a plaid flannel shirt and chamois jacket with a leather collar.

He unmuted his microphone and interrupted the group who were debating among themselves.

"Excuse me, Charles, Marion. You may not have noticed the land intensity study in Appendix J. This development is not meant for such mass construction, so the utility lines can in fact be buried. We don't want to spoil that skyline."

The online group mostly turned their attention to Portals. A few opened their documents looking for Appendix J.

"This is the higher-end section we have planned for this side of the lake. There are no lots under a half-acre and all have at least 100 feet of lake frontage."

"So this is not where the condos would be planned?" a man Portals recognized as one of the investment bankers asked.

"No, sir," he answered with a smile. "That development is near Turlington Creek, all the way over on the McCormick County side. What we are discussing today is the timetable for moving ahead with the development of Minor Hills Estates in Hurrt and Carson Counties."

A man abruptly entered Portals' office, quickly realizing that Portals was online. He closed the door quietly and stayed off camera.

Portals kept his professional, competent attorney smile but cut his eyes toward the intruder.

"There is no finer fishing than this side of Minor Hills Lake in Hurrt County where Terrible Creek flows into it."

He muted his mic. "Quiet," he warned the intruder.

Opening the mic up again, he said to the meeting members, "Please excuse me one minute, I need to confer with an associate on a separate matter." He then re-muted his microphone and closed the web camera.

"Apologies, Uncle Mark. I forgot your lake thing was this afternoon."

"Quiet, I said," Portals snapped. He reached across his desk and paused a digital recorder.

The man stroked his beard as he walked over and casually sat in a client chair.

Portals spoke in a low tone. "I think this is going well. We'll get our investment back tenfold or more."

"Well good! Seems like you are always in something, about something, and up to something."

Portals sighed. "What is it?"

"You ready now?"

"Carl, please. Our clients are waiting."

Carl Jack Portals sat up and cautiously looked at the digital recorder and the web cam set up.

"We're good, all muted," Portals said.

"You wanted me to keep my eyes open and to watch out about that Ashe guy. The one who moved back to town from Metro."

"Oh, yes. Okay what about him?"

"Well, I just happen to be in Roger's Café this morning and he was there. Then the sheriff came in and they talked for a while."

"Ashe is a retired policeman, CJ."

"Later, Ashe went back to see the sheriff. I only know because I was uptown getting a late lunch."

"Mmm," Portals said.

"They talked for maybe two hours."

That got Portals' attention back. "Two hours? Well, he *is* a retired cop. Maybe he's getting checked in with the locals. Getting a gun permit or something."

"Then he got a haircut."

"Oh, for crying out loud, CJ. I simply asked you to keep your eyes open, not follow the man around! Did he speak to anyone else at the sheriff's office?"

"How should I know? But he did go see Judge Marsh."

"Judge Marsh, eh? Ah, I know. He was his father's friend and business partner. That's not unexpected. You know the elder Mr. Ashe was sick a long time, but eventually ended it himself."

"I did hear that. Put a gun in his mouth and..." CJ made a popping sound.

"Don't be coarse. We've all been cooped up by Covid and Mr. Ashe got here right as it started. He's just making the rounds with people he's wanted to see."

"Oh, one other little detail. I'm sure you'll appreciate this."

Portals looked at the faces of his clients on his monitor then snapped at Carl. "Hurry up."

"Stevie Collins drove all the way out to Ashe's house this morning."

"Stevie," Portals said flatly.

"Yep. You know she was at the gym this morning and went right over to her old boyfriend's house."

Portals thought about this for a few seconds. He had known they'd been an item but assumed that was over. "That's not entirely unexpected either."

CJ added, "You know she's looking good these days. Quit drinking, too."

"I've got work to do and so do you, but I want to be firm about one thing," Portals said. "You leave Stephanie Collins alone. You stay the hell away from her, do you hear me?"

"I was just doing what you asked me to..."

"I mean it. You keep away from her."

"Aye, aye!" Carl said sarcastically.

"Listen, we have four projects that can proceed now the lockdowns are being lifted. Go find your friend and see if they know anything else, got it?"

Before his nephew could respond, Portals reactivated his system and smiled at the online members.

"Sorry about the delay, ladies and gentlemen," Portals said into his mic.

Carl mock saluted his uncle off camera and left the office quickly.

Mark Portals didn't flinch and went right back into the conversation where he'd left off, but he made a mental note to himself.

He needed to have another personal conversation with Stevie Collins.

CHAPTER 8

Ashe opened his eyes in his bed and without looking at his bedside clock, he felt as if it were still very early. The room was fully dark and he wasn't sure what had woken him up, as the only sound he could hear was his old metal oscillating fan from the corner.

Then down the hall he heard footsteps. Heavy, slow, moving toward his room. He got out of bed and went to the bedroom door, listening carefully.

"Who's there?" he shouted. "I have a gun!" But he didn't. He tried to quickly recall where he'd put his old .38 revolver, much less where the ammunition was.

"Don't mess with guns," his father said through the door. "You leave my guns alone, Chig."

"Yes, sir," Ashe replied, but his voice sounded like he was about twelve.

The door bumped as if his father was leaning against it, like he didn't want Ashe to open it. Ashe stood there a bit. Wanting, *tempted even* to grab the doorknob and throw open the door and see his father. But he didn't. He knew what he might see and he didn't think he could stand to see that image of his father again in his life.

In another second or two, he heard the footsteps walking back in the direction they had come.

"I mean it, son."

"Yes, sir," Ashe said, but in his own grown voice. That startled him and he realized he was sitting up on the edge of his bed.

He looked around but everything was as it was supposed to be. It was three a.m., by his clock, and there was no metal oscillating fan in the corner. At least not since this was his parents' room and he was a child.

Ashe lay back down in his bed, confused. After a long while, he fell asleep again.

The weather had turned more decent overnight and a bright but autumn-like sun was out. There was all but no breeze to chill the air, and so Ashe decided to take some personal time to go check on his dad's cabin and the boat Stevie had reminded him was now his.

Ashe had missed Ms. Marlin at the Land and Title company, and Jacobs hadn't called to let him know when it would be best to talk to Detective Davis. So, having the morning free and knowing Pat was going to drive down, he called Pat and left him a message where to meet.

Just as he was about to leave his house, Ashe had a thought and snapped his fingers. *Lois's email.* So he went to his home office and logged on. *I'm getting forgetful in my retirement.*

After waiting for his ridiculously slow internet to wind up, he finally was able to open her email. There, she had attached his old Metro Outlook account calendar. Ashe flipped through the dates and the notes she'd included according to his request.

There was no mention of Georgia Murphy by name, but a couple of notes to review "Missing Hurrt County Woman" in mid-April two years ago. There was a meeting with his unit sergeants and immediately after that meeting, he had a second meeting with Pat, "Re: Hurrt Co. woman."

Okay, I assigned this to Pat on April 29th, Ashe noted and wrote that down.

There was no further mention of Georgia Murphy even indirectly. That caught Ashe as odd as he always scheduled updates. But looking further through his old calendar he started to see why. "Meet with divorce lawyer" and several follow-up appointments with "re: never-ending damn divorce" as a subject.

Then just a month or so later, he saw calendar events such as "Schedule new doctor for Dad, re: last CT scan," and later, "Look into potential long-term care." Later, a note he remembered well and not but a few days before his retirement, "Hospice care visit with Dad."

In a note, Lois repeated her warning to him that Georgia Murphy was a hot topic. She'd overheard enough to know the Chief of Criminal Investigations, Captain Speakes, had mentioned the investigation to Pat on a couple of occasions just since Ashe had been looking into it. She hadn't heard much, but she'd heard his name, Ashe, and the name of the former ADA in Metro, who had become the State Deputy Attorney General, Rollin Ashad.

Watch it, Ashe, she added.

Ashe switched off his computer and thought for a minute, jotting a couple of notes to himself. *Why were Speakes and maybe Ashad interested now, two years later?*

Pat would know, that was for sure.

As he got his stuff together to leave, he thought he smelled his father's aftershave. Just an impression, less than an actual scent. More like, he had tried to remember what it smelled like than actually smelling it. That brought back the previous night's visit.

It was a dream, he thought, but wasn't sure he bought it. He snatched up his keys and headed to the lake.

The boat was a well-known brand and was a still-decent-looking, fairly clean twin inboard cruiser his dad had bought over twenty years before. It had a small inside cabin that could sleep four with a kitchenette and shower as well.

It needed work, he knew. Then again, all boats always do. Ashe thought it was comfortable enough and equipped well enough that with some technical updates and minor repairs, he might just live on it. Maybe even take off down across the lake, down the Hurrt River to the Stuart River. From there, maybe even the big river to the sea. His dad and mom had done that trip in their day.

Over the lockdown while he'd been alone, he often fantasized about him and Stevie making such a trip. *Maybe,* he thought as he worked. *Maybe after this Georgia Murphy deal gets cleared up.*

Pat had been to the lake house before, so Ashe set out cleaning the boat pumps and generally tending to things he'd left undone all year.

It felt good to be outside working on what might be the last chance before cold weather; to wear shorts, dock shoes, and an old sweatshirt with the sleeves rolled up. He had a radio on playing music as he worked and starting thinking about actually getting some old friends together and having a run at fall fishing season. He began making a punch list of what he wanted to get done with the boat before then, when he noticed a familiar face walking down the dock toward him.

Thoughts of fishing and long river voyages drifted away.

They wore sport coats and slacks and ties and didn't look like early autumn fishing at all.

Cops.

The taller of the two was smiling at him and called out, "Ahoy! Chig! How goes it? You stealing that damn boat?"

It was Pat Keagan. He actually hadn't expected them to make it before noon. The man with him was Danny-somebody-or-other. Pat's new partner. Ashe put on a grin for his old friend.

"Pat, how the hell are you? What brings you way down here? I guess they didn't lay you off over Covid," Ashe said and waved him aboard the boat.

"Shit, they couldn't lay me off, I'm their token Irish minority now," Pat said. "Your lazy ass on the other hand..."

Ashe grinned some more. This was just the verbal crap-filled greeting cops gave each other. It didn't mean anything and never lasted too long with him and Pat. They'd grown older and tired of it quicker.

Pat looked the part of the stereotypical Irish cop, if such a thing still existed. He was big, 6'3 at least, and thick in the neck. Ruddy faced with curly light-brown hair turning grayer at the edges. And he had the thickest, scarred-up hands Ashe had ever seen.

"Hey, heard you were all holed up at your daddy's place over the pandemic."

Ashe continued his work on the boat deck, coiling up a drain hose under his right elbow and up over his palm.

"News flash, it's my place now," he corrected. "Did you 'hole up' at that crappy Irish bar on South Street with one of your old female informants?"

"Hey! It ain't crappy. They mopped the place out only last month. And my informants are too old to be much fun anymore!" Pat said, feigning indignation over their favorite bar.

"I'm glad to hear you were there. Truth is, that much Black

Bush whiskey and Murphy's Irish Stout is better than the vaccine. You're not only safe from Covid, hell, Pat, you're safe from leprosy!"

"Yeah, yeah. Hey, you know my partner, Sergeant Dan Breslin," Pat said.

"We met," Breslin said first and stuck out his hand. "At your retirement lunch."

Ashe shifted the hose to his left arm and took his hand and said, "I remember. You were a Vice guy last I heard, right?"

Then the two cops spoke at the same time. Pat asked, "You still dating that cute little lawyer with them big brown eyes?" Over top of him, Breslin answered, "Yeah, Narcotics-Vice for four years, five as a precinct detective before that."

Before anyone said anything else, Ashe's boat phone rang, so he dropped the coiled hose to the deck and ducked into the little cabin to answer it.

The caller asked, "Is Lieutenant Keagan there please?"

"Pat! In here! For you!" He held the receiver up until Pat came to take it.

"Lieutenant?" Ashe asked sarcastically with his hand over the receiver.

"Damn straight," Pat whispered back.

Ashe stepped back out on deck with Danny Breslin. "Not much cell service. It's why I still hook up a landline when I'm here."

Breslin nodded and just stood there, as if not sure what to do with his hands. He looked up and down the boat, feigning admiration, but Ashe could tell he wasn't interested in it for real.

Breslin was shorter, fit-looking, about 5'10 or so. He had closely cropped black hair and wore some sort of large gold class ring. He dressed better than Pat, but that wasn't hard to do.

"You two came up through the ranks together," Breslin said, stating a fact, not asking.

"Yeah, I dragged that big hound dog along on my back for years."

"Detectives together too?"

"Yep."

"You retired a couple, three years ago."

"Yep. A little over two. Then I moved back here a few months ago. Just in time for the lockdowns."

Breslin nodded. He was making small talk and wasn't used to it. They were here at Ashe's boat for something official and it was obvious Breslin wanted to get on with it.

So, Ashe turned the tables. "You and Pat have been together since…"

"Right as Covid hit."

"So street to vice to MCU in four years. You must be good."

Breslin shrugged. "I prefer to think I'm detail-oriented."

Ashe smiled. "What happened to…"

"Pat's other guy, Birchfield? He quit," Breslin said.

"Lot of cops up there quit about then."

"Uh-huh." Breslin stopped looking around and focused on Ashe.

"Not me," Ashe said, a bit more sharply than he meant to. "I retired after twenty-five and moved here to take care of my dad. He was 90."

"I take it he's…passed?"

"Yeah."

Breslin nodded again. "I'm sorry about that. Pat talks a lot about him. And you."

This time, Breslin seemed sincere so Ashe pointed at a deck chair. "Water? Soda? I figure you're on duty."

"No thanks, and yes. We are here officially."

Ashe was about to ask more, but Pat burst out of the cabin like a buffalo coming out of a revolving door.

"Hey, so we need to talk about something," Pat said. "Sorry but I got to."

"You want a water or something?"

"I already got one out of your fridge there," he said and threw a second bottle toward Breslin.

Pat walked around to place himself against the rail and between Ashe and Breslin.

"I'll just get to it, Chig. You doing something down here with the Georgia Murphy thing?"

"Why do you want to know? It was a Hurrt County case until it looked like the woman was killed in the city."

"It's a cold case but belongs to Metro and you're retired," Pat said tiredly.

"Ah, so what if I'm retired? It was a local mystery, kind of interesting."

"Well, Captain Speakes heard you were trying to reinvestigate it."

Ah-ha. Just as Lois had cued him.

"From who?" he asked.

"Somebody, I dunno." Pat took a huge draw at his water, almost finishing it.

"Look, that case came to us at Metro through channels. As I recall, I assigned it to you."

"You did. I spent a lot of hours on it, but there wasn't anything we could take to the DA."

"Pat, I'm sorry but I just don't recall it much. Why was it a Metro case and not Hurrt County in the first place?"

Pat looked at Breslin, but Breslin just stared at Ashe.

"Okay, you know she was separated from her husband and he lived in Metro."

"Yeah, Tony Murphy."

"We had him on an attempted armed robbery, cold. Slam dunk. When we picked him up, we searched his apartment."

Breslin sighed and lowered his head. His demeanor suggested to Ashe that he didn't approve of Pat talking this much.

"Hey, why don't you go check in. You might get cell service by the car," Pat said to him.

Breslin stared at Pat a beat. It was obvious to Ashe he was perturbed, but turned and started back to the dock.

"Hey, "Ashe said to him as he left. "You going to…"

"No!" he shouted and tossed the bottle of water back to him.

Ashe snagged the bottle and took a long pull from it. He waited until Breslin was out of earshot.

"Okay, yeah. I remember this part now," Ashe said.

"We found some blood, DNA, and her things in Tony's apartment."

It was as if a lightning bolt hit Ashe on the head. *Things?*

"Huh. So, he didn't get rid of her things. Sloppy."

Easy, don't let on you might know what. C'mon, Pat. Tell me what things you found.

"We were on him too fast with the robbery maybe. Anyway, her stuff was behind the bedroom door."

"Stuff," Ashe said and pretended to look at the deck.

"A leather purse, a dress, a cell phone," Pat said.

Bingo! Be cool. We don't know who all is involved.

"Was there enough blood to prove she could be dead?" Ashe said, still trying to show semi-professional interest.

"Nah, but enough to type. He could have hit her, he's the kind. It would have to be pretty bad but not fatal. Anyway, we didn't find any blood-soaked towels or bandages or anything. Tub and floor were clean too. I Luminol'ed it and the bathroom floor. Nada."

Ashe nodded. If a person killed someone and cleaned up the blood, Luminol would still find it. Especially in kitchens and bathrooms where people tended to try to clean up their mess.

"So, the only reason you know of for Metro taking the case was her things. The blood and her purse and cell?"

"There was other stuff. Her last calls were up there, witnesses said she'd been there and they'd had a fight, other stuff. Anyway, like I said, I can't prove he killed her or for that matter that for sure she's dead."

"But..." Ashe said.

"But, Chig, I'd guess she's dead. No woman runs off for two years without all that stuff in her purse. Especially after all this time and nothing."

"Pat."

"Yeah?"

"Women have a lot of purses. It also might not have been hers; they were separated."

"Oh, it was hers. Driver's license, credit card, some new jewelry, and it was her cell."

Boom! Another bingo, Ashe thought.

"So two years and still nothing?"

"FinCen checks, social security checks, no new cellular phones. She could be using burners, but where? No relatives know anything that they're saying, and all her friends were either in Metro or Seacord."

"Huh," Ashe said. Inside, he felt himself tingling. This would be the first physical evidence to corroborate the photos. The sheriff and the old judge were right. They had evidence things had been manipulated to make it appear Georgia Murphy was abducted or killed in Metro, not Hurrt County.

"I even came to Seacord here to try and prove it was or wasn't Metro's."

That didn't surprise Ashe. Pat was good at his work.

"Yeah. I interviewed her co-workers, friends, even your little girlfriend, the young lawyer. Stephanie Whoozits."

"Collins."

"Not Mrs. Ashe yet?" Pat said and grinned. "Christ, everybody here I talked to said you two were banging each other nonstop! Can't blame you, hell, but she's got to be…"

"Drop it." Ashe wasn't amused.

Pat smiled at Ashe, but he knew Pat was making a mental note about it irritating him.

"Okay, buddy. But listen, she told me Georgia Murphy was going to divorce Tony. And now Georgia Murphy hasn't surfaced anywhere."

"Yes, I heard that." *Note to self, Ashe. Go verify that.*

"Pat, a person could, with some pre-planning, drop everything and disappear. But eventually most people who try that have to use their true identity sooner or later."

"Nah, Chig. You can only get by on cash for so long. And there's no evidence Georgia Murphy had a lot of cash to live off of for two years."

"Plus, almost everyone I know who did take off, attempted to reenter their lives once they figured it was safe to do so. They called a relative or friend," Ashe admitted.

"That's why it's a Metro case…and two damn years ago you agreed!" Pat said.

"She's not going to reappear. FinCen and NCIC will not find her."

Pat nodded, "Nope."

"Because she's dead."

"Yep."

Pat looked out over the lake and drank his water. Ashe watched as he patted his breast pocket then thought better of it.

"You get a private detective license?" Pat asked.

"You don't have any smokes. You quit smoking," Ashe reminded him.

"Answer the question, Chig. You got a client or something?"

Ashe almost told him about his reserve deputy status, then had a thought.

So Speakes was pressing Pat to come talk to me? Why does he think I have a PI license?

"My call, it was from the captain," Pat said. "He wants to know if you're legal with a license and all…and what the hell are you nosing around in this for?"

"None of his business. But if I was, why would it matter to him?" Ashe asked. "Maybe I could shed a new light on it? Or, just maybe I'm researching for a book."

What is all this talk about a private investigator's license? Ashe wondered. *It didn't make sense.*

They both looked back to the dock and saw Breslin returning. Pat shot a look at Ashe straight in the eyes and almost imperceptibly shook his head.

Then louder he said, "State law says retired cop or not, you have to have a private license. I happen to know you don't have a private license to poke into anything. If you're writing a book about an official open case, the department would want to clear it first."

Why would he insist Metro PD clear a book? It was ludicrous.

Ashe played along. "Tell your Captain Speakes he has no authority over me now, and no jurisdiction here. Besides, I might decide to go get a license. Is the captain afraid I might figure something out you and Danny here haven't?"

By this time, Breslin had stepped back aboard and looked back and forth at the two men as they bantered at each other.

"Oh, whatever!" Pat shot back. "Anyway, Captain says he'd call the local guy, uh, Sheriff Whoozits if he has to. And if they approved your private license, then you'd have to have a client and you'd have to file a blue form with us to operate…"

Ashe cut him off. "I don't live in the city anymore. I live here, in Hurrt County. Any forms or anything else I had to do would be filed here."

"So, you are or you aren't?"

Ashe rubbed his arms. *Is Pat still putting on a front for Breslin?*

"Anyway, say I'm not, Pat. Not looking, doing, getting into anything but a hopefully few late fish this fall and cleaning up this boat."

"You're not?"

"No," Ashe lied.

"So, no for sure?" Pat said. "The captain's wrong."

"I'm fixing up my boat." He didn't want to repeat the lie.

"Oh. Gotcha. Just the boat," Breslin said. By his tone, Ashe figured they knew he was lying.

"No, my damned Gulfstream jet too."

Pat laughed at that and stood up. "Let's go, Danny, it's a drive back to the city." He groaned as he moved and resembled a grizzly bear getting to its hind legs.

Breslin hopped down to the dock and started up toward the gate at the far end.

Pat looked at his old friend and patted Ashe on the back. He lowered his voice a bit and said, "You need to stay clean on this, Chig. I mean it. Check your six, whatever you're doing, be careful. You call me anytime, eh?"

Ashe lowered his voice to match Pat. "Pat, listen. I need to…"

"No, you listen to ol' Patrick. Watch your ass!"

Ashe nodded and decided he'd talk to Pat again later. Like after he'd nailed Detective Davis to the wall of her damn office.

"Hey, Pat, one more thing."

"Yeah?"

"I might just go get that P.I. license."

"Huh! You're ineligible. Your parents were married when you were born!"

"Unlike yours. They ever figure out who your mother was? I could look into it for you."

"Blow me, Chig." Which Ashe knew meant, *Take care, buddy.*

Ashe watched as Pat lumbered over the side onto the dock and walked briskly to where Breslin was waiting.

He hated having to talk around Breslin, but Pat hadn't seemed comfortable discussing the case with him around. The sheriff had been clear that no one was to know he was officially investigating Georgia Murphy that didn't need to.

Ashe made up his mind to talk about that to the sheriff, and as soon as he could bring Pat in on it. This would need to be worked from both ends.

But this morning, he'd finally learned more than he'd given out.

Ashe knew there was a dedicated effort to plant sufficient evidence at Tony Murphy's apartment in Metro to mislead investigators. That was one. Two was, he also knew that anything that had happened to Georgia had likely happened in Hurrt County.

Then three, Captain Speakes at Metro Police was so concerned Ashe was looking into the case in Hurrt County, he had sent Pat and Breslin all the way down to ask questions.

Ashe knew Speakes, and he wasn't typically engaged enough with anything other than his own political ambitions to be pulling strings this heavy. Someone was likely pressing him to send Pat at him, knowing they had been partners.

AAG Ashad? Someone else?

But Ashe knew from experience, nobody puts too much pressure on Pat Keagan. Pat came down to see him as instructed and went through the motions.

Then somehow, the idea Ashe had a private investigator's license to look into Georgia Murphy had come up. This meant, they didn't know the sheriff was the one to get him involved and had deputized him. He figured that was number four.

Ashe looked at his boat a little sadly. "Some other day, old gal," he said to the boat and went inside to clean up.

Time to go find Detective Davis and stop waiting for her.

CHAPTER 9

Ashe arrived home from the boat dock to get some things he'd need and to change clothes. His head was trying to sort and collate all he'd found out over the past couple of days.

Stevie. Her face popped into his mind. *Later, this is not helping.* But he texted her anyway and asked her to call him.

He changed into nice jeans and a black sport coat and was ready to head back into Seacord, but this time decided he'd probably ought to be carrying his gun. He strapped a leather holster inside his pants, the one he'd bought from a former Army friend in Arizona who'd custom-made it for him, and took out his worn blued Smith and Wesson hammerless revolver.

It only held five shots and he poked around in drawers until he found some simple flat but accurate wadcutters. With the just-under-two-inch barrel, there was not much advantage to using sturdier rounds. He also found in his bedside drawer a firm rubber strap that held five more rounds in a row by their base. These were lead hollow point rounds that protruded past their brass case and were thus easier to load in a hurry.

If he actually had to reload, he knew it'd be a very bad day.

Ashe hitched up his pants and looked in the mirror. With his jacket, the tiny revolver was invisible. This was okay for now, he figured. Having worked in Metro, and having had to pull a gun and use it before, he knew he needed something better.

Walking out to the living room and kitchen area, he grabbed his portfolio and decided to give Sheriff Jacobs a heads-up.

Ashe called the sheriff on his cell and updated him first as to what the judge had said. Jacobs said he was at the courthouse running errands.

"So Harold Marsh is figuring Mark Portals is pulling Stevie's strings somehow? Why?"

"At this point I can only assume. Let's you and me avoid doing that from now on."

"Agreed."

"Now, Sheriff, hang onto your hat," Ashe said.

He wanted Sheriff Jacobs to know that the photos were more than ever critical evidence, given Pat's comment that Tony Murphy had had Georgia Murphy's purse and cell. But he didn't want to throw Pat under the bus with whomever was manipulating this in Metro.

"Secure those photos you showed me. Lock them up. I think we will be able to back them up with the hard evidence you need to prove your theory."

"Really? You think her purse and cell are in Metro? The same ones in our photo?"

"I'll know soon for sure," Ashe promised.

"Dammit!" Sheriff Jacobs started fuming. Ashe could feel it even over the phone.

After a beat he added, "Shit! I should arrest Tracy Davis right damn now! For...for...tampering and changing evidence from...for what happened to Georgia Murphy!"

"Whoa, hang on!" Ashe shouted. "She'll just lawyer up, and like you said, all we have is evidence of sloppy police work."

"I thought, well maybe before, but now, I definitely...she's..."

Jacobs was mad as hell. Ashe had to smile to himself because he'd known the feeling many times. He decided he needed to talk Jacobs down off the proverbial roof.

"Hey, hey! Let me talk to her first, get her to admit or deny what happened. Either one will work for us, but we need to know *why* she would do this before we start taking this to the Portals-related ADA."

Ashe could hear Jacobs breathing hard. "Yeah?"

"Yeah. You accuse her of anything and she just clams up. I want to know the why and the how those things went missing and how they got to Metro. I want to see her case file and inventory of evidence. And you and I need to know what the hell was up. What would be so important to ghost Georgia Murphy," Ashe said, trying to get him to settle a bit.

"Yeah," Jacobs said more flatly.

"You asked me to help…"

"Okay, yeah. I did."

"Well this is how I can help."

"I'm a bit over my head here, Ashe. Sorry I blew my top."

"I got it. One other thing."

"Okay?"

"If we are right and the purse and cell that Metro might have *are* the same ones from Deputy Clark's photo…"

"Yeah? Oh…I think I get you."

"Yep, you have a damn probable Hurrt County murder and a conspiracy on your hands. Anything we do now will impact the bigger investigation later."

"Yeah, gotta be smart. Got'cha. So what can I do?"

"First, stay away from Detective Davis if you can help it. As mad as you are, she'll pick up on it. I want her to keep thinking everything's normal."

"Probably smart," Jacobs said.

"And I…I just want to be sure how Stevie Collins is involved," Ashe said.

"Yeah, the ol' judge was worried about her too. And I get it, you and her."

"Sheriff, I'm not suggesting if she were on the wrong side of this, somehow…"

"I get it," was all he said.

I have to know, and fast.

"So what next?" Jacobs asked.

"We divide and conquer. You sure you trust Deputy Clark?"

"Uh, yes. I guess I have to, right?"

"Get him in private. Get his camera and see if the photos you showed me are still on it. Especially the one with the two purses and the cell. Then, for God's sake, lock it up. It's crucial evidence."

"Ok, he works nights. I'll just go wake him up at home."

"Are he and Davis close? You think he'd tip her off?"

"I honestly don't know, but I don't think so."

Ashe thought for a minute. He wanted to back up the first crime scene photo with the original digital image. It'd have the metadata with the exact date and time, and depending on the camera, the location.

"We'll have to chance it."

"I think he'll do what I tell him," Jacobs said.

"Then convince him to, better yet, *order* him to keep it close hold. But don't mention Davis. Just tell him to talk to no one."

"I think I can get him to do that. He might be on his three-day off, too."

"Oh, and another thing. Can you get with the clerk's office at the courthouse and, without alarming anyone, see if Stevie actually filed Georgia Murphy's divorce papers? I've been assuming things too much. We can't afford a single mistake; this will blow open pretty soon."

"Yeah, I'm in my car at the courthouse now."

Ashe had another thought. "And another thing," he said.

"Damn, I feel like I should've been writing all this down..."

"You have access to NCIC and the State Criminal Database yourself?"

"I can have my dispatcher..."

"No. You, personally. Do you have access in private?"

"Okay, yeah."

"Get me everything on Tony Murphy. Criminal history, everything. I've heard all about what a bad dude he was, so I want to see."

"You got it. *Anything else?*"

Ashe smiled. "No. That will keep you busy today, huh?"

"It's okay. I feel like I'm doing my damn job now. Wait, what are you going to be doing?"

"Is Detective Davis at the S.O.?"

"Just now, I think."

"You're at the courthouse still?"

"I'm walking in. Just outside the clerk's office as we speak."

"Good, stay gone a couple hours. Let me have time with Detective Tracy Davis."

Ashe heard the sheriff sigh heavily again. Just the mention of her name got him upset.

He said, "She asked about you. What you were doing. I wasn't sure what to say so I told her you were just an old retired cop that was bored and I wanted you to look over any of our unsolved cases."

That was smart.

"Good. I'll call you back when I know more," Ashe said and hung up.

He went out, locking his house for the first time in months. *Better to be cautious.*

As he hopped in his old Jeep Cherokee, he said out loud to it, "If you pull any shit today, you're headed to the damn scrapyard!"

Ashe arrived about twenty minutes later back at the HCSO and went inside. The same woman from before buzzed him in without him having to ask.

"Your daddy and my daddy used to go fishing, back a long time ago," she said as he walked into the hall. She leaned out the top of the split door again.

"Oh, cool. Yeah, he loved to fish."

"Sheriff Jacobs isn't here."

"Oh, darn. Um, is Detective Davis here? Maybe she could help me."

"Tracy's office is right by where the sheriff's is."

Ashe started to head that way when the woman, her name tag said Janet, asked, "Are you a private investigator?"

Ashe just mock-laughed. "Oh my gosh!" was all he said to her and moved off to see Davis.

Why not keep this rumor going?

He saw Davis was at her desk and tapped on the doorframe.

"Excuse me, Detective Davis?"

She looked up without any surprise. "You Chig Ashe?" she asked.

"Guilty. But just Ashe, please."

"Okay, Mr. Ashe. Yep, I'm Detective Tracy Davis. Come in, the High Sheriff ran over to the courthouse and will be back in a bit."

"Thank you," he said and stepped in.

She gestured toward a seat and said, "Give me a minute, Mr. Ashe," and finished up something on her computer.

It was a small office, cramped almost, and the exact opposite of the spacious office Jacobs had. On every flat surface, there was some sort of paperweight, mini statue, toy police car, photo cube, or general clutter—all related to law enforcement. The walls were covered with training certificates and group photos of deputy sheriffs, including the obligatory Hurrt County Sheriff's Office official calendar that matched the one the sheriff had.

Davis was short, maybe 5'4, and wore gold aviator-style glasses and 5.11 khaki pants with an embroidered green polo with a sheriff's star and the word *Detective* in an arch above it. She wore the polo tucked in, which showed her belly that pooched out over a thick black nylon rigger's style belt. A compact Glock pistol was in a soft nylon holster on her hip.

Ashe hadn't noticed her shoes yet but bet himself she was wearing either 5.11 or Blackhawk brand tactical boots.

She sat in her chair behind her desk and reared back a little. Given the stuff all over her desk and the large computer monitor, Ashe had to lean forward and left a bit to see her.

"So...Sheriff Jacobs said you wanted to look into our cold cases," she said as she finished typing.

"I'm retired, Metro Major Crimes Unit, thought maybe I could help."

Davis seemed to be staring at him, but the way she was leaned back in her chair meant the overhead light put a glare on her glasses.

"You have a case in mind, Mister Ashe?" She put an emphasis this time on the word, *Mister*.

"Like I said, I worked MCU for nearly eighteen of my twenty-five years so, robbery, kidnapping, homicide."

"Well, I have a few unprosecuted assaults." She shrugged and half smiled.

Ashe could understand why the sheriff had gotten so mad at just the mention of her name. She was just screwing around with him.

Time to go work, ol' boy.

"Assaults? That's it? Well that is impressive work, Detective. I'd be excited to see what your case load-to-solve ratio is for this year and the past five years? Or, as long as you've been an investigator, if that's less than five years."

"Six years," she said defensively. "My ratio is...good."

"Good? I see. So, okay, how many higher-level NIBRS cases, Group B or above, have you yet to successfully clear?"

"Uh," she said. "NIBRS..."

Exactly, Ashe thought. *Good's ass.*

Ashe opened his portfolio and put on his reading glasses. He flipped a few pages in his pad and took a pen. "National Incident Based Reporting System. Group B or even Group A crimes. You do report case work to the DOJ and FBI. Through the state police. Yes?"

She sat up a bit. "We, um, they do UCR reporting…uh, we have two cold cases that are a Six to them."

"UCR? Six? Oh, well there you go. We're all transitioning from UCR to NIBRS over the next year or so. Hey, I'm here to help. So, tell me about those two cases."

Davis looked around her office at her cop souvenirs and crap, and then to the pile of additional crap on her desk. None of it was of immediate help. So she went back to her computer.

"Let's see," she started and began to wiggle the computer mouse.

"Hey, Detective Davis," Ashe said. She stopped and looked at him.

"Just tell me what you remember."

"Well…" she said, and again she was just stalling.

He'd thought about this. Small-town deputy sheriff being asked to cooperate with the big city detective on a local case. Of course she'd be a little defensive.

"Look, I'm from here. Born and raised. Played baseball and football here at the high school. Left for the Army then got hired in Metro. My dad and granddad were both from Hurrt County. I moved back here to take care of Dad when he went into hospice."

"I know," she said. "He was sheriff here too a long while back, I heard. Sorry to hear he passed."

"Thank you. May I call you Tracy?" Ashe pointed at her large brass nameplate on her desk.

"Sure."

"Tracy, I assume you have an active case load that keeps you…busy. I've been asked by the sheriff just to try and see what I can do to help. We're on the same team."

"Sure." But she didn't sound convinced.

"God knows the sheriff couldn't do it without you," Ashe said, playing a gambit.

She smiled at that. She turned her chair a bit to better look at him from behind her monitor.

"Samuel Brooks. 1979 case. Allegedly killed by his brother-in-law. No prosecution. But I'm guessing you don't care about him."

Ashe just sat and looked at her over his glasses with a faint smile.

"I'm guessing you want to see Georgia Murphy's case file."

"The missing woman," Ashe said.

She nodded, twirling a pen in her hand. "I'm guessing from what I heard, we handed this case off to you back then. Up in Metro."

"My office, the Major Crimes Unit. I assigned a detective to take it on."

She kept twirling the pen. "So, somebody up there is handling it now."

"I assume."

"Pardon me, Mister Ashe, but what are you supposed to do down here? She went missing up there?"

"I'm guessing the sheriff wants me to review what was sent to Metro, since as you say, I accepted it there. But he wants a simple relook. Just covering his political butt, I guess."

She smiled again. There was no love lost between them, Ashe knew.

He waited. She twirled her pen. A full minute went by. She looked at her cell phone. Finally, she kicked her legs and her chair went back upright. She pulled a file folder out from under other ones skewed across what little free space there was on her desk.

"This is what we sent Metro on Georgia Murphy."

Ashe took the file then pulled up his reading glasses and opened his portfolio. There was nowhere to lay it all out flat except in his lap. So, he decided to read through the file first.

There was an initial offense report by Deputy Bill Clark. The report from just over two years ago was very basic but surprisingly well written. Georgia Murphy's supervisor, Susan Marlin at Hurrt County Land and Title, had been trying to find her after she'd not come to work or called in for two days. Ms. Marlin had also mentioned that Georgia's husband, Tony, had been in criminal trouble a lot and had moved to Metro six months before.

So that would be six months of separation before Georgia's disappearance.

Ashe wrote a note after swapping the file for his portfolio in his lap.

The report continued that Deputy Clark had run a check with surrounding counties, including Metro, for any report of an accident or any other type of contact with Mrs. Murphy. The file had several copies of return NLETS emails where departments had responded negative. He ran her name and address and got a car registration. He ran that to see if there had been any LE contact with the car. He had a dispatcher call all area hospitals as well as the Highway Patrol. Nothing and nothing.

Clark had also run an NCIC criminal history through the state and FBI. Nothing on her but Tony's took up a full page. Even two years old, it showed an escalating pattern of minor to medium run-ins with the law here in Hurrt then more major problems in Metro.

Deputy Clark is a hunter.

Then there was a memo in the file showing a full copy was provided to Metro, at the assistant district attorney's directive. A hard copy was made and packaged and turned over to an official messenger. That was the 30th of April. About two weeks after she'd disappeared.

"Hey, Davis," Ashe said. She'd been staring at her computer screen while making slow random moves with the mouse. Ashe guessed solitaire.

"What?"

"I don't see anything much in here about her husband, Tony, except his history. Did you guys interview him?"

"No. I think you guys in Metro did."

"Ok."

Ashe's cell phone abruptly buzzed loudly. He ignored it.

Ashe made a note to call Pat, or better yet, Lois.

What date and time was Tony Murphy arrested compared to the date Georgia was last seen? Did he ever make bond after his robbery arrest? Is there any way he could be out and on the street between his arrest and eventual conviction?

Deputy Clark and Davis had gone to Georgia's apartment the night she was reported missing, April 15th. With the landlord's help, they searched her place. At this point, the file was officially handed over to Detective Davis, and Clark was relieved. A photocopy of her field notes was in the file.

Ashe made himself a note. *Susan Marlin reported Georgia missing the afternoon of the 15th. Georgia Murphy hadn't been at work for two days but she had been at work the day before, the 13th. Right here in Hurrt County.*

Back to the case file. A search of the apartment showed normal clothing, personal possessions, toiletries, and belongings. No indication to Ashe she'd packed and left on her own. In fact, there was every indication she'd soon return to this apartment.

Davis had run a check of Geogia's cell phone. It pinged a tower in Metro that night and was still active at the time. Davis had called it and got no answer. She got Tony Murphy's cell phone number off a scrap of paper stuck to Georgia's refrigerator and called it. No answer, no voicemail was set up.

A detailed inventory of items of interest was in the file. Notably there was only the one purse listed. A small bejeweled clutch with a thin silver strap.

And we have another bingo. If everybody else was accurate and the leather purse and cell were in Tony Murphy's apartment, Tracy Davis likely has doctored this case file.

Ashe's phone buzzed again. A short buzz. Text message. *Ignore it for now.*

He shifted in his chair and a heavy envelope of photos fell off his lap onto the floor. Ashe recovered them and set them under his portfolio. He wanted to examine them carefully.

Ashe finished up with the file.

Georgia Murphy had been at work here on the 13th, he wrote and circled it.

"Tracy, you interviewed Ms. Susan Marlin?"

"Me and Deputy Clark."

He handed the file back to her. "I don't see any statements or interview notes with her in here."

"Oh, maybe I have them here somewhere," she said and started fumbling through a drawer.

"Just answer me this, do you know about what time Georgia would have got off work that night?" From his own experience, the office closed at five.

"I'm not sure I recall asking…it's been two years."

"Okay, I'm not here to critique your investigation, but I have to ask questions. Same team, remember?"

"Same team? Sounds to me like you are trying to prove she went missing here. I guess that would clear up that you didn't find her or prove anything in Metro?" She was back to being smug.

Ashe took in a long breath. He wasn't sure how she made that leap, but it was not yet time to confront Tracy Davis.

"Hey, Tracy. Let's back up. This is a missing persons case here. In Metro, it's still a missing persons case. Let me ask my questions. I don't mean anything negative by them, certainly nothing personal to you or the HCSO. But I wasn't here, you were. I just want to know what you know."

Davis didn't relax a bit, but she lowered her voice. "She's dead, you know."

Ashe wondered why she was being quiet but lowered his to match her.

"You're probably right. But we have no evidence beyond circumstantial she's dead. That and it's been two years."

She nodded.

"Plus," he continued, "you're too busy with today; the crimes of right now. I can focus just on this. Anything I see, I hand over to you."

"Okay," was all she said.

"Like I said, I've been an investigator a long time. So, I can tell you; you've done a very professional job from what I see. But all this in the file is two years old. I have to ask or I don't know. I mean, for instance, at that time of this report, Tony's arrest would not have been in the system when you guys were checking that night."

She nodded. A half a degree up then down.

Her cell phone made a loud *bing*. She looked at it and seemed to be reading a text. Whatever it was, it was good news because a wide smile spread across her face.

"Everything ok?" he asked.

"Oh, absolutely." She sure sounded to Ashe like her cockiness index had gone up.

"Let's spread this stuff out somewhere besides my lap and bring it up to date. Maybe something else will catch *our* eye," Ashe said.

She chuckled a little and led him through the warped door that adjoined her office to the sheriff's.

Davis spread out the photos from the big envelope on the table.

Ashe went and looked over the photos. It was the second set, shot in daylight. Most were common crime scene pictures he'd expect to see for a missing person and not yet a suspected homicide.

And there was the shot of the bedroom closet door. One fancy purse, no cell phone.

"Have you shown these to Ms. Marlin? Does she recognize the purse? Did she know of any others?"

"Oh, I don't recall."

Yes. Since that text, she is definitely cockier, he thought.

He made a note or two about the caliber of clothing that belonged to Georgia. Much of it still had price tags.

"Hey, Mr. Ashe," she said.

"Just Ashe."

"Okay, 'Just Ashe,' answer me this. You still chasing after Stevie Collins?"

The question caught him off guard but he tried to not let it show. "Uh, no. Not for a while now," he said as he kept his eyes on the table of pictures.

"You know she was close pals with Georgia Murphy."

"Yeah," he said. *Don't get distracted. She's trying to get a rise out of you to draw off your focus on this crappy case file.*

"She's going out with Phillip Crews nowadays. Hot and heavy, I hear," Davis said.

That news hit Ashe in the stomach, but he knew he had to not look at her and stay focused on the paper in front of him. He bit a corner of his lip to keep from reacting.

Ah, Stevie, he thought. *What are you doing?*

Instead, he said, "None of my business but hey, check out this call list from Georgia's cellular phone company."

"What about it?"

Two years ago, they'd requested her call records back two weeks before her disappearance and had kept a check for any new calls for a week afterward. The last ping on a cell tower was on the 15th. Nothing after that night.

"You say in your notes you called her phone but she didn't answer. That would be the night of the 15th?"

"I did," she said but leaned over to look at the document.

"Leave a message?" Ashe asked. He had his finger on the list of calls from the 15th. "I mean, I don't see where you called?"

"They don't always have incomplete or unconnected calls on the log."

Bullshit. "Do you remember leaving a voicemail?"

Fifteen degrees of cockiness left her tone. "Actually, Clark called. I'll have to ask if he left a voicemail or not."

"Can you look at these numbers on her log and show me Clark's phone?"

"I don't...no, I don't recognize his number."

"Can you get his number for us to compare to these call logs?"

"I reckon," she said. But didn't make a move.

"May I make a suggestion?" Ashe said. "You looked at this disappearance at the time like she might *want* to be found. Or maybe she was alive and in trouble."

"Okay. But we agreed she's likely dead."

"But we can't *know* that for a certainty yet. Certainly not at the time. So run it like this, what if she left *and didn't want to be found*? What would you do different?"

Davis looked at him hard. Wheels were beginning to turn in her mind, it seemed.

"What if," Ashe continued, "all this was staged?"

"Why would she do that?"

"Who said *she* did the staging?"

Davis sullied up some. "Look, she was in Metro that night. Her phone proves it."

"No, Tracy. This only proves her phone was in Metro."

Then Davis gave Ashe a huge smile. It was unnerving and out of place. Before he could say anything, his cell buzzed again.

"You need to get that?" she asked and pointed at his phone.

He looked and saw he'd missed a call from the sheriff and then there were two text messages.

"Yeah, I'll walk outside."

"It's okay. I need to 'hit the latrine' myself," she said.

Ashe watched as she went up the hall then read his first text.

Jacobs texted, *Call me back, ASAP. Divorce filed by Portals, not Stevie.*

Ashe frowned to himself. *That contradicts what Stevie said.*

Then the next one read, *Clark not home, but wife says camera gone.*

Shit, shit, shit! Ashe thought. *No wonder she'd been stalling and putting me off. She knows she is covered.*

Then Ashe had another thought. *Was this what Davis's text message was about?*

His last text was from Stevie: *We need to talk.*

Yes, we do, he thought.

Meet me for dinner-1730, he texted Stevie back.

Davis strolled back into the office as she was closing her cell screen. She had called or texted someone. She then started picking the photos and the case file off the desk.

"So, tell me, 'Just Ashe,' are you a private investigator? If I had known that, I wouldn't have shown you this file and the photos."

"Oh, despite what the sheriff instructed you to do?"

"He said we could talk."

Ashe felt himself getting hot. "Oh, well then. No, I'm not a private investigator."

"Whatever," she said.

"I have an idea. Maybe to get this investigation back on track you could show me the other photos?"

"I don't know what you're talking about."

"Yes, you do," he said as calmly as he could. "Of course you do, Detective. You know, the first set of photos that were shot the night she was reported missing?"

"Not true!" she barked, then composed herself. "You need to more careful who you listen to! Have a good day, Mister Ashe." Then she got up to walk through the connecting door.

"Hey, Tracy," Ashe said softly. She turned and glared at him.

"I'll leave you for now. But I'm not going anywhere. I've been here in this county since before you were born and now, I'm back. And... I am never leaving."

She just glared at him, but Ashe could see her façade of toughness crack just a bit.

"Ever."

She left him and then tried to pull the warped door shut, but it never fully closed.

He left the HCSO and found his Jeep. Hopping inside, he scanned his notes again and took out his cell to call the sheriff.

It was obvious by her attitude toward Ashe that Tracy Davis knew Georgia Murphy had been abducted from Hurrt County. Davis also seemed confident there was no remaining evidence to the contrary. That's why she was so cocky. Her comment of, "She's dead, you know" had a much darker meaning to it.

And she was daring Ashe to do something about it.

CHAPTER 10

"You know, Sheriff, I now understand why you get pissed off about Tracy Davis," Ashe said over his phone.

He'd called the sheriff to update him and after a couple of tries finally got him leaving Deputy Clark's house. Apparently, the signal was sketchy out there, but Ashe did his best to fill him in on their conversation.

"Now she says there *never were* a set of photos of Georgia Murphy's apartment taken that night," Sheriff Jacobs said and huffed. "And so we're all liars!"

"Told me to be careful about it. About who I listened to."

"You think she was threatening you?"

"Nah, I rattled *her*. Wasn't my intent going in, but rattled she got," Ashe said. "And come to think about it, that might stir the pot a bit."

"Okay," Jacobs said, his signal crackling and fading in and out. "Meaning, her denial tells us a lot."

"Right. I'm assuming they've had it pretty easy since Georgia vanished. Pretty smooth. Likely they're not used to anyone coming at them with direct accusations. They are overconfident, like she was with me. No offense, Sheriff."

"None taken. It's why I came to you. Maybe now someone will start making mistakes on their side."

That's when Ashe saw him. The man who had been watching from before. He was walking onto the town square toward a burgundy Chevy sedan. He didn't act like he'd noticed Ashe, although he walked right past his Jeep without looking, but on the other side of the street.

Probably getting my car tag number, he thought.

This time, he wore jeans, a dark fleece jacket, and a dark-blue ball cap and sunglasses which hid most of his face and hair, but it was him.

"Ashe, any sense in us searching Georgia Murphy's apartment?"

"Has it been rented since she disappeared?" Ashe asked.

"Yeah, you're right," Jacobs said.

"Doesn't hurt to check into it."

"I think I will. Oh, hey, Laney Clark, Bill Clark's wife, says he left about 1100 hours without saying where he was going. He said it was work-related."

Ashe looked at his watch. "Yeah, that would be about the time I was at my boat."

"Says she doesn't know if he had his camera, but it's missing."

"So maybe he has it. Maybe we're still in play here?" Ashe wondered aloud.

"Don't know. But, another thing though, she says he seemed upset and had his duty pistol with him."

"Uh-oh. You headed back here?" Ashe asked and checked his watch. It was already four thirty.

"Yeah, an hour or so. With Clark missing, I'm picking us up some backup."

"Okay. I'll meet you at the sheriff's office. I'm headed to the Land and Title office."

Jacobs acknowledged and before they could hang up, the signal was lost.

Ashe wanted to see where his shadow guy had gone, so he had to risk turning around in his seat. He didn't want this guy to know that he was looking. Anyway, the Chevy was gone.

Ashe started his Jeep after two tries and drove back up the direction his shadow had come to try and figure out where he'd been. Uphill a little past the sheriff's office was a four-way stop, but to his left was the rear of Judge Marsh's office building and also the Hurrt L&T.

The back door was open. Ashe pulled over and parked. He took a slow breath. This might not be good. *Did Shadow Guy just leave the title office?* He thought for a second. There was no way to tell.

He hopped out of his car and adjusted the gun on his hip. Then walked around the corner to come in to the Title Company from the front.

A chime sounded as he stepped in the door. The office lobby was brilliantly lit and newly furnished in a modern office motif. Bright tan and gold patterned wallpaper, stenciled lettering of the company name on one wall, huge fake plants, and floor tile that looked like light wood. Tiny LED lights circled the celling's white crown molding.

There was a big counter with fake ivy just under the ledge with more little LEDs to one side of the open hallway directly ahead. Additional stenciling on the wall behind it said *We are here to bring you Home!* and *We are how Hurrt County settles in!* in huge letters behind the counter. No one was seated there.

"Hello?" Ashe called out.

"Hello!" a woman's voice answered from way in the back. "Give me one second."

Ashe could hear someone closing and locking what he figured was that back door.

After a minute or so, he saw a woman coming up the hall to the lobby. She walked on tall high heels and looked about his age or just a tad younger. She was very well dressed in a skirt and jacket that were maybe a little tight but fit her figure well. Her light reddish-brown hair was neatly styled and fell just below her shoulders. She wore a large gold necklace and jewelry that looked real but not overdone. Everything about her looked professional and successful, Ashe thought, and somehow familiar.

"Chig!" she said excitedly and trotted toward him with her arms wide open.

"Hi, yeah, my name is Ashe and…"

"You old dog you, I heard you were back in town and wondered when the heck you were going to come see me!" She gave him a big squeeze-type hug then stepped back to look at him.

He still didn't quite recall her, but the look and the voice and the hug were familiar.

"Susan?" he gambled.

"Yes! But I'm a Marlin now. In high school, I was a Webster!"

"Of course! I knew the second I saw you," he lied. "I had no idea you were still living here."

She hugged him again and took him by the hand back to her office and sat beside him on a small couch. She quickly filled him in on everything she'd done since high school, including college and her marriage and divorce from Mr. Marlin. She punctuated her sentences with a grab of his hand or by popping him on the thigh.

He remembered her better. *Still flirtatious.*

Ashe caught her up as to his divorce, retirement, and move home without mentioning the reason for his visit. Yet.

"I just thought the world of your daddy. I worked for him here and we did a lot of business together even after he and Judge Marsh sold the company to the current owners."

"Well thank you. People still call you Suze?"

"People still call you Chig?"

"Only you and a couple others still remember that. I'm just Ashe now."

She cocked her head cutely to one side. He remembered that move. "Just your last name?" she asked.

"It's an Army-slash-Cop thing. You can still call me Chig. Just, not in public please!"

She looked at her watch and trotted back up front to the office. He heard her set the phones to voicemail.

When she returned, she gave Ashe a cute mock-frown and said, "You didn't come here to catch up with me; you didn't even know I was here."

"True, I want to pick your brain about something."

"Your daddy's estate? His land holdings? That was all settled I thought?"

"No. I mean, yes. But not about that." Ashe stood as he knew what he was about to say would completely change the mood.

"It's about Georgia Murphy."

Her smile fell. "Oh, lord," was all she said.

She settled in beside him back on the sofa and Ashe scooted around to be able to face her.

"You and she were not just co-workers, you were friends."

"Yes, she was a wonderful person. A tragedy! It was so good to see her learning so much so fast while working here. Her up and vanishing is not just a mystery, it's a shame."

"Talk to me about the month or two before she disappeared, or however far back you want to tell me what you know."

Susan looked him in the face hard and then averted her eyes as she started to speak. She had gone from a bright, happy, with an effervescent attitude to what appeared to be cautious and hesitant.

"I don't know what I should say to you, Chig. She seemed happy and was palling around with your, um...friend, Stevie. I was still married so I wasn't going out and all like they were."

"I know about Stevie's drinking. I didn't know the depth of it until lately. Was Georgia also..."

"Oh, she was a *fun* girl alright and might drink a lot sometimes, but Stevie was the hard partier according to Georgia," Susan said firmly. Like she was still defending her.

"You said she was happy. I take it the decision to divorce Tony was easier for her, given they'd been separated so long."

Susan frowned and seemed to Ashe to be thinking about what she was going to say.

"She never told me she was divorcing Tony. I mean, she was off and on mad at him for his *behavior*, shall we say, but I think they were trying to work it out."

"Huh. I'll be. They were separated for six months," he said.

She wrinkled her nose. "Well that was only because he worked up in the city. He did construction and got a job with a concrete company. He was back here often, or her and Stevie would go up to Metro to see him."

Ashe felt himself getting a bit warm under the collar. He'd been lied to quite a bit it seemed.

"So, Stevie never filed for a divorce for her? Georgia was trying to actually *stay* married to Tony."

"I really couldn't say. I'm sure whatever Stevie says is correct."

Uh, no. Actually not, he thought as he took out his cell and again return-texted Stevie.

Call me when you're in town. Then he put his phone away and turned back to Susan.

"Suze, why do *you* think she disappeared?"

"I don't know. It scared me then and it still scares me to think that sweet poor girl just dropped off the face of the earth. I still to this day pray she's safe and sound."

Ashe closed his pad and took off his glasses. "I think after all this time we should assume she's gone."

She nodded. "Yes, and never coming back. I hope she is happy and..."

"No, Suze, I mean she's likely dead."

Susan drew in a halting breath. "Oh, lord in heaven. I guess that's probably right."

"I need you to remember as much as you can about those times before she disappeared. It's important and I want to find out what happened, don't you?"

"I do. Okay," she said, her voice shaky.

"Was there anything she was doing that might have been unusual? Was she seeing anybody before trying to reconcile with Tony?"

Susan just shook her head and got up and walked over to her desk. Ashe followed her.

"Was she working on anything important? Sensitive?"

She frowned and just looked at her desk.

"*Anything* unusual? Any strange behavior? By her, or someone toward her?"

"I don't know, what all do you mean?"

"Well, I need *you* to tell *me*."

"I just don't know. I told Metro Police and the sheriff everything I knew at the time. I probably shouldn't even be talking to you now."

Oh?

"I want to discover what happened to her, the same as you."

"Yeah, but, Chig, you're not a cop anymore, you're a private detective or investigator, or whatever now," she said. "I shouldn't be seen talking to you!"

Ah, that again. It's not funny anymore. Time to get to the bottom of that.

She had flopped heavily in her desk chair and he sat on one corner of her desk to face her. Then she abruptly hopped up and went back to the small sofa and sat. Ashe just pivoted on her desk to face her.

"Suze, I'm not trying to hurt or embarrass you. I don't want you to be afraid. But I am not now, nor have I ever been, a damn private detective." He took out his deputy sheriff's badge and showed it to her.

"This is an official reinvestigation in the disappearance and likely death of Georgia Murphy."

"But they said…"

"Who? Who said?"

She turned and looked toward her back room and rear door.

"He… You're telling me you weren't hired to try to pin this on a local?"

"I was asked by Sheriff Jacobs to look into this case. He deputized me officially."

She sank back in the couch, her eyes darting back and forth as if replaying the past couple of hours or so in her mind.

"Well," she said after a long beat. "Son of a bitch."

"Indeed. Who told you that about me?"

"Son of a bitch," she repeated. This time more perturbed. "I don't curse like this normally and I hope my pastor never hears about it, but it's all I can think of to say!"

"Does the SOB have a name?"

"CJ Portals. Carl Jack, but we call him CJ."

"Oh? So I assume he's kin to…he's what to Mark Portals?"

"Nephew."

It made sense. This CJ Portals was checking up on him and telling everyone he was a P.I. to keep them from talking to him.

But why? And why did Portals not want me to figure out Georgia Murphy's disappearance? Unless the people I am talking to somehow could help prove what happened.

Ashe described the man who'd been shadowing him to Susan.

"That's him," she said. "CJ Portals."

"And, Suze, he was here tonight, correct? Right before I got here?"

"Oh yeah. He came to the back door and told me not to talk to you. He said you were a P.I. and were covering up for not finding her in Metro and trying to pin it on someone local!"

"Uh-huh. And have you talked to Detective Davis at the sheriff's office recently?"

"No, not at all."

So now I can assume CJ Portals and Tracy Davis spoke or texted tonight. It's why Tracy asked me the same stupid P.I. thing. That puts her in with him.

"Tracy Davis told me just now that she interviewed you the night you reported Georgia missing."

"Just asked me if she worked here, what all she did, and if she had been having any troubles. I said no."

"Did she ask about a divorce from Tony?" Ashe took out his pen and made a note.

"No, not that I recall."

"Did a big detective from Metro come see you later on?"

"Yes, I might still have his card." She got up to look on her desk.

"Pat Keagan."

"Yes," she said and sat back down. "That's him."

"Tell me about your conversation."

"I told him basically what I told Davis. He never asked me about a divorce," she said.

Yeah, Pat got that from Stevie later.

Ashe stopped writing and looked at her. "Did he ask you about Tony?"

She crossed her legs. "Maybe, I think so."

"What did you say?"

"Well, this is so long ago, I don't know. He said he wanted to get my impression on Tony Murphy and if he could do something like this. He said they thought Tony Murphy may have taken her in Metro and asked what I knew about that. Heck, that's what Tracy Davis and everybody else said. She went to Metro and was missing because of Tony."

"But you've told me she and Tony were getting back together. That just doesn't make sense."

"No, it doesn't," she said. "I told him I didn't know anything. But now, as I say it out loud doesn't fit with what all Georgia told me. She was finally happy, Chig!"

She uncrossed her legs and crossed her arms. "You know, Chig, I was working with Georgia to train her to get her license one day. I had her working on a set of title transfers for Mark Portals' office. He was managing some property acquisitions for some people."

She got up and motioned for him to follow her to the back room.

"I'm probably not supposed to show you this. It's actually not part of the L&T. It's leased by a couple of companies as kind of a 'war room,' I think they call it."

She walked him into a large rectangular room that took up the whole back half of the building. Large ten-foot square county and town maps were under plexiglass on the walls.

Dry-erase marker and thin strips of colored tape showed

surveyor lines and lots and zoning lines. A large table with a raised glass top that was possibly twenty feet by fifteen feet, by Ashe's estimation, sat in the center of the room. Instinctively, he looked for his property and found it, and also on another map, his lake property.

At the edge of Seacord township was a large section of properties, mostly undeveloped or pasture that were covered by a blue-tinted plastic overlay. As if bringing them all under one large new property.

"Wow," he said. He took out his phone and starting taking some pictures. "Suze, what is all this?"

"That's a rezoning plan. I don't know for what yet, but we've been doing title work for a company called DBA through Mark Portals' office."

"DBA? You mean as in, *Doing Business As*?"

She shrugged. "I don't know if it stands for anything, but if so, likely somebody's initials. DBA, LLC has some kind of future development plans. It's mostly unutilized land or old farms."

"That's a big damn development," he said, and photographed it all.

She noticed him taking pictures for the first time. "Hey, you shouldn't do that."

He put away his phone. "How much is all this going for?"

"The county assessor could tell you, I guess. I'd say the better part of four hundred and fifty, maybe five hundred million dollars' worth."

Ashe whistled. "Whoa, Nellie!"

"It's all we do now. We handle just these clients. Regular home closings or whatnot, we send to Heartland Title."

He went back and looked at his dad's old lake property where he had the boat. Beside it were several other lots going around the lake and several behind those. Probably a half mile deep or more in places. Many of these lots around the shoreline of Minor Hills Lake were in Hurrt County and all had a plastic red striped overlay cut to cover them into several new shaped lots. *S.C.E.A.* was penciled on the overlay.

"Ess-see-ee-ay?" he asked.

"Seacord Cultural Enrichment Association. It's informally pronounced 'Skee-Ah.' You should have heard about it, but then again maybe not."

"So what does this mean?" he asked and pointed to overlay.

"That's Skee-ah's planned zoning request. The county had already been through one public reading, but the investors asked for an extension until later this year. I guess they want to work on adding more to the project."

"They have actually bought these lots?"

"Some, but those they have, they are asking to change the density of how the residential lots are zoned."

"So they are planning to build more homes here?"

She shrugged. "Could be, or condos. I don't know for certain and they don't have all that worked out yet. I think he is being proactive with the rezoning."

"He? You mean Portals."

She looked at him. "No, this is Phillip Crews' project. Together, he and Mark rent this room and are our sole clients."

"Crews and Portals."

"Yeah. But this is all pretty normal stuff. They're working on projects in Carson County and McCormick County also. It seems big for here because nothing has much changed in years, but a lot of older property owners around here are selling. This is…progress, I guess."

"Georgia was working on DBA?"

"Not alone. I had her doing some of the basic research and she carried papers for me back and forth to Mark Portals or Phillip Crews. She processed some of the environmental impact statements and the ground stability inspections. I don't think we were doing the Skee-ah project yet. Before she got disbarred, Stevie did some of the legal work too."

Another icy finger traced a line down Ashe's spine. All along, he had wondered what was the *why* to her disappearance. What could be so important that someone would want Georgia gone?

And not be in Hurrt County.

"Who has seen all this?"

"Oh, everybody in Mark Portals' office, some men and women from out of town, investors maybe. I think the county assessor. It's only been kept a little private because there's some big future project associated with the DBA acquisitions. They put this together to help keep track of all of it and show off to their clients."

"This...war room, you called it. Would Georgia have seen all this?"

"Well, yeah. She put some of the new lines and shading up on the glass. Of course, there is a lot more to it now. Two more years of work and of course, the Skee-ah project is all new."

Ashe looked at it all. This was obviously years of planning, easily going back to when Georgia Murphy worked here. He studied the maps and knew he couldn't make sense of it, but he knew one thing he didn't know before.

He was looking at why Georgia Murphy had disappeared, and was likely dead.

"Suze, think for me. What is CJ Portals' involvement in all this?"

She looked at the maps and then back at Ashe.

"Nothing that I know of. I mean, he's like an unofficial go-between sometimes. Bringing papers and such, guiding surveyors and maybe business people out to the property and stuff."

"But tonight, he tried to get you to not talk to me," he said.

She hesitated, then said, "Again, he said you were covering up that you hadn't really done your job in Metro. CJ said Georgia went missing up there but you were trying to bring the case back here. They didn't want anything to mess up the project here, and a scandal might scare off their investors."

Ashe nodded. It was adding up. "Suze, what does this gray shaded area represent?"

She walked over and pressed herself against his back to look over his shoulder.

Again, is she flirting with me?

"Oh, those are a test pouring of concrete. It's pretty large. I think Mark hired Tony and his crew from Metro to come pour it. Our normal guy couldn't do it that fast."

She didn't move to separate her body from him, so Ashe stepped forward and turned to face her.

"Why? Seems expensive as hell," Ashe said.

"They said something about wanting to show some investors they could manage large-scale projects like this."

"For who? What is DBA building?"

"I don't know, but I think that DBA is just going to build a facility, not actually *do* anything out there," she said. "Then lease it or sell it."

Ashe nodded. "And you. You stand to make the L&T quite a profit, too, right? Handling all these titles and closings, being their sole title company."

She bristled a little at that. "Okay, sure, CJ mentioned that. Said to be careful or they'd change companies. But, Chig, I don't own the company and I swear I've done nothing improper or illegal with any of this!"

"I'm not pointing a finger at you. But I bet CJ was letting you know that for a reason. Didn't you feel like he was trying to intimidate you?"

"Maybe, a little bit." Then she smiled a subtle smile. "Look, he's only tried to get me in bed about a thousand times! Don't worry, I can handle him."

Ashe smiled. "Well, I understand his attraction to you. I guess I will just have to have a talk with him."

"Before you do, talk to Stevie," she said.

That was out of nowhere. "Huh?"

"She was seeing him for a while, if you know what I mean."

For the second time in the span of a few hours, he felt like he'd been gut punched. He decided to not address it with her, but would definitely talk to Stevie.

"Um, Suze, do me a favor." He took her hand. "Be very careful now. I do not know anything yet, but this is the first important thing that somehow might be tied to Georgia's disappearance."

She made a face and threw up her hands. "Oh, c'mon! I can't see how any of this could add up to her disappearing. Or being worth it to make her disappear!"

"I know. It's not clear to me either yet, but I think I've found the string to start pulling on."

"Really?"

"Plus, everywhere I've been the past couple of days, CJ Portals has been there first. Telling people I'm a P.I. and not to talk to me about Georgia."

She shook her head. "He…maybe he just doesn't know you're a deputy now. He's just protecting the investment. This could be a Big. Damn. Deal."

Yeah. Five-hundred-million-bucks worth.

"Well, don't *you* be the one to tell him I'm working this officially, eh? And look, he probably knows I've been here with you this long for, what? An hour maybe? So, he'll be back to ask what it was I wanted. Please, Suze, protect yourself. We were just catching up, all right? Nothing about this deal or Georgia."

"You don't seriously think CJ had anything to do with...he wouldn't. Well, I don't think."

Ashe shook his head. "I don't know the answers yet. Please trust me, just until I get this worked out. And be cautious, please?"

She sat and he could see her thinking hard.

"Oh my God. Chig, this...this could be..."

"Yeah. A Big Damn Deal."

CHAPTER 11

Ashe left the Hurrt County Land and Title through the front door. He wasn't sure anymore if he was being watched constantly or not, so to hedge his bet, he smiled broadly and gave a big silly wave back at the office as if Suze were watching him.

Just high school buddies, catching up.

She wasn't. He'd left her back in the DBA war room. He'd trusted her quite a bit, not having seen her since high school, but had also given her a lot to think about as well.

As he walked to his Jeep, his phone rang. It was Stevie.

"Hey," he said. "We still on for dinner?"

"Yeah, I'm a few miles out yet but I think I'll be there by five thirty or five-forty-five."

Her voice in his ear was like a tonic. "That's okay. I have a meeting I'm going to now myself," he said.

"The Fireside has a ribeye special!" she said in a sing-song voice. "I will let you buy a bottle of wine if it's ludicrously expensive and I can watch you drink it!"

"Fireside?" Ashe had never been there and it was miles out in the country. "Hey, my meeting is at the sheriff's office. Can we make it Roger's Café?"

"Oh good god!" she huffed. "Roger's? *Come on,* Ashe! Is your old girlfriend going to stare and give me the stink-eye the whole time? Our first dinner in months and I get a blue plate special?"

Ashe grinned at that. "Tilly works breakfast and lunch so, no. Please? Fireside's ribeye and vicariously imbibed wine next time."

"Fine, whatever, fine. Make it five-forty-five," she said and clicked off.

He smiled still, but the thoughts of what he'd learned at the L&T dulled his high mood a bit. He had a lot of hard questions for this person he still saw as his girl. He hoped in the end she still could be.

But it was looking more and more like not.

Then Ashe realized he'd been walking and thinking, engrossed as always in Stevie, and had not been scanning the streets as he arrived at his Jeep. He looked around for CJ Portals but didn't see him.

What he did see were several people beginning to filter out of the town's businesses and offices and start toward their cars. Shrugging on light jackets and standing around and finishing up conversations in pairs or small groups, standing beside their cars. A few more were smiling and looked to be trying awkwardly to break contact with someone and just get home. This was great camouflage if you were watching someone, Ashe knew.

It was still a little light outside despite the days growing shorter, but someone hadn't adjusted the streetlights. A few on the shaded town square began to pop on. He looked at his watch and saw it was later than he thought, so he hopped in and tried to start the Jeep.

The starter missed on him. He tried again, same result.

"Well to quote the great Susan Marlin, Son of a Bitch!" he shouted to no one.

He grabbed his portfolio and started walking back toward the town square and across it, to the Hurrt County Sheriff's Office. As he crossed the square, he saw a pair of county cruisers swing down from the main route, across the square, and then pull in outside the sheriff's office. After five minutes of fast walking, he made it there.

Sheriff Jacobs was outside his cruiser and smoking. A big uniformed deputy Ashe didn't know was leaning on the other car.

Jacobs saw him. "Hey, Ashe. Didn't see you drive up." He gestured to the other deputy and introduced him. "This is Ed Bell. Been with me since I took office. I figured we might want some help and someone else to know what all is going on."

Ashe shook his hand. Ed Bell was six-foot-five if he were an inch, Ashe figured. He looked to be in his thirties and at first glance, Ashe had thought he was a bit heavy, but in fact he was thickly muscled with little to no fat.

Bell had a big, light-brown moustache and bright blue eyes.

Ashe met his eyes as he shook his hand and immediately sensed that he was not just a big man but intelligent as well.

"You're Lieutenant Ashe from Metro," Bell said, not a question. "The one people call Chig?"

"Just Ashe, please. Good to know you."

"So we've been talking about Bill Clark," Jacobs said. "Ed here knows him pretty well and has been checking. Bill is still not home. His wife's worried sick now."

"Billy Clark would not leave his wife and kids at home all day for no reason," Bell added.

But Ashe had a bad feeling. "First, I hope he's fine. But, Sheriff, we need to find him and we need his camera."

Jacobs nodded and said to Bell, "Go over to his in-laws, go check the Fireside and anywhere and anybody you know that might know where he'd be. Find him and call me."

Bell nodded to his boss then turned and looked at Ashe again, then got in his cruiser and peeled out.

When he'd left, Ashe said to Jacobs, "I have a sick feeling."

"Ain't saying anything out loud but Christ, I hope that kid's okay."

Ashe jerked his thumb back toward where Bell had left. "If he's Clark's friend, I'd hate to be the one to have pulled something," Ashe said dryly.

Jacobs only offered a faint smile at that. He was worried.

"Listen, I checked on the Murphy divorce like you asked. The clerk was hesitant but I leaned in on it a bit and she let me have this," Jacobs said.

He handed Ashe a printout and he saw it was a schedule for court filings from two years ago on April 29th. It showed a divorce proceeding filed by Mark Portals on behalf of Georgia Murphy, vice Anthony Murphy.

"The 29th of April?" Ashe asked. "That's like way after…"

"Yeah. It's the same day Mark Portals and Stevie spoke with Sheriff Laughton about Georgia."

"Shit. She could have been missing since the night of April 13th, but for sure by the 15th. That's two weeks later! Stevie told me she'd delayed telling the sheriff that *she'd* filed for Georgia's divorce for several days, because, well she insinuated she was drunk and Portals was helping out her law practice by then. She said she thought she'd filed it way before Georgia disappeared but couldn't find the papers."

"Well, that might still be partially true. I know you two were an item later on, but two years ago, before I was sheriff, I lived here in this town. Everybody knew she was partying pretty hard. It could be she was supposed to file the papers but didn't, so Portals helped by covering for her."

Ashe leaned against Jacobs' cruiser beside him. He considered what the sheriff had said.

"I guess. But let me tell you something. Stevie and Georgia were hanging out together quite a bit then."

"Yeah, everybody knew that."

"So she would know that Georgia was back to seeing her husband, Tony. Off and on, true, but according to Susan Marlin, they were about to reconcile. Hell, Stevie and her had even visited him at his apartment in the city."

Jacobs frowned. "So why all this about a divorce? Why did Mark Portals file for one…"

"After she was dead?"

Jacobs lit a cigarette. "Oh hell."

"Yeah. Hell indeed," Ashe said. "Throws the whole disappearance on Tony Murphy's back and up in Metro."

"I did check with the manager at Georgia Murphy's old place," Jacobs said.

"Yeah?"

"Was professionally cleaned up after her disappearance as Tracy told them it was ok. Been painted twice, rented three times, and had the carpet replaced."

"We could call the forensics people and try," Ashe offered.

"Not too likely anyone'd find anything," Jacobs said. Then he drew on his smoke hard. "Oh, and Tony Murphy's criminal history. You know what? He was arrested April 13th on the robbery charge."

Boom! Ashe thought, then said, "So depending on what time he was arrested compared to the time Georgia left work on the 13th, then…hell, he may not have been able to have had anything to do with her disappearance!"

"And Detective Tracy Davis provided the damn evidence he did!"

"I think we should ask her about it. Together."

"Damn straight!" Jacobs said and they walked into the sheriff's office.

Tracy Davis was in her office and Ashe watched her as they walked up the hall. When she saw them, she started putting away papers and stood as if leaving for the day.

"Tracy," Jacobs said. It sounded more like a bark. "A minute in my office, please."

"I was about to go see Ms. Teller about the break-in at..."

"Now," is all Jacobs said. His voice sounded harsh and Ashe could see he was shaking.

"Sheriff, let me start, please," Ashe whispered.

Jacobs nodded and opened his office door; Davis came in through the adjoining one. Jacobs walked over to his desk and reached in a drawer. After a beat, he caught Ashe's eye and nodded. Ashe figured they were being recorded.

"Detective Davis, uh, Tracy, I need to ask a couple more questions," Ashe started.

She had been about to sit at the sheriff's long table but stood back up.

"Sheriff, do I have to talk to you in front of this P.I.?" She pointed at Ashe.

Before Jacobs could answer, Ashe jumped in. "Hey, that's a great place to start. You know I told you I wasn't a 'private eye' but you should know who I actually am."

Ashe took out his deputy's badge and showed it to the sheriff under the table where Davis couldn't see it. He nodded at Ashe, so Ashe set it on the table and slid it closer to Davis.

"I told you I am a retired detective lieutenant, former chief of the Major Crimes Unit in Metro. What I didn't tell you is here lately; I have been duly deputized and had my state commission reactivated by Sheriff Jacobs. That makes me a Hurrt County deputy sheriff."

Davis looked at the badge, looked at the sheriff who nodded, then looked at Ashe.

"So as I told you earlier, I am reviewing the Georgia Murphy case. Oh, and I have a couple of more questions for you."

"This is crap!" she said loudly, but with less conviction in her voice.

"Yes. Yes, it is," Ashe said and opened his portfolio and flipped to a blank page. He put on his reading glasses and looked at her.

Sheriff Jacobs had a form in his hand. "Tracy Davis, you have the right to remain silent..." he started and continued to read her rights. When he was done, he signed the form and pushed it over to her.

She was still acting confident, Ashe noticed, as she signed the rights waiver form, agreeing to be questioned.

Probably thinks she can talk her way out of this.

"Tracy," Ashe started. "We left off at the photos you said never existed. The ones we know Deputy Bill Clark took at the scene of Georgia's apartment the night of the 15th. The night she was reported missing. You know, you were there."

"Sheriff, that's not true. I told him that it never happened. The only photos are the ones I took the next day because it was too dark that night."

Jacobs must have been a great Army NCO, Ashe thought, because Jacobs didn't say anything or show any emotion, but went over to his office safe and pulled out Clark's photo. The one that showed both of Georgia's purses and her cell phone on the floor.

He slid the photo over to Ashe who straightened it so Davis could see it clearly.

"Like this one. This set of photos Bill Clark shot that night. You know, Tracy. You were there."

"That's...got to be some kind of trick, Sheriff! Did he give that to you? It's bullshit! It's staged to look like she was taken from here! He knows that she was in Metro when...whatever happened to her happened!"

"No," was all Jacobs said.

"Tracy," Ashe said, redirecting her to him. "Sheriff Laughton kept that photo and gave it to Sheriff Jacobs long before I moved back here. Laughton asked him to look into this case."

The temperature and air density seemed to have gone up by double in ten minutes. Davis squirmed a little in her seat. She looked at the photo and then wiped her mouth with her hand. For a couple of seconds, it was as if she didn't know what to do with her hands, but she recovered and clasped them loosely in front of her. She fixed a hard contemptuous glare on Ashe.

Ashe kept a slightly calm smile and firm composure, trying to keep his breaths even and unhurried. He took the photo and placed it in his portfolio.

He started again. "Tracy, you need to think clearly now. You did in fact go back and reshoot Georgia's apartment the next morning, the 16th. But something else happened. I don't know if it happened overnight or right there with you in her apartment."

She shifted and looked at Jacobs, but his face was harder and firmer than Ashe's slight smile.

"The burgundy purse with the broken logo was gone when you returned, alone, the next day. Later, they were found in Tony Murphy's apartment up in the city. Can you explain how that could happen?"

Ashe was offering her an out and if she took it, it was a partial admission of her involvement.

"No, not true," she said. But her confidence in her own words was failing.

"Bill Clark will testify he shot this photo, and that this other purse was there."

Tracy looked up at Ashe. Her face relaxed a bit.

Oh hell. She knows something. Dammit, I hope he's still okay. He concentrated on not letting his face or tone change.

"Now, I know you took possession of his photos," Ashe said as he tapped at the one in his portfolio, "as evidence, and I'm sure you also took his digital film card from his camera. I'm guessing you were ordered to destroy them. What we want to know is, who is pulling the strings here? How did they get you to do this?"

"Nobody. I am saying this for the last time, I did not destroy his photos or that camera card!"

His photos. That card. They did exist.

"Let's assume that's a lie. Who told you to do it? Is it the same person who told you I was a P.I.? Is it the same person who took the purse up to Metro?"

"I do not know!"

Ashe pressed in. "Did you remove the purse before shooting the pictures, or did someone else do it?"

"I…I don't know!"

Ashe nodded. "Okay, that's not a denial, Tracy. So you saw it the night before. Did someone tell you to go back and reshoot the scene? Were you surprised it was gone, or were you told ahead of time it'd be gone?"

Tears formed around the edges of her eyes. "This…this is all just crap!"

"Tracy, do you know what happened to Georgia Murphy? Is she for sure dead?"

"I do not know…nothing but what I have said all along," she said. She was trembling all over and half crying as she spoke.

"Tracy, I need you to write the sheriff a statement. If this is, as you say, 'all crap,' then tell us what really happened. I want to hear your side of things and only you can tell us that."

"It's like I've been saying, all along," she said.

"Well, we know that's not the case anymore, don't we?" Ashe said. He looked over his notes from their morning discussion and glanced at the photo Clark had shot, then added, "You said this morning that you weren't sure if you called Georgia's cell phone or if Bill Clark did."

Ashe was lying to her to try and trip her up. Her notes had said she had tried calling that night and also the cell records at the time showed her phone had pinged a tower in Metro on the night of the 15th. So it was removed from Hurrt County and activated up in Metro that same night.

"Um…" she muttered and paused a minute as if thinking hard. "I think Clark called her," she said.

"Oh. Huh," Ashe said. "But you didn't get her, right?"

"No."

Jacobs handed her a statement form. "Tell me the truth, Tracy," he said.

She looked at the blank statement form for several minutes. Then slid it away from her.

"No, sir. I…don't think I'm going to write a statement," she said.

Jacobs had stood beside the table like a statue the whole time but moved over to face her.

"Okay, Tracy. I gave you a chance," Jacobs said. "Now you hear me. Tracy Davis, you are suspended immediately pending an investigation into charges of being an accessory to the disappearance and possible murder of Georgia Murphy."

That seemed to crack her demeanor.

"Sheriff, no, please! Don't! Look, I just don't know what he's talking about!"

He continued. "Gun, creds, and badge, Tracy. On the table."

She looked around and started to tremble as she stood up. Ashe had been a part of this scene before with other bad cops. Some broke down, he knew, but some went for broke.

She took out her wallet and dropped her credentials and badge on the table. She slowly started to reach for her Glock.

Ashe was seated across the table from her so he lifted his portfolio just enough to conceal his right hand drawing his gun and holding it under the table.

Davis hesitated a bit. Jacobs obviously hadn't considered she might resist, but it must have just occurred to him so he stepped back. After a long ten seconds, she drew her pistol and set it on the table. Jacobs snatched it up and immediately unloaded it.

Ashe reholstered his revolver, and the sheriff saw for the first time that he'd had it ready.

"Hey, Tracy," Ashe said. She turned and looked at him, no longer so cocky.

"Let me tell you something. Something I'll bet you haven't thought of," he said.

She was too stunned by what had just happened to her to remark, so Ashe continued.

"Now, you don't have to say anything. I know I'm probably off by a few degrees, but we can fill that in later."

"The day Georgia was reported missing, you went out with Bill Clark to her apartment. He shot the photos and you looked into it because I don't think at this point you were a part of what had happened to her."

He paused to let that sink in.

"But at some point, someone got to you. Either you removed the evidence from the apartment or knew it was going to happen before you went back the next morning. You took everything Bill Clark had and must have done a great job of intimidation to keep him quiet. Or maybe, just maybe, he didn't know what had happened to the purse and cell he had intentionally photographed."

She started to say something, but Ashe held up a finger and stopped her. He spoke in short pieces to be sure his words sunk in.

"What you need to consider is this: Whatever reason it was they wanted Georgia gone is still there…"

She seemed to think about that and didn't try to interrupt.

"But since you did as you were told and destroyed any evidence that disputes their story, and since you're not a detective anymore, you're not on the inside *helping* them anymore."

Ashe spread his palms open across the table.

"What good are you to them? Whatever you did for them, you can't do anymore. So, and this is the important part," he said.

She looked at him and he could almost feel the wheels turning in her mind. She hadn't considered what he was saying.

"Tracy. The people who would kill an innocent woman and conceal their crime successfully for two years, why should they leave you walking around?"

"I…I should," she said and then swallowed hard. She stared at the photo in the portfolio.

"Well, I think, Sheriff, we should start with a hard search of her office and car. Then we get a warrant for her house," Ashe said. "Unless you want to show us something, Tracy."

The sheriff sat beside her and handed her a box of tissues. Ashe saw how his whole demeanor became softer.

He's better at this than he thinks he is.

"Tracy, please. Tell me, do you know anything about Billy Clark? Do you know if anything happened to him?"

"I swear I do not know anything about him," she said.

"Tracy, please. He's got kids, like you."

She sat there and started crying softly and shook all over.

"Tracy, please," Jacobs said. "Just tell me about Billy, then tell Mr. Ashe here what you know."

She wiped her face and blew her nose. The two men waited a long minute for her to compose herself. Then she spoke.

"I want to call my lawyer, Phillip Crews. I won't answer any more questions until he's here," she said.

Jacobs patted her on her shoulder gently then stood up. "Okay, Tracy, okay."

Ashe closed his portfolio and took off his glasses. "Well then, I guess there's just one other thing," he said. She looked up at him, red-eyed.

"You're under arrest."

Ashe made notes on the conversation while Sheriff Jacobs did his job. Davis cried and pleaded with him to not lock her up in the Hurrt County Jail with those she'd arrested before, but to take her to another county for her own safety. Jacobs agreed, but took her over to be processed and ordered she be kept in holding. Away from the inmates.

After a half hour or so, Jacobs came back and went to his desk and removed a digital recorder from behind his nameplate. He motioned for Ashe to follow him outside.

"I need a smoke," he said.

"You did a good job tonight, Sheriff. That had to be hard."

He nodded, but it was apparent that this was eating at him, having to arrest one of his own. Jacobs had said he'd had a suspicion about her for a while, but Ashe knew this was a tough time to be the Hurrt County sheriff.

"You got someone who can transcribe that recording?" Ashe asked.

"Yeah, a private court stenographer from over in McCormick City I know," he said.

"Well make sure he or she knows to keep this absolutely..."

Jacobs wasn't listening but said, "I hope her lawyer talks some sense into her and she tells us what she knows."

Ashe shook his head. "She asked for Phillip Crews. From what Susan Marlin tells me, he might be involved. Plus, he's a former ADA. He'll know the score and won't let her talk to us without some kind of a deal."

"Dammit, I'd give one to know Billy Clark's all right."

Ashe had a thought. "Hey, see if you can get a clean record of Georgia Murphy's cell records. All we have are what Tracy gave us."

Jacobs nodded.

"And get Tracy's cell phone records for back then all the way up to now. Oh, and Bill Clark's. It might nail down a lot."

"Hey, what was that all about, 'did you or Clark call Georgia' back in there?"

"I'd already seen her notes in the case file where she wrote that while in her apartment that night two years ago, she'd tried to call Georgia Murphy."

"Okay?"

"That was a lie she wrote back then to cover what really happened," Ashe said and handed Jacobs back the Clark photo. "See?"

Jacobs looked hard at the photo, then he saw it and smirked. "Well, hell."

"Yeah. Why would she try to call Georgia with the cell phone right there in front of her. I didn't mention the missing cell phone tonight on purpose, and then she lied about it. She said Clark tried to call her."

"Maybe..."

"If she did call, it was after she knew the phone was moved to Metro and it would ping a cell tower up there. Her or Clark," Ashe said.

"Clark," Jacobs said, and fished his keys out of his pocket and opened his cruiser. He grabbed his microphone.

"County One to County Four," he said.

"Four," a voice answered that Ashe recalled was Ed Bell.

"Any luck?"

"Negative so far, but I may have a lead," Bell said.

"Keep me apprised," Jacobs replied and switched off.

Ashe suddenly looked at his watch. It was five-fifty.

Stevie.

"Sheriff, I'm not going to knock off for the night just yet. I have one more interview to do."

"Okay, I'm going to lock down her office. I want you there when I search it, Ashe."

Ashe nodded. "Sure. Later tonight though?"

"Yeah," Jacobs said. "I do want to say...well, I would never have gotten this far without you helping out. You're a hell of a detective, my friend."

Ashe smiled. It had been a while since he had heard that about himself.

"Well, I appreciate it, but I still think I'm just blundering my way through this."

"You keep blundering, then. As for myself, I'm going to ruin the circuit court magistrate's dinner, ruin the ADA's dinner, not have dinner myself, oh, and go arrange a transfer to Carson County for Tracy."

"Let's hold off on her transfer until we see if Phillip Crews actually comes here to see her."

Jacobs nodded and stubbed out his cigarette.

"Hell of a thing," he said and walked back into the jail.

Ashe took out his car keys, looked around, then angrily put them back in his pocket and headed on foot for Roger's Café.

CHAPTER 12

Ashe shuffled his notes and zipped up his portfolio as he walked across the town square. As he approached Roger's Café, he could see it was brilliantly lit against the darkening night. People were moving in and out, a few still wearing surgical or cloth masks.

It felt good to see things open and lit up again. The people he saw, even recognizing a few of them, were still keeping a distance from each other but were talking and fist-bumping and being polite. Just seeing them out and at the café, Ashe felt it was an incremental step the town was taking toward normality. A tiny, onion-skin-thin layer to be sure, but his little hometown was crawling its way back from loneliness.

Ashe thought about how since his first day out of the house, he'd been involved with Georgia Murphy's disappearance and how he'd let it consume him.

Did I need this? Is this what it took to draw me back into the world of...people?

He thought about how of all the people he knew orbiting this case, he'd actually spoken the least to Stevie. She reportedly knew Georgia Murphy better than anyone, and Ashe realized he didn't really know much about Georgia. Who was she really? What was truly going on between her and Tony Murphy and everything else?

Time to fix that, he thought, and approached the café.

From outside, he could see through the windows the brightly lit interior. The small marquee sign proudly stated this was their first full-dinner menu in months.

Then he saw Stevie. She was in a booth next to a window looking at her phone like people did whenever they could these days.

Before going in, he leaned against a small brick retaining wall on one side of the sidewalk. He wanted to clear his mind before talking with her again. He needed answers without the diluting influence she had on him.

Looking at her through the window, she looked better than good to him, and immediately Ashe felt that strange combination of aching and longing that rose from his chest to his throat. Like no other woman he'd ever met, she held his whole person captive.

He drew a deep breath, let it out. She had been his last connection to people and to love after he'd lost it all. After his divorce, then retirement, then his dad's death, he had felt alone in the world. No kids, no relatives. Then Stevie.

He'd known deep inside she was wrong for him, and it wasn't just the age difference nor the drinking. But despite his instincts, she'd seemed so infatuated with *him*. So he'd allowed her to pull him along into a sometimes clumsy and risky relationship.

He loved that she touched him, often and so playfully. She held his hand, caressed his chest, his face, nibbled at his neck, and tussled his hair; even occasionally slapping his butt in front of people.

He smiled to himself. She had made him feel like the person he hadn't been in years. As the head of MCU, he'd been logical, controlled, on time, and lived by an agenda. With her, he could be spontaneous, relaxed, and enjoyable. He let her drag him into the laughter and the flirting and the touching and pure, intoxicating fun. Back then, just being with her, he *wanted* to make a fool of himself; loudly, publicly, even if it was only for a short time. To make her smile and laugh was his everything. To have her want to come to him in the night was the raw renewing energy that empowered him to be that new man.

Like no other woman.

Ashe wasn't living in denial; he knew why he'd taken her into his life. During their brief tumultuous affair, he had cast off a little of the dark finality of his life. The series of endings he'd endured in a short time lost some of their power over his heart. She became both his focus in life, and as he knew, his kryptonite. Even back then in the quiet, repressed closets of his mind, he'd always known it would end, and likely disastrously.

He knew it was over between them forever. Her drinking and the loss of her daughter to her ex, followed directly by the damp cloak of Covid had collectively brought a gradually brightening, eventually blinding illumination to the perils of their affair.

Ashe thought how the pandemic lockdown in the middle of it all was actually like a thunderbolt. Destructive but also cleansing. It shook them back in time to the people they had been before, bringing both sobriety and separation to them. Stevie's knowledge of Georgia's disappearance, and his involvement, all combined to reveal how close they both had come to the edge of disaster.

Georgia Murphy had not survived it. Neither Covid nor a bolt from Olympus had killed her. Somebody in Hurrt County had.

Ashe watched her a second or two longer then sat up off the wall and walked into Roger's Café.

"Hello, handsome," Stevie said. She held a glass of white wine and sipped at it.

Ashe drew in a breath and the essence of the café at night. There was a difference with the flavors in the air, tailored to the night, of steak and fish and pasta. The people here were also evening people. There were overlaps from the breakfast and lunch crowd, especially in a small town, but the rhythm of everything changed as the night came. The clothes, the conversations, and even the tone of voice each person used seemed to adapt to night.

"Hello, yourself," Ashe said. "I didn't know they served wine here."

"They don't but you can brown bag," she replied and from a huge black leather bag she had on the seat beside her she produced a half-empty bottle and another glass.

This caught him off guard. "You...okay?"

"Very. And not at all. It's okay, my doctor has said I can have a glass or two if I'm not emotionally drinking. Which I am, but I am also not!" She smiled and poured Ashe a glass.

"I'll—hey that's enough—have an iced tea too," he said and waved a young waitress over.

He ordered the tea and then across the restaurant he saw Tilly. She was behind the counter adding up her checks and glaring at Stevie.

"Oh boy. She wasn't supposed to be working. Tell me this

doesn't have anything to do with Tilly," he said.

Stevie smiled a little at that then turned a little in the booth to find Tilly.

"Ha! God no. But your old girlfriend has been shooting daggers at me with her squinty wrinkled little eyes since I got here."

"Um, what's going on?" he asked, pointing at the wine.

"Well. First, I am fine." She took a long drink of her wine but didn't finish the glass. Then she ceremoniously set the glass down and away from her on the table.

"See, I'm fine. I am not going to be a drunk tonight. This doesn't count because I have a perfectly logical excuse."

"Stevie, honey, you either can or cannot..."

"My ex, Michael, is getting remarried. It's where I've been all day. I got to see my baby and they wanted to tell me face-to-face."

Ashe sat back in his seat. "Ah shit."

"Yep. Good for him. And my precious little wonderful daughter Nora, she is so excited. She's going to be the flower girl!"

"Oh, that must make you feel so...low."

"It's okay. I just had a toast to him and I wanted to drain that bottle and get more, but look! I will not let his sorry ass kill me. I will prove to my sweet baby that her mother, her *real* mother, is not a drunk!"

Ashe took her hand and she let him this time.

"You are a strong woman, the most resilient I know. You have made such a comeback and are on the brink of getting your whole life back."

Stevie shook her head a little and made a small hand wave, dismissing what he had said. "I don't think even Harold Marsh can help me get custody of Nora if she's living with a happily married couple!"

"You don't know that. Look, you'll be reinstated and get your practice..." Ashe didn't finish the sentence.

Practice. Mark Portals was involved in her law practice and had, while she was a total drunk, filed for Georgia Murphy's divorce. Weeks after she'd disappeared.

"Well I guess we'll see. Harold doesn't know this yet," she said.

"I know it will be all right."

She took her hand back from him and dabbed at her face with a napkin.

"I'm fine."

"You're fine," he said and smiled a little at her.

"Fine! Everything's just fucking fine!" she said, then they laughed a little together.

She dried her face again and sat up, drawing in a deep breath. "I hear you are back on the job. Hurrt County's newest law officer."

"Small town I guess," he said.

"Harold told me. Again, told me I should talk with you about Georgia now you're officially on the case."

Ashe looked into her eyes. She'd had a terrible and emotional day.

"Look, it can wait until after dinner. I know this is a classically inappropriate time to ask but…"

"No, no. I'm…"

"Fine!" Ashe said again smiling.

This time they laughed harder. She looked at the wine but didn't reach for it. She took his hand again and slowly raised her eyes to meet his.

"I know you love me," she said in a low voice.

Whoa! Ashe thought.

"I'm going to need to count on that," she said. "Now, I know you want to talk about Georgia."

Ashe's phone vibrated in his pocket. He set it on the table and ignored the call.

"You and she were good friends while you were drinking. I've talked to Susan Marlin and she told me you and Georgia were both involved in different ways with a big land business deal."

"Yeah, you mean DBA," Stevie said, and turned and looked for the waitress but saw Tilly again.

"Is she going to stare at us all night?"

Ashe looked across the room at Tilly and made a face at her. *Knock it off!*

"Uh-huh, probably," he answered. "Now try to think for a minute. Before, you told me you didn't remember if you had filed for her divorce from Tony, but are you sure she wanted a divorce?"

"Oh. Yeah, well…it's hard to say because we'd go out and she'd think about dumping him. She was a big flirt with guys we'd see and I guess she was envious that I was single. But then she'd swing the other way and talk about how she was still in love with him."

"Huh. Well Susan seems to think they were reconciling."

"I guess Susan might have a clearer recollection than me. But, to my knowledge, and subject to the record," she said with an officious tone, "Georgia wanted a divorce."

"But you didn't file it."

"I didn't? I figure I probably did. Sorry, that is my best answer. Is this important to finding her?"

Ashe's phone starting vibrating and walking across the table a little.

"No, I meant, *you* didn't. Mark Portals did. The same day you two talked with Sheriff Laughton."

She frowned. She looked at the phone but didn't say anything about it.

"Ashe? The day we talked to the sheriff? Seriously?"

"Yeah. By the court clerk's printout, about an hour afterward."

"Wait, no that can't be right. You're saying an hour *after* we told the sheriff that Georgia had wanted a divorce, that I had filed for a divorce, *then* Mark went and filed for one?"

"Yep," Ashe said. "Now, turning back to this land deal, DBA. How were you and Georgia involved exactly?"

Stevie thought for a second. Then, as the waitress arrived with iced tea for Ashe and coffee for Stevie, Stevie abruptly stood up.

"You need to get that," she said and pointed at Ashe's still-buzzing phone. "I'm going to the ladies' room. And get rid of this wine please?"

There she goes again. Dammit, I get her on the topic and she dances off.

Ashe answered his phone. "What?"

"What?" shouted Pat Keagan. "Hey, what the hell is going on down there?"

"I can't hear you, Pat, hang on," Ashe said and walked back out to the sidewalk. He stood against the low wall again where he could still see when Stevie got back.

"Can you hear me?" Ashe said.

"Yeah, buddy. Hey, what is going on down there?"

"What do you mean?"

Ashe noticed a man in a dark coat and ball cap walking briskly down the sidewalk toward him. He strained to see his face but couldn't make it out yet.

"I just talked to your sheriff; he's looking for you. And yeah, I know he deputized you—thanks for letting me make an ass out of myself before!"

"I wasn't supposed to... Oh never mind, Pat, what do you want?"

"Your man, Bill Clark? I've got him up here."

The man on the sidewalk paused briefly and looked over toward the town square and the pavilion there. *He doesn't look like my shadow guy, CJ Portals.*

"Oh, Pat! Wow, hey is he okay?" Ashe took his phone away from his ear and put it on speaker so he could hear Pat and see if Jacobs had been calling him.

"No, Chig, I'm sorry but I'm at a crime scene. He's dead!"

Ashe's heart sunk. "What happened?"

"Somebody killed him! I got us here plus state homicide, everybody!"

The man on the sidewalk then turned and suddenly started jogging straight toward Ashe. There was something in his hand, like a phone or...

Gun!

The man fired a shot at him and it hit Ashe like a hot hornet on the left side of his head. Ashe stepped to one side and drew his revolver.

Front sight, press!

Ashe fired a pair of shots, the first going wide but with his second, he took an extra quarter second and hit the man dead center. He bent over and turned to try and run away before falling to the ground.

Ashe scanned quickly and checked his six. He felt warm blood on his face running down to his shoulder. White-hot pain ran across his skull and face. He was breathing hard and shallow and couldn't control it. A high-pitched tone rang in his right ear; his other seemed deaf.

From Ashe's left, a louder blast went off. Pieces of the retaining wall exploded and peppered Ashe with flying pieces of brick and cement. He pivoted and took a knee, partially behind the wall, gun at the ready.

He scanned and ducked then popped up over to scan and then

moved again, staying low and as much behind the low brick wall as he could. He looked, never more than a second before moving, but couldn't find the new shooter. The square and pavilion areas were too dark and he knew he was in a bad spot, backlit by the café.

"Ashe!" It was Stevie. She came out of the restaurant and was between Ashe and the first shooter.

"Stevie, no! Get back inside! Get back!"

The first shooter was still crumpled over on his knees holding his gut, but when he heard Stevie, he straightened himself out a bit and raised his gun in the direction of both Stevie and Ashe.

A second shotgun blast hit the wall near where Ashe just had been. Ashe drew a quick breath and aimed carefully at shooter one. He fired a shot and this time, the man went over flat on his face.

"Ashe!" Stevie screamed his name again and started toward him.

He sat back on his butt for better cover and quick peeked over the wall. He felt the left side of his head, face, and shoulder covered in his blood.

The second shooter racked his pump shotgun. That motion, even in the dark, was all Ashe needed to locate and target him. He was kneeling behind a tree near the pavilion. Maybe twenty yards. Ashe gripped his revolver with both hands and used the top of the wall to steady his gun.

"Ashe!" he heard her scream, but he ignored her to stay focused on the shotgun shooter.

He fired a shot and the second shooter dropped his shotgun. The man tried to stand but fell forward in front of the tree he'd been behind.

Ashe was quivering all over but somehow struggled to his feet. He again felt the hot slipperiness of his own blood all over his left side, but he moved toward Stevie while gesturing for her to get down behind the wall. He pulled his reload strip out and tried to reload.

"Ashe! Behind you," Stevie screamed, a second too late.

The blow from behind caused Ashe to drop his gun and reloads. He stumbled and tripped on his own feet. He went sideways into the wall of the café but regained his footing enough to turn around.

A third man. Big, young looking, swung a fist hard, but Ashe moved his hips enough that the haymaker only clipped his shoulder. Ashe jabbed and connected with his stomach, but it didn't seem to have any effect, so he pushed up fast through his knees and connected an undercut to his jaw. The man staggered backward and sank against the wall, but that's when it was over.

Ashe collapsed, dropping to the sidewalk. He felt nauseous and was losing consciousness fast.

"Kill him?" he heard a voice say from somewhere close beside him.

"Too many people. Beat it," another man said.

"Ashe!" he heard Stevie scream again as if miles away.

Darkness came, and he let it.

CHAPTER 13

Ashe had flashes of pain and only brief moments of consciousness. He had a glimmer of Stevie holding his head. There were a lot of people, cops, later medics. Roger Clancy, of all people, sitting beside him on the sidewalk. Then he was out again.

An ambulance ride, no, a helicopter maybe. *Must be pretty bad for that.*

Ashe woke later for a bit and could feel them putting something down his throat and in his arm. He felt them lift him onto a table, then he went into a tunnel. *CT scan?*

He opened his eyes. It was dark in the room except for a little ambient lighting. At the foot of his bed was a door to his room that was partially open but dark on the other side. Beside it was a large burgundy leather chair with brass tacks and a man was seated there. A man whose face he couldn't quite make out.

He had trouble focusing his eyes, but in one corner, he thought he saw Pat in a different chair underneath a small florescent light. He looked to be checking his phone.

Ashe was drawn back to the dark door and it looked like it was slowly opening; still pitch-black on the other side. Ashe had a strange awareness of a woman trying to open the door. But the man in the leather chair leaned forward and with one hand pushed on the door and closed it. Ashe heard the man's voice, a familiar voice, saying to someone at the door, "No, not yet."

He looked at the man and could only just make out his eyes. The rest of his face was dark and out of focus, but he recognized the shape of it. The eyes, that voice…

Dad.

With that thought still in Ashe's mind, his father's eyes locked with his. They were warm and comforting, and also seemed to be acknowledging the strangeness of his being there with Ashe.

Hot tears came to Ashe's eyes and also a feeling of gladness. Glad he had a few moments still with his father. He tried to speak, to tell Pat, *Hey, look, Pat! It's Dad. He's here!* But he couldn't get the words out.

Then abruptly, as if hearing his thoughts, his father's eyes changed. He was glaring at Ashe and in some way, he sensed his father's disapproval. He knew that if he did actually manage to call attention to his father's being in the room, and Pat or anyone were to notice, this moment would be gone.

Just be glad he's here now. He's here for me.

Then Ashe fell asleep.

He woke again much later for a couple of minutes. Someone, maybe a nurse, was checking his eyes with a light. He was in a hospital. There were devices making soft noises connected to him. Ashe tried to lift his head and immediately regretted it.

"Hold still and tell me your name," she said in the medically loud fashion through a mask.

"It's on my driver's license in my wallet," Ashe replied.

"Okay, smart guy, that's what you said last time."

"Chig, behave yourself and hold still," a familiar woman's voice said. But it wasn't the nurse, nor Stevie.

"Do you know your birthdate?" the nurse said.

"Also on my…oh hell," he said and then just told her his name and birthdate.

She asked several more questions and he was too groggy to banter with her, so he answered them straight. Then he closed his eyes.

Much later it seemed, Ashe opened his eyes. He could see he had to be in the ICU as there were no windows, and a big sliding glass door to his right opened to a nurse's station outside. There was a curtain half drawn as well. It smelled like a hospital; sterile, antiseptic.

There was no door at the foot of his bed. There was no leather chair.

He was fully awake. The lights were dim so he assumed it must still be night out. Beside him holding his right hand and wearing a Covid mask was Tilly.

"Hey, you," he said weakly.

"Hey, yourself, Chig. You scared the shit out of us. The whole dang town, too! Nothing like this ever happened in Seacord!"

"You're at Metropolitan Memorial in the ICU," he heard a man say from off to his left where he couldn't see.

"Pat?"

"Yeah, Chig. Your sheriff and State Homicide wanted you covered, so I took the first watch. It's four a.m."

Ashe recalled the man jogging toward him. "Did I…"

"Yep. You got them. And the one that clobbered you. Your girlfr…uh, that lawyer friend of yours and a couple of guys from the restaurant sat on him until the sheriff got there."

Tilly said, "It was Roger and a couple of my customers. You knocked the SOB down but they held him for the sheriff."

Ashe's recall of the incident was still flashes. Small pieces.

"Ah hell, Stevie?"

"She's good. She's here, or was here anyway. I got Breslin on her."

"Hey, Till, Dad was here," he said and pointed at the foot of his bed where the leather chair had been.

She cut her eyes at Pat, then said, "Good, Chig, that's good."

Ashe closed his eyes and tried to think. There was something else important. Then he remembered.

"Any word on Bill Clark?"

Ashe turned in small moves, Tilly helping him, until he could see. Pat was in a chair with some papers in his lap going over them. The surgical mask he was supposed to be wearing was on a table beside him. His jacket was off and the big Colt 1911 he wore on his hip was positioned where he could get to it easier while seated. His backup compact .45 was in a shoulder holster.

"Am I still in that much trouble?" Ashe asked.

Pat cut his eyes at Tilly.

Ashe got it. "Hey, Til, thank you tons for coming up, but it's late."

"Oh. Cop stuff, huh?" she said. "I understand, Chig."

She looked at Ashe, worry all in her eyes, then leaned over and kissed him on the forehead. Then she seemed to think better of it and leaned in again and kissed him firmly on the lips.

When she stood up, her eyes were moist but she smiled.

"Chig? You get out of here? I'ma kill you," she said, then

kissed his hand and left.

Ashe looked over at Pat who had watched them the whole time.

"We, uh, dated some in high school," Ashe said.

"Yeah, uh-huh. I went to high school with ten to twelve girls. They don't make their husbands drive them up here to kiss me!"

"Ah, Pat. I..."

"No shit, Chig, he's in the damn lobby!"

"Okay, okay," was all Ashe could think to say.

"Your, um, *other* girl? The lawyer, whatz-her-name, the one with the legs," Pat said.

"Stevie Collins. Yes, she has two of them."

"She's been with you the whole time too. Rode with you up here and wouldn't go until we pointed out she had your blood all over her and her blouse was all torn."

"Really?" Ashe remembered her running toward him.

"Took her high heels off and threw them at the guy that hit you."

Ashe blinked. "She did what?"

"Yeah! They said she was running right at the guy. They said she was going at him with a damn high-heel shoe! Then she tore her blouse to stop the bleeding from your thick head."

Ashe remembered more. "I was shot," he said.

"Nine mil, head shot. Cut you pretty good but grazed off your skull. Ripped a nice piece of ear off."

"And Stevie ran at him? What was her plan if she'd caught him?"

"Oh, not him. You nailed him. The other guy with a tire iron behind you. And we couldn't hardly get her off you until nurses used the damn jaws of life to pry her off. She was here with you until your...other, ah, lady friend showed up."

"Don't start. Where is she?"

"Hotel. Like I said, Breslin and a female officer covering her. She needed rest and a clean shirt."

"Okay." Ashe raised himself using the bed control a little.

Pat shook his head. "Both of them women, huh. Me? I retire? I'm thinking maybe I'll get a place in Hurrt County," Pat said with a wry grin.

Ashe ignored him and tried to think. His head hurt and he was hoarse from something having been in his throat. A white foam cup with a straw was on his bedside table so he sipped some water. After a minute, he was clearer.

"Bill Clark."

"Yeah," Pat said slowly. "I think maybe he gave as good as he got. But they worked him over pretty damn good. Place out in Allensville area, you remember, deserted warehouses. Had to have been trying to get something from him. But whatever they wanted; I don't think he gave them. They finally put a bullet behind his ear."

"Damn," Ashe said.

"We're doing all the checks, pulled out all the stops. Somebody kidnaps, tortures, then kills a deputy here in Metro? Bullshit. We'll get them," Pat said firmly.

"Who were the ones…came at me?" Ashe asked.

"Local guys, local to Metro I mean. MacNeal and an Everitt. Both DRT."

Dead Right There, Ashe knew what Pat meant.

"The guy that clobbered you…"

"I *tried* to clobber back," Ashe said, weakly.

"He's one Paul Milton. You got him some, enough he fell over. Your friends in Seacord did the rest. He's in Hurrt County Jail."

"None of these names mean anything to me," Ashe said weakly. He was trying to stay awake, but exhaustion was all on him.

There is something else. Something or someone I heard, Ashe thought, but trying to remember was too painful.

"Yeah, they should, Everitt anyway. You indicted him nine years ago on a strong-arm robbery here in Metro. He did eight up at state."

Ashe shrugged. "You say so." The name didn't ring a bell. Maybe when his head quit hurting.

"MacNeal's daddy was in for a racketeering. Died in prison," Pat mumbled on as he looked back at the papers on his lap.

Ashe noticed the papers Pat was reading through for the first time. It was his portfolio.

"Hey, that's mine."

"Uh-huh, I'm reading your notes. You've been busy, my boy."

"Well just keep reading, then. I'll need your help."

"Yes, you do. I've also been making some corrections as I go," Pat said.

"Whatever. Oh, and Georgia Murphy? *Not* a Metro case but Hurrt County," Ashe said.

"I read your theory on that," Pat replied, not convinced. He stood up, yawned, and stretched.

Ashe realized his friend had been with him the whole time as well. *Not too many MCU lieutenants take a watch on a vic.*

"We'll talk tomorrow. I got a uniform outside," Pat said.

"Pat. Thank you for watching over me," Ashe said in a serious tone.

"Huh, I got a floor show for my trouble. First, one young hot girl crawling all over you, then, another hot older one making out with you…"

"Pat, please."

Pat leaned over and mock-whispered, pointing back at the door. "Her damn husband right down the hall, Chig! What the hell?"

"Pat, I can't…oh, whatever."

"Hey," he said, more seriously. "I got a guy outside your room like I said. I got an undercover in clothes downstairs watching the night entrance. Hospital security has got a guy on the cameras and a uniformed security rover in the parking lots."

"Okay. Maybe I can sleep better if you get yourself and all your armament out of here."

Pat raised Ashe's portfolio. "I'm taking this to make copies. You don't mind that," he said flatly.

"No, please. Flipping help yourself."

Pat shook on his jacket and yawned again.

Ashe felt his weight sinking him into the bed. "I think I'll retire again. Never should have let them catch me off guard like that. I'm getting too damn old."

Pat turned and looked at Ashe, still serious. He shook his head slowly and stared at Ashe straight in the eyes.

"They sent three at you. Two were armed. They braced you from three different sides. You got them. In the dark. One had at you with a nine, the other with a twelve-gauge pump gun. You killed them both with a damn J-frame. Then even after being shot, you hit the third guy who'd hit you with a tire iron, hard enough he didn't get away."

Ashe took in a shaky breath and looked at his oldest friend. They held each other's eyes for a long minute.

Then Pat said, "Too old?"

Ashe couldn't think of anything to say for a second and just nodded. Pat turned and opened the big glass door to his room.

"Hey, was there a door there?" Ashe said and pointed at the foot of the bed.

"Huh?"

"With a big chair beside it?"

Pat looked at him, obviously confused. "You had a hell of a smack on the head, buddy. Get some rest."

"Thanks, Pat. Good night."

"But," he said over his shoulder. "*I'm* damn well not kissing you!"

The next morning, the press had found out where Ashe was, but between the Metro PD protection detail and hospital security, they'd been held at bay. Ashe had no desire to talk to them and had let everyone know to not let them in.

Right after breakfast, the Deputy Attorney General Rollin Ashad had arrived with Sheriff Jacobs and a State Homicide Bureau investigator.

Ashe recalled Ashad better. He had previously been an assistant DA for Metro about the time Georgia Murphy's case was transferred to Metro, so Ashe decided to be cautious with him.

What did he know at the time about her case?

"Lieutenant Ashe, or I should say retired," Ashad said warmly as he entered the hospital room wearing a mask. "It's good to see you alive and not too worse for the wear after what happened. You know Sheriff Jacobs; this is Special Agent Rachel Hume of State Police Homicide."

"Yes, sir, good to see you too. Everyone, good morning."

Ashe was sitting up in bed and had a polo on. He fist-bumped hands all around and an orderly brought in enough chairs for the group.

"I want to start by assuring you that you are not the target of an investigation into a crime at this time. This discussion today is fact finding in nature. But I will read you your rights anyway," said Hume and tugged her mask down to speak clearly.

Ashe initially waived counsel and told them essentially the facts into how the attack and shooting took place outside Roger's Café. There were a few questions, all from Agent Hume, clarifying the sequence of events. Ashe told her everything he could remember; except he left out his thoughts on how this was all connected to his inquiry into Georgia Murphy.

However, it became apparent Sheriff Jacobs had told them at least some about their investigation to date.

"So, Mr. Ashe, you feel as if these men were sent to kill you because you uncovered that the first crime scene from two years ago was meddled with in order to make her husband look guilty," Ashad said, like he was talking to himself, not like a question.

Ashe cast a frustrated look at Jacobs who seemed to catch on. "Not exactly. It's just the theory I was looking into. Regardless, I don't know *for a certainty* how that would connect to the men from Metro trying to kill me," Ashe said. Not exactly lying.

He knew if the state bought into his theory and took over the investigation, he'd have no way to protect Stevie. However she might be involved, he wanted to keep her clear of this as much as he could for as long as he could.

"I'm also fuzzy on why a team of hitters from up here would want to drive all the way down there and eliminate you because you were asking around about Mrs. Murphy?" asked Agent Hume. She was a short woman, mid-forties. Attractive with intelligent eyes.

"I indicted one of them years ago. The one in Hurrt County custody is an associate of Tony Murphy, who was arrested while I was head of MCU," Ashe said.

This was conveniently true, he thought, even though intentionally a diversion.

Hume made a note and then shrugged. "So, you think Tony Murphy, while in prison, orchestrated this hit on you and Clark with his former associates because…"

"He had never been charged with his wife's disappearance or her probable death. I am guessing only, but maybe he didn't want me digging any further into it," Ashe said, this time stretching the tar out of the truth but not necessarily lying.

Jacobs looked surprised but didn't say anything.

"And Clark? Was he also assisting you in your inquiry? What

did they want from him so badly to kill him?"

Again Sheriff Jacobs thankfully stayed quiet.

"I don't know for sure," Ashe said to Hume. "What do you think?"

Ashad and Agent Hume looked at each other, then Hume said, "That case is under investigation by Metro MCU. Given my belief these incidents are connected, I'm staying coupled with them on it."

"Well," Ashad said suddenly. "I've reviewed the matter at hand and given the work of Agent Hume with the assistance of Sheriff Jacobs on the attempt on your life in Hurrt County, I can't see where this was not a justifiable use of defensive force. I will of course ask this be reviewed by the Hurrt County ADA, Mr. Price, and then by a Hurrt County Grand Jury as soon as their next session convenes. But, I do not see how you will have any problems."

"We will *of course* also continue to look into the connection between the murder of Deputy Clark and the attempt on your life, Mr. Ashe," said Hume.

"People, my, uh, head is killing me. Can we finish up later, please?" Ashe said.

Ashad and the others nodded and said, "Of course" and "Get better" as they stood. Ashe signaled for Jacobs to linger behind.

But as they headed for his hospital room door, Rachael Hume turned around and looked right at Ashe. "I'll be available as soon as you're ready to *really* talk," she said.

And right then Ashe knew that Special Agent Rachel Hume was not about to let go of this.

"Thank you, Agent Hume," Ashe said. He and Jacobs waited to be sure the two of them were gone.

"Damn, son, you just lied your ass off to the Deputy AG and one of the senior state homicide investigators!"

"Not really. More like *evaded*. We'll need them later, Sheriff, but right now we can't prove anything with the larger case of Georgia Murphy."

"They did a professional job with your shooting scene. I called them in on it," Jacobs said. "You sure we don't want them to just take everything and run with it?"

"You notice Ashad wanted to go along with the current party

line, that Georgia went missing from Tony's apartment?"

"Hey, yeah, how come you didn't tell them we knew he couldn't have done it? That he was arrested the same night and at the same time she went missing?"

"You didn't show them that?" Ashe asked.

"No. Of course, they were too busy working your shooting to ask, maybe."

"Good. For now let's keep it that way. The more it's a Metro case to figure out, the more room we have to maneuver."

Jacobs seemed further confused. "But why?"

"Because I want to know a lot more about all these big land development deals Georgia was working on first," Ashe said. "Because there's maybe a connection between me and Clark and Georgia Murphy. Because…"

"Because you want to look after Stevie Collins," Jacobs replied.

Ashe grinned a little. "Okay. But also, we still don't know for sure what would cause someone want to make Georgia vanish. And Crews in Hurrt County as the ADA sent this case to Ashad who was one of the ADAs in Metro at the time."

Jacobs shook his head. "I guess I see."

Ashe changed the topic.

"Where is Tracy Davis? She was the one who got this case transferred. Both Crews and Ashad would have to review evidence and approve for there to be a change of venue in a potential homicide."

"She's still in jail but over in Carson County now. She's being represented by a lawyer from over there, but as of this morning she's not made bond."

"You search her office like we discussed? Her cruiser, phone records?"

"Yeah, about that." Jacobs leaned back in his chair, crossed his legs, and took out a cigarette. He looked around then quickly put it back in the pack.

"Nothing in her office beyond what we've seen. Nothing in her car. She must have cleaned house between when you talked with her and later when we both did."

"No camera or camera card?"

"No. Her momma even let me look through their house. Nada."

"Dammit! I have to assume Clark had his camera and then Paul

Milton and his buds got it after torturing him."

Jacobs narrowed his eyes and started to fidget in his seat a little. "Let me tell you, Ashe, I saw those crime scene photos of Billy…" Jacobs' voice cracked and he paused to clear his throat. He made a fist and slowly knocked on the arm of his chair.

"Paul Milton will pay. You got two of them, and I'm glad you did. I will make sure he pays up now," Jacobs said.

"He talk to Hume?" Ashe asked.

"No, lawyered up. Lawyer named Danvers from Metro. You know him?"

"No. When I get out of here, we'll have a go at him, plus Tracy, and even Tony Murphy."

"I want in on Milton," Jacobs said firmly.

Ashe closed his eyes again. He'd had a busy day already and was tired even though it was still morning. "Sure, I'll even hold him for you," Ashe said as he started to drift off.

"Sounds good. Hey, I've missed you back home, Ashe."

"Okay." Ashe laid his head back; his eyes went closed. "I really am woozy now, boss."

"You get better, I'll be in touch," said Jacobs. "And don't worry. I'll take care of your girl."

Ashe opened one eye. "Yeah," was all he said.

With his eyes closed again after less than a minute, he drifted back to in front of Roger's Café. Stevie was there stroking his hair. He started to reach for her but couldn't.

He was on the ground and heard a familiar set of voices in his mind.

"Kill him?" a voice–Paul Milton's asked.

"Too many people. Beat it," a second voice answered.

Ashe bolted awake, momentarily confused. He was still in his hospital room.

"Sheriff?" Ashe said and sat up a bit.

"I was just leaving," he said.

Too many people, said a separate voice in his mind.

The man he'd fought was Milton. A separate person, a different voice was there, too. He didn't see his face.

"There was a fourth man."

"What, where? That attacked you? No, Ashe, there were only three men, several people have already confirmed that."

"No, there was a fourth. And I'm pretty sure I know who it was."

CHAPTER 14

Mark Portals pulled his Lincoln Navigator into a parking spot in the alley behind his office. After several years of building his practice, he'd finally gotten the town of Seacord to clean it up. He had sunk his own money into having the alley better paved and lit, and all the brick and block washed clean. He'd pressured the town council to get all the trash cans and dumpsters relocated, and he'd widened the alley by buying then demolishing all the old structures that had made it seem seedy. It looked good, he thought. In another couple of years, he would press for this alley to be named a street.

Named after himself, of course.

Portals entered his office building by his private entrance and took the elevator to the second floor. His office door was open but dimly lit with a couple of people in there. The adjoining conference room was lit up and as he stepped into his office, he noticed his partner, Phillip Crews, at the conference table with a woman he couldn't see.

As he opened his office door more widely, he saw a county commissioner, a realtor he knew named Jasper, and a local banker named Crawford.

"I want to know…" Mark started, but from a dim corner stepped CJ Portals who pressed a finger to his lips.

"Please, Uncle Mark," he whispered and gestured toward the adjoining conference room door.

Mark narrowed his eyes at CJ, not even trying to hide his anger. "I'll be having words with you in a minute."

From the conference room, he heard Crews speaking. "I do not know, I mean, this all just happened. Right here on the streets of little Seacord!" he said.

There was a woman's voice speaking in reply, haltingly, as if crying. Mark could not make out what she said.

"Nobody knows why. Could Ashe have torqued off people here in town with these wild insinuations about Georgia Murphy," Crews continued.

The woman again replied unintelligibly to Mark, but a couple of words were clear.

She said, "DBA" and then seconds later, "commission."

"I'm sure it's fine, Susan," Crews said. "Let me poke around a bit and then I'll come see you tomorrow."

Mark silently mouthed, "Susan Marlin?" toward the banker Crawford, who nodded.

There were a few more muted words between them, then Mark heard the sounds of his heavy conference chairs on deep carpet shuffling, followed by the woman's heels walking aggressively down the hall.

Phillip Crews stepped into Mark's office as CJ moved over and quietly closed the office door so the woman couldn't look back and see them.

"What the holy hell?" Mark raged at CJ.

"*Somebody* killed a Hurrt County deputy named Clark, and *some other people* tried to kill that P.I. named Ashe that I told you about, Uncle," CJ said.

"I know that!"

"We don't know *anything else*, Uncle Mark! They caught one of the attackers though, a Paul Milton. *From up in Metro*," CJ added, speaking carefully.

Mark caught the hint. He knew the name, and the others in the room didn't need to hear this.

You son of a stupid bitch!

"What do we know?" Mark asked more calmly and gestured for the men to have a seat.

"I can tell you one thing," Commissioner Jasper said. "That Ashe isn't a P.I. from Metro like you've been telling people, CJ! Sheriff Jacobs commissioned him as a deputy!"

"I got that from a trusted source," CJ said defensively.

"Who gives a shit!" the banker, Crawford, cut in. "Once the DBA and Skee-ah investors see this on the news, they'll pull their financing. We are shut down!"

"Everyone, please!" Mark said and held up his hands. "Give me a second to process all this. Was anyone else hurt?"

"Milton has some minor cuts and bruises. The café crowd were not too gentle as they sat on him for the sheriff," CJ said.

"Who gives a shit about him?" Crawford said.

"Good!" said the realtor, Jasper. "I hope they kicked his ass a little."

"Dammit, CJ, I mean the public! Mr. Ashe shot up the town so did anyone else get hit?"

"No, I don't think so," CJ said.

"Gentlemen," Crews spoke for the first time. "I've calmed Ms. Marlin for now. Her apprehension is that the man, Mr. Ashe, who is investigating the disappearance of her co-worker and friend two years ago, was attacked so soon after speaking with her. She's afraid there's a connection between then and now. *And* for her personal safety."

"Poppy-cock!" Mark said. "This Ashe may simply be covering up that he did nothing in Metro to find her and now is living here. He likely wants to clean this stain from his name."

"Well, she also expressed a high degree of concern for the terrific amount of billable hours we've done so far to both DBA and Skee-ah."

"Mmm," Mark said. "Sensible concern."

Crews wrinkled his brow a bit. "Well, I think what we should, as a community, be worried about is the kidnapping and murder of Deputy Clark. A heinous crime that likely started here and wound up in Metro. Sound familiar?"

Crews looked first at Mark then CJ. Neither spoke.

"And," Crews continued, "a professional-style assassination attempt on Mr. Ashe, another deputy sheriff, right here on our town streets."

"Blood is actually on our streets. Right here in town," Jasper added.

"National news is here! They have a satellite truck in the park. By dawn, this will be on every national channel!" Jasper said.

Crews said, "I should also mention, Mark, that Deputy Tracy Davis was arrested by Sheriff Jacobs this afternoon. Somehow, he has proof she's tampered with evidence in the disappearance of..."

"Okay, okay," Mark said, cutting off Crews. He stood slowly and walked over to the bar area of his office and poured himself a dark bourbon. "Anyone else?"

They all mumbled, "no" or "no thank you." Mark had done this to quiet the room some and to ensure he had the floor.

"I am sure that none of this is connected in any way to our plans to develop and improve Hurrt County and the Minor Hills Lake areas. But as Mr. Crawford has so rightly reminded us, we are at a critical juncture in our final negotiations through DBA to bring new industry here."

Several of the men nodded but Crews stared hard at Mark.

"That means more people. More homes needing to be built. More room necessary in our schools and our public facilities. Gas stations, grocery stores, utilities, and every other type of economic expansion we cannot yet foresee."

"Hear, hear," said Crawford. "Over time, millions in investments."

"Ms. Marlin is correct. We have nearly a million in already committed personal funds between us and our local team. We cannot afford to lose our outside investors just now because of this mess," Mark said.

"So what do we do?" asked Jasper.

"Excellent question," Mark said. He dramatically paced the room. After a few moments, he continued.

"I think we first need to throw our full support behind our Sheriff Jacobs. One strong community. Seacord Strong, maybe, eh?"

The men looked confused. "What does that do?" asked Crawford.

"Well, we cannot let this be how our home is perceived to the outside world. Ideas?"

Mark listened as the other men began to discuss ideas of how to show public support, especially while the news cameras were in town. They talked about how they could show the investors they were a resilient and close community. A couple took Mark up on his offer of his very expensive bourbon.

Mark noted however, a subdued but surprised look on Phillip Crews' face. Mark shook his head softly and privately to him as if to say, *not now*.

CJ Portals had sat quietly almost trying to disappear into a dim corner, but occasionally Mark ensured he caught his eye. Mark

Portals was not yet done with his damn nephew.

After another twenty minutes or so, the group stood and decided to head out and share their plans to start a funding website for the Clark family and for Ashe's hospital bills. They also wanted to get started on a "Seacord Strong" campaign and "Hurrt County Helps." A large "Support Hurrt County Sheriff" event was going to be planned.

Mark was happy. "You men get this going and get it big. Get it on the news fast. Anytime anybody talks about the murder of Clark and the attempt on Ashe, I want fifty or more citizens chanting they support law enforcement and that these families will be supported and not be out a cent!" Mark said encouragingly. He took the banker, Crawford, by the arm before he left.

"Now you get these accounts set up fast so we can make up signs with those little square things people can click on."

"QR codes?"

"Yes, yes, that. And listen, whatever we are short of in setting this up, I'll transfer from my personal account," Mark added.

Crawford smiled and shook Mark's hand aggressively.

"You're right. This is not only good for the people, it might get the investors excited again as well," he said.

"Let's go one step at a time. You get this going. If you need legal help, I'll have my other partner, Tom Fischer, do it pro bono."

The men shuffled out slowly still pitching ideas to one another. But not before finishing their bourbons, Mark noted.

You boys don't let free five-hundred-dollar bourbon go to waste.

Neither CJ nor Phillip had moved from their chairs. When he closed his office door, he circled around to sit behind his wide, imposing desk.

"Phillip," Mark said.

"Mark, you know Tracy Davis contacted me to represent her. We discussed this."

"Out of the question, she cannot afford us," Mark said curtly. "She should be handed over to the Public Defender's office."

"Are we sure that's wise? She's sure stuck her neck out and..." CJ started.

"Yes, helped with any issues we needed to know about," Mark

cut him off for the second time. He turned back to Crews, who was staring at CJ.

"Phillip, given we are going to be a part of the public support for this community and its sheriff, I don't think we can logically also defend a disgraced deputy who is alleged to have tampered with evidence, can we?"

Phillip Crews stared at Mark with a strange and slightly confused look on his face.

"Mark," he said flatly.

Mark sighed. "Yes?"

"Let me be sure I'm hearing you correctly. You say that we should not be representing a person that is accused of altering or destroying the evidence of a two-year-old disappearance case. Even though she has provided, um, services of some sort to this firm."

"Well, yes," Mark said. "But her services were strictly in assisting us with land owners and ensuring certain civil, *legal* processes were served. That is all. It was, eh, her job."

"And this decision is based purely on a belief she may be guilty and therefore not congruent with a desire to support the Hurrt County Sheriff's Department during these times."

"Yes!" Mark said sharply. "The disappearance of a woman whom we worked closely with on early DBA business. I do not know what happened to her but it was a tragedy. If Tracy Daniels had anything to do with it, I don't want to be associated with her!"

"I see," Crews said.

"Davis," CJ corrected.

"Whatever, whomever," Mark snapped at CJ. Then to Crews he said, "It's not good for us and you don't do criminal work anymore, Phillip. Refer her to another criminal attorney if you must, but our firm cannot be involved with her."

Crews nodded and studied the ceiling for a second or two then said, "Mark?"

Mark breathed out slowly. "Yes, Phillip?"

"Tell me something, partner. Did we have anything whatsoever to do with tonight's events?" He jabbed a thumb toward CJ. "Anything in any way. Direct or indirectly?"

"Fuck you," CJ said.

Mark held a hand up at CJ and then sat back in his big leather chair and smiled reassuringly toward Crews.

"Oh, Phillip. Of course not."

"I'll remember that, Mister Crews," CJ said.

"You do that, Carl Jack," Crews replied calmly. Mark noticed his partner was not intimidated by CJ at all.

"Phillip, I brought you on because we both shared a vision of how to build something special here in the place we live and call home. I could never dishonor that idea."

"All right, Mark, but answer me this," Crews said. "On the disappearance and probable death of Georgia Murphy two years ago. Given our stated past relationship with Ms. Davis, who stands accused of evidence tampering in that case, I feel I have to raise a question."

"Of course not," Mark said quickly.

"I'll ask anyway." Crews turned his chair enough so he was looking at both Mark Portals and CJ Portals. "Did we have anything whatsoever to do with the disappearance of Georgia Murphy?" he asked firmly.

"Phillip," Mark started, but Crews cut him off.

"I am serious, Mark! If the firm, you, *him*, or anyone here had a hand in her abduction, I want to know right now!"

"Dammit, Phil, that's an insulting and acrimonious accusation!" Mark shouted. "You and I will hash out why you would even *think* such a terrible, rancorous thing of me at another time! But I should not have to even say no to you!"

Mark then pointed a thick finger at CJ and said, "And I'll add something else! I am well aware of my nephew's reputation and sullied history as well as his father's—my brother's—criminal record. *But it is not mine!* We are not involved in any way. Neither is CJ here. You and I have…well, oh…dammit!"

Mark glowered at Crews and put on his best intimidation face. He'd melted witnesses at depositions, cowed insurance agents, and lorded over opposing council with his imposing stare. But Phillip Crews matched Mark's eyes and did not blink. Mark had to remind himself, Crews was a highly experienced former prosecutor before joining the firm. This was not someone who intimidated easily.

You have to convince a man such as this, he thought as he tried to regain his composure.

Crews thought for a minute then rose from his seat. "Alright,

Mark. I will go see the ex-deputy and deliver her the bad news. She's to be transferred to another county early tomorrow before breakfast."

"Listen, Phillip. We are all a little high strung, given the emotionality of tonight's trials," Mark said. "I apologize if in denying your rightly asked question, I was rude toward you. It was good to get everything out and, on the record, so to speak."

Mark stuck out his hand. Crews smiled and took it. "You were passionate in what you said. I would trust you less if you weren't."

"Let's agree to meet privately, at my home in a couple of days," Mark added.

"I look forward to it," Phillip Crews said. Then just before he opened the office door, he turned and emitted his own gravitational fix toward CJ but spoke to Mark.

"One addendum. I assume that Susan Marlin's concern for her own safety is unfounded. To be perfectly clear, she is in no danger," he said.

"I don't know what *those who have perpetrated* tonight's horrors would want with her," Mark said. "But certainly she has nothing to fear from any of us. We are in business together."

Crews continued to seemingly try to bore holes through CJ Portals with his eyes for a minute then turned to Mark. "Well just know I am going to take a personal interest in her safety from now on," he said and walked out of the office.

CJ got up and looked out the window to be sure Crews was gone.

"He doesn't believe a word we've said," CJ said. "He's a real obnoxious bastard."

"You stupid son of a bitch!" Mark yelled.

"Hold the hell up, Uncle Mark!"

"Stop calling me that! I took you to all but raise years ago when my brother Dale went to prison. And I have kept your sorry ass out of jail more than once ever since."

"You told me to make sure this didn't come back to bite us in the…"

"Shut up! Shut up! I don't want to hear it! I never told you to have anybody kidnapped, or for Christ's sake, killed!"

CJ walked around and sat on the corner of Mark's desk and leaned over him.

"I have done whatever needed to be done for you in Metro for years, Uncle. Nothing or nobody ever has connected us with anything, ever."

Mark drained his bourbon and stood to loom over his seated nephew.

"Chicken shit compared to this," he said, and went to refill his glass. "I'm going to have to do more than just call in some favors. I'm going to have to go into hock over this with the state attorney general's office."

"There's a state police homicide investigator already here."

Mark looked at his glass for a second and said, "That's to be expected, I guess. You know who it is?"

"No, just that it's a short and sort of serious-looking woman," CJ said.

"That doesn't help." Mark swirled his bourbon around in his glass while thinking. "Maybe my man at the AG's office can help. They do too good a job, and if they make the right, or wrong in our case, connection…"

"Even the high and mighty Mister Ashe up there, when he was in charge of investigating, he never connected anything we did there to *here* or you," CJ continued.

"Oh good God, CJ! You can't compare a few coarse, raw-sided business dealings to…to this! They will not rest, you fool, here or in Metro, until they've nailed *whoever* might be responsible for killing a cop on their turf!"

"They won't be able to…"

"Shut up and listen! And by *someone* trying to kill Mr. Ashe here in Seacord, that shows even a blind man the connection between the two!"

"We can't be implicated. They can suspect us all they like."

"Dammit, CJ, the implication is all they need to shut us down. I've tried to build something important. Something good for the people here."

Mark took a big sip of his bourbon and suddenly grabbed CJ's arm. "And a clean, legal sustainable income for all of us. Years of high-level income, get it?"

CJ sighed at Mark and nodded his head.

"You have likely…possibly, fucked this all up, m'boy."

"Ok. I'm sorry but I don't see how. I should never have left

Ashe there on…"

Mark waved his hands and closed his eyes. "No, I do not want to hear this," he shouted.

"None of these people even know who I am, much less you!" CJ finished anyway.

Mark went back and flopped in his office chair. He knew he'd used CJ and a few local and dependable people to help move things along in business before.

He knew he'd hidden witnesses, destroyed documents, even hinted to CJ that maybe a building needed to be damaged for insurance to have a hold over the owner. *Coarse*, he'd said, and raw. The rougher but realistic side of corporate operations.

But he looked at his nephew and took another slow sip to help him stall a bit. This was different. Georgia Murphy, Bill Clark, Ashe, and…Tony Murphy, too.

"Alright, Carl Jack," Mark said. "Now, and for the last time, I never want to hear about this from you or anyone, understand?"

"Of course," CJ said.

"You have a couple of problems, m'boy." The bourbon was having its desired effect.

"I do?"

"Yes. The man that was arrested after attacking Mr. Ashe. He's in custody, I believe here in Hurrt County."

"Yeah, you mean Paul Mel…"

Mark shot up his palms and closed his eyes for a second.

"Okay, okay. Sorry, Uncle."

"He was an associate of Tony Murphy, you know," Mark said, then covered his ears and closed his eyes again for a few more seconds. CJ said nothing.

"I do not know of *anyone* who had *anything* to do with Deputy Clark, but if they are the same ones from Mr. Ashe's assault, that is a damn connection."

CJ looked a little concerned but still said nothing.

"And your other issue is of course your relationship with the ex-deputy, Tracy Davis."

CJ nodded. He stood and walked to the door.

"I'm guessing," he said, not turning to face Mark Portals, "I'm not going to be living on that lake in a big damn house beside you anymore, am I, Uncle?"

"Your investments are secure. You'll have ample resources to go wherever you want to go. I promise you that, CJ. Wherever you want to *go*."

CJ paused at the door, reached over, and took the most expensive bottle of bourbon off the tray and walked out.

CHAPTER 15

"**O**kay, Mr. Ashe. You can go," his doctor said through an N95 mask. He was staring at a computer monitor and reviewing Ashe's latest CT scan. "But behave yourself for a week or two."

A technician came in and asked a ton of questions from a checklist, and he tried to listen and answer dutifully, but his mind was preoccupied.

They'd come for him. *I am closer to something than I thought.*

Ashe dressed with the clothes he'd been wearing four days ago when he'd been admitted, but they'd been cleaned and pressed. His head hurt less and the bandage on his left rear skull and ear was considerably smaller. He still had occasional flares of nausea if he moved his head too quickly, and he wasn't as steady on his feet as he wanted. He did feel overall like going home despite knowing he wasn't anywhere near fully recovered.

The hospital provided him with a fresh surgical-type Covid mask they still required, so he hung it off one ear while he waited as instructed for his ride.

It was five a.m. He figured his doc must have been on the night shift. He looked around but saw no one he knew; he'd half expected maybe Stevie would be there to drive him home.

He switched on his room TV and the news came on. They were still covering the "Small Town Assassinations" and a talking-head reporter was describing his shooting in front of Roger's Café. All over the windows in the background were posters with *Seacord Strong!* and *Hurrt County Helps!* printed in the high school's colors. A website for donating scrolled across the bottom of the screen as well as donation drop-off locations for the Clark family.

A woman and man Ashe didn't know were interviewed saying they were witnesses and had known "Chig" Ashe all his life.

Ashe rolled his eyes. *Dammit, did they have to say that name on TV?*

Another small group interviewed said they were neighbors of Deputy Bill Clark and that he had two children, the youngest just two years old. The segment ended with the reporter pointing at a QR code on the posters for those who wanted to donate.

Ashe switched it off and noticed a Metro cop was still stationed outside his door.

"Hey, Officer."

The cop stood up and walked in the room, pulling his mask up while tucking his phone into a pocket. "Yeah, Lieutenant?"

"You can let them know uptown to call off the watch. I'll be going home in a bit...once I figure out how."

The officer gave a mock salute but returned to his seat. "I'm here as long as you are and my directions are to walk you out. Your lift home has been arranged."

A nurse with a cloth mask came a few moments later and he pulled his mask on correctly for her. She went over everything he needed to know for discharge and follow-up care. Then a female orderly in powder-blue scrubs appeared with a wheelchair. The nurse, who'd said her name was Audrey, cut him off before he could object.

"Don't even start. Just get in, Lieutenant," she said like she was used to giving orders.

"You don't have to call me Lieutenant. I'm retired," he said to her.

"I'm not. I'm just tired," Audrey said, and pointed at the wheelchair.

The orderly handed Ashe a plastic bag with his wallet, cell phone, and his deputy sheriff's badge. The police officer next handed Ashe a big Level 4a ballistic vest to put on and no one moved until he did. As the orderly rolled him out, Audrey the nurse accompanied him, and a few feet behind walked the police officer. They escorted Ashe to an elevator and down several floors to the main level. Ashe watched as the officer went out first and spoke into his radio.

A second uniformed officer and a plainclothes man that Ashe couldn't tell whether he was Metro or hospital security, stepped into view. They were in what looked like a wide corridor leading to a side service entrance. His escorts were taking him out a service entry of some sort and the two men had been securing this area. Once he'd been rolled off the elevator, they quickly moved toward the entrance.

His escorts had paused just outside the elevator but right at a large polished cement column.

Cover, Ashe realized. Apparently as they'd rehearsed or at least been directed, they waited to wheel him forward until the two first-floor officers had gone out and scanned the covered side portico area.

After some radio discussion and a hand signal, he was wheeled down the long empty hallway to the covered entrance. With its large metal doors open, Ashe could feel a chilly breeze blowing and it smelled moist out. It was still mostly dark due to the clouds, and the pavement out from under the portico cover looked damp like it'd been sprinkling rain.

Just out of the doors, and near another large concrete column, the orderly stopped Ashe's chair as if on a preselected mark. *Cover again.* The officer who'd been his escort stepped directly in front of him.

Ashe sat quietly observing. He knew this drill. They'd used similar plans for hospitalized high-priority protectees and witnesses before.

Looking out, he picked up another Metro officer in tactical clothing standing beside a dark-blue sedan in a visitor parking lot with an M4 carbine slung high across his chest. In the other direction, near a closer handicap parking lot, another tactical officer stepped out from behind a blacked-out Chevy Tahoe.

I must have been in real trouble. He felt around his hip and his jacket pocket for his gun, then realized it'd had to have been taken as evidence. *Crap! And I'm unarmed!*

Within a couple of seconds of his arrival outside, a dark charcoal Dodge SUV with blacked-out glass drove in aggressively under the covered service portico and stopped suddenly in front of him. On cue, the officer in front of him stepped quickly around the vehicle to cover the far side of it, as the plain-clothed security man with him jogged to its rear. They all drew their guns and faced outbound; watching the area they'd obviously been assigned to and must have rehearsed.

The nurse stepped forward and locked the wheelchair wheels for him, but Ashe stood without her help. Behind him, he noticed the "orderly" in scrubs who had wheeled him out had a SIG 9mm in her hands at high ready and was facing back into the hospital entrance. She wore an earpiece and spoke into her wrist where a microphone was attached.

At the same time all this happened, the back door to the Dodge opened and Detective Danny Breslin got out and opened the front door for Ashe. He had a folding stock HK MP5 in his hand.

Inside behind the wheel was Pat. "Let's go, Chig! It's raining! I need coffee, and it's a long damn drive!"

Ashe did his best to get right in quickly as Breslin slammed his door and got in the back. Pat hit the gas and the Dodge surged forward.

"You guys are spending a lot of Metro's resources on me," Ashe said. He started to wiggle up out of the vest but Pat put a hand on it and pulled it back down.

"Coffee," Pat said and Breslin nodded. Breslin spoke a location Ashe thought sounded familiar into his wrist mic.

"Damn, Pat," Ashe said. "You have some intel I don't know?"

"Give me a minute, Chig," he said and focused on his driving.

The streets seemed a little more empty than usual for the hour. Ashe turned in his seat and saw the black Tahoe behind them. An unmarked unit surged past them and then blocked the next intersection, so regardless of the traffic light, their vehicle and the Tahoe could fly straight through.

Ashe broke the silence. "You've done very good preparation work, gents. Except I should be in the back and buried under bomb bunkers with a pair of patrol canines sitting on me."

"I figured you'd prefer to sit up front, head wound and all. Might get a little nauseous. Also, it lets Danny shoot out either side," Pat explained.

"Oh. Well, when you put it like that," Ashe said.

A couple of more intersections went as before then Ashe recognized the location where they were headed. Pat slowed a bit and pulled into the DCT Shack drive-through. It was a Metro tradition, the Donut-Coffee-Taco Shack that had been in town since the seventies. But in addition to having good donuts and coffee in the morning and excellent street tacos for lunch, this location was one the police had used for other purposes on several occasions.

The small drive-up-only restaurant sat back off the street about seventy-five yards in a huge paved lot where a train depot had been in the 1950's. The DCT Shack itself was far off the street which allowed for the frequent long drive-up lines. An old railroad track that was closed ran along the far side of the lot and the river was across the street on the other side. There were no other buildings close by. If you came down here, you had to *want* to come to the DCT Shack.

Ashe remembered using this place as a meet because anyone following you would stick out and could not hide from view. Two marked Metro units were already stationed near the lot entrance waiting. Ashe smiled to himself. Pat was less about coffee than clearing his obliques and rear, and ensuring they were free of a tail.

I must have really been in the shit.

Pat pulled through to the drive-up window. They were the only vehicle in line. "I'm having a large black coffee and plain donut. Danny? Chig?"

"Nothing for me. I've got a bottle of water," Breslin said. He was keeping his eyes on the far side of the lot.

Ashe grinned. "Coffee, black as well. Pat, how the hell did you get the streets so clear and the Shack to be free?"

"Huh? Oh, it's Sunday. I guess you got hit so hard you missed a few days."

"But the Shack isn't open on..."

"Yeah, yeah, today they are."

Pat ordered at the window and Ashe looked back at the Tahoe that had moved as if to block anyone else from pulling in. The big vehicle's glass was blacked out but through the windshield, he could see his undercover police "orderly" in the front passenger seat pulling on a tac vest. He gave her a little two-fingered wave and she waved back.

Pat handed him his coffee and rolled forward lazily. Brelin was on his earpiece and wrist mic. They were in no hurry to leave, which meant other units were buzzing around and checking any traffic for a tail.

"Ok, Pat, we're clear," he said.

Hearing that, Ashe suspended his coffee out and away from his body and braced one foot against the door and one against the transmission hump, because he knew Pat. Sure enough, Pat floored it and they took off for Hurrt County.

One by one as they left Metro and drove through the less and less urban outlying areas, their escort vehicles dropped off. The Tahoe with his officer/orderly stayed with them for another thirty minutes then turned back as well. They were alone on the road except for a very few other local vehicles. Pat slowed to sub-light speed. It was still early morning.

"Am I in that much danger?" Ashe asked. "Lot of people's Sunday ruined just for me."

"We don't know, but after your buddy Clark was tortured and killed up here, we ain't taking any chances," Pat said. "Them that hit you were semipros. I got to assume whatever the reason they wanted you dead still exists, plus they got a new reason now."

"Well, they might be a little short on manpower," Ashe mumbled over his coffee.

"You're good," Pat said. "But anybody can be got. And you're slower now."

"Pat, there's something else."

"Yeah?"

"I'm pissed off. These mothers came at me in my town," Ashe said. "They killed one of our own, tortured him first, too."

"Yes, they did. You try to rest some. We'll get you home and when you're better, you can get back after them," Pat said.

Ashe nodded and just sat back. If the situation were reversed or if he were still in charge, he'd be doing the same thing. He looked at his watch. Five-twenty a.m.

"But," Breslin added from the back seat. Ashe looked at him with his visor mirror. "You got help now. No more Lone Ranger bullshitting-the-Metro-guys act."

Ashe looked at Pat who said, "Yeah, he read your notes too. I didn't know what was up when he was assigned to me by Captain Speakes. But, Chig, he's one of us."

"Glad to know. Welcome to the club, Danny," Ashe said tiredly. In his mirror, he could see Brelin didn't take his eyes away from scanning the sides and rear, but he smiled.

Ashe laid his head back and closed his eyes.

When Ashe next opened his eyes, he realized despite the coffee, he'd dozed off. Breslin and Pat were talking in low tones.

"Good morning again," Ashe said. Ashe saw that it was six thirty by the dash clock. He sat up a little and looked around. They were almost back in Hurrt County.

"Ah. Good, you're up. We'll be in Seacord in fifteen minutes," Pat said. "Hey, where's your Jeep? Danny will drive it home for you."

Ashe rolled his eyes. "Never mind," he said. "It likely won't start."

"Ok. Well, I got some news, then." Pat pointed at his cell phone.

"Go ahead." Ashe shook his coffee cup to see if there was any left. There wasn't.

"The investigation into Clark; we got some impact DNA off his body and touch DNA from his skin. We're running it and hope to hear something this week."

"Wow. Good, that's good," Ashe said.

Then Pat grinned. "Also, the stateys that are working your attack here in Hurrt County—you met Agent Hume—anyway, they recovered the bullet that hit your dense head."

"Also good. I'm guessing by your shit-eating grin it must be a match to something."

"Yep. Same gun and bullet type that killed your Deputy Clark."

So, the men I shot were involved in killing Bill Clark. He took a breath and thought about that, then realized he was actually glad.

Not that he'd been forced to kill two men, but that if he had to shoot someone, he'd at least gotten some justice for the Clark family.

"So, Pat, if the disappearance of Georgia Murphy is all a Metro case, as so much evidence has tried to make us believe, why bring a hit team from the city to Seacord and try to 'off' me?"

Pat nodded as he drove. "I'm starting to see your way on that a little."

"You add that to the purse and cell we believe Tracy Davis removed from Georgia's apartment or had them removed, then staged in Metro. Sending us the case up there and out of town, you might come all the way over to my point of view."

"Maybe. Maybe closer but you're still missing quite a bit. Like for instance, why?"

"I'm curious about that as well," Breslin said.

"I have a theory, that's all. And it's damn thin," Ashe admitted. "It's all wrapped somehow in this big real estate development project in Hurrt County. A really big deal worth hundreds of millions."

"Seriously, real estate?" Breslin asked.

"I'm thinking Georgia Murphy maybe found out something about this huge deal and they killed her to keep her quiet," Ashe said.

"I read that in your notes. Oh, your leather thing is in back. I'm done with it," Pat said.

"It could be that she was silenced. Then they had to make it look like it happened in Metro so as not to spoil the deal in Hurrt County," Ashe said.

"You're right, that's damn thin," Breslin said.

"Guys, what if I told you I can possibly prove through court records and a timetable of events that Tony Murphy couldn't have been involved in Georgia's murder?"

"Ah, well. Now that would send the Georgia Murphy case back to you," Pat said.

"I agree. And I think I need to interview Tony Murphy. They dropped all this *insinuation* of murder on him and the whole time, he's been in prison."

"Well, he's not in jail for her disappearance," Breslin said. "Or what is likely now her murder. He may cooperate to get that insinuation off his back."

Pat shook his head. "By the way, your ADA and your sheriff are waiting, Chig. Not to mention you are *literally* a head case. You're going home and staying home today."

Ashe thought for a minute. It made sense to get home and catch up with the sheriff.

"There's something else. Something I remembered last night. There was a fourth man there that night," Ashe said.

"Four?"

"He didn't touch me, probably blended in with the crowd. But he knew Paul Milton and spoke to him before Stevie and the crowd got to him."

"Shit," Breslin said. "They're better than we thought. They had a guy on overwatch, maybe quarterbacking the whole attack!"

"Well, they just made their first unforced error."

"Yeah?" Breslin asked.

"Yeah," Ashe said. "They missed me."

CHAPTER 16

Ashe felt his spirits lift a little as they arrived at his home. He had spent his childhood here, seen the passing of many he loved within its walls, and had come here to heal after his divorce. Every moment of his life was soaked into its old wood, and every dream he'd had was imprinted into its walls. Every childhood prayer was lifted through its windows. This was home in the truest, most enduring sense. Simply being here would help him to heal again.

Pat pulled in slowly and without discussion let Breslin out with his MP5 a couple of dozen yards up the drive. They weren't taking any chances.

As he pulled forward, Pat pointed to an older model Ford pickup off to one side of Ashe's stand-alone garage. There was a man sitting behind the wheel and when he saw Pat's Dodge, he started to get out. But before he made it, Pat slammed the Dodge into reverse and started backing up aggressively.

"You know that truck or that dude?" Pat snapped as he was driving backward.

"No," Ashe said and instinctively reached for his own gun then remembered he didn't have one.

But it didn't matter. In less than a minute, Breslin had moved up behind him and had his MP5 against the man's neck. Pat stopped about a hundred yards back and dialed in the Hurrt County sheriff's frequency on his handheld. They waited a beat, then Pat suddenly exited the Dodge and from the back seat grabbed his own MP5.

Ashe threw off his seat belt and looked around the cab of the SUV for something he could use and found an old Metro-issue Glock 40 mounted to a magnet up under the dash then opened the passenger door and propped his right foot in the doorjamb and braced the pistol on the windshield frame. He was still mostly seated, but lower in the vehicle.

Pat maneuvered ahead to one of the big tulip poplar trees that lined the drive and to where he could see Breslin with the stranger. Ashe couldn't see them except as glimpses between trees from his angle.

Then Ashe started sweating, profusely. His gun hand was steady enough but damp. He felt his chest start shaking and his breathing went shallow. He forced himself to take as deep a breath as he could which was not much, then try to blow it out through his lips, slowly as if through a straw.

Breathe, again, slow, slow down. It's adrenaline, it's natural, like from before.

He heard the radio. "We're clear here," Breslin said. Pat didn't move, so Ashe stayed in his position too.

"Buster. Blue Cap, buster," Breslin said. It was the code for all clear and also for a cop on scene.

Pat hopped back in, noticed Ashe had his Glock, and drove down to the house and garage. As he pulled up, he reversed and backed the Dodge up against the garage.

"What the hell?" he yelled as he got out and walked over to the truck.

Ashe drew another couple of breaths and he put the Glock back where he'd found it. His hands were shaking as well so he focused on just breathing as deeply as he could and climbed out of Pat's SUV. He stuffed his hands in his pants pockets to hide the shaking and tried to look natural about it.

Through the windows on the front of his garage door, he saw a familiar car inside as he walked over, but didn't say anything.

"This is Reserve Deputy Sheriff Jeremy Franks," Breslin said. "He was sent out here a couple of hours ago to watch the house until we arrived."

Franks was an older fellow, older than Ashe, and had a thick gray and black beard. He wasn't in a uniform, just jeans and a flannel shirt with a tarnished sheriff's badge clipped to his belt. Ashe looked at him and nodded, although they'd never met.

Breslin returned an old Colt Double Eagle .45 to Franks who stuffed it in a worn holster then stuck out his hand to Pat.

"Good to meet you boys. You must be ol' Chig," Franks said.

Pat rolled his eyes and looked at Ashe. "Your sheriff might have at least told us he had a...*man* outside!" Then he strolled off toward the front porch.

Franks looked from Pat to Ashe. "Oh, sorry. So you're the one. You're..."

"Ashe. *Just Ashe.* Thanks and hello," he said and headed for his front door as he pulled off the heavy body armor.

"Well, all's clear! Nobody's been here!" Franks called out to his back.

Once inside, Ashe felt better and his shakes subsided a little. He went through the foyer and into the kitchen to the fridge and started for a beer but switched to a bottle of water.

Pat returned from the back rooms to the front and walked into the kitchen. He'd made a quick check of the house. "Nice place. You've done a lot since, ah, well since you took it over."

"Thanks, you want something?" Ashe held up his water but Pat shook his head.

"This was all hand built back when, eh?"

Ashe nodded. "My dad and grandfather built it."

Thinking of his father, he'd wanted to hold a reception for him here after he'd passed. Something casual so friends and what little family was left could come together and mark his passing. What they called "celebrations of life." He wanted to and had starting planning it, but the pandemic was still raging then and there had been restrictions on such gatherings at the time.

"So," he said to Pat. "I guess I'm good now. I mean, with Deputy Franks outside and all."

Pat roared, "Haw!" then said, "Your sheriff said last night he'd be out with your county DA this morning. He asked us to stick around until they get here."

"Again, Metro's not going to pay for you and Breslin down here in Hurrt County," Ashe scolded. "You two should get back."

"What Metro and what pay? This is Sunday. Me and Danny are on our own time."

Ashe dropped his face and shook his head. "Ah, for the love of...well now I feel like crap, Pat. Look, I'm fine! You guys go and have what's left of your Sunday."

"First, you're not so fine, Chig, and you shouldn't be, with what you been through. Don't think I didn't notice them shakes. That's normal, I had them myself a time or two after…"

"Yeah, I know, but I'm okay now. This place is a fortress."

"Besides, I'm having a hell of time, buddy! Now Danny outside there, he lives for the tactical stuff. He was SWAT and all for years." Pat leaned over and looked out a window so he could see Breslin.

"Well I owe you both, then," Ashe said.

"Damn straight," Pat said. "Look, your high-speed bodyguard is fingering Danny's MP5 like it's a damn diamond-plated laser gun or something."

Pat appeared to have a sudden thought and walked over and shouted out the door. "Danny, you and your new buddy might ought to check the garage building and the shed in back!"

"They're all good," shouted Franks and waved.

"Danny?"

"On it, Pat!" Breslin answered and moved toward the garage. Franks followed him like a puppy.

Pat looked at Ashe and said, "I'm going outside to make a call and check on things, you just settle down and rest some. I'll lock up, I got your keys."

"I'm having a shower."

Pat walked off past his Dodge and took out his phone. Ashe just stood in the kitchen a second and drank his water.

After a minute of silence, he said, "You may as well step out here. I know you're here."

From the hallway and into the kitchen, Stevie emerged.

She wore a form-fitting gray knit sweater over a white tee and charcoal leggings and socks on her feet. Her hair was pulled back and she wore no makeup. Her eyes looked tired.

"I'm sorry. I wanted to see you when you got here so I let myself in. I still know where you keep your other key," she said in a whisper.

"You snuck past the deputy outside?"

"I got here before he did. It was raining so I parked in your garage and waited for it to stop. I walked over here as he drove up. I didn't know who he was so I came in here and hid."

"Then when I come home with an entourage, you…"

"Oh, I don't know why I hid. I'd slept some in your bed waiting and when I heard your men come in, I just hid in that old attic entry. Your friend, the detective..."

"Pat Keagan."

"Yeah him, he stuck his head in and looked around, but he was looking at his phone too and missed me."

Ashe smiled at that. At some point, he knew he would let Pat know he had missed a five-foot-six woman while checking his house. He figured somehow, he'd make a comparison between him and Deputy Franks.

"Well, you're here. We are going to talk, and talk about your involvement. This is getting out of hand."

"God! That's an understatement, Ashe! I almost lost you! Talk about getting out of hand!"

She walked over and hugged him hard. She buried her face in his chest for several minutes and didn't let go. He let her. Outside, it looked to Ashe like Pat was finishing up his call and was headed back inside.

"Honey? Pat's coming in. I'll tell him why you're here."

"No, I don't want to talk to you in front of him or anyone else yet."

Ashe pulled her away and looked her in the face. "He's my old partner. With Deputy Clark being killed in Metro, he's got a right to know everything now."

"Not yet, please? Please, Ashe."

"Okay, go to my bedroom. He won't look there again."

She turned and padded off in her socked feet toward the back of the house as Pat burst back in.

"Your people are on their way and the state police are sending someone to replace Ol' Grandpa Hatfield out there."

"I'll take all the help I can get. You always explode through doors like that?"

"Kiss my ass, and I thought you were showering?"

"I am now," Ashe said innocently and left Pat in the kitchen.

Ashe entered the bedroom and saw Stevie was standing in the master bath. He peeled off his coat and shirt and kicked off his boots and socks and walked into the bath.

"Help me with this," he said and pointed at the bandage on his head and left ear.

She made a cringy face but found a small set of scissors in a drawer and slowly started to cut away at his dressings. "Eww," was all she said, and in the bathroom mirror he could see her making all kinds of faces.

After a few minutes, she said, "I got most of it, but, eww, some of it is...stuck to your skin and stitches."

"Be as gentle as you can, but get it all off. I want to see."

Stevie sighed loudly and pulled at the last of his bandages. Ashe could feel it tugging at his stitches as it finally gave way. She grabbed a washcloth and soaked it under hot water then dabbed at his head and ear.

"Does this hurt?" She was still cringing but focused on her job.

"It's good, yes it does, but the hot cloth feels good," he said.

After wiping away the old antiseptic and cleaning everything off, she stood back. "There," she said.

Ashe looked at himself. It wasn't near as bad as he'd expected, but that side of his head was still a little purple from bruising, even five days later. The top of his left ear was squared off flat from the bullet.

"Thank you." He took her hand and kissed it. "Now I've had four to five days of bed baths, I have to shave and shower."

"Sure, um...what do you want me to do?" Stevie asked.

"Maybe go hide under the bed?"

Afterward, Ashe dressed in navy jogging pants and gray sneakers with a lightweight gray sweatshirt. He could hear muted men's voices in his living room, so he looked at his watch; it was still only eleven a.m., so after plugging in his dead cell to charge, he left Stevie on his bed looking at her phone to go check on who had arrived.

Between the living room and the kitchen were Sheriff Jacobs, Pat, Agent Rachel Hume, and a younger man Ashe had never met but assumed was the Hurrt County Assistant District Attorney John Price.

"Hey, Ashe," Jacobs started. "Glad to see you home again. You know everybody I guess."

Ashe nodded and shook his hand then turned to Hume. "Hello again, Agent Hume," he said.

She shook his hand and said, "Morning. And this Special Agent stuff will get to be tiresome pretty quick. I'm just Rachel."

"Good. I'm just Ashe," he said.

Rachel was short, about five-four and full figured without looking heavy. In fact, she looked as if she worked out. She wore her hair up and pulled back in a professional look and had hazel eyes that seemed to catch everything. He could see already that she was quiet, smart, and observant.

Ashe decided to be careful what he said at first around her. He then turned to the new man in the room. "And I assume you're John Price."

Price smiled and hopped to his feet from the sofa and strode confidently over to give Ashe a firm double-pump handshake.

"You bet, John P. Price. I'm damn glad to meet you! You're something of a hero I guess around here now."

"Well, there are at least a few people who don't share that opinion," Ashe said and smiled.

Price chuckled politely and returned to his seat on the sofa. He and Rachel had pulled his coffee table over closer to it and they had papers arranged on it.

Ashe gave Price his five-second look over. He was tan even here in autumn and wore a heavy, expensive-looking watch and a big college ring.

Ashe noted he had a large black and gold bracelet that had to be real gold. He wore neat and appropriately-casual-for-Sunday pressed jeans and a powder-green sweatshirt over a yellow polo, and Ashe bet himself there were designer labels on everything. His wide and trendy tortoiseshell glasses completed the look of a young, well-educated lawyer on his way up.

ADA of Hurrt County? Or an Eddie Bauer model? Ashe thought and went into the kitchen where Pat stood beside the coffeepot.

"You make this?" Ashe asked.

"Yeah, and you're out of coffee now," Pat said quietly.

Ashe looked at the assembled men who all had a cup for themselves or were drinking water, so he didn't make an offer but poured himself a mugful and took a sip.

"Uh-huh," he mumbled to Pat. "Precinct coffee. You could stand a shotgun barrel up in this mud and it wouldn't tip over. No wonder I'm out."

Ashe walked over to his dad's—and his—favorite chair. It was a huge reddish-brown leather high-backed rocker chair with big brass tacks, and he sat down in it, leaning forward to see the table. Pat pitched him his portfolio so he could take notes.

"Let me start by saying, Mr. Ashe, er, *Ashe*, that the deputy attorney general has turned the case concerning your ambush, over to me to present to a local grand jury. That way, we can validate our initial finding that you were justified in defending yourself against the deceased, Mr.'s MacNeal and Everitt."

Ashe just nodded.

Price continued. "The aggravated assault against you by Mr. Milton, currently being held awaiting bond here in Hurrt County, will go to a preliminary hearing this coming week. He is represented by a local attorney, Phillip Crews."

"Crews? The ADA before you?" Hume asked just as Ashe was about to ask, *Crews, the partner of Mark Portals?*

"Yes. We have a meeting tomorrow. He wants to discuss some options," Price said.

"Just a damn minute!" Jacobs roared. "He murdered my deputy and my friend! He shouldn't get any deals!"

"Gentlemen!" Price said above them. "It's routine and normal for me to hear any offers from the defense. At this point, we have yet to charge him officially with the torture and murder of Deputy Clark. That, I am saving for a Metro grand jury the end of this month."

"And, guys," Ashe added. "If ADA Price were to refuse to meet with Milton's defense, it would look bad and wouldn't help us at the preliminary or in front of the grand jury or circuit court later. The defense could claim they were prepared to do or say anything and we couldn't counter them."

"Oh, got it," Jacobs said. "Sorry, guys, but I want to personally pull the switch on the electric chair with that dude strapped in it!"

Price and Hume looked at each other, then Price turned to Ashe and Pat.

"As all of this is multijurisdictional, I've officially requested the AG to have the state police homicide commander take this case. I think as everything I've read and seen so far from your independent investigations seem to lead; these crimes were carried out across multiple venues in this part of the state. The state homicide commander has assigned…"

"Well now hold on," Jacobs injected again. He stared at Price hard. "I want Ashe here to be fully involved. He got this thing with Georgia Murphy moving again at my request and got shot and beat because I asked for his help. He's got more done on this in one week than you got in two damn years!"

"Yes, well, Special Agent Hume has, um, been assigned as lead," Price said.

Ashe decided the air had stiffened in the room. He started to try and diffuse things when Hume raised her hands and smiled.

"No objections from me! Look, I know of Mr. Ashe's lengthy investigative background and would welcome the professional local insight," Rachel said.

"Good," Price said. "As this is also a Metro matter, I'd like Lieutenant Keagan here to be involved as well. Sort of a 'task force' I guess."

"Absolutely. Myself or if I get occupied, Detective Sergeant Dan Breslin will represent Metro Major Crimes Unit," Pat said.

"Great, I'll have the AG write something formal up," Price said as he scribbled a note. "We've already discussed with the Metro ADA office. I will be the prosecutor for both counties."

Ashe sipped at his coffee as Jacobs nodded and winked back at him. Ashe figured the sheriff thought his objections had worked with Price, so he let it be.

Ashe was about to say something when from the back of the house, everyone could hear a toilet flush.

Uh-oh. Stevie.

Pat looked at Ashe with his brow wrinkled and started toward the hallway.

"It's okay, Pat. Old house…it does that," Ashe lied. Pat nodded and seemed satisfied for the moment.

"What would help me get started is if you two would fill me in on everything. From the start and leave out nothing," Rachel said.

"Well, what we can prove is one thing…" said Ashe.

Rachel waved a hand. "No, everything. Tell me what you know but can't prove as well."

Ashe opened his portfolio and remembered Price was Mark Portals' nephew. He decided to feel him out a bit more.

"Uh, firstly, what about Tracy Davis?" Ashe said to stall a bit.

Price nodded and said, "Ah, yes. It seems you have a decent circumstantial case of evidence tampering. But I don't think, minus a confession or the discovery of any additional evidence…"

"Like Deputy Clark's camera," Ashe said.

"Yes, like that. I don't think we will get a conviction. I'll hold fast through her preliminary appearance to see if we can get her bound over to circuit. Then likely have to, to…"

Price looked over at Jacobs and shrugged. "We'd have to cut some kind of agreement."

"I believe that Deputy Clark was abducted, tortured, and ultimately killed to get his digital camera, so nothing or no one could corroborate that Tracy Davis manipulated the Georgia Murphy crime scene," Ashe said.

"She got the case thrown up to Metro and away from here, Ashe will tell you," Jacobs said.

"You could be right. Or, they could claim she was simply the unknowing or even innocent victim of someone else who manipulated the evidence," Price answered. "You see, by shooting to death those men who ambushed you, one of whom can be connected by his gun to the Clark murder in Metro, we are limited in the ways we can know for sure," Price said.

"Yeah, Chig. You should have let them take you," Pat said.

Price smiled. "Not at all. But now we have only Tracy Davis who can tell us her end, and Paul Milton, your surviving attacker, left to fill in the gaps. Right now, both have attorneys and are not talking."

Price then turned to Jacobs. "And that, Sheriff, is why I will meet with Mr. Crews to discuss what his client knows. Mr. Milton may solve a great many things."

The clock on the huge hand-hewn oak mantle over the living room fireplace chimed and everyone took notice. It was eleven forty-five a.m.

"Which brings us back to you," Price said, turning to Ashe.

Ashe took a deep breath and let that comment hang in the air for a minute.

How do I tell it all until I know if this is Mark Portals' guy?

Until I know what Stevie knows, how can I trust anyone?

"I need a bit more coffee," Ashe said and started back to the kitchen. "Pat got me up too early this morning. Anybody else?"

As he poked around for a can of coffee, he saw Price shrug and Rachel mouthed, *What the hell?* to Price.

Pat coughed and looked at Ashe with confusion and as if to repeat her sentiment.

"Hey, maybe Ashe here doesn't quite feel up to this yet. It's his first day out of the hospital and all," Jacobs said.

But Ashe noticed it was Price who seemed to get it.

"Mister Ashe, you don't know me and you have some concerns. I've read your notes," he said.

"Actually I wanted more coffee, but okay since *you* brought it up," Ashe said. "I was told you got your appointment here because your, ah, uncle, Mark Portals, pulled strings for you."

Rachel looked at Price and relaxed. He smiled and stood to face Ashe.

"I get it. You've been through hell for this Georgia Murphy case, literally, and you don't know who to trust. You're from here, at least you were, but I'm not."

Pat stayed quiet and looked back and forth between them. This was the first he'd heard of this.

"Ashe, my uh, uncle I guess, is actually my aunt's ex-husband. We're not related and I'm not sure that qualified even back then."

"He didn't get you appointed?"

"Oh my God," Rachel said almost laughing, but Price just waved a hand over his head like he was clearing smoke.

"No, no! It's okay, really. If we're going to be working together, I'm glad he brought this up now."

Price turned back to Ashe. "Yes, he did, but I was looking into a prosecutorial job right out of school and figured at best I'd be buried as the rookie in a twenty-person office in Metro. Here, I'm it. I get to do it all. I'm glad he helped out with his connections at the capitol, but I don't consider myself unduly indebted to him, and I'm not really sure I ever liked the guy."

"I think Georgia Murphy knew something sour about some big land deals that Portals and company are working here, and maybe that got her dead," Jacobs said.

Price nodded. "That's the root of this whole case. That's what I want you to lay out for me and Rachel here. But let me say this, Ashe, Mark and I are very different kind of lawyers. I am not on his payroll; I am on the people's payroll."

Ashe saw his face flush a bit as he continued. "If the evidence leads to criminal activity by Portals, you'd have no issue indicting him?"

Price sighed heavily. "I take my job damn seriously and whether you trust me or not, I am the assistant district attorney for Hurrt County, and I am going after *whoever* had a hand in the disappearance and murder of Georgia Murphy, the torture and murder of Bill Clark, and the attempted murder and aggravated assault of you! Now are you going to help me or not?"

Ashe looked at the sheriff who nodded back at him, then he looked at Pat who looked convinced as well.

"Okay. I guess I'll help you," he said.

CHAPTER 17

It started raining outside again only harder. Ashe found a can of coffee Pat hadn't wasted and made a fresh pot. This time Rachel Hume joined him in the kitchen.

"God, I was worried I'd have to drink that other stuff again," she said.

"Pat's coffee is a lethal weapon," Ashe agreed. "See, if you drop a cup of it and the cup shatters, the coffee will just sit there quivering in the shape of the cup for a full second before slowly spilling."

Rachel laughed. "You two worked together long?" she asked and looked at Pat.

"All our lives," he said, "or so it seems."

"I could tell you two were close."

"I joined Metro PD after I got out of the Army. Pat was an academy class ahead of me. We were partners as detectives. Then I was his boss at MCU. I think his wife was sort of jealous for the time we spent together."

"What about now? I imagine she'd be less so now you're retired," Rachel said and looked around for Pat.

"No, not now," Ashe said and focused on the coffeepot.

"Oh, sorry. He divorced?"

"Widowed. About six years ago I guess."

"Oh. Really?" she said, and kept looking around for him.

Ashe noticed and wondered to himself if Pat were even open to someone. He realized he had no idea if his friend had a woman in his life. He looked around for Pat and didn't see him, but continued to poke around his cabinets and found a couple of big thermoses with lids and cups.

To the group, he said, "Before we get too cozy inside here, I imagine Franks and Breslin might like some of this."

"I'll take of it," Jacobs said and took over filling them. "As old as Franks is, I'll bet his old bones will be locked up. I'll add some WD-40 to his!"

"Okay, let's get back to telling me everything," Price said. He had sat back on the sofa and waited patiently but he seemed eager to start.

Rachel sat on the far end where she could see Ashe's face directly as he went to his chair again with his fresh coffee.

"This started the day the café reopened. I met Sheriff Jacobs there for the first time and he told me how the former sheriff named Laughton had doubts with how Detective Tracy Davis worked the disappearance of Georgia Murphy."

Price and Rachel began taking notes and didn't interrupt.

"Laughton had a set of photos taken by his deputy, Bill Clark, of Georgia Murphy's apartment. The initial complaint of her having gone missing was from her boss, Susan Marlin. She'd last seen Georgia on Wednesday the 13th at about five p.m., give or take a half hour."

"Where they worked at the Hurrt County Land and Title?" Rachel asked.

"Yes, Ms. Marlin didn't report Georgia missing until the 15th, after she'd not shown up for work on Thursday and Friday. Anyway, Deputy Clark took the initial complaint at five forty-five p.m. and then went to Georgia's apartment. Now, Laughton told newly elected Sheriff Jacobs that Clark shot several photos of the apartment with his personal digital camera. Detective Davis by this time had joined him there that night."

Ashe opened his portfolio. His notes and papers were shuffled around by Pat, but he found everything and arranged it all back the way he had it. Especially the photo.

"This is one of the photos Laughton gave to Jacobs, saying it was from Clark."

He handed Rachel and Price the photo that showed Georgia Murphy's closet and closet door. It showed the purse with the broken *A* on the latch and the new-looking dresses still with tags. It showed a cell phone on the floor.

"The very next morning, without Clark or anyone, she for some reason felt the need to go and reshoot the apartment. This of course formed Laughton's first doubts against Tracy Davis. This is her set of photos Sheriff Jacobs recovered from her office."

Ashe handed them the set. There was a shot similar to Clark's photo of the closet door, only this one showed only the fancy purse and no cell phone.

"The former ADA, Phillip Crews, reviewed the evidence, and I can only assume he'd never seen the Clark photos at the time. Based on what he must have figured was evidence he lacked venue, he forwarded the case to the Metro ADA at the time, Mr. Ashad, on or about the 30th of April that year."

Price and Rachel looked over both photos carefully. Rachel made notes to herself then looked up at Ashe as if to say, *go on.* About then, Jacobs returned from tending to the men outside.

"Now, understand the original Clark photos are gone from the case files Tracy Davis maintained. She told me to my face they *never existed.* I knew that was a lie as I'd seen the other shot. The only way we have this photo is from Clark's digital camera. See, Detective Davis got his digital film card and all the original prints, but apparently these original images were also in its internal storage drive. Clark gave them to Laughton."

"This phone and purse, and some of these dresses," Rachel said, "They are on photos of Tony Murphy's apartment that Metro took, along with some of her blood."

Huh.

"Yeah. So somehow, Davis or an accomplice removed them and built a crime scene in Metro to hang this on Tony Murphy. They built up, through Mark Portals, the fiction of a pending divorce between Georgia and Tony to give him a motive. Given their separation and his criminal history, it was easy enough to convince Metro authorities he'd had a hand in her disappearance."

"You mean, me and you," Pat said. He'd been down the hall and rejoined them in the living room.

Ah, shit. Stevie.

"Yeah, me and you. When her case came to me through ADA Ashad, I assigned Pat to investigate. We proceeded on what we couldn't know was a false premise; that she'd been at Tony's apartment that night."

"But…she couldn't have, right?" Price asked.

"Correct. Not while Tony was there," Ashe said. "It's the first flaw in their scheme. I time-lined this out. Assuming she went missing the night of the 13th, she'd have had to really flown her car to Metro for Tony to have had maybe fifteen minutes to kill her while he was also about to be arrested for an armed robbery."

"Her car?"

"We found it at Tony Murphy's apartment. Wiped clean of *any* fingerprints," Pat added.

"Any? That's interesting."

"Yeah, why would Tony wipe Georgia's or even his own prints from a car they both still owned? Even the outside door handles and mirrors."

Price made a note then said, "So, Ashe, from your records, you say everyone told you Georgia was divorcing Tony, but then later you say that's not true. I see nothing else here to indicate where this information came from. Why is that important?"

Ashe nodded. "Because Mark Portals filed for the divorce about ten days after her disappearance. It was a sloppy mistake, but an attempt to add to the insinuation Tony killed her," Ashe said, leaving out Stevie altogether. "It's the second mistake they made. See, Mark Portals and an associate went to see Sheriff Laughton to tell him about the divorce filing. They were insinuating a motive, initially leading everyone toward Tony Murphy."

"Well, Ashe, this is convincing, but it hinges on her disappearing on the 13th. What if she went off on her own and fell into trouble afterward?" Price asked.

"I had the same question. See, her cell pinged a tower in Metro late on the night of the 13th and then never again. She had to go missing the 13th so they could say Tony did it. He was in jail later that night and has been since. He never made bond."

"Why did it have to be Tony?" Price asked. "Could've left it a mystery."

Pat answered that. "Because, well, an unsolved case is a problem. A mystery. I hate mysteries. Now a case where you have a viable suspect, one like Tony with a criminal history and a solid-seeming motive but no proof, well that's another thing. I mean, he was going to prison anyway so we thought we had time. There wasn't a killer on the loose, so to speak."

Rachel made some notes but then just stared with what looked like admiration at Pat as he spoke.

Look out, buddy.

"I see," Price said.

"Plus," Ashe added, "why else go to the trouble of relocating her purse with her driver's license and her cell phone to his apartment except to frame him. And him getting caught just as he was about to...huh. Hey, Pat?"

"Yeah?"

"How did you guys get onto Tony Murphy so fast? You caught him right as he was robbing the pawnshop, right?"

"Yeah, we were there before he could... You know, I think Danny can back me up here, but we got a tip from someone who said *they saw it* going down!"

Ashe looked at Rachel and Price. They all seemed to get the same thought.

"He was set up," Rachel said first.

"But I'm still not there yet with the *why*," Price said, shaking his head.

"This is where we still have work to do and that's where my interview with Susan Marlin comes in," Ashe said, and described how Georgia had worked there with the DBA land acquisition and the S.C.E.A. He showed them the photos he'd taken of the wall charts in the "War Room" on his phone.

"And this is about where I was when I got clobbered," Ashe said. "I think there is something wrong with the deal, and the murder of Georgia Murphy triggered a panic. Someone, I have my ideas on who, but someone then made it all look like it didn't happen here in Hurrt County to preserve their investment."

"And Clark? Why?" Price asked.

"I think they needed his camera. So once we cornered Tracy Davis, the only one who could dispute her story and her photos was Clark. Heavy-handed? Way too excessive? Sure, but we're talking half a billion dollars of outside investors, according to Susan Marlin," Ashe said. "Deputy Bill Clark was tougher than they figured."

"Do we know if they got it from him?" Rachel asked, still looking at Pat.

"No, not for sure one way or the other," Ashe answered.

Rachel closed her notepad and finished her coffee. "I think I need to go introduce myself to Ms. Marlin and see this 'War

Room' for myself."

"Before you go, you wanted me to tell you what I can't prove, right?"

"Yes, Ashe, of course. Please do," she said and sat back down.

"The night I was hit. Right as I passed out, Paul Milton was on the sidewalk beside me trying to get up. But I heard another voice there. A fourth man," Ashe said.

"Fourth?" Price looked up, surprised. "You sure? I mean, you took a hell of a hit."

"Yeah, I believe it was Milton who asked if he should kill me. This fourth voice said 'no.' And that there were too many people around and for Milton to beat it."

"A fourth man," Price repeated. "It's good that never got out. People might be terrified. On the other hand, since this man doesn't know you remembered him, we might can use that to our advantage."

"Of course, I only know what others have told me, but apparently as Paul Milton tried to escape, several customers of the café tackled him and held him for the sheriff."

"Yeah," Pat added excitedly. "And then Chig's…"

"Friends," Ashe interrupted. "My *friends* prevented Milton from leaving."

Years of working together meant Ashe knew that Pat was about to tell his favorite part of the story. That Stevie threw her shoes at him. *But not just yet.*

"And you think you know who this fourth man is?" Rachel asked.

"No way to know until I hear his voice. But Carl Jack Portals has been following me since I started looking into Georgia Murphy's disappearance. Talking to everyone in town trying to keep them from talking to me. Told half the town and even Detective Davis that I was just a cheap private investigator."

"What?" Rachel asked. "Why?"

"I think he was trying to convince people I'd screwed up her case in Metro and was covering up for my own reputation's sake," Ashe said and shrugged. "It's part of how I figured out Tracy was involved with the cover-up. She and Susan Marlin asked me if I were a P.I. within an hour or so of each other. When I spoke to Davis, she was defensive and edgy, then she took a call from someone and got all cocky. Accused me of being 'just' a private detective."

"Earlier," Ashe continued, "on the same day, Susan Marlin asked me about whether I was a P.I. right after I had seen CJ Portals leave the vicinity of her office. It's not conclusive of course, but it adds up that CJ Portals had talked to both of them."

"Ah, shit," Pat said. "You know I asked the same thing because Captain Speakes in Metro told me you were a private license."

"Where would he get that?" Price asked.

Ashe watched Pat, whose eyes flickered a micromillimeter. Just the slightest bit.

You had to know him and be looking right at him to catch it.

"I don't know. You guys should ask, he's my boss now and all," Pat said convincingly.

"I will," Rachel said. "Anything else I should know?"

"Yeah, my head is now really hurting. I think I should eat," Ashe said and closed his eyes.

Rachel looked at Price and said, "Fourth suspect, interesting. I'm going to town and interview Ms. Marlin and try and look up this associate of Mark Portals, Stephanie Collins."

Pat and Ashe shot a quick look at each other.

"Well I'm going to sit here a minute and digest all this," Price said. "So where does Mark Portals come into the picture here?"

"Again, so far as we know only because of the DBA project that Georgia had a small hand in," Ashe said.

"Well that's nothing to…" Price said, then looked at his watch. "Oh hell!"

"Yeah?" Rachel asked him.

"Yeah, uh, let's all meet at my office in town tomorrow about ten-ish. Right now, my wife has a thing; she's coordinating a fundraiser for the Clark family this afternoon I have to be at," he said. "Mr. Ashe, I think a lot of people might like to see you there. Feel up to it? I could drive you?"

Ashe smiled and shook his head. "I'm just hours out of the hospital, Mr. Price, and please, don't mention I'm back here yet to anyone."

"Yes, please don't," Sheriff Jacobs added. "Hopefully that's obvious as to why."

"Of course," Price agreed, and they got up and put on their

raincoats and gathered their papers. Pat sat cold still and made no attempt to move.

"I'm guessing you and Detective Breslin need to be getting back to Metro," Ashe said.

"Yes. Yes, we do," Pat said flatly but did not move.

CHAPTER 18

As Sheriff Jacobs prepared to leave, he mentioned that he had Ed Bell coming out to relieve Franks outside, but Ashe drew a line.

"No need for that. You're shorthanded as it is. I'm good, I'm home now, so call it off, Sheriff."

Ashe shook hands with him, and Jacobs extracted a promise to have breakfast that next morning before meeting with Price. He left and a few minutes later, Franks rolled off as well.

Looking outside, Ashe could see that Breslin had repositioned the Dodge SUV where he could see up the driveway, but the increasing intensity of the rain made any kind of observation unlikely.

"Pat, you want Breslin in here?"

"He'd drown before he made it to your door. Go get Stevie Collins," he said.

Ashe smiled to himself. Pat had missed finding her once but not twice.

"How?"

"*I* wasn't shot in the head. I had Breslin run the tag of the car in your garage."

Ashe went back and opened the bedroom door. Stevie was napping so he went over and sat on the bed beside her.

"Come on out. They know you're here," he said, startling her a little. He then left her alone to get herself together.

He came back down the hall and found his coffee cup but realized he hadn't eaten anything, as his stomach rolled and reminded him he had downed three coffees this morning. He went into the kitchen to make some eggs for himself when Stevie timidly entered the living room.

"Hello there," Pat said officiously. "You remember me from the other night. I'm Lieutenant Keagan with Metro Police."

"Yes, you were at the hospital when…anyway, call me Stevie," she said and sat on the sofa where Rachel Hume had been.

"We first talked, oh, two years ago about your friend Georgia Murphy."

Ashe figured Stevie had to be hungry so he added a pair of eggs to the scramble he was making. He microwaved some bacon and made toast.

"I'm sorry I kind of hid earlier. I came here and then that old man outside arrived and then all of you. I wasn't sure who was who," she said.

"Uh-huh. Why would you be hiding from anyone?" Pat asked but Stevie didn't answer.

It was something Ashe knew she was good at, so there was a thick silence in the room for a few minutes while Ashe cooked.

"Just a minute," Pat said. He took out a Miranda Rights card and read it to Stevie.

Dammit, Ashe thought. He wanted to hear what she knew before she gave a statement.

"Here," Ashe said to her and handed her a plate. "Eat and we'll go over everything."

Pat got up and helped himself to some bacon and toast and Ashe stood at the kitchen bar and ate. Finally when Pat was picking up bacon crumbs, Ashe went ahead and made more of everything for him. When everyone was eating, Ashe turned to Stevie.

"Let's start before you met me. When you were friends with Georgia Murphy," Ashe said.

"I was finalizing my divorce but still had Nora, my daughter," she explained to Pat. "I was a single mom and Georgia was about my age. I was just sort of going downhill. See, Georgia was a pal. She was not legally separated but her husband worked in Metro, so we wound up going out a lot and I started drinking way more than ever before."

She took a bite and then added, "Not her fault, I know, it's on me. But I found out she was a hard partying gal."

"What did Tony do in Metro?" Pat asked.

"Technically construction. Mostly concrete work I believe. But…and this is just rumor," she said between bites, "I take it he worked with the men who tried to kill you, Ashe."

That was news to Ashe. "Why do you say that? You knew them? You recognized them? Did Georgia tell you Tony worked with Paul Milton or the others?" Ashe asked.

"She mentioned it but, well, you'll find out anyway." Then to Pat, "Mr. Keagan, I was a mess, as you may have heard. I was a barely functioning drunk. At some point, Georgia and I started going to this place she knew, a club in the city called The Hot Event."

"I've heard of it," he said.

"We were drinking a lot. Almost every other night. We usually hung with this group of regulars; I don't remember the guy Georgia was always hanging all over by name. But then later, there was a sort of gang of buddies she knew who started coming there. 'The Concrete Crew' as they called themselves. They had T-shirts with a company phone number on them, so they worked together. I later knew it was an LLC that CJ owned."

"Go on," Ashe said.

Stevie averted her eyes and paused breathlessly for a minute. "I'm so damn ashamed of this, and I know how much this is going to hurt."

"You're stronger now, go ahead and tell us," Ashe said.

"No, not hurt me. *You*. This is going to hurt *you*, Ashe."

Ashe leaned back and drew in a breath. He had already sort of heard the rumors of what he figured she was about to reveal to him and Pat.

"I got involved with CJ Portals. I don't think it was ever anything serious, he was just a lot of fun and he paid for my drinks and dinners. He seemed sort of edgy and thrilling at the same time. We hung out a lot, especially at night, and mostly in the city. Georgia was always flirting with some guy there too, teasing Tony I think."

"So Tony Murphy was there as well? There's a motive for you. So he also knew CJ Portals. Was he a part of 'The Concrete Crew'?" Pat asked.

"Yeah, he was. They all knew each other pretty well." Stevie drew a sharp breath and continued. "CJ was just…charming. He was the guy with big rolls of cash and everyone in the club knew him. He was the king of that place and he bought me anything I wanted. All my drinks and…other, well, I was all fucked up by then. I even did ecstasy with Georgia a few times. A little coke once or twice—but I swear that was all!"

Ashe turned and put his dishes in the sink and was glad Pat had started asking questions. He knew he had to hear this, but she was right. It hurt.

Damn you, Carl Jack Portals!

"Who all worked with The Concrete Crew?" Pat continued.

She continued to Pat. "There was Tony Murphy, Paul Milton—he's that bastard who hit Ashe—and a couple, three others. Sometimes they'd bring on a guy and then I wouldn't see him again, so I don't know how many for sure."

"MacNeal? Everitt? You hear those names?" Pat asked.

Stevie nodded and focused on Pat. She didn't look at Ashe who decided he wasn't looking at her either.

"MacNeal, yes, I'm not sure about the other name."

"And CJ, he hands-on ran The Concrete Crew?" Pat said.

"The Concrete Crew definitely worked directly for him. A lot of their conversation was mostly work related, construction talk. I mean, they were always *about* to do something, something sketchy I took it. But I don't have a great memory of that time. He was buying my drinks and paying for everything, it all seems like it was in a haze now. It was like being a Wise Guy's girl in that movie…"

"What did they do, Stevie?" Ashe asked a little harsher than he meant to. She didn't look at him. "I don't mean at work, either. What sketchiness did they do?"

"I don't know of anything serious. No big drug deals, nothing like that I know of. It was more like they acted tough and rough and talked *around* things more than *about* them when I was there."

"CJ, he worked for Mark Portals?" Ashe asked.

"Well yes, but in a different capacity. It was like here in town, CJ was a nice professional-acting man working for Mark. Oh, a man with an edge and a history, and always flirtatious, but otherwise completely…normal. Up in Metro and with The Concrete Crew, he was, oh, darker."

"Did The Concrete Crew ever come down here?" Pat asked.

"No. Not that I know of. Not until the other night," she said. "Oh God, Ashe, I'm so sorry. This was all in my past and I swear I had no idea they even were a thing anymore until they actually came here."

Ashe decided to set aside the idea she might have been used as bait.

Willingly? God, I hope not.

"So, Mark Portals?" Pat asked.

"Of course I knew Mark professionally here in Seacord, he handled my divorce. And I knew CJ was his nephew, but I never thought back then they were actually criminals or I'd have never..."

"Never have..." Pat asked.

She made an angry face at Pat who just said, "Oh."

Slept with him, Ashe thought, completing her sentence for her. His stomach rolled more.

"I began to break it off with CJ or at least slow it down a lot. Mark wanted to help me in my practice. I had, um, slipped up some. I was day drinking and losing clients by then. You know how I was, Ashe. Mark and Phillip Crews were good to me when I needed it. Look, I thought CJ was entertaining but I needed to get my act together. I wasn't serious and CJ moved on pretty quickly, so I guess neither was he."

"He just dropped you? After all that good time?" Pat asked.

Ashe shot a glare at Pat who acted as if he didn't notice.

"I was... I started to go out with...okay, Phillip Crews. Phillip was with Mark Portals' firm by then. He was nice, very mature, gentlemanly, but we knew it would never, ever go anywhere," she said to Pat. "CJ backed off me then."

"CJ. Talking about CJ, you said he moved on to...who? Georgia Murphy?" Ashe asked.

"No, she was trying to get her marriage back on track with Tony. I think he started hitting on Susan Marlin pretty hard. I know she kind of egged it on a little. She liked the attention but I think CJ was too intense for her, so she shut him down."

Ashe slapped his palms against his thighs several times like a drum.

"You lied to me about her filing for a divorce. Right over there in my kitchen, you lied about that," Ashe said.

"I had to!" Her eyes widened. "I mean, I didn't know for sure what you were doing asking me about it. And honestly, Mark had told me a thousand times we'd taken care of it and, Jesus, between the stuff and the booze, I didn't really remember. I am sorry."

"Did you know Mark filed the divorce as her attorney ten days after she disappeared? The same day you and he went and saw Sheriff Laughton about her disappearance."

"Oh…lord. No. Maybe. I don't know," she said.

"So, back up a bit," Pat pressed. "You said you and Crews would *never, ever* go anywhere? You mean out of town?"

"I'm sorry, Ashe," she said. Then to Pat, "No. I meant, I knew he was married. I think he realized that himself again and was very kind about our not seeing each other anymore."

Everyone sat still for a few minutes and listened to the rain beating down on the tin roof. Ashe found himself wishing he was back in the hospital. Or, as Sheriff Jacobs had suggested, that they'd turned the whole thing over to the state to work.

Of course, it was also Jacobs who'd insisted that I be included in the investigation. Next time, I'll ask that he shut up.

"Speaking of Georgia and Susan Marlin, what was Georgia's involvement in the land deals?" Ashe asked, wanting to get off Stevie's love life.

"Honestly, Susan Marlin can fill that in better than me. I know Georgia was learning the L&T business and apprenticing with Susan. She ran errands, put together closing paperwork, sort of processed the environmental inspections, but I don't really know details. Georgia and I, we, sort of just ran around together."

Ashe rested his eyes for a second. He'd heard way more than he'd wanted to, but not yet what he'd really expected to. So he began again.

"Tell me what you did when you found out Georgia was missing?" Ashe asked.

Stevie stood up and started pacing the room. It reminded him of the day they'd broken up at her office, when she couldn't be still.

"One of the worst days of my life. I loved that gal. She was always a little more in with those guys, the Concrete Crew, because of Tony, I guess. There was a wild side to her that, even as low as I got, I just couldn't follow. Susan told me one morning Georgia hadn't been to work in a couple days, so I called and called and went to look for her."

"Went to look for her?" Pat said, echoing her to get her to keep going.

"Yeah, but I found CJ and asked him about her and he was weird. 'How the fuck should I know?' was all he said. When I brought her up any time after that, he got mad and yelled at me over nothing. For months. I checked with the sheriff and even called a few former clients in Metro. Nothing. I heard how they accused Tony of killing her but couldn't prove it."

"Yeah. Us," Pat said.

"I didn't believe it. I knew Tony some by then, he's no angel, but no. It just didn't fit. Then out of nowhere one day, CJ just came over to my apartment. It'd been a few months since we'd been together. He wanted me to start going out to dinner and having drinks with him again. He brought over expensive liquor and nice bottles of wine. As bad off as I was then, I think I knew better. I talked to Phillip about it and he got CJ to stop."

"You know CJ was trying to keep you a drunk," Pat said flatly.

"Yes, I figured that one out myself. I also found out over the next several days, this was late last year, they'd been using me and my practice to run through certain client's legal papers, investment documents, legal opinions, all in my name to keep their name off of things. Mark just said to sign them; he was helping me I thought, so I signed everything he said to. Oh, nothing obviously illegal at first, just dishonest representation to their clients. I can show you some of it, but there was enough to make me quit."

"This is about the time I met you?" Ashe asked.

"Yeah, about. I started out with you like with...um, just fun. But, Ashe, you were different. You were such a good guy, and actually seem to care about *me*. I just wasn't in a place I could accept I deserved that."

"Okay, so tell us about these actions, or papers. You said they weren't illegal, *at first*?" Pat asked.

Stevie finally circled back to the large stone fireplace and flopped down in front of it.

"It's kind of chilly, don't you think? With the rain and all? We should start a fire."

"Stevie," Ashe said firmly.

"Well, your man outside, he should eat too, right?"

"Ah, c'mon. Danny Breslin's as tough as hard-boiled mule leather!" Pat said with a chuckle. "He's probably outside doing pushups in the rain!"

"Stevie," Ashe repeated.

"Okay!" she said.

"Tell us about the land deals Georgia and you worked on for Portals. DBA and that other one," Ashe asked. "What was illegal about this?"

She sat by the fireplace and stared into it for another full minute. Every now and then, she'd pull at her hair and tuck up it, then let it go to one side.

"So first, you need to understand that DBA is a large investment company with twenty or thirty big investors from all over the state, region even maybe. It's probably millions and millions of dollars. They're going after some big company to locate here in Hurrt County. It's huge and Marks Portals and a handful of local investor's part is to secure the land for construction. See, Mark wants them here and wants DBA to be their big fat landlord I guess."

"Who is *them*?" Pat asked.

"DBA?"

"No, who is the big company?"

"Oh. Yeah. You ever hear of Doorbella?"

Pat whistled as Ashe exhaled at the same time and they looked at each other.

"Damn," was all Pat had to say.

"*The* Doorbella, not a subsidiary or support company?" Ashe asked.

"Nope. *The* Doorbella. The third or fourth largest online retail company in the US. They are looking to build a major distribution center and we are on the short, short list. Mark and Phillip have been working this to the exception of all other work. Hurrt Land and Title has no other clients except them now. It means six to seven hundred jobs, maybe more, with at least three to four hundred jobs hired locally."

Ashe thought of Hurrt L&T's war room and his conversation with Susan Marlin. *That's a big damn deal.*

"So this is a good thing, hell, a great thing for Hurrt County," Ashe said.

"Think of all the peripheral impacts. Stores, housing, apartments, school expansions. It will change the nature of this town and this whole area. They're looking at building a loop from the interstate to pass by here, just north of town," she added.

"Incredible. It's amazing this has been kept so quiet," Ashe said.

"But you said there was something *illegal* going on, remember," Pat said.

"Yes. This is where I think Georgia and I sort of came in," she said.

Ashe said, "I saw the 'war room' as Susan called it."

"Right. See, first this was before when Mark Portals was *helping* my practice and CJ was keeping me in free booze and..."

"And?" Ashe asked sharply.

"And...I think they didn't want me clearheaded."

"Ah, goddamn it," Ashe said not quite under his breath.

Pat shot Ashe a *calm down and step away* look. He said, "Tell us what they didn't want you clearheaded about?"

"Okay, so some of the land was just old pasture. That was cheap enough to acquire if you knew how to do it. First, you just sort of trick the environmental reports for our banker, Mr. Crawford. Now DBA wasn't really financing their land deals but they ran everything through a couple of shell companies that did. Something about making money off the interest and paying themselves back, I dunno. But land they needed with homes on it was tougher," she explained.

"Tougher how?" Pat asked.

"Tougher in that there were more issues with the transfer of deeds. Most of the owners in that end of the county were older. Retired couples, former farmers and the like. So they figured out how to intentionally compromise the titles to older people's homes by something called a 'vampire' mortgage. That's where they muddy the water by filing a claim against a title, usually where there's no survey on file or a very old property line description. Then they use the title to request funds from a bank or even better, a shady lending company. They didn't even have to actually receive funds, just hand us the documents so we can scare the owners."

"Huh. That's pretty cold-blooded."

"Now the owners, they've heard of title theft on TV, so they panic. They run to the biggest, best real estate lawyer they can get. Mark Portals."

"He was doing this all himself?" Pat asked.

"Oh, *hell no*! He was the man behind the curtain for sure, but he had *me* do it!"

"Ah. The *illegal* part," Ashe said.

"Yeah, I'd be sent to meet with these people, now mind you, CJ Portals was always nearby and I was high as a kite. We'd tell them, as their lawyer, they had to pay the mortgages or…if they wanted to, they could sell, screw over the false mortgage crooks, and with the local bank and our help, even make a little profit doing it," Stevie explained.

"You know, I actually thought I was helping people out. Then I found out the local bank president, Crawford, was in on it. He was also a private local investor. I had no idea it was a master con and my name was all over those papers," she said.

"So in fact, there never were any false mortgages?" Pat asked.

"Oh no, Crawford saw to it that they were real. Applications and all the necessary documents in case an owner went outside our circle," she said. "Once the property sold to one of DBA's shells, the loans were satisfied internally and the titles were repaired."

"By Susan Marlin," Ashe said.

"No, I don't think they ever had her that close to the con. She probably smelled a rat but she was making what she thought was honest money, and a lot of it."

"So they used you and your law practice to make it seem like there was an appearance of business separation, and all in case it didn't work. Then Mark Portals would be in the clear. Jesus, lady," Pat said.

"All this and I found out some environmental statements were doctored, home inspections fixed, and more, I'm sure. I walked out the day I half sobered up and I went and saw ol' Judge Marsh."

"Harold actually helped you," Ashe said.

"Yes. He eventually helped me stay sober, gave me a job," she said. "But before that, right after, I mean *right after* I left Mark's firm, complaints about me started rolling in to the state Bar Association's Board of Professional Responsibility. I was suspended. Hell, I deserved it. Maybe more."

"I remember the day you got that letter," Ashe said.

"Then, suddenly as well, my damn ex gets custody of Nora!"

"I know, honey," Ashe said.

"All because his lawyer said in my client's formal complaints that I was high and a drunk and dammit, I was!" She stopped and started crying. Ashe went and got her a box of tissues.

"They were trying to either bring you back into the fold or see your reputation shot to shit so no one would believe you," Ashe said.

She shook herself and made herself sit up straight. "Harold Marsh is the one man around here that Mark Portals knows he can't lean on, or he'd be torpedoed. So I gave copies of whatever I had on these guys to him. To keep safe."

"So why doesn't Harold just stomp him? If he knows any part of this, he should get Portals disbarred!" Ashe barked.

"Me," she said.

"Huh?"

"I was the price Harold extracted. Our silence in exchange for me being left alone."

Wow, the old judge is craftier than I'd known. He'd sent me to look into Georgia Murphy's disappearance without breaking his confidence with Stevie or his shady agreement with Mark Portals.

Ashe had another thought. *Did Marsh use me? Yep, sonofabitch he did. But, in his own crafty way, he'd also sent Stevie to me that day.*

"And Georgia?" Pat asked. "Did she know about any of this?"

"She must have, especially the environmental stuff and any ground stable-somethings they had to have. I'm guessing, but yeah, especially if they got 'fixed' after she'd seen them. Plus, CJ Portals to Tony Murphy to Georgia Murphy. Especially once they got back together. See, as long as they were separated, CJ or Mark could manipulate one against the other."

"But together again? They both knew too much," Ashe said.

"I don't know what she knew, maybe Susan does, but I have to believe Georgia Murphy knew all about this. I really haven't had *anything* to do with *these men* in months."

"Could this be worth killing her?" Ashe asked.

"It was worth killing you! And Bill Clark," Pat said. "We should go get Rachel Hume in on this."

Stevie started shaking her head but Ashe nodded to Pat.

How do I get these people without using Stevie? Without her incriminating herself?

"Ashe?" Stevie said to him. "Remember when I said I was going to have to count on you. That I knew you loved me and I needed to count on that?"

Pat shot a look at Ashe, but Ashe ignored him. "Yes. The night I got shot."

"I want you to know I swear I didn't know they were going to come for you. I thought CJ just wanted to talk to you."

Ashe's throat tightened and he could feel his pulse pounding in his head.

"I was going to finally answer your questions and tell you the truth. Tell you about the big land development and what we had done to get the land. But CJ ran into me that afternoon in town. It was about to rain so we sat in my car and talked. He said he wanted to straighten things out with you. He just wanted to be sure you and he were on the same page. That *I* was protected."

"Honey, what did you do?"

"He asked me to tell him when we were going to see each other again," she said, flatly, still staring into the dark cold fireplace. "Then he would stop by and talk."

Pat's face flushed. It was his turn to be angry. "You just said you didn't have anything to do with Portals!"

"Well, I haven't!" she yelled back.

"What did you know about what they did to Bill Clark?" Pat asked.

Stevie looked at Pat as if he'd slapped her.

"God, no! I was here in town. I haven't had anything to do with them!"

"Until you did!" Pat said.

"Uh, actually, Stevie. I was on the phone with you. You were driving back to town that night," Ashe said.

She turned and looked at Ashe. "Oh my God! Ashe, no! I was driving home from seeing Nora, you can ask my ex! I was coming from Metro, the opposite way!"

"Oh, you can be sure we will ask him," Pat said.

"You didn't know they were going to try to kill me," Ashe said as fact. He was directing this to Pat as much as to Stevie.

"Oh lord, no. I didn't know that was what was going to happen."

"You would never intentionally…" Ashe said.

"God, no," was all she replied.

Pat exploded up out of his chair and walked toward the front door.

"I need a stretch and some fresh air!" he said quickly and went out onto the covered porch.

Ashe stood on uneasy feet but walked over to Stevie and put a hand on her shoulder.

"I swear, Ashe, this is the worst of it," she said.

"There is a special agent with the state police assigned to this case. She's in town talking with Susan Marlin now. I hope you've told me everything so I can try to…I can…"

"Yes. Thank you. I am so sorry. I did not set you up, Ashe, and dammit, I did not have anything to do with Deputy Clark's death either."

Ashe turned and started for the front door to follow Pat, but stopped and without looking back at her and said, "You still seeing CJ or Crews?"

"No. I swear it. I've been focusing on sobriety and getting my law license back and getting in shape. Clean. For Nora. It's about my girl Nora now."

"Well from what I've heard today, think about this. What if that night the Concrete Crew were coming to kill you as well?"

She turned and stared at Ashe. The thought obviously hadn't occurred to her.

"You know a lot they don't want out. It was luck that I was outside on the sidewalk on the phone with Pat. I surprised them. They had an ambush set up for when we left Roger's," he said.

"I…I," was all she said.

"They had to know we'd leave together, Stevie. Me and you."

Ashe turned and stepped out on the porch with Pat who'd been listening.

The porch was stone floored with thick wood pillars and a wide roof as it wrapped around the house. The underside of the porch roof was finished with burnt edge slats, and big outdoor fans hung every so often. They were covered with tarps for the winter.

The rain was pounding on the tin roof as Ashe walked up and stood beside Pat who was watching the rain and looking toward Breslin in his Dodge.

"Pat," he said.

"Jeez, Chig. I know in general they're all crazy, but this one!" He wiped his face with his big paw and just stared.

After another minute, he added, "You know they'll make out she set you up, and hey! I don't know I disagree. They'll arrest her for that then indict her for the land fraud and roll all these assholes into one big fat gang. RICO maybe. At least."

"No," Ashe said slowly.

"She was out of town when Clark died," Pat said. "She lied about that. Damn, in the past we'd hold her just for that lie! And what else?"

"No, she didn't lie and come on! You don't think she'd stand there and help them, so knock it off. I don't deny she maybe was had by that bastard CJ, but she'd never let me be killed."

Pat closed his eyes and took in a long breath. "Ah, for Christ's sake, Chig. Tell me you're not going to just wash over this! Clark is dead. You could be dead too now!"

"She'll talk to Rachel Hume tomorrow. She'll tell everything. She was impaired and under duress. She will work an immunity deal to testify against Portals—both of them. If they bring up the night I was attacked, then...she'll have to deny that part."

"Why the fuck should I go along with that? That's collusion! I just heard what she said," Pat roared.

Ashe let his friend's anger be tempered by the cool rain all around them. It was cold and he shoved his hands under his sweatshirt.

"Because I ask you to," Ashe said, almost a whisper. "Because no matter what, and knowing she isn't ever likely to wind up with me, I still..."

"Don't fucking say it! Damn you, Chig!"

"I need the recording," Ashe said, again in a low, quiet voice.

"You used to be one stainless steel cock. Hardest guy I knew. Now look at you!"

"I know you recorded us."

After what seemed like several minutes of silence, Pat reached inside his jacket pocket and took out a small digital recorder. After another beat, he handed it to Ashe.

Ashe took it and said, "I am being hard. I am going to nail these bastards. But not her. Not Stevie. If Hume figures something out, well, then I won't interfere. But I can't..."

They stood there, side by side on the porch, listening and watching the rain as it began slowly to subside. It slackened from a gully-washer to a steady, even pulse.

"You don't really think she set me up, or had a hand in Clark's death, do you?" Ashe asked seriously.

"I don't get paid to read minds. I'd lock her up if it were me," Pat said. Then as a friend, "And, buddy, this might be both our asses."

"I can't think of any other way to get at those who had Georgia and Clark killed, *and* protect her," Ashe said.

After another long thoughtful pause, Pat kicked a small rock off the porch.

"Okay. Your way for now," Pat said and walked off through the rain toward his SUV. "I'm taking Danny to get some food. I'll…I'll call you later," he shouted as he left.

"Pat. If you see Rachel Hume, do not say Stevie was here today?"

Pat thought about that a second, then said, "Fine, whatever."

Ashe knew he was asking a lot and was pushing their friendship awfully close to the breaking point. Maybe past that.

Ashe watched as Pat got in and Breslin drove them off. He wondered what he'd tell Danny Breslin. Pat had seemed to have gotten closer to his new partner, and he hadn't asked Pat for Breslin's cooperation.

Ashe walked back in and saw Stevie was stuffing kindling and newspaper into the fireplace. She didn't turn or look at him as he came in.

"Stevie, stop that. I need to talk about one more thing," he said.

"Can't it wait? I'm just…*done*. I'm beyond exhausted and I just napped half the morning."

He walked over to where she was sitting on the floor in front of the fireplace and sat in front of her.

"I'm all beat up too. But I'm about to commit a crime here. So please listen to me carefully. I want to talk about what you have to say to Agent Hume. I think I bought us until tomorrow, at least I hope Pat will buy that for us."

"What *I* have to say?"

"For me to try and keep you out of jail."

CHAPTER 19

The entire left side of Ashe's head was pounding and felt swollen as he'd rested on the sofa. When he opened his eyes, it seemed to him like it was later that afternoon. Stevie had apparently finished making the fire and was sitting on one of the sofa's extensions with her feet and legs curled under her. She stared at the fire and held an empty heavy-bottomed bourbon glass.

"Hey," Ashe said groggily and pointed at the glass.

"Shut up," was all she said.

He obeyed and closed his eyes again.

The next time he came to, his head still hurt but not as bad as before. It was early to mid-evening he guessed, as he couldn't focus his eyes on the mantle clock. The fire was hissing and popping and only a few flickers of flame were left.

Stevie lay on top of him asleep, her head on his chest and her arms around his neck and shoulders, their legs intertwined. The fire had warmed and dried out the room. She had peeled out of her leggings and taken off her sweater to sleep, and he hadn't woken up whenever she'd crawled over to him.

He was still a little tired, maybe thirsty some too from the dry heat of the fire, but she felt so warm and it was too good a feeling to disturb. He drew in a long slow breath and tried to absorb her body into his, her weight, the smell of her hair, and the softness of her skin against his.

This may be the last time I get to hold her, he thought, then drifted off again.

When he woke next, it was late. The lights in the living room that were controlled by timers were off, so it was after eleven p.m. Stevie had rolled over between him and the back of the sofa, meaning, he was unceremoniously about to be dumped off it. He slowly got to his feet trying not to disturb her.

She barely mumbled something without waking as he did.

He padded into his bedroom, used the toilet, then checked his phone that was still plugged in. Twelve fifteen a.m. There was a message from Jacobs to meet at Roger's Café at eight the next morning. There was nothing from Rachel or Pat, so he hoped that was good news.

Either Rachel found out Stevie was here and doesn't care, or she doesn't know because Pat didn't tell her.

No, he decided. *If Rachel had known Stevie was here—and had been here all day—Rachel would have been out to see her.*

Ashe pulled up the throw blanket that was tangled around Stevie and re-covered her gently. On an index card, he wrote, *Don't take off, I need a ride to town.* He got her a glass of cool water from the kitchen and placed it on the coffee table with the note where she could see it, poked the fire a bit, then reached down and stroked her hair and her cheek.

Then he went to *his* bed for the first time in a week and set an alarm for six a.m.

He woke five minutes before the alarm went off and got up. Stretching, he went to the bath and got some ibuprofen for his head then walked to the living room where Stevie was still sleeping on the couch.

"Hey," he said and tickled her bare foot. "Get up, I need you to drive me to town."

She drew back her foot and twisted around on the couch, looking about with one eye open as if not remembering where she was, then suddenly jerked her whole body in an explosive spasm and half sat up.

She didn't say anything but looked at Ashe with one eye and a menacing face as she stretched and ran her fingers through her tangled hair.

She never has woken up as pretty as she slept.

"Hey, lady. One hour. We have to turn and burn," he said.

She saw the water and drank it, looked at his note but obviously couldn't read it yet, then started to lie back down.

"Nope, no time for snoozes."

"I jus' haf nof is stin," she mumbled.

"Yeah, okay, *that*," he said with a grin. "One hour to take off, I'm showering again."

When he had shaved and was half done with his shower, she appeared in the bathroom. She seemed to want something but couldn't find it then said out loud to no one, "Screw it."

She peeled off her underwear and got in the shower with him.

For a half second, he couldn't catch a breath. She was so beautiful, even more than before when they'd dated.

"Please, make yourself at home," he said, chuckling, and handed her his soap.

She reached past him, her breast rubbing against his chest as she did so, and grabbed the back brush. "I'll do your back and you'll do mine?" she said and they both started laughing.

"Well, we haven't had a good, deep shower conversation in a while," he said.

"I see you still like it," she said and rubbed her belly on his. "Conversation, eh?"

She lightly kissed his neck, he felt himself rise against her, and she pressed into him. She touched him there and grabbed playfully at his buttocks. He rubbed her back and let one hand caress her inner thigh.

Ashe smiled. It felt so wonderful. *Like no other woman.*

He was about to kiss her, then he remembered.

He saw CJ's face and thought of him touching her, holding her just this way. Of CJ Portals giving her cocaine and ecstasy. His mind saw flashes of her *wanting it. Craving* it. Wanting *him.* Then her *wanting* Phillip Crews and not giving a damn if he was married or not.

She had wanted them both.

He pulled back from her a little more quickly than he'd meant to and bopped his head against the tile wall.

"Oh shit, Ashe! You okay?" she asked, still half giggling. "Is that the sore side?"

"I'm fine," he said and then got out of the shower.

She told CJ Portals where and when I'd be at the café that night.

They were dressed and about to leave for town, her in her same clothes, and Ashe wore a black shirt with a dark charcoal sport coat and dark jeans. He'd put on black and gray trail jogging shoes.

Outside, a state trooper was stationed in a marked car, but it was farther down the drive, so Ashe figured they could make it to the garage without being seen. The rain was gone and the sun was clear and bright. It was still wet everywhere from the rain and the air had a cool snap to it. Autumn was going fast.

"You have Harold Marsh's private number in your phone?" Ashe asked, all business.

"Yeah," she said and started looking it up.

"Call him and have him meet us at his office in twenty minutes."

"I'm not going to breakfast with you? Or to Price's office?"

"No, we're going to your apartment. You're packing a bag and going to Marsh's until I can talk with Rachel Hume. Tell Harold everything, including what I told you to say. He's to be your attorney for when Hume wants to interview you," Ashe said. "Now come on."

They walked out carefully and got to the garage and into her car. Ashe got in the driver's side and had Stevie duck low and out of sight. He drove out and up the driveway, pulling up slowly alongside the trooper, who rolled his window down.

Ashe flashed his retired Metro Police shield out his window to the trooper. "Lieutenant Pat Keagan, Metro PD. The guy's still inside asleep—he's all yours now!"

Ashe snapped his badge case shut and pulled off without waiting for an answer. The trooper seemed surprised that anyone would be leaving, and Ashe had to wonder what he'd been told. Likely to just stop people from coming in. It would've been embarrassing, Ashe knew, if the trooper had a photo of him, of the man he was supposed to be protecting.

So Ashe just figured the guy would either accept this or not, and if not, come pull him over. He didn't.

In town, Ashe pulled up to his old Jeep behind the Hurrt L&T and prayed it would start. Stevie walked over toward Harold's office as Ashe walked to the Jeep. He sat inside and cranked it. Nothing. He tried again and it whirred and thunked but almost caught. Once more, he tried and it fired to life.

He took out his phone and looked at his watch. Seven thirty, too early for her to be in the office, so he tried her cell. After a couple of rings, Lois answered.

"Hey, baby," he said in a gravelly voice. But it didn't fool her this time.

"Don't you 'hey baby' me! Damn, I thought I lost you, Ashe!"

"I am fine, can you drive to work and talk?"

"I'm parking outside now. I see Pat's here early," she said.

He thought for a minute. He wasn't sure if Pat had seen Rachel or even if Pat was still going to cooperate with his plan for Stevie. *Hell, he might still be really pissed off.*

"I need a teeny-tiny favor?"

"Un-uh. I think Captain Speakes is on to me. I'm on my best, non-favorish behavior for a while," she said.

"Okay, I'll buy you dinner."

"Nuh-uh."

"You can bring your husband," he said.

"No."

"Okay, leave him at home."

"Call me later, I'll explain," she said and hung up.

Ashe drove over to Roger's Café and parked across the street. The last time he'd been here two men had died and he had come damn close himself.

He drew in a shaky breath and got out to walk in. Standing beside his Jeep Cherokee, he remembered he didn't have a gun. His Smith J frame revolver would be state's evidence, so he was of course, unarmed. That thought he didn't like at all and it made walking into Roger's a degree or two tougher.

On the glass windows facing outside were the posters he'd seen on the news, all supporting Hurrt County and Seacord. Several were asking for donations for Bill Clark's family. Others were simply pro-law enforcement and were decorated with little blue-line American flags.

He was glad he hadn't been in Seacord during all the hullabaloo following the shooting. The press, the fundraising, and protests against crime would have been more than he could have taken.

One poster had a large picture of Deputy Bill Clark, and it struck Ashe hard that this was the first time he had ever seen Clark's image. He was young. Younger than Ashe had assumed. Even through the pixelated poster photo, his picture showed an exuberant-looking and proud family man. Another poster that was asking for donations showed Bill Clark's widow and children. Ashe stared at it a few seconds then on unsteady feet went to the door.

As Ashe stepped inside, it hit him that this is where it had all started. The first day the café was back open after Covid when he'd walked in hesitantly and wearing a mask. The café had only a few customers back then and they were scattered about the place socially distancing. A lot had happened in the past few weeks; Roger's Café was packed.

The smells of thick grease, bacon, and coffee were still there but multiplied by the throng of breakfast eaters with their phones and newspapers. The normal conversational tone of the early risers in the place was amplified and back to where it had been pre-Covid, but as the first person in the place saw him, it stopped dead.

In waves from the front of the café to the back, as people saw him, they stopped talking. Others turned in their seats and stared.

It halted him by the front door for a second, then several people shouted, "Hey!" or "Ashe!" and a few even clapped. It got Tilly's attention and she half jogged over to him.

"Please, Till, don't make a scene," he said to her as she approached him.

She grabbed him in a big hug and a lot of the customers cheered.

"Too late, Chig," she said and then looked him in the face, smiling. "You look better than the last time I saw you."

"I'm fine," he said and pried her off. "I may need to go back to the hospital after I eat here…"

"Behave yourself and go sit with the sheriff. He's in the back, in my section."

People stood as he passed and gently slapped him on the back or tried to shake his hand as he made his way through the café. Jacobs was in a back booth talking with a couple of other men but shooed them off when Ashe got close.

"Morning, boss," Ashe said as he slid into the booth.

"Morning, Ashe. You just missed John Price, he's on his way to the ADA's office now. He says last night him and Phillip Crews and Rachel Hume talked," Jacobs said.

"Huh," Ashe said and looked around for coffee.

"Did you know Rachel Hume and Crews went to college

together?"

Ashe turned around. "I did not," he said. "Does that help?"

"I guess her and Price have him convinced to make Paul Milton cop a plea."

"Well, good. I assume that deal will include a statement to us on Clark."

"And one on you, too. I damn well will insist it does," Jacobs said.

The throng of conversation in the café had returned but perhaps a bit louder. He could hear pieces of conversation here and there, bits of sentences. People claiming they'd known him or known the family well. Been to high school with him. That they knew him as *Chig*.

"Everybody is happy to see you, even if they don't know you," Jacobs said.

"I don't think everybody should be."

"Huh?"

"Billy Clark's family, I just now saw his picture and the picture of his family. I'd never seen them before," Ashe said and pointed at the front glass.

"I think they'd be fine knowing you...got the ones that did it."

"Really? Will they when they find out someday that I goaded Tracy Davis by mentioning that Clark's photos were still on his camera? And why? Because she pissed me off?"

"Ashe, come on, you can't think..."

"I can and I do. Tracy got a call or made a call and walked back in asking if I was a P.I. and where did she get that? Goddamn CJ Portals. So of course she told him about Clark and bam! The same ones that came for me came for him."

"I think that no matter what, they'd have circled back to him and that camera. You should not be blaming only yourself. Hell, I asked you to go after this, and Tracy. It's my fault as well, by your logic," Jacobs said.

"I just think if I had gone slower, waited to spring that piece of information on her, and then of course to CJ Portals, then maybe we would not have lost him."

"You don't know that, Ashe."

"Well, you're about to hear today from Stevie Collins the damn direct connection between CJ and the men who killed Clark."

"Oh, yeah? Good, Agent Hume wants to talk to her."

"And she will, this morning."

Jacobs went back to his coffee while Ashe waited for Tilly. For a few minutes, Ashe watched Jacobs who had started looking around and waving silently at a few people he must know. At first, Ashe turned to see who it was, but he didn't directly recognize but a very few.

He was more reserved than Ashe had expected, muted, almost embarrassed by the bright focus of everyone in the place. But Ashe could see that just a little, just at the edges of Jacobs' eyes, he clearly knew he was getting his share of the good political will in the room.

Ashe didn't begrudge him anything; he had to get reelected someday. But sitting there, all the way in the back, with no gun on him, Ashe began to feel as if the crowd was somehow moving closer. He took a couple of deep breaths and tried to let them out slowly like before, but it didn't help this time. The comforting aromas and sounds he'd known and loved just moments before were becoming stifling and deafening.

Too many damn people.

He felt himself tightening up in his chest and his throat. He wanted to just get up and walk out. He kept deep breathing and tried to hide it; it was embarrassing and he didn't want anyone to know he still shook when he thought about that night. Or sat in here.

Then abruptly Jacobs reached over and took Ashe's arm.

"I was in Desert Storm," he said. "First Brigade, Third Battalion, 504th Infantry."

Ashe looked at Jacobs as he held his arm a minute more.

"Oh, yeah? Airborne, huh. I guess I knew you were Army," Ashe said.

"You?"

"Yeah," Ashe replied. "Grenada and there in Qatar and Kuwait too. I was with the first of the third, 187th."

Jacobs smiled and patted his arm. "I saw something just now I've seen before. Guys I served with and had seen some...stuff. I was a first sergeant and saw some action myself. It takes a toll."

"Yeah. It took Pat's son as well."

"I didn't know that. He seems like a hell of a guy," Jacobs said.

"He is. We're family."

"Listen, you're okay, Ashe. I hear what you're saying about Clark's family, but nothing you or I could've done would have changed what MacNeal, Everitt, and Milton did. You did what you had to do then to be here today because that's what was supposed to happen. Believe it."

Ashe nodded and reached over and grabbed Jacobs' arm in the same manner.

You must have been one hell of a soldier.

"Today, right here in Roger's, it's a big first step, eh?" Jacobs asked.

Ashe let out a shaky breath. "Yes. Thank you."

"Look, if you need more time to…"

"No," Ashe interrupted. "No more waiting. I want coffee now," he said and smiled.

"Airborne," Jacobs said quietly and grinned. "Hundred and worst! Good grief! You know…I think Roger ought to be paying *you*. This place has been packed."

Tilly walked up and looked at them. "What are you two jackals smiling about? You want this coffee, or should I leave and…"

"God, no!" Ashe said. "Please," and held up his cup.

After breakfast and standing outside, Ashe looked at his watch. They still had time before meeting with ADA Price, so Ashe had Jacobs call Rachel and send her over to Harold's office to interview Stevie. It would help a good deal to know what Stevie knew when Rachel went in to interrogate Paul Milton.

Jacobs put his cell on speaker.

"So she is there at former Judge Harold Marsh's office now?" Rachel asked.

"Yeah," Jacobs said and motioned Ashe with his cell to speak.

"Agent Hume, this is Ashe," he said.

"Yes, Lieutenant."

"No, just Ashe. Listen, she is scared so please go easy. I found her and she wants to cooperate. She told me a good deal about the motives for these crimes that Mr. Price wondered about at my house."

"Okay, Good. I'll be there in five."

"Agent…Rachel, if we can get one thing nailed down by Milton, other than the facts of the murder, it'd be the fate of

Clark's camera and if it contained the original crime scene photos."

"Got it," she said and hung up.

"They likely won't let us be in on that interview," Jacobs said. "It will be up to her and maybe Pat Keagan to grill Milton."

Ashe stood for a minute thinking. Then he turned around and around looking at the side of the square outside Roger's Café. He didn't see anyone suspicious.

"Sheriff, take me to your office. I need you to do me a favor."

CHAPTER 20

The courthouse that sat in the middle of the Seacord town square was built in the 1970's after the original burned down. Although more modern a building than many in the area, especially for such a small county, Ashe could see it was in bad need of updating.

Sitting in Assistant DA Price's cramped outer office with the sheriff, Danny Breslin, and Price's part-time clerk, drove home his observation. There were extension cords everywhere running under the carpet and on flat rubber tread strips. The walls were painted cinder block and the windows showed signs they leaked. Wearing Covid masks that the courthouse still required made it feel stuffy as well.

"You know there are only two power outlets in this whole room?" the clerk complained through his mask. Ashe had once known his name but couldn't recall it.

"Back when this was planned, all you plugged in was an electric typewriter," Ashe said.

"Well, I have a computer and two monitors, a printer, the main phone, my cell charger, a lamp, a mini fridge, and a coffeepot," he said and then pulled his headset back on to continue transcribing something from a voice recorder into digits.

"Well come work at my jail and you'll think this is heaven," Jacobs said. His mask was hanging off one ear.

"Price and Hume are with the judge? This circuit?" Breslin asked, looking at his watch. They were fifteen minutes past when they were to interview Paul Milton.

"No, not *the* judge, *a* judge, as in retired. Harold Marsh. He's representing Stephanie Collins," Ashe said.

Breslin just nodded and made a note of the name. He was wearing a white dress shirt and dark-green tie under a gray wool sport coat with brown and green threads in it. He had dark brown slacks on and brown dress shoes with well-worn soles. If Ashe didn't know him, he could have picked him out for a cop by his outfit alone.

And Breslin just looked *cop*. The way he sat, his demeanor, and most of all his eyes. He watched before talking. He rarely gave an opinion or answered a question without considering it for a minute first. His default expression resembled a blend of bemused indifference and mild disgust.

Ashe put aside any doubts he'd had on Breslin. He and Danny Breslin weren't friends, but Ashe decided he could trust him. If by nothing else, he figured his own instincts told him so, but also because it was obvious Pat trusted him.

After another fifteen minutes, Ashe could hear ADA Price and Agent Hume through a glass-windowed door walking into Price's inner office, still talking to each other.

"I think given her willingness to cooperate, I can get on board with Mr. Marsh's request," Price said. He pulled off his cloth mask as he entered.

"Not for nothing! Come on, John, what do you think an appropriate penalty would be for her?" said Rachel.

The clerk tossed off his headset and ran to tap on the adjoining door. "Sir, the rest of the group is in here," he said, signaling to Price and Hume they could be heard.

"Have them join us in the juvenile courtroom. Is Phillip Crews here?" Price said through the door.

"He said he will be over whenever you are ready."

"Send for him. Take them to the conference room when they arrive. And, Jerry? I don't want these two groups to see each other."

"Yes, sir," said Jerry the clerk.

Ah, Jerry, Ashe remembered.

As they moved to the empty Juvey Courtroom, Ashe saw that Price was dressed in a pale-gray suit with subdued burgundy pinstripes, cordovan oxfords, a pink dress shirt, and a gray and burgundy tie. Ashe bet himself it was Italian.

Rachel wore a sensible navy suit with a mid-length skirt that fit her well. She had a bright white blouse and a yellow-and-blue striped scarf and, on her jacket, she wore a tiny gold lapel pin shaped like a bird. Ashe thought she looked like the opposite of Breslin, meaning, she could have been any other sort of professional person. She had a surgical-type mask sticking out of her suit pocket, and Ashe wondered where, if at all, she wore her issued 9mm pistol.

As they entered the courtroom, Rachel looked back then said to Breslin, "Is Pat Keagan here, or is he coming?"

"No, ma'am. I'm here for Metro," he said, then cut his eyes at Ashe.

Rachel nodded, but Ashe noticed a slight microscopic note of disappointment.

Well, now. Mister Patrick.

They gathered around a table in the empty room and Sheriff Jacobs posted himself at the door so he could see whenever Crews and Milton arrived. Price took off his suit jacket and hung it over the back of his chair. They all pulled off their masks.

"Thank you, Lieutenant, ah, *Deputy* Ashe for finding Ms. Collins. She has given us a rather damning preliminary statement against both of the Portals'. Of course, we'll have to have her give a full deposition and testify as to these fraudulent land deals," Price started.

"Not to mention, I'll have to contact the investors both locally and nationally. For that, I'm going to bring in the state attorney general's Fraud Unit. This is a RICO case from hell," Hume said.

"Speaking of that, how did it go with Susan Marlin?" Breslin asked.

"Well, she is a little ticked off that she is likely out of business. The Portals, Crews, and Fischer firm and the DBA project was her bread and butter for these past couple of years. But she gave us a full tour of that 'war room' you mentioned, Ashe. Then she stopped and called her lawyer," said Rachel.

"Let me guess, Mark Portals," Breslin remarked.

"No, a Mr. Fischer. He's one of Marks Portals' partners who works in the city. We'll circle around to her later today. John, I want you to subpoena her files so nothing is destroyed while I interview Mark Portals this afternoon," Rachel said. "With Ms. Marlins records, we can authenticate Ms. Collins' documents and avoid having only her to depend on."

"Which brings us back to this morning," Price said.

Ashe said, "I know you wanted to focus on the murder of Billy Clark and the attack on me today, but I thought what Stevie Collins had to say, given what little she said to me until she invoked her right to an attorney, went straight to the motive behind all this."

"She didn't say how you came to talk to her, Ashe," Rachel said. Ashe didn't answer her.

Don't lie except if you absolutely have to.

"This morning, just now, we were discussing Harold Marsh's request of immunity for Ms. Collins in exchange for the documents she had preserved and her testimony," Price said. "I will want to see what she has before extending any deal, but I think we are on much stronger ground with what we know from her and Ms. Marlin when we go in with Phillip Crews here in a bit."

"I don't like it," Rachel said, "I don't like letting her off so easy. She should do some time for defrauding those property owners."

Ashe started to say something but Price cut him off.

"I know you have had a personal relationship with Ms. Collins, so I think you might consider letting us work this from here on out, Mister Ashe."

"Hey," Sheriff Jacobs cut in. "It was because of his *past relationship* that he was able to convince her to come forward and cooperate!"

Ashe waved his hand and said, "I was going to say, Mr. Price, I have not had a relationship with Ms. Collins in months, but it's a small town. I can't help tripping over her just inconsequentially here and there," he said, more to Rachel than Price.

Not a lie, he thought. "I don't know what she told you, but I agree. I don't want to participate in any interviews of her from this point forward."

"She only told us that you and she were over a long time ago and that when you did confront her in the course of your investigation, she lied to you," Price said.

"Plus, you are one of our vics," Rachel added. "I'd feel better if you provided us whatever insights you have as we proceed, but…" She looked at the sheriff. "I think if actively continuing to investigate you could compromise the case. Sorry."

"I agree," Ashe said. "I'd like to stay on as a team member and provide insight."

"I'll have to think about that. I'll speak with the DA and get his read. I think it could be seen as populating your future testimony with new and inside knowledge," Price said and jotted down a note for himself.

Then he added, "Sheriff, Ms. Collins will surrender herself to be arrested and processed this afternoon after making some arrangements and gathering the records she promised."

That is to be expected. But being arrested will hit her hard.

"Ok with you if I just listen in to your interview with Paul Milton?"

Price sat back and looked at the ceiling and chewed on his pen a minute. Ashe waited for Rachel to object but she didn't.

"I understand, Depu...Mister...uh, Ashe, I really do, but I can't have you in the room."

"I see."

"Uh, and you, Sheriff. I think you normally could sit in as the sheriff, but I think Agent Hume and I will get better cooperation from Mr. Crews if we handle this one," Price said. "You two can watch from my office on a monitor."

That surprised Ashe. He had figured he was being asked to leave altogether.

"Phillip Crews is here with Paul Milton," Jacobs said, looking through the little window in the courtroom door.

"Okay, let's go," Price said and they all stood up.

Before Price collected his jacket, Ashe saw the label. Canali. *Damn.*

They walked toward the conference room once Crews and Milton were inside and behind closed doors, but before Ashe turned away to go to Price's office, Breslin caught his arm.

"I'll let you know what I can," he said.

Then without being invited or told otherwise, Breslin walked into the conference room behind Rachel. Ashe and Jacobs went back to Price's office, and Jerry took them to the inner office and set up the monitor and speaker for them. Once they were working, Ashe could see it was a ceiling-mounted camera that was perhaps concealed. He reached over and turned up the speaker.

There was Paul Milton. To Ashe, with over twenty-five years of policing experience, he looked *exactly* like the sort of turd that would sneak up and hit you with a tire iron.

He was about five-nine and had wild unkempt black hair and well-grown beard stubble from his time in jail so far. He had a pot gut from too much beer but strong-looking arms and thick wrists from working concrete. He wore the issued bright-orange jail scrubs and socks with flip-flops. His ankles were shackled and his hands cuffed in front.

Jacobs must have noticed Ashe looking at him. "You recognize him?" he asked.

"Hmm, no. Maybe if you had him creep up behind me and bean me with a steel bar, I might," Ashe said.

"Well, because I know that *you* would want to know, I have a deputy in the parking lot outside and a couple of men I know and trust around the square with their phones, watching. I got the jailor who brought him here standing by right outside that door, and my SWAT team close by if we call," Jacobs said.

"SWAT team?" Ashe asked.

"Yeah, Ed Bell. He's our SWAT team."

That made Ashe laugh out loud.

"But seriously, I don't think all shackled up like that he'd be able to go very far. Or fast," Ashe said.

Jacobs said, "I wasn't thinking he could escape. I was thinking of who might not want him to talk."

That makes good sense, Ashe thought, then he turned back to the monitor.

There were the usual introductions and preliminary discussions. Crews had known Rachel would be there with Price but seemed surprised that Breslin, a detective from Metro PD's MCU, was involved. He didn't look like it bothered him too much though.

Phillip Crews appeared taller than Ashe by quite a bit, and had a very successful look to him and wore a black suit with banker stripes. Ashe couldn't tell too much else through the monitor except that Crews had gray sideburns and some well-styled graying up front.

Ashe couldn't help noticing, but Crews also looked to be quite a bit older than Stevie, and he certainly was vastly more experienced as an attorney. His entire look and demeanor, even filtered through the camera and monitor, still came across as mature, confident, *experienced*. And yet, as far as Ashe knew he was a cohort in Mark Portals' fraudulent conspiracies.

Crews had preyed on Stevie when she was weak, Ashe thought, under the guise of helping her with CJ. She had all but insinuated they'd slept together, and yet, she defended him still. To Ashe, this was the horrible part; the depth, breadth, and width of Crews' polished and well-orchestrated malevolency.

He manipulated her. He made her feel so guilty inside that she actually thought he'd been kind to her.

Ashe had never met Phillip Crews in person. But now that he saw him with his tall, tan, crisp, competent persona, knowing he had been with Stevie despite his being married and knowing she was an alcoholic, *and* knowing full well that his firm had taken terrible advantage of her in the worst possible way...

Ashe decided he absolutely hated the son of a bitch.

Somehow, someday, I am going to knock you on your ass.

Ashe felt himself shaking a little but took a breath and forced himself to calm down. To be clinical, less emotional, and still. At least for now.

In the conference room, the overtures were done and Crews spoke to Price.

"I'd like to know if we agree to cooperate, what we can expect from the state?"

"*Expect?* Well, Phillip, let's review. I have a dozen eyewitnesses and some video from the bank across the street that shows your client taking a tire iron and beating Deputy Ashe in the head. I have both impact and transferred touch DNA that shows Paul Milton was present when Deputy Sheriff Bill Clark was tortured and murdered."

Pat's DNA came in that quick? Ashe thought. *Must help to have the state deputy AG interested.*

Rachel passed some still photos over to Crews, who looking at them, made some notes.

Milton started to say something to Crews but he waved Milton off.

"And," Price continued, "I have a witness who will testify that Mr. Milton here was part of a group of co-workers who often engaged in extracurricular criminal behavior. They were a criminal group prior to the murder of Clark and the attempted murder of Ashe. That's not an ad hoc gang; that's a team of men scheming a pair of murders to hide crimes. That's a conspiracy."

Ah, Ashe thought. *Enter Stevie.*

"I think we have information to counter some of what you allege," Crews said. "Plus, we'll have to request a change of venue. My client could not possibly get a fair hearing anywhere near here."

"Request away. Maybe you can, maybe you can't get that. The state assistant AG is involved now. But, anyway, I seriously doubt you have a counter to *everything* I'm alleging," Price said. "Let me say this, right now, pending anything you might offer to change my mind, I see this as a winnable death sentence case."

"Oh, come on, John, surely you do not believe…"

Price cut in sharply, "I believe this is a very pro-law-enforcement county, hell, *region.* I believe I have scientific evidence to support the indictments of murder, conspiracy to commit murder, torture, and kidnapping. Oh, and another attempted murder, a second conspiracy, an especially aggravated assault with a deadly weapon…and I'm sure, given time, we can think up more."

Crews sat back a little then whispered to his client. Milton nodded.

"Oh, and I have the weapon, the tire iron used. It has Mr. Ashe's blood and tissue on it and Milton's fingerprints. It came from a 2009 to 2018 Chevrolet truck. Your client owns a 2010 Chevy found very near the scene in Seacord that is registered to him. It's missing its tire iron!"

Rachel passed another photo, that Ashe assumed was of the tire iron he'd worn like a hat that night.

Ashe looked at Jacobs who smiled and winked. *He'd said the state did a great job at the scene. But if they have video, does it show CJ Portals as his fourth man?*

"So, Phillip, before your client can *expect* so much as a cigarette before his electrocution, what does Mr. Milton have to offer the state?"

Right then and there, Ashe decided as much as he hated Phillip Crews, he was beginning to like ADA John Price. Snooty Italian suit and all.

Ashe turned to Jacobs as Crews and Milton on the monitor went to a corner to talk.

"Sheriff, did you know Crews from before? When he was

ADA?"

"A little, but I can tell you this, he's slicker than snot on a doorknob," Jacobs said.

Ashe grinned at that. "I take it you work well with ADA Price?"

"Yeah, some. Of course, we didn't have a lot of cases before *you* showed up. He rotates here from Carson County three days a week."

Ashe nodded then saw on the monitor that Crews and Milton were back at the table.

Crews began again. "My client will plead guilty to the Hurrt County case. He maintains that despite being present, he did not assault nor in any way cause the death of Bill Clark. He will give a detailed statement and testify as to what he knows and observed in the murder of Deputy Clark. In return, we'd like the death penalty taken off the table and your recommendation for minimal sentencing."

"Is that *all*?" Price asked mockingly.

"We'd like to have dropped the Conspiracy to Commit Murder and the Attempted Murder charges on Ashe. We will plead to the Especially Aggravated Assault charge. Because, seriously at the end of the day, John, that's what actually happened."

"I see," Price said and turned and spoke quietly to Hume.

"That's a ton of bull!" Jacobs exploded back in the office.

Ashe signaled him to wait. He knew these were simply the opening salvos.

Back over the monitor, Price said to Crews, "I need to know exactly what Mr. Milton here can tell us about Clark's death? Heck, we know the firearm that Everitt fired and killed him with is also the gun that was used on Deputy Ashe. We know that Ashe then shot two of those responsible for Clark's death. So what can Mr. Milton possibly testify to? That the other guys did it? That's useless. Sorry."

"My client can give you the details as to the kidnapping, the torture, and the murder."

"I'll expect that anyway. But let me guess, Phillip, he'll describe in detail how he was a helpless bystander, a victim almost, scared to go against his buddies lest they kill him too."

"Not so dramatic but essentially..."

"So no dice. I don't need any help punishing MacNeal and

Everitt. They're before a higher court about now," Price said.

Crews just nodded, and he and Milton returned to their corner to whisper.

Ashe took out his cell and texted Rachel. *Camera.* Then, *Georgia Murphy.*

On the monitor, he saw her check her phone. She made no facial indication of what she'd read but handed a note to Price who nodded then tucked it away.

Crews and Milton returned to the table.

"Is there anything you want to know that might bring you around to our offer?" Crews asked.

"Nuh-uh," Price answered. "That would be seeding your client's statement and thus also planting a time bomb for an appeal. No, I want to know what he knows, then I will consider discussing your offer. But I will not accept anything less than Accessory to First-Degree Murder and Aggravated Kidnapping on Bill Clark, and Attempted First-Degree Murder on Ashe. I'll take death off the table. Those charges are nonnegotiable. Oh, and this all expires in ten minutes."

"Ten..." Crews started.

"Minutes. Then your client goes back to jail and I convene a grand jury in two weeks," Price said flatly. "Clock is ticking."

This time, Crews and Milton didn't huddle. Crews knew what he had to offer.

"We can give you information about the death of Clark that will greatly assist you in another case. A capital case you will be highly interested in, involving currently unindicted co-conspirators who are not dead. We can also give you information as to the men, including my client, who together perpetrated other, lesser crimes in Metro, but...how they were *directed* to do so. Including the kidnapping and killing of Clark."

"And the assault and attempted murder of Mr. Ashe?"

Crews paused for a long breath. "Yes. How he and the others were...*directed* to make the assault on Mr. Ashe."

Price nodded. Then he looked at Rachel but said to Crews, "Does your client have any direct knowledge of the disappearance and probable death of Georgia Murphy?"

Phillip Crews looked at his own notes, stalling for a minute as Ashe held his breath.

"He did not directly participate in any way with her…going missing, but may have information that would close that case," Crews said. "In exchange for Life on both cases, to run concurrently."

Ashe felt a terrific swell of emotion rise up in him. It was like a great hot expanding mass rolled up and filled him from his chest to his throat. His head was tingling; his hands felt numb.

For the first time, someone said they knew what happened.

He knows, he knows what happened to Georgia Murphy.

Ashe looked at the sheriff who was also obviously about to go bust. As if on the same mental wavelength, neither said anything. They didn't want to jinx it.

"Full cooperation, now and in the future," Price barked. "A detailed written and sworn statement under penalty of perjury. No retractions, and dammit, no lies. He lies once, *just once*, all deals are off. He goes on the record with Special Agent Hume here. He testifies against all others involved, whether he fingers them or we get them independently. He assists in any way possible to help us verify anything he says."

"Yes, of course," Crews answered.

Then Price turned to Milton and stood up, leaning across the table to speak directly at him. "You point out everybody involved whether we know about them or not. You give us whatever you know and hold back nothing. You tell us where her body lies and take us there. Even if you think of something you figure we won't find out, you better offer it up."

"He will," Crews said, putting his hand on the table between Price and Milton. "And in return?"

Price sat back down. "What you said, Accessory to the Murder and Kidnapping of Bill Clark. Attempted Murder and Especially Aggravated Assault on Ashe. Show us where Georgia is. I'll recommend double life sentences to run concurrently."

"He did not kidnap Clark! He was only an accessory to the planned assault on Mr. Ashe!" Crews shot back.

"The DNA from the Clark crime scene and one bloody tire iron say otherwise! Four minutes left."

Crews spoke to Milton, then said, "Accessory to Murder on Clark, drop the kidnapping. Attempted Murder on Ashe, drop the Agg Assault. He wants at least a shot in 25 years at parole."

"Maybe. Oh, one last, small note," Price added.

Crews looked surprised and turned back from Milton. Watching from the office, Ashe thought perhaps Price must have sensed he'd gotten too little.

"Deputy Clark's camera," Price said, as if it were only an afterthought. "I'm certain your client knows its whereabouts and whether it is still in fact, intact as evidence."

Even through the monitor, Ashe could sense Rachel and Breslin holding their breath. He and Jacobs sure did.

Milton leaned over and whispered to Crews who nodded. "We can give you a very solid lead as to its current whereabouts. We cannot guide your investigation further on that note. We also cannot be held responsible if someone else unknown to us has tampered or destroyed it."

"I tell you what," Price answered, then again spoke directly to Paul Milton. "One minute left. Tell me directly everything you know about the camera right now, and name who it was that directed you, and the deal is on."

"One minute extra, please, first," Crews said, holding up his hands. Price nodded but checked his watch. Crews took Paul Milton over to the corner again, but they quickly returned.

"Deal," Crews said.

"Deal. The camera of Deputy Bill Clark?"

Paul Milton spoke for the first time. "It's why at first, they had to go get Clark. He was going to turn that camera over to the sheriff, or Mr. Ashe."

"Where is it?" Price pressed.

"Tracy Davis knows. Clark told us where he'd put it but I guess she found it first."

"How did she just *find* it?" Price asked.

Milton hesitated but Crews nudged him.

"CJ Portals."

"Carl Jack Portals told her where to find the camera? Bullshit, she was in jail before you Concrete Crew boys ever kidnapped Clark," Price snapped, using their nickname for the first time. Ashe figured he did that to intimidate Milton and show he knew more than he said.

"No. She found it before that, but CJ didn't know. He sent them to make Clark give it up."

"So how did *you* find out she had it?"

"When CJ called Everitt and told him to head to Hurrt County and for us to…*shut up* Mister Ashe. He said she had told him from jail to get her out or she'd turn it in. That's why we hurried down here and didn't…finish up with Clark."

"*Finish up?*" Price asked.

"We were going to, uh, hide him…put him in concrete."

Ashe leaned in toward the monitor.

"Our, um, *their* plan was to just seal him up in a garbage bag and put him in one of our jobs."

"You were going to dispose of Clark's body at one of the Concrete Crew job sites," Price said.

Ashe thought about the war room maps at the L&T where Georgia worked and had shaded areas where a lot of concrete had been poured for DBA.

Milton blurted out loudly, "I know you don't believe me, but I was scared to death!"

"So!" Crews jumped in, stopping Milton. "Sounds like you have some camera hunting and questions for CJ Portals ahead today. When can I get the deal we made in writing, John?"

"You and I can go to my office. I think Special Agent Rachel Hume and Detective Sergeant Daniel Breslin can continue to get Mr. Milton's full statement."

"Um, I should be here when they are…"

"Something else you are holding back? Anything he might say you wouldn't want him to?" Price asked, hinting darkly at Crews.

"No, uh, but let us have a break. We'll go over the written offer, then they can do the interview."

Price shrugged. "Comme ci, comme ca."

In Price's office, Jacobs asked Ashe, "Why only Accessory to Murder for Clark?"

"Well, since I shot MacNeal and Everitt, it'd be all ADA Price could prove."

"I guess," Jacobs said. He seemed disappointed.

"Oh, one other thing, Sheriff. Why isn't that scumbag CJ Portals arrested yet?"

Jacobs' nostril flared and he said, "By god, Ashe! I'll have that ass-wipe in orange in fifteen minutes!" Then he jogged out barking directions into his radio.

Ashe started to switch off the monitor, since he knew Price would want him out of his office before Phillip Crews came in. But just before he did, Rachel Hume asked Paul Milton one last question, seemingly out of the blue.

"So, by *finish up*, you guys were going to use concrete to get rid of Bill Clark's body?" Rachel asked, like she was just curious.

Milton nodded. "Yeah. It's what we know. Everitt said it was a cold thing to do, but that he'd be in the dark and stay silent."

CHAPTER 21

Ashe sat on a bench in the third-floor hallway of the courthouse. There was no court scheduled until that afternoon, so he was alone. He was tired and his head started throbbing some again, so he tried closing his eyes to try and calm his aching. It might have worked if his mind wasn't still sprinting around on what Paul Milton had said.

He knew that Paul Milton and the Concrete Crew planned to dispose of Billy Clark's body by using *what they knew*, as Milton had put it.

Concrete.

He had a vague idea in his head, one he wasn't sure of yet, but it nagged at him because those guys worked almost exclusively in the city, and would know better up there what job sites would work to forever entomb a body. This was their plan for Billy Clark's remains. Had CJ Portals not rushed them to abandon Clark and directed them to hurry to Seacord that night, it's unlikely anyone would ever know what happened to Clark.

He said it was a cold thing to do.

To permanently hide his body. To deprive the family of any closure, any knowledge of how and maybe even why he'd died. Had he been brave? Was there any meaning to be discovered in the knowing?

Ashe had seen a lot of cruelty and death, both in the Army and as a cop. He thought of some of the bodies he'd seen over the years, casually discarded or brutally burned and disfigured to try and hide their identity and delay justice. It always haunted him, the way human animals could just dump the remains of their victims. Like so much garbage they burned them, buried them, abandoned them in dumpsters, or even chopped them to pieces.

This is different. Is Billy Clark my fault?

He'd even seen a murdered cop before, but never had he known of a man to be tortured to death then his body condemned.

Condemned to be forever in the dark, he'd said. And silent.

Although Paul Milton didn't know it, he'd actually revealed a deep truth. Clark's friends and family would have forever been in the dark. Sheriff Jacobs and ADA Price would never have known, and so justice for his unnecessary murder would never have come.

No one would ever be able to speak for him. Ashe could not imagine a worse fate.

To be sealed into dark, wet...

He snapped his eyes open. Rachel had hinted at it. Had they done this before? Ashe looked at his phone again but the war room photos were not clear enough. So he hopped up and ran down the courthouse stairs. He had to see them again.

As he rushed down past the second floor, he heard his name.

"Ashe!" said Stevie. She was alone and motioned for him to follow her into an empty room, so he turned around.

He looked both up and down the stairs and all down the second-floor hallway. People milled about, all several yards away doing county business, but no one was paying them any attention. So he went to her.

He hadn't seen her since before she met with Harold Marsh and noticed she'd put herself together quick for that meeting. She was wearing a business outfit and had on subdued but professional-looking makeup.

"I'm not supposed to be talking to you," she said in a low voice.

"Uh, that's actually my line. Did you turn yourself in?"

"Yes. I can add 'booked for fraud' to my resume. Anyway, the sheriff let me sit in his office until Harold made my bond."

"Damn. I'm sorry, Stevie."

She rushed forward and threw her arms around him, burying her face into his neck. She held him tightly and although caught off guard at first, eventually he held her as well.

She pushed back from him after a minute or so. "Well Harold says he will thank you someday, somehow, but for now, he and I are on one side of this and you are on the other."

"Meaning?"

"Meaning, he is trying to keep me out of jail. You of all people know what I have to lose now. My Nora, my freedom, my career."

Ashe knew the old judge was right; he should just shake hands and walk out. If anyone saw or heard them in the busy courthouse, they'd be done for. Especially so soon after his meeting with Price and Rachel.

But instead, he said, "They are not sure about his request for your immunity. Hume wants you to do time. Is there anything you can give them you haven't?"

"Time? Jail time? That bitch!" Stevie said too loudly and then caught herself. The room they were in had an echo.

"No! Now stop that," he said quietly but sharply. "She is doing her job, and given the people that were probably defrauded, she has a point."

"Oh, god. I knew it, Harold knew it. You're going to help them to…"

Ashe stepped forward and kissed her. Long and deeply.

When he released her face from his hands, he said, "Never, ever think that ever again."

They just stood there, both stunned, and stared into each other's eyes for a minute. Ashe had never felt so resolute in his life. He knew no matter what hell came for it, no matter that in the end she could never be his, no matter the cost to him, he would do whatever must be done to protect her.

Like no other woman.

She shook her head and looked at the floor and smiled to herself. "I just, I just…"

"I know, honey," he said.

"No. No, you really don't, Ashe. Get CJ and put him in jail. As long as he's out and free, there's no telling what he will do to stop you, to stop all this," she said.

"You know where he is?"

"No, he just keeps texting me. Says he thinks he loves me. Wants me to go away with him."

"You're not helping…you're not considering…"

"Of course not, Christ, Ashe!"

She ran her hands down from his neck to his back as she stepped back. Then her face changed and she gave him a worried look.

"Are you…armed?"

"Um, actually no. They haven't returned my gun to me yet."

She pulled her hair back with her hands and straightened her clothes.

"My God, don't you think you should be?" she said and walked out of the room quickly.

Ashe stood there for a moment longer. It was as if her ghost was left behind to haunt him. He could still smell her and taste her on his lips.

Then he remembered where he was going before, and took off himself.

Ashe looked across the town square at Third Avenue at the Hurrt Land and Title company's rear door and saw it was open. As he walked, he looked around and behind him, half expecting to see his shadow, CJ Portals, but there was no such luck.

Stepping into the office through the rear door, he was in what Susan had told him was the war room leased space. Leased to Mark Portals.

Three people he did not recognize, two young men and a woman, were working at boxing up piles of documents. All the maps were down off the walls. The plexiglass had been removed from the big center table and its maps were being folded.

"May I help you?" the young woman asked. She looked up from the clipboard she held and was checking things off on what was probably a punch list. She looked to be maybe twenty-five and wore jeans and a polo shirt.

The two young men turned and looked at him. One, who was about twenty or so, stepped forward.

"I don't think you can be in here," he said and gestured for Ashe to leave by the rear door.

"No, it's okay," Ashe said and smiled his sixty-watt smile. "It's all good."

The man who'd spoken to him relaxed and smiled back, offering his hand. "I'm Glen, you with the title company?"

"No," the woman said. "He's that guy from the news. The one who got beat up. He's a cop."

Glen withdrew his hand. "Hey, you have to leave. This office is closed."

"Sure. Just please tell me where I can find Susan Marlin. Is she here?" Ashe said.

"Get out of here, Officer!" the woman said sternly. She pulled out her phone. "I'm calling our lawyer. This is private property and you have to have a…a thing to even be in here."

"Mark or Phillip? Tell them I said hi," Ashe said. "And it's called a warrant. But FYI, your door was wide open."

"Hey," the second man said, grinning. "You're the one! You shot those two dudes."

"Are you leaving?" she said.

"I'm leaving," Ashe said and walked back to the door.

As he stepped out, he turned and said to the woman, "And for the record, I didn't get *beat up*. That implies I lost a fight. I shot two of them and the third snuck up and hit me with a tire iron but I still had enough gas in me to knock *him* on his ass."

"Whoa. Hard core," the second man said.

Ashe walked out and back down Third and onto the square. He had hoped to get a better, fresher look at the maps in the war room from out where DBA was developing the area for Doorbella Corporation. In particular, where they had poured the test concrete that Susan had mentioned. He needed to know if there was a record of the dates the work had been done and if the Concrete Crew under CJ Portals had done the job.

It's what we know, Paul Milton said. Rachel needs a subpoena now.

As he crossed the town square, he had that feeling again. Just an itchy feeling like when he'd been watched. He looked around but saw no one, but the feeling reminded him maybe Stevie was right.

Just then, Sheriff Jacobs and Danny Breslin pulled around in an unmarked Dodge cruiser and honked the car horn.

"Ashe!" Jacobs shouted out his car window as they pulled over to a parking spot and idled. "What are you doing out all by yourself?"

"Thinking, walking. I was at the Hurrt L&T but they're closing it up," he said and got in.

"We do everything possible to keep you alive and you think it's cute you should just wander around by yourself?" Breslin said from behind the wheel.

"I thought your trooper guard drove you to breakfast," Jacobs said with a grin.

"Yeah, oh, and very funny using Pat's name this morning," Breslin said. "I told the trooper he was good to go so he doesn't know the difference."

Ashe shrugged. He'd forgotten about the trooper at his house.

"You get a full statement from Paul Milton?" Ashe asked.

"Oh yeah. He puts a noose around CJ Portals, but that's just a co-defendant statement. We need proof of CJ's direct involvement in your attack and for Clark," Breslin said.

"And Georgia Murphy," Ashe said.

"He says CJ was trying to scare her, but it got out of hand. They buried her around here somewhere. He doesn't know Hurrt County and says it was at night, so he can't say where. But he says CJ knows, and that body could be all we need to fry him."

"Sheriff, you get CJ Portals yet?"

Jacobs turned in his seat to half face Ashe. "No. Nobody's seen him today so far. He's around, we know that, thanks to your little favor this morning."

"A favor? And how do you know he's still around?" Breslin asked, looking occasionally at Ashe in his rearview mirror.

"Ashe here asked me to run all CJ Portals' vehicle registrations and all the vehicles registered to the Concrete Crew, LLC. Also, all of Everitt's, MacNeal's, and even Milton's vehicles," Jacobs said. "Then everything registered to Mark Portals, his law firm, Phillip Crews, their secretary, and—I got a kick out of this—even Stephanie Collins."

Breslin cut his eyes at Ashe in the mirror. "And?" he asked.

"We have a list and I have my deputies and your cops in Metro running them down."

"That could take a while," Breslin said.

"Sheriff?" Ashe asked.

"CJ's Chevy Tahoe is missing from town, but a truck from the Concrete Crew, LLC is parked behind Mark Portals' office," Jacobs said.

"Do we have a warrant and a BOLO out on him?" Ashe asked.

"No," Breslin answered. "Price wants to bring him in for questioning without arresting him first."

Ashe nodded. Made sense to him. "Okay, are we headed to

check for him?"

"No, I got everybody in the county I know watching for him. Ed Bell is on standby if he moves. Right now, we're going to Carson County to talk to Tracy Davis. Wanna come along?"

"You'll be an observer," Breslin said firmly.

"No problem. Can we make a stop first?"

Ten minutes later, Ashe walked into Knob Street Hardware with Breslin and the sheriff in tow. The owner had all the recent fundraising posters up both inside and out.

"Hello, Chig!" he said, warmly, although Ashe had never met him. There were only a few people in the cramped store. Jacobs used the opportunity to go shake hands.

There were rows of shelves lining the floor close together that rose from the old wooden floor to above head height. The only open area was about halfway back in the store along on one wall. The owner wore a new trucker-style ball cap with a plastic mesh back that said *Seacord Strong* on the front. He wore coveralls and sat on a high stool behind a counter with a flyswatter in his hand and an open Mountain Dew in front of him.

"Hey, um, is it *Eddie*?" Ashe asked.

"Yeah," Eddie said as he grabbed Ashe's hand and pumped it hard.

"Eddie, I need to buy a gun."

Mark Portals finished a phone call in his office and made himself a reminder to follow up in a few days. He looked up and saw his nephew waiting for him, staring at something out the window, so he waved him in.

"CJ," he said, as if identifying a bug he saw on the carpet.

"Uncle Mark, I'm a little surprised, I guess, that you're here," CJ said.

Mark shuffled some papers in front of him into a file folder, clearing his desk. "I don't know why you would be. I hear the DA and the sheriff are looking to talk to you."

"Oh, I'm sure they'll be around to see you, too," CJ said.

"I already have an appointment to speak with Agent Hume, and my friends at the capitol tell me the state Fraud Unit is planning to come down here, likely early tomorrow morning."

CJ laughed to himself. "You don't seem anxious at all, but why should you? You're Mark 'By-God' Portals."

Mark smiled, not warmly, at his nephew. "I have absolutely nothing to worry about as long as *you* stay focused. Is everything set?"

"Yeah. You know Stevie is talking to the state now? They also got guys from Metro down here," he said, and pointed back at the window. "And I just saw Ashe walk out of the L&T."

"I have already had a heart-to-heart with our girl Stevie."

"She might sink us!"

Portals gestured with an open palm toward CJ. "You. You mean she might sink, *you*. Not I. And she cannot sink *you nor I* without tarring herself in the process. The good Judge Marsh and I have an understanding and we have discussed her at length. What I need from you is to stay away from her."

"Oh, for Christ's sake, Mark, she's going to tell them anything to keep herself out of jail!"

"She has already spoken with Agent Hume and she has given her a statement including her own involvement. She has revealed to them exactly what Harold Marsh and I agreed to."

CJ flopped in a chair and thought for a minute or two while stroking his beard then popped back up and began pacing the office floor.

"They have Paul Milton," CJ said.

"That's your problem. I told you what I thought of your little disaster on our town square."

Mark leaned back and looked his nephew up and down. He was too much like his father, Dale, who was still in prison. All action, too little thought ahead of time. It was time to begin prepping his nephew for the inevitable.

"The final assessment team will be here in ten days and this needs to be a dead issue by then," Mark said.

"How? Seriously? They usually meet with Phillip and by the way…where is he?"

"That is troubling, but Phillip is my issue, not yours. We need a sacrificial lamb."

CJ shook his head and smiled. "I knew all along we'd need a scapegoat and I thought we all agreed that Stevie was going to take the fall. That's why you had her name and signature on all the documents."

Mark shrugged and looked at the clock over CJ's head. It was a little too early for a drink, so he buzzed his secretary for some iced tea.

"Well," he said while he waited for the tea. "Unfortunately my arrangement with Harold prevents that."

"Crews?" CJ offered. "I'd like to see that sanctimonious prick get his."

"Because she preferred him to you once she was clear-eyed? No. Phillip is too deep with DBA and to ensure we bring this home; he will have to stay. I think we need to feed ADA Price someone actively involved, someone believable as having the wherewithal to have orchestrated the sort of large-scale design that could have led to the murder of Deputy Clark and the assault on Mr. Ashe."

"Tracy Davis," CJ said, then immediately shook his head. "No."

"'No' is correct, she is collateral damage and too small a player to convince anyone."

"I bet you anything Paul Milton is talking to the damn state right now."

"About what?"

CJ didn't answer that but slapped his leg. "Susan. Susan Marlin."

"Again, seriously, CJ? She executed every single one of our transactions. If we fed her to the state, she actually *could* sink us. But since you brought her up, are we set for later today?"

CJ just nodded and leaned in one corner. Mark could tell he was beginning to figure it out as their tea arrived.

"Thank you, Betty," Mark said. She smiled and handed him a note folded as always then left the room and closed the doors behind her.

Mark read the note and then rotated his chair around and dropped it in a shredder.

"What was that about?" CJ snapped.

Ah. He has realized his role now.

CJ exploded from the corner over to Mark's desk. "I know you! You are going to send *me* over! You set this up to happen all along!"

"I have to have a conversation with some very influential people so nothing is 'set up' as you accuse," Mark said calmly.

"But as a contingency plan, purely backup mind you, what would you think if we offered you five hundred thousand dollars?"

"To eat this and go to jail? Fuck you, Uncle Mark!"

"Calm down and think!" Mark shouted. "Sit down, right here, sit down!"

Mark knew he had to feed it to CJ, bark and all. He waited for CJ to submit and do as he'd been directed.

After a lengthy pause, CJ flopped in the chair then grabbed a glass of the tea.

"I still say hell no," he said.

Mark stood up and walked around and sat on the corner of his desk to tower over CJ.

"Think of this as one possibility of many, but it's also an opportunity. In addition to your well-managed investments, plus whatever your DBA and Skee-ah shares bring in, you get a half a million, up front. You decide where and how that is managed."

CJ said nothing and didn't look at his uncle.

"Now, assuming the worst and we have to implement this idea, you don't confess at first. I'll be your attorney, mind you, and we work a deal. See, Stevie committed the land fraud, you didn't know about Clark or Ashe until it was too late. And remember, you actually stopped Mr. Milton from killing Ashe."

CJ just nodded, but Mark had his attention.

"But now Georgia. Say Everitt or MacNeal were dating her, and she had an accident. With your record and theirs, you were afraid to call the cops. So, you helped them hide the body. We can counter anything Stevie or Phillip or even Susan Marlin might say otherwise. And of course, Everitt and MacNeal are dead, thanks to Mr. Ashe."

"Maybe. I dunno, I know this sucks. This damn thing completely sucks."

"Oh, inconvenient for you, sure. But, nephew, with the situation with her husband, Tony, *who worked for you*, and what Georgia discovered. It had to be done. Now this *must be done*."

"I want to think about this," CJ said and glared at Mark.

"*Think*? Were you *thinking* two years ago? Huh! I'll do the thinking from here on out if you don't mind. Now, nothing is set yet and if things work out, we may not have to ever discuss this again," Mark said.

He'd noted a hint in CJ's voice that his nephew might be trying to figure out a new angle. *I'll have to act fast.*

"What's this mean to me, time-wise?" CJ mumbled, as if a guillotine hung over his head. "How much?"

"Unlawful disposal of a body? No direct evidence of homicide? Max sentence is about six years. You'll be out in two."

"Damn, two years."

"At two hundred fifty thousand dollars a year," Mark said.

CHAPTER 22

They arrived at the Carson County Sheriff's Office by midafternoon and were escorted by the chief deputy to a dimly lit and windowless interview room. In the car, they agreed Breslin would take lead, Jacobs would back him up, and as much as it would frustrate him, Ashe had to be quiet.

The interview room smelled of long-term cigarette smoke with the undertones of mold and sweat. Ashe assumed they didn't clean in here very often by the dust on the wire-rack shelves against the wall that held spilled stacks of old report forms and boxes of toner that had likely outlived the machines they were meant for.

For once, Ashe was happy to wear the surgical mask the jailor gave him.

In a few minutes, Tracy Davis was brought in by a young man in blue jeans and a Carson County Sheriff's Department T-shirt. Tracy was wearing bright-yellow scrubs, socks, and flip-flop shoes. Of course, at least this week, correctional facilities still mandated masks, so she wore a cheap disposable one that looked well-worn.

At Jacobs' request, she was uncuffed and unshackled.

Her lawyer filtered in behind her and introduced herself as Linda Ingles. She looked to Ashe to be in her mid-to-late forties with bright-blonde hair that spilled down over her shoulders. She wore a black pants suit over a plain white top. She handed everyone a card and after introductions were done, she allowed Jacobs to read Tracy her rights. Ingles and Tracy had obviously discussed this in advance, so Tracy waived her right to silence right away and agreed to talk.

"Tracy, you okay?" Jacobs asked first. Ashe noted an actual note of concern in his voice.

"Yes, sir," she said, looking him in the eye. She then looked at Breslin, and apparently decided she didn't know him, then looked at Ashe for a long minute. For a second, Ashe worried it might have been better if he hadn't come, as she might still be holding a grudge.

She looked at him with dull, almost-uninterested eyes and said, "Mr. Ashe, I'm sorry. I had no idea anyone would try to hurt you."

Lawyer told her to say that.

"Let's start there," Breslin said with a quick *be quiet* look at Ashe. "In fact, let's go back a couple of years to talk about why Ashe here was talking to you in the first place."

"You mean Georgia Murphy," Tracy said.

"Georgia Murphy," Jacobs agreed.

"But first," Ingles interrupted. She took off her suit jacket. Ashe mentally agreed and took off his. It was stale enough in this room, but with five people breathing and no obvious ventilation, it was getting stuffy. She looked at Ashe as he did without saying anything.

"I am curious as to how the state has charged Ms. Davis here with the felony range of Tampering with Evidence and Obstruction when that is a Class A misdemeanor."

"It's a C felony if the evidence and obstruction are of a felony crime. In this case, Homicide," Breslin answered.

Ingles shook her head. "What homicide? You only have a missing person. You can't prove that any felony occurred and my client has no direct knowledge as to how Georgia Murphy disappeared nor what happened to her afterward. I'm going to make a motion tomorrow that the charges be reduced and an appropriate bond be set."

"Well, I'll let ADA Price and Deputy AG Ashad know this. Now, you know we cannot offer any deals without their approval, but…"

"But?" Ingles said. Again, cutting her eyes at Ashe without speaking to him.

Breslin nodded. "But we *could* be convinced to not argue against your motion and possibly even go a bit better."

"In exchange for?" she asked.

Breslin said, "Full statement and an agreement to testify as to…"

"As to whatever she knows," Ashe interrupted. *Don't seed the statement.*

Ingles turned to Ashe. "You'll need to be a lot more specific."

Breslin shot an annoyed look at Ashe then said, "As to anything she knows about the disappearance and probable murder of Georgia Murphy, and the tampering of evidence in connection with that case."

"Also," Sheriff Jacobs added, "the photographs Clark took, the digital film card he gave to her, and the whereabouts of his camera."

Ingles nodded and took notes. She stood for a second and pulled at the front of her top to fan some air down it.

Jacobs got up and opened the door a crack to try to let some air in.

Ashe wrote a note to Breslin and handed it to him. He read it and stuck it in his pocket.

"Ms. Ingles, in addition, we want to know everything Davis knows about the men who kidnapped and murdered Deputy Bill Clark and tried to kill Deputy Ashe, here. Did she know them and know anything about their employer?"

"Gentlemen, this is a lot and I think I might achieve what I want without cooperating with the state. Can you give me a minute with my client in private?"

"Sure," Breslin said. "But keep this in mind. We have full statements and agreements with Paul Milton, Susan Marlin, and Stephanie Collins. We know the approximate location where Milton and the two others hid Georgia Murphy's body," Breslin said. Ashe noted the last part was a bit of a lie. They only had the wildest idea of where.

"Okay," she said slowly.

"If we find her body first, if we find her body in Hurrt County, the felony charges will be hard, if not impossible, to get reduced in court. Your client will be lumped in with those who perpetrated these murders."

Ingles appeared to take that in then nodded to Breslin. She looked over to Ashe as if expecting him to say something, and when he didn't, she just repeated, "A minute in private, please."

They filtered out of the room and walked back through the office to a hallway with a window and some air flow.

"Could the damn air be stuffier in there?" Jacobs said and stood in front of the window to ventilate some then shook a cigarette out and lit it, holding it out the window.

"Makes you appreciate Hurrt County, huh?" Ashe said.

"Guys, I thought we agreed I was going to ask the questions?" Breslin cut in.

"I apologize but I didn't want you to give them exactly what we wanted, or that'd be all we'd get," Ashe said. "It should be a *push* not a *pull*."

"Yeah, okay. I didn't mention CJ Portals' name though," he said.

"Right. It's a stronger statement if she says his name to us," Ashe agreed.

"I think Ashe should be in the interview. He makes her feel guilty maybe," Jacobs said, then added, "And why does Ms. Ingles keep looking at you?"

Ashe shrugged. "Maybe my aftershave? Maybe my scar. Chicks dig scars."

"What is it with you and the young female lawyers?" Jacobs said.

Ashe busted out laughing. It hurt his head but felt good to laugh at the same time.

"I'm walking away from that," Breslin said with a slight grin.

The jailor who had brought Tracy up found them in the hallway and motioned to them.

"Ingles must be ready," Jacobs said, and after taking one last drag, flicked his cigarette out the window.

They assembled back into the interview room in generally the same places they'd been before. Ashe figured the room was too small for improvisation, but he still tried to get closest to the door for better air.

Ingles had untucked her tank top and was sweating pretty freely at this point. She'd grabbed a stack of old cardstock forms from the shelf and was fanning herself. When Breslin entered last and tried to close the door, she reached out and grabbed the door to stop him.

"Please, no," she said.

Tracy was still seated at the head of the small table and had a hopeful expression on her face. Ashe decided this meant they were about to get her cooperation and she was thinking she'd spend considerably less time here in county, and maybe no time in actual prison.

"Can you call John Price and let him know we're interested in cooperation and a plea in exchange for dropping felony charges," she said.

Breslin shrugged. "You'll have to tell me what we can expect. I think regardless, there'll be a D felony anyway."

"My client will describe how the crime scene was changed in Hurrt County. She will provide you with the camera, which as of the last time she was in possession of it, still had Clark's photos of Mrs. Murphy's apartment on its internal drive."

"Okay, is that it?" Jacobs said, staring at Tracy.

Ingles turned to Ashe as she spoke which obviously aggravated Breslin.

"She had no knowledge of what happened to Mrs. Murphy directly, but she knows the name of the person she told about the crime scene and the camera two years ago. She will describe what instructions she received from this person back then and she will describe the conversation she had with this same person during a visit he made with her two days ago here in jail."

Breslin was writing this down, and it took him a second or two to catch up and as he did, Ashe tried not to smile. Ms. Ingles was saying CJ Portals without saying his name yet.

Of course, the jail visitor logs would give them the name, but only Tracy could give them the meat of the conversation from two days ago.

"And as to the crimes against Clark and Ashe?" Breslin asked.

"She has no direct knowledge of either event, except that the person we have mentioned is likely the same person who directed the two deadly assaults you reference," she said. "This person works with all the same people you already know."

"Bullshit. Oh, excuse me, Detective Breslin was supposed to say that," Ashe said.

Breslin shifted in his seat, staring at Ashe, then said, "I think what Mr. Ashe here is implying is, we do not believe her."

"Tracy, when you and I spoke about Georgia's disappearance and I asked you directly about Clark's photos, which you denied existed, you got a call or a text and right afterward started calling me a private investigator. Your whole demeanor changed."

"Yeah," she said.

"Hold on," Ingles said. "Are we interviewing? I thought we were negotiating a deal?"

"She waived her rights, before we try for a deal, I want to be sure on one fact," Ashe said. "I want to know what she was told about this case during that call or text message that changed her attitude from *unsure* to *very confident* when I said we'd have Clark testify."

Ingles looked at Tracy, who looked at Jacobs, then finally back to Ashe. Her eyes were such that Ashe assumed he would not get a Christmas card from her.

"I was only told Clark would not testify. I assumed he'd been bought off. I did not know he was dead," she said in a monotone.

"Gentlemen, do we have any kind of an agreement? If not, this is *over*," Ingles said, fanning herself more vigorously.

"I'll make the call," Breslin said and stepped out. Jacobs took the opportunity as well.

"Jeez, why don't we all step out for a minute and catch a damn breath," Ingles said. She and Tracy stepped into the hall with Ashe in the rear.

"You should…" Tracy started to say to Ashe, but Ingles held up a hand.

To Ingles, Ashe said, "Good for you. I think that's a smart thing for your client."

Ingles looked at Ashe's left side of his head. "Does that…hurt?" she said and started to reach for his ear.

"Only in there," Ashe said and pointed at the interview room. He gave her his low lumen smile.

"I'll bet," she replied. "I'm surprised you're working again so soon after what I saw on the news."

"Well, we Ashes, we're Scottish and naturally hardheaded."

She smiled at that and then turned back to Tracy to whisper to her.

Is she flirting? At my age I have no idea anymore.

After several minutes, Breslin returned and winked at Ashe. Jacobs was behind him with a lit cigarette but suddenly remembered it and went back to get rid of it.

"Okay, ADA Price is emailing some papers to the chief deputy here. Essentially, we have a deal. He stresses full divulgence, complete cooperation, surrender of the camera, agreement to testify, and of course…"

"No lying," Ingles said to Tracy.

"I won't. I have children and a husband who are worried sick."

After a few minutes, the chief deputy brought a printout in a manilla folder, and Breslin and Ingles went over it; then she went over it with Tracy.

"Felony charges dropped?" Ingles asked Breslin.

"At my discretion and Sheriff Jacobs, but after I get her statement. One caveat, if any new evidence appears showing she had any kind of a hand in disposing of the body, Clark, or Ashe here, deal's off."

Ingles signed the papers, then Tracy said, "Okay," she said, "shoot."

Breslin set his digital recorder in front of her.

"Camera first," Jacobs said.

Tracy smiled nervously. "You already have it. I found it in Clark's locker of all places about the time you and I first discussed this. I even had it on my desk when you and I talked, Mr. Ashe," she said. "Afterward, I was going to get rid of it but I didn't have time. So I hid it in your office, Sheriff."

Jacobs was surprised. "Wait, my…"

"In your old file cabinet in the corner. In the bottom drawer full of stuff. I put it in the binocular case," Tracy said. "I figured you wouldn't look there and I could get it later. I actually never considered I'd be arrested that day."

Ashe smiled to himself. As full of junk and clutter as her desk was the day he talked with her, she could have had a French horn on her desk and he might not have noticed it.

"Why did you keep it, Tracy?" Jacobs asked.

"I thought I might need it as a bargaining chip, Sheriff. Looks like I was right."

"A chip for who?" Breslin asked.

Tracy swallowed hard. "I'm not covering up for these sons a bitches. CJ Portals."

Kaboom! Ashe thought. *CJ mother-loving, kiss my old ass, Portals!*

"Ok, start at the beginning," Breslin said.

"Before you start, Danny," Ashe said. "Sheriff, you think maybe you could call someone at Hurrt County and confirm the camera is still there and still has Clark's photos intact?"

"Yep," was all he said and left the room.

Breslin nodded and Ingles prompted Tracy to begin.

"Georgia Murphy," she said. "I never thought she was dead at first. I knew she was a wild child and ran with CJ and his boys. The 'concrete kids' or whatever the name of their stupid construction company was. When she was reported missing, I called CJ Portals first and asked him if he knew anything. He swore he didn't but said it was possible her husband Tony Murphy had killed her."

"So you thought she was dead?" Breslin asked.

"Right from the start, but CJ convinced me Tony was going to get away with it if I didn't help him trap Tony. I had heard rumors they were going to get divorced anyway and it was obvious with his criminal record he *could* possibly kill her," she said.

"And seeing her driver's license in her purse and cell phone all there in her apartment didn't make you stop and realize *whatever* had happened, happened *right there*."

"Yes. But CJ, you have to know him, he's very convincing. I've known him a long time and he was very…uh, convincing. He said I should just leave and go back to her apartment the next morning like it was the first time. He'd do everything to ensure the case got sent to Metro where Tony had probably done it anyway. I mean, he said he figured Tony caught her here and killed her in Metro."

"So you did that," Breslin said.

"I did. The next morning, I saw what was missing. I was shocked but at the same time, I said to myself, 'I got kids and the Portals' run this county' so…I reshot the crime scene. I got the original photos from Clark and his SD card and destroyed the photos by burning them. When I found out about the camera just recently, well you know I got that later too."

"So, you knew right then on the morning of April 16th, two years ago that someone, likely CJ Portals, had removed evidence from what you feared was a homicide crime scene in order to help throw suspicion onto Tony Murphy," Breslin said.

"Yeah, except that part about *likely* CJ. It *was* CJ. He said so later."

"He told you directly that he had removed her items and took them to Tony's apartment in Metro."

"Yeah, he called me a few days later. He said, 'Good job, I took care of it. The mother f'er will pay' and stuff like that. He also said he wouldn't forget me."

"Is that all he said?" asked Breslin.

"So, he told me he had taken her personal stuff to her husband's apartment in the city to hand him," she said. "I just...you need to know I thought I was helping them to find out what happened to her."

Ashe just looked at her with a blank face, trying not to reveal what he really was thinking.

Tracy, you are completely full of shit.

"What was exactly said during the call or text Mr. Ashe here referenced?" Breslin asked.

Tracy sent a hard look toward Ashe but said to Breslin, "Just that I had said maybe Ashe will get Clark to testify about the crime scene and the photos and...CJ said 'not to worry.' He said Clark won't be testifying."

Ashe held her stare. If she thought she were intimidating, she wasn't.

She leaned over to Ingles and they whispered to each other.

Tracy turned back around and said, "Okay, to be clear, I may have had a bad feeling back when I spoke to Ashe, but I did not know he would go and have Billy killed or anything. I still thought Tony Murphy was the killer, until much later when I heard about what happened to him...and to you, Mr. Ashe."

"You said CJ Portals visited you here in Carson County a couple of days ago. What was said then?" Breslin asked.

"That I should be smart and give him the camera. He said he knew I must have it because Clark didn't. That scared me because by then I knew what had happened to Clark."

"What did you say?"

"To that? Nothing really. I asked for him to help get me out but he just promised me in exchange for my silence and my sticking to the story, I'd get fifteen thousand dollars."

"Tracy, do you know for a fact that Georgia Murphy was murdered? Do you know who killed her?" Ashe asked.

"I've always thought Tony did it. But CJ has been acting

strange, so after what all has happened now, I don't know who for sure killed her."

"Do you know more than you're telling us about the kidnap and murder of Billy Clark?" Jacobs asked.

"No, God no. Sheriff, he was a friend," she said.

"What do you know about the assault on Ashe?"

"Nothing."

"Your visit from CJ, he never mentioned anything about it?" Breslin pressed.

"No, nothing."

Breslin made a note then looked at her. "If we discover you had any foreknowledge of the kidnapping and murder of Bill Clark and or, the attempted murder of Mr. Ashe…"

"Look, I said…I swear I don't," she said.

Breslin held up his hand to her. "Any knowledge Georgia Murphy was murdered back then and have concealed that all this time, up to and including today. Or, if we discover her body in Hurrt County and can show you knew where she was buried, this deal is off and you're minimally an accessory to murder."

Tracy started to say something else, but Breslin again stopped her.

"Or any foreknowledge of the planned murder of Mr. Ashe."

"I know. I'm saying everything now to you. I'm really scared," she said.

"Why scared? You are on the same team as CJ and the Concrete Crew?" Breslin said.

"No. I knew, sooner or later, CJ Portals would decide he'd have to shut me up too."

CHAPTER 23

During the ride back to Hurrt County, everyone was mostly quiet, which Ashe was grateful for. The only thing that kept him from dozing was that Jacobs, who was in front of him driving, every few minutes cracked his window an inch and lit a cigarette. The pungent smoke didn't all make it out the window, and Ashe had to breathe it over the half pack Jacobs went through on the trip home.

He felt his energy dropping, and his head went from just beyond achy to well over into throb territory. He searched but didn't have an ibuprofen left in his pocket then looked at his watch and saw it was almost six.

Breslin had let Jacobs drive so he could tap away on a digital tablet, likely working on his notes. Occasionally he'd ask a question about the interview to be sure he'd heard correctly.

"She did say she had no idea at the time *or now* where Georgia is, right? I'm sure I asked that," Breslin said to them both, almost rhetorically.

"Yeah, she said she figured somewhere in Metro. Got that from CJ," Jacobs said. "And hey, I just got a text from Ed. The camera was right where Tracy said it was."

"Pictures still on it?" Breslin asked.

Jacobs read the text while driving. "He doesn't know. Wants one of us to mess with it. He's afraid he'll screw it up."

"Good idea," Ashe said, then had a thought. "You did ask Rachel to subpoena Hurrt County L&T's records on the DBA project from two years ago, right?"

"Yes, I texted her earlier before we got to Carson County. You wanted to know who did a concrete test, right?" Breslin answered.

"Something Suzie Marlin said to me. That they normally used a local contractor but they had to do a test of a concrete pad *in a hurry* to show some investors a while back. Got me to thinking about what Paul Milton said too."

Breslin turned in his seat and looked at Ashe. "You think?"

Ashe nodded. "I do."

Jacobs was looking at Ashe in his rearview mirror. "There's over fifteen hundred acres out there all dug up and leveled. Must be thousands of yards of concrete by now, maybe more, some of it two feet thick."

"Yeah. Looks like hell out there, I hear."

"All of it on private property too. I doubt ol' Mark Portals will just consent to a search," Jacobs said.

Ashe rubbed his head and closed his eyes. "I doubt he personally owns it. Whoever manages DBA's physical assets would have to give us...ah hell, who cares. We should have enough for a search warrant."

"Maybe," Breslin said and went back to his tablet. "But a search warrant for *where* exactly? That whole end of the county?" Then he stopped and looked at Ashe again.

"That's why you want the dates on the concrete pours," he said.

"Yep. Might narrow it down some. Gents, I really hate to, but I need to tap out and go home. Can I see you in the a.m.?"

"I'll take you straight home," Jacobs said. "You may not make it in that damn old thing of yours."

Twenty minutes later, they pulled up in front of Ashe's house and dropped him off. Jacobs said he'd see him for breakfast again and Ashe just gave him a thumbs-up.

Inside was quiet. He could smell the lingering remains of the fire Stevie had started the day before, and her empty bourbon glass was on his coffee table. He felt like a shower and bed, but he knew he should eat something first, so he washed his face and took some ibuprofen. He was staring into his refrigerator when he remembered the gun he'd bought. A Smith and Wesson 9mm.

I guess I need to know if this thing shoots straight.

He went outside and across his side yard toward the old dirt floor barn and thumbtacked a couple of eight-inch paper plates to a big tree that was backed by a small valley and then a large hill beyond, all on his property. Then he backed off fifteen paces and knelt and loaded the gun, holstered it in the Kydex holster he'd bought, and put on safety glasses and earmuffs.

With his head hurting, this was the last thing he wanted to be doing, but he figured when you need a gun, you really need one. That would not be the time to discover you couldn't shoot it worth a damn.

He fired a single shot and saw it hit a little low and left on the first target. He took a breath and was more careful with his trigger press the second shot. That one hit more to the center. He fired again and emptied his magazine. All were on the first plate.

Nothing to brag about. But they're there.

Then he reloaded with a second magazine, wanting to be sure they both worked, and drew and fired while slowly stepping to one side, then the next. He fired pairs and a few three shot hammers until the compact Smith's slide locked back empty. Checking the target, he saw where when shooting fast, he pulled left but he'd only missed the plate altogether once, and that shot was low but still on the tree.

He pulled off his safety gear and took down the plates. *Good enough for tonight.*

And as he did so, he felt his scalp crawl under his hair and the sudden feeling of being watched returned. His gun was empty. His box of ammo was several feet away. Hearing something behind him, he dropped his slide forward and turned, hoping if need be, his bluff would work.

"Damn, Chig," Pat said, holding up his hands. "What did I do to you?"

Ashe lowered his pistol then holstered it. "What in hell are you doing here?"

"I brought dinner. And some Jameson's," he said. "You don't have anything but crumbs to eat out here, remember?"

Ashe collected his shooting gear and they went back into the house.

"You still can't shoot for shit," Pat mumbled as he set out food from Roger's Café onto the kitchen counter.

Ashe sighed. "Tell you what. You let me shoot off the top quarter of your ear *then* bean you with a tire iron, see how good *you* do."

Pat chuckled. "Nah, you already did that. Tell you what though, I'll drink half this Jameson's then go out and chop down that tree with my forty-five!"

Ashe noticed Pat had an overnight bag just inside his front door. "What's this?"

"I had to do my *actual* job in the city today. But since I was planning on being down here to see what's going on tomorrow, I thought it'd be easier if I stayed here. Be, you know, quicker in the morning," he said.

Ashe grinned, but it hurt so he quit it. "I don't need a babysitter, but thank you."

Pat jerked a thumb over his shoulder toward the side yard. "That shitty shooting out there says you do."

There was baked chicken with rice, green beans with almonds, and fried okra. Ashe started eating without waiting for Pat to reheat the food then poured himself two fingers of the Irish whiskey over a single ice cube. Afterward, he went and sat heavily on his sofa. Pat joined him with his second plate of chicken on his lap.

Ashe stared at his glass. He was getting sleepy already. "Did Danny update you?"

"Yeah, he told me about the deal with Tracy Davis."

"You don't approve?"

Pat shook his head then between bites said, "I think she's in this deeper than she says. I can't prove anything but I just think so."

"You're likely right," Ashe said. "But it got us the camera. Do you know if Rachel could get a subpoena this afternoon for Hurrt L&T?"

"I do not. I came straight from Metro to here," he said, still eating.

"Well, my friend," Ashe said and set his glass on the table near Stevie's. "I'm going to shower and go to bed. If you want to watch TV, it's in Dad's old den."

As Ashe stood and walked past him, Pat said, "Chig, hey seriously. You okay?"

Ashe thought about that for a second or two. He was hurting, he felt shaky again, and all day had barely been able to focus without pain. A hot boiling ball of bile and emotion seemed to always be just at the bottom of his chest, waiting for the right time to rise into his throat, creating a lump he had to fight through to speak.

"No. No, I'm not okay," he said slowly. He turned and sat back down and faced his friend.

"I'm beyond tired all the time. What Dad used to call 'old-dog tired' when I was a kid. I'm in pain, yeah, but I don't want to take whatever that is they prescribed me."

Pat nodded and didn't speak.

"You know, I've always been a rule follower. I've tried to be like my dad and granddad, men of certain principles. Principles they taught me. Fair play, honesty, hard work, you know. You were raised the same way. Do right and it'll all be good."

Pat just said, "Yeah."

"But what did it get me? I wound up divorced and lost half my pension. Then I retired from a job I was good at to take care of Dad, because that's what you're supposed to do, right? I wound up spending a lot of time just waiting around. Waiting for him to get better or, God help me, *die*. We went through a lot to get him set up and cared for, then you know what? He did it anyway."

"That wasn't...you can't..." Pat mumbled.

"No, I know. But then, because of all that, I met a woman."

"Boy," Pat said and polished off his drink. "You damn sure did."

"I know you don't think much of her, but I fell in love, buddy, hard and fast. And you know what? Maybe you were right. Maybe she was just playing me. I don't think she did it on purpose, I'm just not sure she knows how to handle it. But I guess I found out too late." Ashe felt his face grow hot and his eyes burn.

Pat looked up at the ceiling and seemed to be mulling over whether to say something or not. Ashe knew he would decide to go ahead, which was the default for Pat.

"You won't like what I have to say about her," Pat said.

"You'll tell me anyway," Ashe said and shrugged. He thought about another drink but it wasn't worth the energy to get up.

"I've held this back because I didn't think it mattered and I knew you were all hung up on her, but the other day when we were here, she kinda left out some stuff."

Ashe waited.

"So, I guess while you were in the hospital and the stateys were working the crime scene by Roger's Café, they found a video from a bank surveillance camera that showed a fourth man all right," Pat said.

"Yeah, I heard Price mention that video to Phillip Crews. I wasn't sure if it was a bluff or not, but I haven't seen it."

"They won't show it to you yet. They were waiting for you to ID the fourth guy without polluting your memory with the video."

Ashe considered that. It's what he would have done too.

"Plus, despite you thinking you're all clever about it, they know you have a weak spot for Stevie. Probably they don't figure you're as over the damn moon for her as you are, but Price and Hume, they are aware of it."

"My head hurts. What does the video show?"

Pat seemed to think about that for a long minute then said, "He comes out of a shadowed area we can't see clearly and approaches you after you're hit in the head and on the ground. Stevie comes out and yells something, we can see that clear enough but there's no audio. Then, and I laugh every time I see this, she throws one of her shoes at him. He gets up and leaves," Pat explained. "Then the crowd pours out of the diner and she throws her other shoe at Paul Milton."

"She didn't say anything about that the other day," Ashe said and rubbed his head. "I forget if I told her then if I thought there was a fourth guy or not."

"Me neither, but in her statement to Hume, she does admit she saw the fourth guy. She says it was CJ Portals and she yelled and threw her shoe to stop him."

I knew it. "Well, that's my girl I guess."

"Or not," Pat said. "Nobody else recalls seeing him and nobody at the scene says she told them she'd seen CJ crouched over you at the time. When interviewed the first time, that night, she didn't mention him."

Ashe stopped rubbing his head suddenly. "Wait, what?"

"She had a thousand opportunities to tell us he was there. She's even talked with you several times. She ever bring him up to you? Now what I don't know, and nobody knows for sure is, if she's telling the truth."

"I don't get you, the video…"

Pat waved a hand as if to clear unseen smoke. "Was she yelling and throwing her first shoe to stop him from hurting you…or was she warning him to run because the crowd was coming. There's enough of a pause in her action there on video to raise the doubt."

They sat quietly for a few minutes then Ashe picked up the pillow that was under his elbow on the sofa and threw it across the room.

"Yeah," Pat said. "It's why I left the other day. I didn't want to sit there and watch her with you, knowing she may have covered up for CJ and even led him to you."

"I can't believe that. That night I was ambushed; she was yelling my name. Not his, *my* name. She even yelled to 'look out' behind me."

Pat seemed to consider this but said, "We have her statement and the video and they seem to match. But, old buddy, this is me, I got a bad feeling about her loyalties. Sorry."

"Nah, don't be sorry. I appreciate you having my back. Besides, I pretty much know she and I are never going to make it."

Ashe was lying. He was dying inside for them to be. Intellectually he might have known it was very long odds they'd wind up together. In fact, he wasn't sure he could ever trust her completely.

He couldn't stop himself. Staring at her empty glass, still noticing her scent on the couch, he kept working her up differently in his mind as his loving, caring, woman. Truth be told, she was all that, and somewhere deep inside, he believed she was fighting for him as much as he fought for her.

But. *But.*

There was always going to be that *but* when he created their life together in his mind. He wanted her. That was it. But he couldn't feel certain *he* was enough for her.

I'm old, she's young. She came to me when she was a drunk.

Then the thought that had lingered in the rear most places of his mind walked up.

When she sobered up, she didn't choose me.

Pat must have sensed his old friend's mood and leaned over and grabbed Ashe's shoulder. "Sorry to drop that on you. It's what it is, Chig. I know it's no fun to hear."

"No. But you always tell me the facts, buddy."

"God knows you been through a lot in the past three years, much less these past few weeks."

"Well regardless of what *I* have gone through, I can't help but think about Billy Clark's family. How this will forever change the lives of those kids? I think we both know the answer to that. And all because I get asked to poke around Georgia's Murphy's cold case. Like a damn hobby, I poked. I had no real idea what I was doing and now a good man, a family man, is dead."

"That's not on you. Look, if you *hadn't* dug into this, we'd be nowhere. Remember Georgia Murphy, her family deserves to know what happened to her. Maybe now they will."

Family, Ashe thought. Something about that bugged him.

Pat continued. "We should bring in CJ Portals any time now. And for Clark? I think you got two of them right off, by God, and the crowd at Roger's nabbed the other one."

"Well, I want one more man," Ashe said, and thought of Mark Portals.

Pat knew who he meant. "You think you can get him? Okay, I'm with you."

Ashe dragged himself upward to stand, his head and whole body complaining, only making it through the force of his stubbornness.

"So, you asked if I was okay? *Hell no,* I'm not okay. I'm pissed off, Pat." Ashe walked off to go to bed. The mantle clock rang nine p.m.

Mark Portals swished his iced diet cola around in his glass. He was at the state capitol for meetings and was asked to come to see his old college comrade after hours.

"You're in a bad way, my friend," Rollin Ashad said. As state assistant attorney general, he had rearranged his crushing calendar of appointments just to meet Mark this late.

"I have done nothing wrong, Rollin. There were some critical decisions that had to be made along the way, some regrettable, but nothing…and I mean *nothing* can be tied to me," Mark said.

"Your firm, your responsibility," Ashad said. He stood and dragged a chair over closer to Mark.

"I know, I know, but everything has been set up to point to Stephanie Collins and my nephew CJ. My name is not on anything remotely illea…ah, *inappropriate*."

"Ms. Collins has turned state's evidence. The DA down there approved an offer of immunity for her. Perhaps a little ill-advised, but she will testify and allegedly has records."

"About what?" Mark snapped, then reined himself back in. "That I was working a project to bring hundreds of jobs and hundreds of thousands in tax revenue to Hurrt County? Hell, Rollin, I've done considerably less business maneuvering than those guys who brought in the paper company years ago. They actually *ran* people off their land! These few people inconvenienced in Hurrt County and Seacord *made* money. They were paid and *agreed* to sell."

"Uh-huh," Ashad started before Mark cut him off.

"And that water park over in Carson County! They had to bribe a state legislator over that!"

"Mark, none of those examples resulted in the deaths of people involved! This woman a couple of years ago, that deputy!"

"None of which I had anything to do with!" Mark shouted, but even to himself, he sounded a little less than perfectly confident.

"Still, they will tar you. There's a search warrant that I sat on until we could talk, but I really can't hold it up any longer. At the request of the DA down there, the state police sent a Special Agent...ah." Ashad looked back at his desk to his notes. "Rachel Hume. She has the Fraud Unit and they will be at your office in the a.m."

Mark smiled a little inside. *That won't go far.*

"They'll come up dry. They'll waste hours of time and a lot of your money to discover just what I've told you. Any evidence of land fraud points only to Ms. Collins and my nephew."

"But," Ashad pressed, "it *will* waste time. Time, we do not have."

Mark finished his cola and set his glass aside. He realized that *this* was the same conversation he'd had with CJ only a day or so ago.

"What do we do?" he said after a minute.

"Well, first, take a back seat with DBA. Do it publicly and the local group of investors will back you. Hell, I'll back you up."

Mark sighed. He knew where this was going.

"We'll get someone else to take over as legal consultant to DBA. You'll still make out."

"As will you," Mark said as a reminder.

"Sure. Just take a different role. Everyone will understand. You make it like you are *recusing* yourself voluntarily. Fully aware of how bad things look, you are being unselfish," Ashad said.

"Doorbella?" Mark asked.

"To them you are just another lawyer—no offense—but we can bring in a clean face probably without their even noticing too much."

"I'm still a heavy investor, I have..."

Ashad patted Mark's leg roughly, collegiately. "Sure, sure. You're not out, just elevated to ah, a more *senior* role. Everything you've done, all the resources you've committed so far are protected."

Mark drew in a deep breath. This was actually better news than he'd expected.

"Okay, fine. So, Rollin, how do we clean this up before they arrive next week?"

Ashad looked at Mark with the immutable face that had worked on politicians and criminals alike for years. "I assume you know what must be done."

Mark nodded. "CJ."

"But not a finger on Ms. Collins. We cannot afford that. She's going to have to pay for what she's done, especially once it's public how she manipulated landowners down there."

"No, of course. I understand."

"We can marginalize her easily enough. But there's been too much loss of life connected with this. Mark, I mean it. Rein in your wild hog nephew!"

"There's this Ashe. He's from a longtime Hurrt County family. He's been the one to..."

"Yes, I know Lieutenant Ashe and worked with him when he was the Metro MCU boss and I was the ADA here. You be careful, he's smart and can be dangerous as you've seen."

"He is...tenacious," Mark admitted. "And a pain in the neck."

"Forget him. But now to Phillip Crews," Ashad said.

"Fuck him."

"No, he'll have to answer somehow, someday himself, but you put him front and center with the DBA board and they love him. He's our guy for now."

"I don't believe he is anymore. I think he's figured this out and is going soft on us."

"I tell you what. I'll meet with him in private. He'll come

around. So, are we set?"

Mark thought about his position. He knew he had prepped CJ for this, but here they were. Right on the ragged edge of it.

"Shit," Mark said softly. "My nephew in prison, Phillip Crews and Collins go free…"

"And you're free, untarnished. Your nephew will be out in seven to eight years, and be a rich man. So will we."

"Hmm, with the judges I know, more like fifteen years."

Ashad held his stoic face and stared at Mark. Mark also had practiced such a face, but he couldn't find it now that he needed it.

"Okay. You want to roll those dice, Mark, roll them. We go to trial. You're a good trial lawyer, but who do you trust to represent you that's as good as you? Everything I've said will come true except that you will face public humiliation, disbarment, be sued by our investors, oh, and you'd be broke on top of all that. Maybe, just maybe, even jailed."

"Ha! I think not."

"Maybe so, maybe no." Ashad held his forceful gaze on Mark.

"You'll be broke as well," was all Mark could come up with. Then after a few seconds, he figured out another angle. "Why is all the bad news on my side of things? Why isn't anyone else having to suffer?"

Ashad never moved. "Well, let's calculate that. You gave a free hand in our two hundred and fifty-million-dollar deal to a cheap thug like your nephew. Scrape him off, Mark. Let me clean-up Doorbella, but you have to step aside and wash your hands of a common bloodsucker like CJ Portals."

Mark only nodded before he pulled out one last card he held.

"Throw me one bone. My brother Dale has served nine years of his sentence. He's a nonviolent businessman, never harmed anyone. Grant his parole, give me that."

Ashad's face finally cracked. He smiled warmly and went back over to his desk.

"Done, but he's your responsibility. And, your nephew will have to plea, I want no trial."

"I'll handle CJ. I get my percentage of DBA. The SCEA isn't connected to DBA so that's mine."

"Well…just be sure you wash it well. And get CJ nailed down. Now."

Ashad sat at his desk and started to go back to work. Mark knew this was a not-so-subtle cue the meeting was over.

But he hated leaving any negotiation where he didn't come out at least even.

"Yeah, I can see why that would be important to you. CJ all tied up," Mark said.

Ashad ignored him.

"I mean, given I hear you're the lead contender for deputy AG next month. That's a hell of a promotion. A much more powerful position."

Ashad never stopped writing or looked up. "Maybe you should remember that, Mister Portals."

Mark didn't press his luck. He wanted to remain friends with Rollin, so he turned and left his office.

He checked his phone for emails or texts and noticed it was nine p.m.

CHAPTER 24

Ashe felt himself awaken softly, slowly. It was still dark and he sensed it was too early to get up, so he didn't move but opened his eyes a little. His head didn't hurt and that was a blessing, so he took extra care not to move it at all.

As he lay there, half awake, he heard his father's morning rumblings in the den. Small noises; the creak of the leather chair where he sat, the shuffling of his slippers against the wood floor, the rattle of his coffee mug on a ceramic coaster. It was his dad's favorite room, where he'd hung his fishing trophies and had shelves of old hardbound books.

It was comforting to Ashe to hear the everyday sounds of his home. His mother would be in the kitchen where after the coffee was made and its scent filled the house, there would be biscuits or French toast. Country ham or bacon, too. After a second of listening, there in his bed, Ashe thought he heard the refrigerator open and close. Not his, but the old one from his youth, with the big silver handle that hinged at the top. A second later, a big glass bowl being set, just so, on an old linoleum counter with grooved aluminum edging.

He rose, carefully, not wanting to break this bubble of time and stepped as quietly as he could to the hall and toward the den. He knew if he made the slightest sound, like so much steam on a bathroom mirror, this moment would vanish. In his mind, he prayed his cell phone didn't go off, as such a thing would be out of time, and thus it would send this warm and comfortable place away.

He stood at the doorway to the den and cautiously leaned in to see. From the corner of his eye, he could see the kitchen to his left and heard a drawer open followed by the clatter of silverware. He caught just a glimpse, just a quarter second of the back of an old-but-still-blonde woman with her hair up, wearing a soft fuzzy bathrobe as she stepped toward the old stove and out of his view.

Mom.

In front of Ashe in the den was a big burgundy leather chair lined with dull tarnished brass tacks. His father sat, his back to Ashe, and reached over to a scarred oak end table and lifted a mug of coffee. Ashe could smell the coffee and then abruptly got a face full of the strong smell of smoke, as if from the fireplace over in the living room.

Through the walls, Ashe heard a toilet flush and knew that was Pat. His father heard it too and turned to look at the wall separating the den from the guest bath.

This can't be right. Ashe held his breath for several seconds, hoping to stay here in this moment, afraid it would disappear, but his father just went back to his coffee. So, slowly he stepped into the room, expecting, yet hoping against, its vanishing.

His father set the coffee back on the table. Ashe stepped forward again, wanting to see his face. He could hear the chair creak softly, but he could not see his father's face.

"No, Chig," his father said. *"You can't be here, son."*

Ashe snapped fully awake. He was in his bedroom sitting in a chair and couldn't remember how he got there.

The realization of the present swept over him, and from a long-ago sadness of the child inside him came the desire to cry. Cry for his parents he longed for and loved, now departed. His mom had been gone for twenty years. His dad, nearly two.

Down the hall, the shower in the guest bath started so he knew Pat was up. He rubbed his face and remembered where and when he was. He got up himself and after using the toilet, he looked at his face in the mirror and saw he wasn't eleven years old but almost fifty years older. Staring at himself didn't accomplish anything, so he pulled on a T-shirt and went to make coffee.

Did that just happen? It couldn't have, it was a dream, he told himself. *But I heard Pat in the bathroom.* He listened as he went by the guest bath and could still hear Pat inside.

From the kitchen, he heard the mantle clock in the living room chime and knew it was five a.m. The odor of the coffee he made brought back all the eerie feel of that brief-but-still-acutely material time he had just experienced.

Did I dream it?

It had felt so tangible, as if he could have stroked his mother's hair, tasted her cooking, held his father's hand. *But why?* There was no cryptic warning of things to come from his father, just his brief admonition not to linger where *he* was out of time. If this had been a dream, why not see their faces? If this was a visit from the beyond, and just the thought of that made his skin tingle, then why present just the smallest, most innocuous of morning routines. It was like a recording from fifty years ago.

Except Dad had reacted to the sound of Pat in the bathroom.

And what his father had said, about not being there. He'd addressed Ashe as he was, an adult, not as if he was still a child in their time.

Ashe felt a shudder rise from his spine and vibrate around his chest and shoulders. It was more than he wanted to think about right then, so as he tried to shake it off. He sipped his black coffee and looked around for his cell. He could tell Pat was done in the shower so he decided to go ahead himself. As he passed the den again looking for his phone, for just for a heartbeat, maybe less, and only from the corner of his eye, he saw the old chair back in its old place. The walls were cedar paneled like in the time before. He jerked his head to see, but no. It was the remodeled den he'd done himself over the Covid lockdown. He took in a still-shaky breath and retrieved his phone from beside his bed.

"You up?" Pat shouted.

"I hope so. Coffee's done," Ashe answered as he checked his messages.

There were four texts, including a couple from Stevie. He ignored those. The rest were from Sheriff Jacobs.

L Burnt, one said, following by *LnT burn 2 GRND*. The texts were from nine-to-nine fifteen p.m. the night before. Right as he'd gone to bed.

"Hey, Pat!" Ashe yelled. "Check this out."

The texts from Stevie were, *LandT gone. Call me*, the first one said.

No, I don't think I will yet, Ashe thought. Pat had made him see things with her slightly differently.

The second one was, *CJ texting me. Covering his tracks. B*

Careful.

No shit, lady. Ashe knew who she meant.

"Hey, Chig, Price wants a meeting of everyone involved this morning at ten a.m.," Pat shouted from the kitchen. He had been checking his phone too.

"Give me ten minutes and we'll roll out. I want to see this," Ashe said.

"Meet you at my car!" Pat said.

It was still dark out as they arrived in town. Firefighters and their apparatus still occupied a full half of the town square, and a small crowd stood back on the courthouse grass and talked and pointed. Most shook their heads and gestured with large and wide motions, possibly to equal the shock and seriousness of the scene they were witnessing.

Through the steam produced by the chilly air and fire hoses still raining onto the open lot, Ashe could see the Hurrt County Land and Title was no more. Firefighters poked with long poles through the debris while others were securing equipment. Small piles of blocks and pieces of charred material and wood were all that was left to mark its grave. A few random threads of gray smoke rose like ghosts leaving its body.

Ashe and Pat parked and walked around the back of the courthouse to get to the other side and see the loss from another angle. That's when Ashe saw some damage to Harold Marsh's building which had shared a wall with the L&T. He hoped everything inside was okay.

"Ashe! Pat!" he heard Jacobs call out. The sheriff came out of Roger's Café and jogged over to where they stood with a large coffee in his hand.

"Sheriff, why didn't you call me?" Ashe said a little harder than he meant to.

Jacobs seemed caught off guard by that. "Why would I? You going to come help put it out?" he said and chuckled. Pat shook his head at his old friend and took out his cell phone to make a call.

"Besides, your head was killing you last night," Jacobs continued. "You needed to take a knee."

Ashe drew in a breath and held up his hands. "Sorry."

"So. How is your head this morning?" Jacobs asked.

Ashe hadn't even thought about it. In his dream, it was fine. "I think it actually feels a lot better." Then he said, "Let me guess, Sheriff, everything about DBA and all those boxes of records I saw being packed up, the ones that Rachel subpoenaed, are all gone."

"We won't know until we get with Mark Portals and Phillip Crews and their staff, as silly as that sounds, but I'd take a wild-ass guess and say, *yeah*, they are gone. You know we're meeting with Price and AAG Ashad this morning."

"Yeah, Pat told me." Then Ashe had a thought. "Sheriff, where is Susan Marlin?"

"*That* was my biggest fear last night when this started," Jacobs said. "The fire chief said they have not found any bodies in the rubble. Yet. You can see they're still searching the site. I actually think Phillip Crews was with her last and…"

They had to step back several feet for a group of firefighters to hose off the street of some burnt rubble. As they did so, a full and powerfully pungent smell of fire and smoke seemed to hit Ashe in the face.

Exactly like this morning.

Jacobs continued, "Anyway, the chief says its likely arson but they can't be sure until the state fire marshal's office arrives."

"I think we better be sure she's safe, Sheriff. With the L&T gone, her memory would be dangerous for some people to leave just walking around."

Jacobs agreed as Pat walked over and hung up his phone.

"I just talked to Rachel, uh, *Agent Hume*," he said. "She has Susan Marlin with her and should get here any minute."

"Oh, good," Jacobs said.

"Yeah, as soon as news of the fire got around, she went to where Susan said she'd be staying and took her into protective custody," Pat said.

"Sheriff, Stevie is getting texts from CJ. Can you get a subpoena for his cell company and locate him that way?"

Jacobs looked at Ashe. "I told you we'd done that already. He must be using more than one prepaid phone and switching between them."

"You told me that?"

"Uh-huh."

"Oh, well good," Ashe said.

Ashe watched the firefighters work and started thinking. They'd tried for him, killed Billy Clark. Then they'd burned the Land and Title after conveniently boxing up everything, so there was only Susan left to describe how the land had parceled. Then Ashe had another thought.

There's one other thing they'd have to cover up, he realized, and a bolt of electricity seemed to run through him.

"Pat! Stay here and get with Rachel and Susan Marlin when they arrive. See if she can remember exactly where at the DBA construction site they contracted concrete with CJ's Concrete Crew."

"But…" Pat started to object as Ashe turned and looked for Pat's Dodge SUV.

"Sheriff, get a hold of Harold Marsh, and see if Stevie is safe. She needs protection even more now," Ashe added. "We may need state protection for her as well!"

Jacobs and Pat looked at each other as if surprised.

"Also, we need to know if the records Stevie said she'd kept were in the old judge's office building and got damaged. By the fire or the water fighting it," Ashe said.

"Okay, but just where the hell are you going?" Pat demanded to know.

"Are your keys in your vehicle?" Ashe asked, spotting where they parked.

"Hold it!" Jacobs yelled. He and Pat stepped over and in front of Ashe.

Ashe glared at them both and pointed at the smoking gap where the title company had been. "Don't you see? They figure the gig is up. They know that Milton and Tracy talked, and Stevie too. By now, they know we've got the camera. They're covering their damn tracks and destroying any evidence!"

"Ah, yeah. Susan and Stevie," Jacobs said. "And Tracy too, if she makes bond."

"I'm going to look at one last thing they'd need to cover it all up," Ashe said.

Pat shook his head. "You're not going anywhere, Chig. Did you forget? You're not the lead investigator anymore; you're a victim and a witness."

"He's right, Ashe," Jacobs said. "They may try for *you* again too."

Ashe sighed. If he was right in what he suspected, they might be too late already.

"Okay fine, dammit, fine. Pat, you come with me. Sheriff, can you talk to Rachel and Marsh and call me when you do?"

"Sure, and I can do one better," he said and took his radio off his hip and called for a deputy to meet him on the square. "I think I know where you're headed and you'll need someone to show you where it's at!"

Pat drove, so Ashe decided to text Stevie back. True, he was a little unsteady as to her trustworthiness, but he didn't want her hurt.

Are U safe? he texted, then set his phone on his lap.

"You think they'd try to move her? You know we're assuming she's out here only based on what Paul Milton told us," Pat said.

"Susan Marlin showed me on one of her wall maps where they'd poured concrete to demonstrate to some investors that DBA was serious, or something of the sort. Anyway, all the current work is contracted locally, but one of those concrete pads back a couple of years ago was done by…"

"CJ Portals' Concrete Crew," Pat finished. "Georgia Murphy buried out there. Shit."

"Yep. I'm hoping they haven't already tried to move her."

A deputy sheriff in a marked Dodge Charger pulled past them and flashed his overhead lights, so they fell in behind him.

After about fifteen minutes, the deputy turned left down a long asphalted four-lane road that went through a huge cut in the tall pines. The road was lined with signs notifying them this was private property.

Pat frowned. "We'll need a warrant."

"After that fire, I think we can say 'exigent circumstances' are present where evidence in a capital case is in danger of being destroyed."

"Ok, maybe. But for how much and how long though? You know what it will take to find a body under…whoa!"

As they approached down the paved road, the woods on either side suddenly fell back and widened into a huge open area the size of several stadium parking lots. Ashe guessed it could be more than a half mile wide and deeper than he could see.

The deputy didn't slow down but continued driving on the pavement for several more minutes, which impressed Ashe as it illustrated the size of the place. After a time, the deputy pulled over near a couple of work trucks. A few men stood around them in work clothes sipping coffee, as it was still early, and appeared to take notice of the patrol car. Pat pulled in behind the cruiser.

It was breaking dawn as Ashe and Pat walked up to the deputy who said his name was Dawson—Ashe hadn't formally met him, but he was the surly one from when Ashe had first walked into the jail. Dawson had only gotten sketchy information from Sheriff Jacobs, so Ashe quickly outlined what was going on and what he expected the deputy to do out here. One of the workers walked over as they finished talking.

"Hey, uh, what's up?" the man asked, a cup of coffee in one hand and a cigarette in the other. He was short, about 5'6 and built stocky but with powerful-looking forearms.

"You in charge here?" Ashe asked and showed the man his badge.

"Of this grading crew, yeah." He then pointed across the long flat field toward a man behind a surveyor's level transit on a tripod. "I'm Mike. That guy over there is William something-or-other. He's surveying the area we have to grade next. He's in charge of himself."

Ashe saw there were four other men leaning on the bed of a truck drinking coffee and some were smoking. A big grader and an excavator sat idle nearby. They all had on hard hats and reflective vests, and one or two were taking great pains to see to it that Deputy Dawson didn't look at their faces.

"So, you the law. What's going on? Big murder case?" Mike said with a grin. The men behind him laughed. He swapped out drinking coffee with inhaling his cigarette.

"As a matter of fact, yes," Pat said. "A murder of a woman that may have taken place right here. A particularly brutal one."

The men stopped laughing.

"Mike, if you have time," Ashe cut in. "We're here on official business investigating a probable murder. Would you walk us over to William?"

Mike threw his coffee out of the cup and tossed it into the bed of the truck. "Sure, hang on," he said. Then to the others, "You hands know what to do, get that first pile moving and that track claw into position!"

The men nodded and mumbled and began to file away. Ashe looked at Deputy Dawson and nodded to him, having given him his instructions. *No one comes, no one goes.* Dawson nodded back.

Mike, Pat, and Ashe walked across the patchy dirt and sparse grass until after about forty yards, they came to a huge concrete pad and stepped up onto it. Rebars stuck up here and there in a pattern and some big six-inch PVC piping also rose above the pad. Ashe had seen how thick this pad was above ground; he estimated eight inches, but there was no telling how much more was below the surface. The pad was in large sections and stretched for hundreds of yards in all directions.

William Something-or-other was watching them approach and talked into a small radio clipped to his vest. In the distance, his assistant with a surveying rod waved back.

"You men are supposed to have hard hats!" he shouted. He was taller than Ashe, maybe 6'1 and had on well-worn chinos under a denim-looking shirt that he had half rolled up the sleeves. His face and forearms were still tanned even this time of year.

Mike said, "Whoops, I'll get you some." And trotted back toward his truck.

"This is a work site, who are you?" William asked when they got close, so Ashe and Pat showed their badges to him.

"I'm with Hurrt County Sheriff's Office and this is Lt. Keagan of Metro Homicide."

"Homicide?"

"You're surveying this area for DBA?" Ashe continued.

"No, I work for myself, Simmons Surveying," he said. "I'm Will Simmons. Midstate Construction hired me to help with a few problem areas out here."

"How long have you worked out here?" Pat asked.

Will shrugged. "Three weeks this year."

"*This* year?" Pat asked.

"A couple of weeks a few years ago too. They had issues

they're trying hard to fix."

"*They* being…" Ashe asked.

"Midstate, like I said. Hey, what's all this about a homicide?"

Ashe hadn't brought his portfolio but fished a pen and piece of paper out of his jacket pocket. "So you don't work for DBA?"

"Heard of them, but they likely subbed this part to Midstate," Will said.

"You said there was a problem," Pat said. "What is the problem you're helping them fix?"

Will thought about that for a beat then said, "Uh, do you guys need to have a paper or a warrant or something?"

Pat walked up to Will and put a hand on his shoulder. "Sure, sure, but right now, we have probable cause to believe the dead body of a murdered woman is buried somewhere out here. So Deputy Ashe here and I want to get the lay of things."

"You wouldn't know anything about that, would you?" Ashe asked.

"No shit? Out here? Hell no, I don't know anything about that!" Will said and laughed nervously.

"You been out here every day for three weeks. You seen any disturbed ground, broken concrete? Anyone hanging around without a hard hat?" Ashe pressed.

"No, no, nothing funny. There have been days when just me and my assistant have been out here."

"So what's the problem?" Pat asked, his big paw still on Will's shoulder.

Will leaned in and motioned Ashe closer. "If I tell you anything, you have to say you didn't hear it from me?"

"Maybe," Pat answered. "Try us."

Will looked around. Mike was still pretty far off with the hard hats.

"Sinkhole," Will said in a low voice.

"No shit?" Pat said.

"No shit," Will answered.

Well, that would be bad news to Mr. Portals, Ashe thought. *And maybe bad luck for Georgia Murphy.*

Mike arrived with a pair of hard hats and as they put them on, Will said, "Thanks, Mike. That's all."

Mike looked a little disappointed, like he wanted to be in on the murdered lady deal, but turned and went back toward his men.

"So," Pat started back up. "Sinkhole, eh? Big one?"

"Forty-five feet across and nearly twice that in depth. Midstate brought in sixteen big dump trucks of fill dirt and general construction debris from as far away as Metro to the North and McCormick City to the East. All trying to fill it in."

Pat whistled, "Whoa!"

"Did they?" Ashe asked. "Get it filled in?"

As an answer, Will pointed, and they followed him a couple of hundred yards to one corner of the giant pad. About another fifty yards off it was a second concrete pad, heavily cracked and broken and obviously caving in on itself.

"They tried," Will said. "Then they poured a huge amount of concrete on top of their fill. Finally stretched heavy rebar racks and even steel plating before pouring that pad."

"It looks like a total bust," Pat said.

"Between us? I can't lose my job over this; I had nothing to do with it. But it was stupid and no respectable company would even try it."

Ashe thought, *Lord, if she's buried under tons of concrete and sixteen trucks of dirt and fill, she will never be found.*

"Let me guess, The Concrete Crew, LLC. Right?" Ashe asked.

"Huh? No, it was Midstate using a local concrete company," Will said.

"How long ago was this?" Pat asked.

"Two, maybe two and a half years ago. It breaks up a little more every month," Will said. "So they moved the whole thing over this far. Had a specialist come in and actually test the area first."

"So this big pad, it's good to go?"

Will shrugged and walked over a few yards and pointed at the big pad with his toe. There was some settling, cracking in a few areas.

"You see this part for yourself. A sinkhole like that is typical for this part of the county. Too much underground water running. Moving the pad a few yards is nothing. I give this thing another year or so."

Pat and Ashe looked at each other, and Ashe figured they were thinking the same thing. A year or so is all they'd need to sell it all off to Doorbella.

Ashe and Pat walked off to themselves for a minute to talk.

"Shit, Chig, if she's under there," Pat said.

"No, I don't think so. CJ wouldn't leave getting rid of her to some other contractor."

"So, crap! Look at all this. We could search for years," Pat said and gestured at the whole area.

Ashe had a thought. "Hey, Will. I mentioned The Concrete Crew a minute ago. You ever heard of them?"

Will took off his hard hat and scratched his head. "Yeah. Crew out of the city. They did a test pour a couple of years ago. I surveyed that area."

"Where?" Ashe asked.

"Okay now, look west. See where our pad ends, then another big one is beyond that? Now look to the end of that one and to the right, closer to the woods, out there is a water reclamation pool. They poured that I believe."

"How far *is* that?" Pat asked. He had his hands cupped over his eyes trying to see it.

"Maybe three quarters of a mile."

"C'mon, Will. Let's drive down there and you can show us," Pat said.

"I don't know if I should..."

"Ah, come on. We'll do our best to keep you out of it," Pat assured him.

They got back to their vehicles and Will hopped in one of the trucks. Pat drove and Ashe got on his radio and called Jacobs to update him.

"Bring Rachel out here, we may be onto something," he told him, then looked at his watch. Eight a.m. "We'll also need another person to secure this site." Ashe was hoping he could walk into Price's meeting with something more than they already had.

"I'll be enroute myself," Jacobs said excitedly.

At the place Will had described was a large sunken concrete structure that was below the surface, with walls and a curvature that resembled, of all things, a huge swimming pool. It was twenty yards across and over fifty long. The shallowest part was maybe six feet deep and it sloped down smartly, unlike a swimming pool, to an end depth of nearly twenty feet. From shallow to the deepest end, this "pool" had a nearly forty-five-degree down angle.

"And this would do what?" Ashe asked Will.

"I don't know for sure, but just me guessing," he said, turning and gesturing behind him. "Imagine a three-story HVAC water chiller system. This pool would hold the overflow and then be pumped back around…somehow to somewhere. You'll have to get a guy that knows that stuff to better describe it."

"And The Concrete Crew from Metro, they poured this?"

"Yeah. Two years ago, I think. Some of the first work out here. But they must have screwed it up, because they weren't hired back."

"Pat," Ashe said.

"Yeah, I think you're right," Pat said, and pointed right at the deepest part. "Hey, Will, how thick is that concrete down there?"

"I don't know. I'd guess two feet maybe. There'd be a record and engineering diagram at the company that did the pour."

"You know a Carl Jack Portals?" Ashe asked.

Will looked completely unhappy. He seemed to know he was getting in deeper and deeper into something he had no desire to be a part of.

"Yeah," he finally said. "But just by name, I maybe met him once."

Will Simmons stared at the pool with them for a beat then added in a melancholier voice than before, "Okay. you know you asked if I knew anybody had been out here? I didn't think of it until just now, but a couple days ago, he was out here. Right over there."

"CJ Portals? Here?" Pat pointed at the ground. "This end of the site?"

"Yeah, he had a Tahoe and parked right over there."

Will pointed behind them a few yards, and Pat walked over to where Will had indicated, kneeling down and looking at the dried mud.

"Chig, new-looking tire tracks in dried mud from when it rained the other day. Could be something," Pat said.

"Something all right," Ashe said. Then to Will, "What was he doing?"

"Well, I didn't watch him or anything, but…nothing really. I guess now I say it out loud, it does seem strange for him to drive all the way out here and just stand around and stare at this pour.

Kinda like us. Just stared for several minutes then left."

A cold steel hand seemed to touch Ashe at the base of his spine and it traced a line up his back.

This was it. Every instinct Ashe had was certain of it.

Georgia found out about the sinkholes. She tried to make something of it, maybe blackmailed CJ Portals, Stevie had guessed as much.

But he knew it had gone badly for Georgia.

They knew she and Tony were getting back together. They had lied about the divorce. Tony worked for CJ in Metro and she must have told him about this. They set Tony up to put him away then tried to silence Georgia.

That had gone worse for her.

"Okay, Will, these other guys see him?" Ashe asked as he took out his phone and walked off to try to get a better signal.

"I doubt it," Will said.

"Will, don't wander off, and get your assistant over here so we can talk to him," Ashe said. "And, Pat, I'm calling Rachel and the sheriff. We're going to be late for that meeting."

Ashe took out his cell and walked off as he tried to make a call. He looked back and saw Will kick a clump of mud in frustration and turn to Pat.

He overheard Will say, "Does that old man always just order people around like that?"

Pat grinned. "Boy, let me tell you something. When he's on the hunt, he's as hard as woodpecker lips."

CHAPTER 25

In a half hour, Rachel Hume and Sheriff Jacobs arrived with two uniformed state troopers and another deputy sheriff in tow, which appeared to cause much concern among the workers working with Mike.

"This is it? You sure? Georgia is here?" Jacobs asked, almost nervously.

They stood around the big concrete "pool" as they'd started calling it, staring at it like Will Simmons had described CJ had done.

"What will we need to be sure?" Jacobs said.

"Ground penetrating radar, for one," Ashe said. "Agent...ah, Rachel! Do you know anything about a body in concrete?"

She had been trying to talk on her phone with her boss and only having intermittent success, so she was talking to Pat a few yards away. They both walked over.

"I'm...not sure. I think depending on the concrete itself and how a body is covered with it, we might be able to get DNA. It might, in fact, be fairly intact after two years compared to being buried underground. But I've never..."

"Yeah. Neither have I," Ashe said.

"What about a cadaver dog?" Pat added.

"Through concrete?" Jacobs asked.

"Maybe," Rachel said, staring and tapping on her phone. "I'll have to ask an expert. No damn signal out here though."

"I'll drive you back to the road; you get a signal there I think," Pat offered. "And I'll call Danny Breslin. He'd want in on this."

Ashe noted with a small internal smile that Pat volunteered to help her and she immediately agreed.

"Ashe, you think a damn dog can sniff a two-year-old corpse

from under this thick concrete?" Jacobs asked.

"I think concrete is porous and a decaying body releases gas that has to escape. So, maybe."

"Well I know what we can do in the meantime," Jacobs said and waved his deputies over.

In a few minutes, they had crime scene tape out and, not sure where in the large pool area her body might be, surrounded the whole area using long pieces of wrought iron they found as stanchions. At one end, they tied the tape to the rear of a cruiser Jacobs set up as the sole entry point to the scene. He posted Deputy Dawson there who started a log of who came and went and at what time.

The second deputy, Big Ed Bell, got a camera and started taking photographs of the undisturbed area.

"Good job, Sheriff," Ashe said. "Have everyone be very careful where they step."

"I watch and learn," Jacobs said, then appeared to suddenly have another thought. He went to his car and reached for his radio mic.

"Let's get some other folks off the bench," was all he said to Ashe.

In another half hour, Rachel had all the construction team as well as Will and his assistant separated and one at a time, she and Pat began to interview them and get their full information. A couple of the construction team declined and started to try and walk off, but Bell blocked their path, and through his serious demeanor or maybe the observed size of his boots, he silently convinced them to cooperate.

Ashe was feeling useless, not having a specific task to do, so he stayed near the entry to the possible crime scene and observed.

Looking at the construction team, he felt confident they wouldn't have had anything to do with burying anybody and those that were nervous likely had a legal paper on them at the jail. Will was straight up and provided critical information as to this pool that the Concrete Crew had poured, and that CJ Portals had visited personally and recently.

By itself, CJ having been out here staring at the pool proved nothing. He could always say he was checking on the quality of his company's work after a couple of years.

But taking into consideration his coming out here along with the resurgent investigation into Georgia Murphy's disappearance that he certainly knew about, and his trying to obfuscate Ashe's own inquiry, totaled up to hinky. Factor in the fellow suspect statements as to CJ directing how to dispose of Billy Clark's body in concrete, and criminal conversations with Tracy Davis, then revisiting the scene of the crime might be damning to a jury.

Not to mention the threats, the probable arson of the L&T, and hell, the attempt on *his* life.

He checked his phone and saw a text reply from Stevie. *I am good 4 now.*

Ashe's thoughts were interrupted by the arrival at the pool area of a blue correctional van and a black Explorer. They must have been cleared by the trooper back at the road and they parked where Jacobs had set up a designated area for parking.

From the Explorer, John Price, a distinguished-looking man Ashe didn't know, and Captain Speakes from Metro Police got out. Speakes was likely here to see why his case was being bounced back to Hurrt County and, if Ashe knew him at all, to also check up on why Pat and Breslin had spent so much time here.

"Agent Hume, Lieutenant Ashe!" Price called out and waved them over.

"*Mister* Ashe," Speakes corrected.

Ashe started over and then became aware that he'd dressed hurriedly this morning. He had on jeans and a T-shirt under a half-zip gray wool pullover and a TAG, LLC ball cap. His navy Brooks running shoes were caked in mud. *Ah well, I'm retired. I'm just Mister Ashe.*

"Gentlemen," he said and shook hands. Speakes was less than enthusiastic about that.

"Ashe, this is our Circuit Court Judge, Timothy Brad Fowler. After talking with Agent Hume, I wanted him to see what we had so far to apply for a search warrant. He agreed to come see the scene himself. I assume you know Captain Speakes."

"Yes, we came up through the ranks together," Ashe replied.

"I'm familiar with Lieutenant Ashe from his work as a detective in Metro," the judge said.

Jacobs, Pat, and Rachel joined them, then Pat and his captain walked away to talk.

Ashe addressed the judge. "Your Honor, let me explain first why we've proceeded here onto private property without permission or a warrant so far. I was concerned critical evidence in a felony, a body in fact, might be in danger of being moved or destroyed."

"You did not have permission of the property owners, nor a warrant?" Judge Fowler asked.

"We felt, given the destruction of evidence at the Hurrt County Land and Title due to what the fire chief felt was likely an arson, that we needed to at least secure the area and protect any evidence of a capital crime out here," Rachel cut in.

Ashe smiled. She hadn't even arrived when he'd hijacked Pat to run out here, but here she was, in here pitching for the home team.

Okay. I see why Pat likes her.

Judge Fowler nodded. "Okay. But you want a warrant for this specific piece of concrete to search for a body in this, this…retaining pool? In all this area out here, why *right here*?"

"We have statements from co-defendants who were employed in the concrete construction business by our lead suspect stating they buried a body in concrete out here in April, two years ago. Now, part of the evidence that likely was destroyed under suspicious circumstances at the Hurrt L&T would prove our lead suspect and his men poured this pool at that time using the co-defendant's labor," Ashe said. "However we still have cell phone photos of some of the evidence."

Jacobs waved over toward the van and a correctional officer stepped out and brought with him Paul Milton. Ashe tensed up a bit when he saw him in the flesh rather than over a video monitor.

Give me just one minute alone with him.

"This is the concrete employee who was here two years ago," Price said. "He's cooperating under an agreement made with his attorney who agreed to allow him to assist us today."

"Then I do not want to speak to him nor, he to me. Especially as he is a prosecution witness," Fowler said and stepped back away from the pool.

The CO brought Milton over to the pool but not near the group with the judge. Jacobs walked over and pointed at the terrain features around them to orient Milton.

"Any of this look familiar to you?" he asked Milton.

Paul Milton looked around and shook his head. "None of this was around when I saw them bury her. No concrete, nothing like this yet. It was dark, it was a dirt road, and I don't know this area," he complained.

"Well, try some more. I'll let your lawyer know we tried to help you. I guess if you can't help, it's too bad," Jacobs said, and used his knee to bump Milton behind his knee a bit.

"It's not my fault, hell, it's been two years," Milton said. Then Paul Milton noticed Ashe. Ashe made sure to lock eyes with him.

"Look around harder," Jacobs said in a low voice, and bumped him a little harder. A little closer to the edge of the pool.

Milton looked around some more as he tried to step back from the edge. He only bounced off Jacobs who didn't move. Milton then looked back at Ashe who, while not really close to him, took a small step forward.

Milton sighed and raised his shackled hands and pointed at a grouping of scrub pine trees on a rise in the terrain several yards away. Beside them was a rusted cattle-fence T-post with a surveyor's flag on it.

"That…" he said. "That was supposed to be one corner of a…" He looked at the large pool. "Something like this. I don't know, I never knew, but I recall CJ saying that was one far corner of something deep we were going to pour!"

"This is where you helped put Georgia Murphy's body?" Jacobs pressed.

"MacNeal,Everitt, and CJ Portals did. I…I only held the flashlight."

"They had concrete trucks out here to bury her?"

"Just one. They decided to pour this job in large sections. There was the frame and iron in place for one twenty-foot by twenty-foot section."

"I'm a country boy so I know you don't pour into concrete molds separately like that!" Jacobs said.

"I know, but they…were in a hurry," Milton said.

"So, right there. In the center of the deep end," Jacobs pointed. There was a section that was slightly off color from the rest. It had cured differently.

"Yeah. They had her in a black garbage bag, a big one. They put her, oh…about over there," he said and pointed toward the deepest end of the pool. "That's about right. They just covered her in concrete. A day or so later, they must have come and done all the rest of this. I wasn't with them, I was sick."

Ashe shook his head. If he'd wanted to kick Paul Milton's ass before just to even things up, now that he saw what a sniveling, lying sack of shit he was, he really wanted to beat the snot out of him now.

Pat must have noticed Ashe getting a little hot because Ashe felt his big paw on his shoulder. When he looked at Pat, Pat just frowned but winked at him, as if to say, *not now, he'll get his.*

Jacobs motioned for the CO to take Milton back to the van then walked over to where Price, Speakes, and Judge Fowler stood with their back to him to say they had a specific target for a search.

The judge nodded; he was convinced it seemed, and after a few muted words to Speakes and Price, walked back toward the Explorer.

Speakes looked over at Ashe and seemed to nod a little. Ashe figured it had to be only his own imagination that this meant the captain was acknowledging that he'd been right.

Someday I'll want to know why you, Mister Speakes, told Pat I was a private investigator. Just like CJ Portals told everyone. Can't be a coincidence, eh?

As they all headed to the Explorer, Price took out his phone then scoffed at the lack of signal. "Okay, good work, Sheriff. I'm calling Phillip Crews when we reach the highway to let him know his client has cooperated but needs to amend his statement. Put someone in charge out here and keep up the security until we get our warrant."

Then to Rachel, Price said, "Rachel, order whatever you need. Get a forensics team out here! Archeologists, pathologists, oncologists, Rin-Tin-Tin, the Red Cross, whatever and whoever!"

"Already on it," she said, laughing a little.

"Okay, we're a little late but let's head back to the courthouse and meet with AAG Ashad before he leaves. Say, one hour?" Price said. Then, grinning broadly he added, "You guys are awesome!"

Ashe figured this was the biggest break in the biggest case Price had ever worked, and Ashe recalled how that had felt himself a long damn time ago. He was on stage in front of his circuit judge and soon to the assistant attorney general.

Everyone agreed to the meeting time, then the correctional van and the Explorer departed. Pat came over to Ashe.

"Go team," he said flatly.

"What did ol' sour face want to talk to you about?" Ashe asked him.

"He wanted to know how hard you got hit in the head and if you were in control of your faculties."

"And you said?"

"Only half as much as you ever were." Pat smiled a sly smile and went to help Rachel finish up their interviews with the work crews.

Ashe was tired of standing around and had a thought. "Hey, Pat, I'll ride back now with the sheriff. Rachel, can you ride back with Pat?"

They looked at each other and then nodded to Ashe. *You're welcome, Patrick, old pard.*

Once in the sheriff's cruiser, Ashe took in a long breath and let it out slowly.

"I think this is it, don't you, Ashe?" Jacobs said. He turned back onto the paved road and floored it. Price wasn't the only giddy one.

"I think I'll feel better once we've covered that pool with GPR and whatever else Rachel can scare up."

"I'm thinking this is really, really it. And you know what? I'm going to by God call Tracy Davis up and tell her!"

"Hold off until you have something to brag about, boss! And by the way, I need a small favor if we have time?"

"Sure, after all this, anything for you!"

"Hell, Boss Man, I'm starving."

At the courthouse, Ashe finished off a cheeseburger from a food truck that had set up outside. He'd foregone taking the time to get home and change clothes but retrieved his portfolio and had washed his shoes in the janitor's closet to get the mud off. He and Jacobs stood in the second-floor hallway waiting.

As everyone arrived, they were ushered by Price's clerk, Jerry, into the grand jury room where a long table was they could gather around. Knowing Pat hadn't eaten either, he passed him a burger in a paper sack.

"Oh, God bless ya, lad," he said and sat in a corner to eat.

In a few minutes, Ashad, Speakes, Price, and Rachel entered and Ashe looked at the assembled group. Including them, there was Pat, Jacobs, and himself. Price looked considerably less giddy.

Ashad spoke. "I have been reviewing all the evidence and statements made by victims, witnesses, and suspects all morning. I'm glad you may have found some more evidence because as I've discussed with ADA Price, as of now, there is damn little actual hard evidence."

Jacobs about came out of his seat, but Ashe put a hand on his arm. There was a lingering unspoken *but* coming from AAG Ashad.

He continued, "But, there is enough probable cause to continue to investigate the disappearance and possible murder of Mrs. Murphy here in Hurrt County. Captain Speakes concurs, this case's venue was erroneously transferred to Metro based on what was known at the time."

"Little evidence?" Jacobs finally said. "All the land fraud and forged mortgages Mark Portals led, not to mention the cover-up of a crime scene by one former deputy and the murder of another!"

Ashad had obviously prepared for this, by the way he spoke slowly and distinctly. "Most of the evidence of fraud and illegal land transfers were destroyed by the fire last night. I have a computer forensics team arriving tomorrow to go over Mr. Portals' records as well as the county bank's records."

"Tomorrow? It will all be..." Jacobs bellowed, but Price cut him off.

"None of which we've seen implicates Mark Portals at all. Unless there's more I haven't seen, this all points to Stephanie Collins," he said.

"A probable co-defendant whom you may have *prematurely* given immunity to," Ashad said with a small wave of his hand toward Price. "In any event, her statement lacks any supporting evidence now unless we can turn up anything at Portals' office tomorrow."

"I thought she said she had copies of some of the files," Rachel said.

"Well, yes, but they tend to incriminate her more than anyone else," Ashad said.

"So, what can we prove?" Rachel asked. She seemed frustrated as well but kept her tone professional.

"Nothing against Mr. Mark Portals or even Phillip Crews. Ms. Collins may as well have implicated my pet dachshund for all the good her word is now."

"Nothing? All this for nothing?" Jacobs said loudly.

"No. We still have time on our side and your crime scene out at the construction site," Ashad said. "We'll have a full search warrant within the hour so keep it secure. But, with what we have now, we can prosecute Mr. Paul Milton for his part in the kidnap and murder of Deputy Sheriff Clark. We can, within the agreement made, also prosecute him for the attempted murder of Mister Ashe here. His co-defendants are…" He looked at Ashe. "Already serving their time."

"But CJ Portals…" Jacobs said. "He's been all over this. He directed the kidnapping and murder of Clark, *and* Ashe!"

"I have no doubt you may be correct, Sheriff, but the best evidence against the younger Mister Portals we have are only the statements from co-defendants who are also involved at best, and hearsay evidence from liars and cheats at worse. I cannot waste taxpayer money attempting to prosecute him knowing we would likely lose," Ashad said.

Ashe felt his neck getting hotter. When saying "liars and cheats," Ashad was lumping Stevie in with Paul Milton and Tracy Davis. *I'm going to remember that.*

"We still have a statement from Susan Marlin implicating CJ Portals and his company at the scene we have locked down for now. We also have the original photos taken by Deputy Clark and then covered up by Tracy Davis for CJ Portals," Ashe said.

"Yeah, uh," Price started. "Now that the Land and Title has burned, Ms. Marlin is a little fuzzier in her facts. As to Tracy Davis, her confession proves she committed an act of Official Misconduct and Tampering with Evidence in her cover-up of the crime scene here in Hurrt County. Until we have a body, we can only prove misdemeanors. She'll never be a cop again but may not even do jail time. The real problem is, like everything these Portals' allegedly orchestrated, someone else actually committed the crime."

"Yeah," Jacobs said. "Shit."

"Davis covered up the crime scene. No proof or witness that CJ Portals moved the evidence to Metro. Stevie Collins cajoled people out of their land, not Mark Portals. Mr. Crawford at the bank fixed up the vampire mortgages, not Portals. Everitt, MacNeal, and Milton kidnapped and killed Clark—by Milton's own statement CJ was never there—then *they* tried to kill Ashe."

"At the direction of CJ," Pat said.

"Well actually Mr. Milton says the deceased Mister Everitt *told* him that. Milton never heard CJ Portals at all," Ashad corrected.

After a full minute where everyone was silent, Ashad said, "From what I've seen on the bank video, I could actually make the case CJ Portals tried to help you, not harm you, Mr. Ashe. Ms. Collins' statement corroborates that as she said, he may have stopped Mr. Milton from further assaulting you."

Ashe felt that hollow core in his gut roll. *Ah, Stevie. Dammit, honey.*

After another tense minute, Ashad added, "But, like I said, we have time. Perhaps our forensic examination of Mr. Portals' and the bank's records we seized will yield something. Perhaps not."

"Perhaps we will find Georgia Murphy's body in the concrete pool CJ Portals poured. And it will yield some further evidence for us," Price added.

"Perhaps," Ashad said and yawned. "But you need more than what you've given me so far."

"Mr. Ashad," Rachel said. "I have a request. Whatever we do find at the concrete pool, can you use your office's influence to give that forensic examination a priority?"

"I will volunteer Metro's forensics lab assistance," Speakes said, which surprised Ashe.

"Thank you, Captain. But, Agent Hume, I can do better than that. I will assure you that anything found will have the number one case priority in the state. You find it, in twenty-four hours, you'll have your results," Ashad promised.

"Anything else?" Price asked and looked around the table. Then we proceed with what we have in hand and continue to investigate. Good job, everybody."

Everyone stood and began filing out of the room, but Price motioned for the cops to stay. Ashe nodded but made his way over to Speakes.

"Damn lucky I was a private investigator down here, huh, Cap'n?" he said.

Speakes was caught off guard and by his face was surprised Ashe knew he'd said that. Then he apparently regained his composure and looked at Ashe's left ear and head.

"Bet that smarted," he said with a faint grin, and walked out.

Price closed the door and gestured for Jacobs, Rachel, Pat, and Ashe to have a seat.

Pat leaned over to Ashe. "Dammit, Chig, I have to work with him."

"What the holy fuck was that?" Jacobs roared. "It's like he doesn't *want* to prosecute anything!"

"I've gone to bat with less evidence in the past and won, *with* Mr. Ashad as ADA. I've taken people to court with more evidence a time or two over the years and lost," Ashe said. "Not like him to be so cautious."

"He's likely concerned the state will get sued, and all of us, for wrongful prosecution. Mark Portals is an experienced and well-known litigator. What Ashad said actually makes sense. We keep digging," Rachel said with a sigh.

Price held up his hands then looked at Rachel. "We drop the land fraud element of this investigation for now, it's secondary despite evidence of motive. Focus on the big enchilada, the homicide. You need to find Georgia Murphy and prove murder."

"Can't indict CJ even with a body. We need something physical tying him to the scene there," she said. "The ground radar team will be out in the morning. Cadaver dogs tomorrow afternoon. I have a forensic archeology team on call if they find anything."

"Paul Milton says CJ was there at the actual disposing of her body," Pat said to her.

"Not enough. Makes him maybe an accessory, maybe even a co-conspirator. Unlawful Disposal of a Corpse. Big whoop!" Jacobs said.

Everyone started talking over each other, then Ashe said, "We need DNA." They stopped and looked at him.

"Is that possible after two years in concrete?" Pat asked.

"We have to hope so. I seem to recall reading about a case from years ago where they recovered intact hair and some tissue from concrete," Ashe said.

"I've got a call in to a university criminologist asking just that. I guess we'll have to wait and see," Rachel said.

"Ok, Rachel, you have your job. Sheriff, here's what I need you to do. Go find CJ Portals. Get him in here for questioning," Price said.

Jacobs nodded. "We're on it. He's taken to cover somewhere, but we'll find him."

"Of course, this is all academic if there *isn't* a body out there," Pat said.

"There's a body out there," Ashe said flatly. "I'd stake my reputation on it."

Price drew in a long breath. "Mr. Ashe, you already have."

CHAPTER 26

Ashe walked out of the grand jury room with Pat and Rachel who paused to talk to each other, so Ashe checked his phone.

Stevie had texted him. *He's coming to see you,* was all it said.

Ashe had to assume her text meant CJ. *But why is he still texting her?*

Ashe texted her back, *Are you in a safe place? How do you know he is coming?*

Yes. w/Harold, she replied, but didn't answer his other question.

Ashe looked around to see if anyone was approaching him but saw no one. Pat and Rachel were quite busy talking.

Case notes, no doubt. Comparing investigative techniques.

The second floor was mostly quiet as there was no court in session. A few people who worked there walked from office to office or down the stairs. Routine. There was a kid, a girl of about ten, sitting on a bench. An older woman was talking on her phone nearby. Beside the little girl was a Hello Kitty backpack.

Another one for foster care.

So Ashe turned and walked back in the direction of Price's office to give Pat a little more privacy, when he heard his name from behind him.

"Mister Ashe!"

Down at the other end of the second-floor hallway stood his Shadow Man. Carl Jack Portals. "Wait up, I'd like to talk to you!"

CJ waved at him, smiling, and all but trotted down the long hall toward him, as if he were glad to see Ashe. He passed Pat and Rachel, who were just as surprised.

"CJ Portals, I assume," Ashe said.

"Yes, hello. Sorry I'm a bit out of breath. I've tried to catch you a couple of times but we keep missing each other," CJ said, still smiling.

He was taller than Ashe and wore a precisely trimmed gray-streaked beard. His clothes were rural professional, costly and new.

Ashe had expected him to skulk up all hunched over. *Maybe an eye-patch?*

CJ was trim, fit looking, handsome. All in all, not what he'd expected.

"I was supposed to talk with you the night you, ah, were attacked by my former employees."

Ashe smiled back. "Yeah, I heard. We've been looking to speak with you about a number of things concerning…"

"Georgia Murphy," CJ finished for him. "Yes, Stevie told me."

Ashe tried hard not to react at all to his throwing her name out there. It wasn't easy.

"Among some other things," Ashe said as calmly as he could muster.

Pat and Rachel walked over and she was on her phone.

"CJ Portals, this is Lt. Pat Keagan of Metro Homicide and Special Agent Rachel Hume with the state police," Ashe said and gestured back toward the grand jury room. "If it's okay, we can talk in here."

"You know I was there," CJ said, not moving.

"There?"

"The night my men, ah, *former* associates attacked you," he said as calmly as if discussing lunch.

"Price is on his way up," Rachel said.

"Actually, Ashe, I think Agent Hume and I should speak with Mr. Portals alone," Pat said.

But CJ continued, "You know, Mr. Ashe, I may have, in a small way of course, saved your life."

"*Saved* my life?" Ashe said, a bit more harshly than he meant to. "*Your* Concrete Crew set an ambush for me, fresh off murdering Billy Clark. They shot me, hit me with a damn tire iron, then when Milton asked *you* whether he should kill me, *you* told him there were just too many witnesses and to beat it. Too bad he couldn't!"

"Ashe," Pat said firmly. Then to CJ, "Mr. Portals, will you come with us now?"

From behind CJ, down the hall about twenty yards, a tall thick-looking man came up the stairs. He stared at Ashe and CJ and walked about halfway down the hall then stopped. He was decently dressed but his clothes misfit him, like he wasn't used to wearing business attire. He looked like a wrestler or maybe he was auditioning for a bad Mafia movie. Regardless, he was there and meant to be seen. Ashe watched as he unbuttoned his sport coat, but he made no other furtive motion.

"Wait, wait, Mr. Keagan. I want to clear the air here. Mr. Ashe is probably a little confused due to the savage attack and the wound to his head."

"Ashe, *Chig*, c'mon—*walk off*," Pat insisted and placed himself between them.

Rachel cut in, "Mr. Portals, I'm with the State Police Criminal Investigation Bureau and I'd…"

"Excuse me, one minute," CJ insisted. He took a step backward away from the jury room and closer to the center of the hall. "Mr. Ashe, or *Ashe* as I hear you prefer, what you said is kind of right, but you have a few things confused."

Both Pat and Rachel did not want to have this conversation out in the hall, but both were smart enough to let a key suspect, who was not in custody, make a spontaneous statement. If he admitted to anything, it would be admissible in court so long as he felt free to leave.

"I was waiting for Stevie to call me and tell me it was okay for me to come talk with you. At Roger's café, remember? She told you about that, right? Well, she never called so I waited in my Tahoe until I heard gunshots! I looked and saw *you* shooting at someone. God help me, I had no idea what was going on, but I saw you shoot two of my former employees, Everitt and MacNeal, dead! Right there in front of me!" CJ said. "It was terrible."

Ashe saw Pat reach in his jacket pocket. *Likely a recorder.*

"I was horrified. I've known Lawrence Everitt five years. Gerald MacNeal almost four. You shot them both."

"They were actively trying to kill me, but I guess you didn't see that part," Ashe said. He motioned with his eyes toward the new guy, but Pat was looking intently over Ashe's shoulder at the other stairwell.

CJ smiled and said, "Oh, yes, I read that in the papers, saw it on national news. All the posters and fundraisers for you in town.

They all told *your* story. What *you* say happened. And now that he has a deal with the state, Mr. Milton, who I've only known a couple of years, is saying the same thing."

"*My* story?"

"Well, there's no one to counter *your* version, now is there? But despite your new friend Paul Milton backing you up, it was *me* who stopped *him*."

"Why did…" Rachel started, then, "Never mind."

"Well, Miss Agent," CJ said, and turned toward Rachel slightly.

As CJ spoke, Ashe took a quartering step back and without moving his head could partially see the stairs behind him. A second man in a sport coat and slacks had arrived on the second-floor hall, likely the same time as the Wrestler Guy. He was also big, not tall but muscular. Very short hair, Oakley's, some kind of athletic-style tan boot under dark jeans and a green flight jacket.

Former military. The hair on his neck stood up. *This could be an ambush.*

"I saw Milton sneak up and hit Ashe here, viciously, from behind. Mr. Ashe hit him back hard, a great effort given his wounds, but I rushed forward and stopped Milton from trying to hit him again."

CJ paused, but no one asked him anything. Pat was watching Military Guy, and Ashe was watching Wrestler Guy.

"See, you're right, Ashe, Paul Milton did ask if he should kill you. He was hurt, having hit his head on a brick wall, and was somewhat dazed. He recognized me as his former boss and asked me if he should kill you. He must have been half out of it to even consider asking me such a thing. I of course said 'no' and made up that, 'oh, there were too many people around' or something—*anything* to get him to stop. I think I even said 'you've beaten him' to prevent him from going back after you and, uh…"

"And?" Ashe said, then immediately regretted it, knowing it was a mistake. No leading questions during spontaneous statements.

"Well, *our girl* Stevie. I was worried Milton might have finished you and then gone after Stevie. *She is a witness*. You see, we both care about her, and I was just in a better position to protect her," CJ said. "I will always be the one that protects her."

Wait, is he telling me she's in danger now? Is he hinting that he is the only one keeping her safe now?

"*Even now...*if, ah, need be, *I am with her.* But, hey, as far as you and I *and Stevie,* Mr. Ashe, it's probably better *we don't dig up old bones.*"

"I see," Ashe said. CJ was threatening him and Stevie. Ashe wanted to ask about a lot of things, like why they'd moved evidence to set up Tony Murphy and why he'd been trying to spoil his early inquiries into Georgia Murphy. But Ashe wanted someone to read him his rights first, and it had to be someone other than him.

"Well, that's an interesting take on it," Pat said. "If you don't mind, the ADA Mr. Price would like to hear this."

"Yes, Stevie," CJ pressed, ignoring Pat. "You see, she even threw a shoe at me and yelled for me to run. *Me!* You know deep down inside she still cares about me. She knew if I was caught near your *helpless body* on the ground, people would connect me with my former employees and assume just what you three have. That I had something...anything whatsoever to do with their actions. Which of course, I did not."

Everyone was still. Ashe watched Wrestler Guy as he started to move slowly, adapting to CJ's step. Five feet away and directly behind him was the little girl.

Price arrived suddenly upstairs and saw the group. Unknowingly, he pushed right past Military Guy. "Mister Portals! Hello, I'm John Price, the assistant district attorney for Hurrt County. If you have time, I'd like to speak with you."

"About the assault on Mr. Ashe here?"

"Among other things, yes," Price said.

"Well, everyone, yes of course. I would love to give you a statement and clear up all the misunderstandings. Let me do this, let me grab my lawyer, Uncle Mark, from across the street, then I'll be right back."

As if on cue, the two men moved forward toward CJ. Ashe locked on Wrestler Guy who returned his stare and reached inside his coat as if going for a gun.

Pat focused on the other man as he swept his coat back and calmly gripped his 1911. At the same time, Ashe cleared his pullover sweater by grabbing it up with his supporting hand and grasped his Smith M&P 9mm.

As he did, Ashe stepped to get a better angle on Wrestler Guy without putting the little girl in danger. The woman near the girl dropped her phone and screamed.

Price saw this and flattened himself against the wall. Rachel pulled up her blouse and exposed a spandex band holster across her chest, and drew a compact Glock.

CJ's men, seeing the guns out, paused reaching into their clothes but were not stupid enough to try and beat guns already drawn. After a second and a quick look between them, they stepped forward and moved beside CJ, shielding him.

"Ladies, gentlemen, I will return after conferring with my lawyer," CJ announced. The trio moved down the stairs and out of the courthouse. "Say, one hour?" he shouted as he exited.

Ashe and Pat followed. Military Guy had waited at the foot of the stairs looking back up and securing their rear. He didn't have a gun out, but his hand was inside his jacket. As soon as he heard the courthouse door open, without taking his eyes off Pat, he followed.

Pat ran down and ensured they'd left the building and were in fact, headed toward Mark Portals' office.

"Clear," he said as he thumbed the safety back on his big 45 and holstered it. Ashe and Rachel reholstered as well. "He's going into Portals' office now."

"What the fuck was that!" Price shouted when he caught his breath.

"Well, CJ Portals wanted to make a show of innocence today," Rachel said. "He knew what he was doing and knew we would listen."

"Christ! Did our lead suspect in a homicide just walk in here with two hoods and then walk the fuck right out?" Price shouted. "Why didn't anybody arrest him?"

The little girl was crying loudly in the arms of the woman with her. They huddled on the floor. Several other people ran in different directions to get out. Rachel walked over and showed her badge trying to calm them.

"Because we didn't want a goddamn bloodbath!" Pat yelled back at Price as he climbed the stairs back to him.

"Oh, for the love of..." Price mumbled. "I want him in custody. Those two men, them too!"

"They never showed any overt hostility and never displayed

their arms," Ashe said.

"To hell with that, go arrest them and get that arrogant CJ Portals in handcuffs!"

"I'll get Jacobs and some backup," Pat said.

"He was sending us a message," Ashe said.

"Yeah, that he wasn't going to be arrested without a fucking gunfight," Pat said, still breathing hard.

"No not...well, yes, but also that he knew we're on to him out at the construction site," Rachel said as she returned. "I heard that comment about digging."

"He also was letting *me* know that he had his finger on Stevie, that he could get to her! She's not safe," Ashe said.

Jacobs arrived at the corner of the courthouse opposite Mark Portals' office building and met up with Ashe, Pat, and Rachel. Pat had kept a watch on the front of the office and CJ had not emerged. The last pair of deputies Jacobs had, came running across the square toward them. One came running from the jail, and the other wearing civilian work clothes came from the hardware store, a Winchester lever action rifle in hand.

Jacobs waved the plainclothes deputy with the Winchester around back and signaled for the uniform to join them. Rachel called for another trooper, but it'd be an hour as they already had one tied up at the construction site with Jacobs' other two deputies.

Price came out the side door with a couple of papers in his hand. They were warrants for the arrest of Carl J. Portals for Felony Racketeering and another one for Felony Fraud. Behind him, slowly and as calmly as they could, came several of the courthouse workers with Jerry ushering them out. They stayed on the far side of the square where they couldn't be seen from Portals' office. Among them was the little girl and the woman escorting her.

Good, Ashe thought.

Then Price took a deep breath and stood beside Ashe. "I'd prefer you not to be here."

"You're running out of troops," Ashe said to Price. "Sheriff, is the back covered?"

"Yep, I've had a couple of friends watching for CJ since yesterday and my part-time deputy is there now."

Ashe nodded. Pat was watching the office front, so Ashe gave instructions. "Okay, everyone. Breathe. This is not a raid. We should walk in calmly and, Sheriff, you should formally arrest CJ. Right?"

"Yes," Price said. "I'll actually try to speak to Mark. It might actually help deescalate things if I'm there."

Our young DA has balls.

"Oh, and if CJ tries to hide in his uncle's office, it's legally not a sanctuary from a lawful arrest. We can go in and get him," Rachel added.

"Rachel, I recommend you stick with Price. You're the senior law enforcement official on the case after the sheriff. Pat, you and I will walk in and brace CJ's bodyguards with Deputy...um, what's your name?"

"Jim Minor," said the uniformed deputy. He looked like he was maybe twenty-two and was wide-eyed and excited.

Ashe looked around and realized he'd taken over. It was an old habit. "Uh, I don't mean to be giving orders..."

"You're doing fine," Jacobs said. "I'm in charge, with ADA Price, so I say go ahead."

"Ok, Minor, you're in uniform, so stay centrally located in case any of us needs assistance. You're our first backup, got it?"

"Yes, sir!"

"Anyone tries to come in behind us, stop them."

"Yes, sir!"

"Where the hell is Danny Breslin when I need him? I called him from out at the site. Hell, he would eat this part up," Pat mumbled.

"Everyone make a note of the hard cover between here and there. If anything starts before we make it inside, head to solid brick or those monuments. Cars are not great cover so only as a last resort," Ashe added.

As if on cue, an unmarked, blacked-out Charger pulled up to the courthouse and Danny Breslin stepped out calmly, wearing a black suit.

Pat pulled out his cell and called him. After taking Pat's call, Danny casually strolled over to their end of the courthouse and out of sight of Portals' office.

"Don't worry, Danny, we weren't going to make a tactical arrest and not tell you," Pat said flatly.

Breslin nodded and drew his SIG P320 compact and press checked it. Although his clothes fit him well, Ashe noted he wore concealed body armor under his shirt.

"What do you want me to do?" is all he said.

"Ashe is making the plan," Jacobs said.

"Hey, CJ has never seen him, right?" Rachel asked.

"That's good, we can use that, Rachel," Ashe said. "Sergeant Breslin, do you think you can walk into the office as a civilian and ask to make an appointment, anything? Just be positioned inside as we walk in. Stay uninvolved unless you have to engage."

"Sure, Ashe."

"That's dangerous," Pat said.

Ashe and Pat gave Breslin the descriptions of the bodyguards and that while not having displayed their weapons, they were likely armed.

Breslin took Ashe's portfolio and walked all the way around the square and then up to Portals' office building. Jacobs called his deputy guarding the rear and gave him Breslin's description so there'd be no mistake.

Breslin took his time, checked his watch indifferently, and then stepped inside.

It was two p.m.

They broke into two groups. Price, Jacobs, and Rachel in one and in the lead, then quartering away and spreading out in case anyone started firing from a window were Ashe, Pat, and Deputy Minor.

Walking across the square and around the old courthouse was no issue, but crossing the street to the office meant they'd be right in the open.

Portals' office building was brick and two stories and actually sat back fifteen feet or so from the street with well-manicured grass on the other side of a short sidewalk that led to the main entrance. There was an ornate black iron fence around the grass so without awkwardly trying to hop over it, forced them to walk around it to the sidewalk entrance.

A funnel. A choke point. Dammit.

As they got to the last of the courthouse grass and prepared to cross the street, Ashe noticed all the windows in the office were covered with one-way mirrored gold tint, to reduce heating costs. But it also meant anyone could be watching them, *hell, pointing a gun at them*, and they'd be blind to the danger.

Price looked back at Ashe. Rachel cut a glance at Pat, but he was watching the second story.

They were across the street, so Price took lead and walked down the fence to the front walk with Jacobs and Rachel and they walked up to the main door. Pat broke right, Ashe left, and they stood watching the corners and the second-floor windows as best they could. Deputy Minor wasn't sure what to do, so he walked up to the front walk and waited.

If shit started, hopefully they'd try to raise a window rather than just shoot through it.

Nobody did. So almost as one, Pat and Ashe turned and all but jogged to the front door taking Deputy Minor in tow. Ashe drew his pistol but held it close in front of him under his pullover.

They entered Mark Portals' office and immediately surged forward looking for Military Guy and Wrestler Guy. They were not in sight.

In the front foyer sat Danny Breslin in a chair talking on his phone with Ashe's portfolio open in front of him. He sure enough looked like was just waiting to see someone.

A long receptionist desk impeded any foot traffic, but Price and company were already past that. Price and Rachel were talking to Phillip Crews. Ashe didn't see Jacobs.

He and Pat went right past the receptionist who started to say something but saw Ashe's gun. She turned and went back to her computer, like that was an everyday occurrence. Another woman in business attire had her phone in her hand talking quietly but quickly to someone.

Ashe and Pat moved past Price, Rachel, and Crews; Ashe heading straight down the center hall, Pat broke right again and covered the stairs and a second-floor balcony overlooking them. At least as best they could.

Ashe made it to the back of the first floor, and there he found Jacobs at a rear door talking to his deputy out back.

"I think he's gone," he said.

"Portals' office?"

"Second floor," he said.

As speedily but cooly as possible Ashe, Pat, and Jacobs headed up the stairs. Ashe went up backward, gun out, covering the overhang as Pat and Jacobs led. From the corner of his eye, Ashe could see Breslin also covering the upstairs balcony from a better, longer angle.

"He's not here," Crews shouted at them from the lobby. "CJ left and Mark is in the city."

Suddenly Breslin shouted, "Watch it! Threat left!"

At the top of the stairs, Wrestler Guy stepped out suddenly from a door. He started to sweep his misfitted coat back but it got hung up on his gun and holster, slowing his presentation.

Ashe was closer, so he holstered, stepped forward, and grabbed the big man's gun arm locking his gun into his holster. Pat slid his arm in under Wrestler's other, stepped around, and then Pat locked his arms around the Wrestler's shoulder. Ashe duplicated the move, and together, they took him to the ground. Jacobs stepped over and handcuffed him.

"You're under arrest," he said.

"I have a permit!" Wrestler said.

"Not to pull it on law enforcement or wear it in a courthouse!" Jacobs shouted right down in his ear. They got him to his feet and moved him roughly downstairs.

Crews looked at Wrestler Guy and said, "What are you doing here?" Then to Price, "John, Rachel, I didn't know he'd stayed behind. I thought he left with CJ."

"Mr. Portals told me to stay and protect the office," Wrestler said to Crews.

"And you called out to us right as we got to the top of the stairs, Phillip!" Ashe barked at Crews. "Nice signal."

Crews shook his head, ignored Ashe, and said to Price, "Whatever you're charging him with, add Armed Criminal Action and Felony Criminal Trespass. I'm a partner here, not CJ, and I never authorized these men to be on the premises, much less armed!"

Deputy Minor and took control of Wrestler and escorted him outside.

Jacobs, Ashe, and Pat jogged back up the stairs and searched the second floor including Mark's office. There were a pair of administrative assistants who got the fire scared out of them, but otherwise, the top floor was clear.

Price gathered his team. "Mr. Crews, who by the way still swears he has nothing to do with anything, said he threw CJ out of the office. Apparently, CJ came in demanding to see Mark, but Mark Portals is in Metro this week. CJ threatened him, so Crews ordered him off the grounds. Seems he came in and went out a private alley entrance. Looks like that other bodyguard is with him."

They all started talking over each other. "Lying sack of..." Pat started, "How long ago?" Jacobs interrupted, "Thirty minutes or more!" Rachel said, "Shit, shit, he's halfway to Metro by now!" Jacobs cursed.

"Okay, okay," Ashe shouted. Everyone stopped talking. "Let's do this methodically. Sheriff, you're right, he'd head to the city to find his uncle and hide out where he knows people. Let's get out a BOLO on him with Metro and on all his vehicles we pulled up the other day."

Jacobs turned and grabbed his radio and started on that.

"Sergeant Breslin, please follow the deputy to the jail with Rachel," said Price. "Maybe we can get something out of the bodyguard we have."

Pat nodded. "Chig, I think you and I need to consider he may not have gone there. He's slick, maybe he's still local somewhere," he said.

"Pat, I think we should just find Stevie," Ashe said. "Then maybe we'll find CJ."

CHAPTER 27

The most likely scenario Ashe decided was that CJ would run home to the city to hide where he was on his own ground. But Ashe also knew CJ wasn't just boasting about being able to get to Stevie, especially as she was the principal witness against him and Mark Portals. He had also made a not-so-subtle threat to Ashe to stop digging into Georgia's disappearance, and hinted darkly Stevie would pay a price if he didn't. So Ashe located Stevie at her office, where she apparently had, off and on anyway, been staying overnight.

If I know where she is and when she'll be there, then CJ knows.

Once the appropriate entries of CJ's warrants were entered into the state and federal computer systems at the sheriff's office, Pat got on the phone and had his people start scouring Metro, starting with CJ's house, the Concrete Crew office, and the club where he used to take Georgia and Stevie.

Stevie.

Just in case he was still nearby, they decided to split their forces. Ashe and Breslin sat on her office while Pat and Jacobs and a couple of deputies checked everywhere they knew to check, searching for CJ. They used cell phones to stay in touch and off the radio.

After four hours canvassing Hurtt County without results, it was dark and beginning to smell of rain. It turned sharply cooler as the sun went down.

"Any progress with the bodyguard?" Ashe asked Jacobs over his cell.

"He refused a waiver, but did say he never meant to draw a gun on us. He said he was startled by us coming up the stairs but stopped his draw when he saw my uniform."

"That it?"

"Name is Mick...something, I have it written down. He's with Alpha Omega Security, city address."

"Alpha Omega Security," Ashe said so Breslin could hear it. He grabbed his own cell and called his office.

"Yeah. Then he clammed up, called a lawyer up there, and they already made his bond," Jacobs said.

"Anyone we know come to get him?"

"Took an Uber," Jacobs said and hung up.

"We'll have Alpha Omega give us the name of the bodyguard and hopefully have them turn in CJ," Breslin said.

"They'll resist that," Ashe said.

"We can subpoena their records and activity logs; plus, any electronic tags or trackers they have active. If they fight us too much, given we have felony warrants, they'll lose their license."

"Time to play hardball. You guys in MCU know what to do," Ashe said.

"Pat says you were a damn hard cop yourself in your day," Breslin said.

"Were?"

In the meanwhile, they sat and watched it start to rain as they kept an eye on Judge Marsh's office. More hours passed and still nothing happened. The rain that was expected came in and sat down right over Seacord, making everything colder and more miserable. In spurts, it went from only drenching to a blinding downpour. Ashe cursed to himself.

Radar and dogs won't work in this.

Stevie stayed at the office; still unaware they were watching her. Unaware she was bait. Every now and then, they could make her out as she walked by a window. Her car stayed parked out front. The rain beat a loud tempo on the top of Breslin's Charger.

"Ashe?"

"Huh, what?" Ashe said and sat up quickly. He had dozed off. *Ah shit!* It was after one.

"Pat's here," he said and rolled down his window.

Pat had parked beside them. "Uh, hey. We should head back to Metro, Chig. Likely as hell that's where CJ is anyway," Pat admitted.

"I've been thinking. He hired those bodyguards up there in the city. The one with him probably is advising him where to hide out until we get a subpoena," Breslin added.

Ashe nodded and fought off a yawn, knowing they were making the logical call. They decided to give up the surveillance on Stevie as they couldn't see much anyway, and Ashe had Breslin drive him to meet Jacobs at the jail.

As he did, Ashe called her.

"Hey," he said as she answered.

"Busy boy. Lots of fun today, eh?" she said. To Ashe, she sounded tired; he'd obviously woken her.

"Doors locked?"

"All secure here, Lieutenant. Harold has gone home but I'm staying. I didn't bring my galoshes."

"Keep your phone handy and stay in tonight, please."

"I was," she said and hung up.

Walking into the jail, shaking the rain off him as he walked, it occurred to Ashe that this was the first time he'd been to the jail since he'd questioned Tracy Davis in the sheriff's office weeks ago.

"Sheriff!" he called out as he walked down the hall.

"Hey, in here! See anything?" Jacobs asked.

Ashe entered his office. "A lot of water. Pat and Breslin left for Metro."

"You look whipped. Rachel went home a while ago too. Said she'd be here early with the radar team in the morning unless it's still raining buckets."

Ashe nodded and then remembered his old Jeep Cherokee, which was probably still at the rear of the judge's office where it'd been for over a week. He looked around for a minute before asking, "Sheriff, um, I need to borrow a car."

Jacobs grinned. "Oh yeah, they towed that old Jeep of yours to the Adams Street Garage after you went in the hospital. I guess I forgot to tell you."

"I was kind of hoping you'd have pushed it into the L&T fire for me," Ashe said.

Jacobs laughed. "I can loan you Tracy's old car. It's an unmarked Impala," he said, and fumbled through his desk for the keys.

"I actually need something a little more...discreet," Ashe said.

Jacobs frowned as he thought. "I got you," he said. "And hey, we know where she is, we'll keep tabs on your girl tonight. But you? You're running yourself ragged and you look like hell, Ashe. There's only so much a man can do. Go home."

"I think given what he said, CJ might…"

"We can handle him if he shows up. I'll put someone trustworthy in Marsh's office downstairs, I'm sleeping here in my office myself, now go!"

Fifteen minutes later, Ashe was on his way home in an eight-year-old GMC pickup with a departmental handheld radio. The truck was dirty inside and out with scrap lumber and PVC pipe in the bed. In the gap between the cab and the bed were a pair of brown mud boots. It was perfect.

Earlier that evening, Mark Portals sat in his Metro office conference room surrounded by his closest staff there. He'd asked them to stay after business hours to break the news to them.

"Given recent events in which you and I had no involvement, there has been a cloud of impropriety cast over the Seacord office. To best ensure we stay on track with Doorbella, I will be turning over my day-to-day involvement with DBA to…Phillip Crews."

There were audible sounds of surprise by those assembled who had worked this project with him since the start. Mark knew they hadn't seen this coming, and also knew one or two had an idea of how much he and Crews, despite their partnership, disliked each other.

"This in no way impacts our SCEA project, nor does it mean we will not continue as a key consultant to DBA. I am deeply invested both financially and emotionally in DBA, and will always work to ensure its success, no matter my role."

"Mark, does this mean…" one woman started, but he held up his hand.

"I expect some of you know of the events in Seacord that members of my office, namely Ms. Collins and my nephew have allegedly been involved in. Allegations of racketeering and fraud and of deceptive legal practices. Phillip and I became aware of these activities only recently and are cooperating with the authorities. While we have done nothing but work to bring jobs and prosperity to Hurrt County and the greater region, I and others of the principal investors feel I should take a less public role."

"That's not fair," someone said.

"Are we losing our jobs?" the woman he'd interrupted asked.

"No, but you will be working more closely with Mr. Crews from this point forward. Michael, Suzanne, I will set up a teleconference tomorrow with him that you two need to be on," Mark said.

There was a flurry of overlapping questions from several of the employees, but Mark held up his hands.

"People, please. This is painful for me and I assume for many of you as well. The good news is everything seems to be on track for next week's visit by Doorbella corporate. Our investments are safe. But, I have much to do myself and while this is not how I would have preferred my role to evolve, the project is progressing on time. Right now, we need to pull together and keep at it. I'll meet with you individually over the next week or so and answer any personal concerns you have, but I need to take care of a couple of things, so please. Have a great evening."

The group began to file out of the room with only Suzanne remaining. She obviously wanted to have further discussions, but Mark shook his head and went out another door to his office.

On his desk, an assistant left him a message from Rollin Ashad. *Later,* he thought as he went and closed the door to his office.

He took out a cheap burner phone from a drawer and saw where CJ had called him twice. Mark dialed him back.

"Damn!" CJ said after only one ring. "Took you long enough!"

"What the hell is going on down there? What was that shit at the courthouse about?" Mark said.

"I guess it just wasn't the day to give myself up," CJ said. "Not here and not yet."

Even without seeing his nephew, Mark could tell by his tone that CJ had that smart-assed grin on his face.

"We have a great plan. You have a great deal. I went to bat for you with the attorney general's office."

"You were covering your own ass, Uncle. I have an idea; *you* go to jail for a few years and *I'll* run the project."

"Have you lost your mind? Dammit to hell, you are the one that mucked this all up with that woman!"

"Stevie is still…"

"Not *her*, idiot! Georgia Murphy!"

There was a long pause, then CJ said, "Well, I might just be able to change things a little. Like, instead of turning myself in, I might *make them* catch me. I also figure I just might take care of…"

"Shut up! Now listen. Go to the DA's office there in the morning and surrender. I'll have Fischer down to represent you initially and post your bond, then I'll submit to the AG's office our plea and arrange a change in venue to here in the city. Mr. Price there won't have a say in it."

"I'm not so sure," CJ said.

"You better do as I say, and fast. If they find her body and you don't have your story and an agreement on record first, well…God help you," Mark said and hung up.

It was Wednesday morning. Ashe jumped up, wide awake at six thirty. He'd fallen into bed last night and almost immediately passed out. He checked his phone and saw Rachel had texted just a few minutes ago that they were on the way to the construction site with the GPR team. Ashe looked outside and saw the rain had stopped, so he dressed in clothes that wouldn't get ruined at a muddy construction site, grabbed a thermos for coffee, and headed out to eat breakfast.

At Roger's Café, he found the sheriff with Ed Bell in the back and they waved him over. As he walked through the restaurant, the conversations of several patrons paused as they looked him over, then resumed more quietly after he'd passed.

"I think I'm still a topic or something around here," Ashe said and he sat down.

"Our little stunt at Portals' office yesterday got some attention, and not just around here," Jacobs said.

He motioned with his thumb covertly over his shoulder and out the window. A big news van from the city was parked just outside that Ashe hadn't seen.

"They've already been out to the site and tried to get in. Said they had Mark Portals' permission," Bell said. "I didn't let them in."

"I think you were right in that it's a probable felony crime scene plus our active search warrant," Ashe said. "But maybe we'll have something to talk about today."

"Well I'm headed out to relieve the trooper who's been there all night," Bell said and left.

Ashe shook his hand then after he left turned to Jacobs. "Sheriff, Stevie?"

"Still in place at old Judge Marsh's office. She ordered breakfast delivered a little while ago," he said. "I'm out of deputies but I have some dependable people watching her. Probably better anyway, CJ would likely spot a deputy in the daylight."

"Hey, before Tilly comes over, I want to throw out an idea to get your thoughts," Ashe said.

"Too late," Tilly said from behind him. "Your usual? Fresh eggs from a *too-young little chicken*? Fill your thing there with *warm milk*?"

"Usual, and black coffee in the thing," Ashe said and handed her the thermos. "Smart-ass."

"I don't see yours doing any tricks, dumbass," she said and headed for the kitchen.

"You two should've gotten married," Jacobs mumbled over his coffee cup.

"We actually thought about it. By the time I got home from the Army, she was married the first time to Tommy."

"Oh, I didn't know that. Well maybe you dodged a bullet."

Ashe smiled at that. "Now, hear me out. So sitting in the rain last night, I had a thought. Consider now CJ can't run forever, and we can't sit on Stevie waiting forever either. We don't have the manpower and I'm running out of patience."

"All kidding aside, you still look a tad haggard. You're not a young man anymore, Ashe. Hell, my ass is dragging a bit too."

"CJ still has a thing for her and she's the chief witness against him. He also likes using Stevie to try and provoke me, which means he wants *me* for upsetting his plans."

"Yeah, okay," Jacobs said. "But with his family's money he could be gone and stay hid in style a long, long time."

"Yes, but also no. First, I think the Doorbella deal is too big for his uncle to put up with him much longer. Next, he's a huge egomaniac, the courthouse show is proof of that. Just running away won't work for him. I think he needs to feel like he's wrapped things up here with me first. And Stevie as well."

"If he's as angry with you and obsessed with her as you say, we can use that," Jacobs said.

"You headed out to the site?"

"Yeah, right now. You coming?"

Ashe shook his head slowly. "Not until after breakfast."

At the Doorbella construction site, it felt colder than in town and although the rain had stopped, the air was wet and there was a snappy wind. Ashe wore a warm-enough jacket and had layered his clothes underneath, so only his ears and nose felt the cold.

At the concrete pool area, the state forensics team had tarps staked down and plywood laid out over much of the muddy ground so they could work and walk around without sinking. They had erected canopies over their equipment and had a couple of pumps running to clear out the rainwater. Large, battery-powered lights on tall tripods were stationed to illuminate the deep end of the pool in the dark. The sun was barely starting to rise as Ashe walked up.

The GPR team was comprised of a pair of young college-aged men and a young woman who held a wired controller to what looked like a push lawn mower. The two men were pulling and pushing this wheeled contraption slowly across the concrete pad where Paul Milton had indicated. The trouble they had was the concrete angle was so steep there, and Ashe watched as they slid sideways every few steps on the wet concrete.

Rachel stood talking to a middle-aged man with a state ID clipped to his jacket, so Ashe guessed crime lab. She was dressed in jeans, a fleece sweater, and mud boots but her overcoat was more for rain than cold. It was obvious she was getting chilled standing in the wind.

"Morning," Ashe said. He stood close beside her and tried to block the wind.

"Hey there," she said. "Thanks, Ashe. Uh, Pat with you?"

"No, but he'll be along. Anything?"

"Yeah. The sheriff is on his car radio, let's grab him and get out of this wind. Dr. Dufflin, uh, Bob, can we see the raw data you showed me?"

Bob walked them over to one of the canopied areas that had big side tarps tied as panels to block the wind. Rachel waved at Jacobs and he trotted over. Underneath the canopy was a table set up with a laptop computer connected to a pair of monitors.

"I've linked us live to the GPR on this screen so we can watch the progress," Bob said. "On this monitor, I can show you what we got fifteen minutes ago."

Bob clicked on the keyboard for a minute then pointed at the screen. Ashe fished his glasses out to see.

It was a bunch of uneven vertical gray lines very close together with occasional tiny black specs, with thicker regularly spaced horizonal lines.

The screen showed this pattern moving from right to left, then seemed to flip and move the other way. Almost at the end of the file, a larger-but-still-thin dark irregular shape appeared.

"There," Bob said. "It's a cavity that doesn't belong."

"How large is it? Could it be a body?" Jacobs asked.

"Possibly eight to twelve inches thick, maybe four feet long. You see the straight black lines are rebar. The vertical lines are slight irregularities in the concrete itself and…"

"Bob," Ashe cut in. "Is it big enough to be her?"

"Only eight inches thick?" Jacobs asked.

"Under this much concrete, possibly a couple of tons, yes. It might be a crushed body. It's consistent with what we've been told to look for by my associates in other states, but hell, nobody's done this before."

Ashe drew in a deep breath. This could be it. Jacobs was still staring at the screen with an unlit cigarette in his mouth.

"They're running the scan again," Rachel said. "Coming from a different angle to compare the results. Once done and we give them a little time to compile the data, we'll have a three-dimensional image to look at."

Jacobs stepped outside the canopy and, cupping his hands around his mouth to shield it from the wind, he lit his cigarette and stared at the team working in the pool. Ashe followed him and they stared for a minute together.

"I wish Sheriff Laughton were here to see this," Jacobs said.

"Let's be sure it's her first. So I wonder what's involved now to…hey, Rachel! What's the process to, well, dig this up?"

Rachel leaned out of the canopy. "I'll call Price and the DA and get a firm go-ahead. Essentially from what I've read, and Bob here, we cut around the area to get a block out, and then chisel in," she said. "It's not a fast process."

Bob waved over two people, who by their name tags were from the university, and had a quick conversation with them. They went and started prepping air-powered jackhammers and large circular saws.

"Those are forensic archeologists," Rachel said. "Bob and I will oversee the preservation of evidence with the main goal being anything that identifies this anomaly as Georgia. And of course, any DNA."

"Rachel, I probably don't have to tell you this, but according to Milton, she was in a plastic garbage bag. If it even survived the concrete, there might be trace DNA on the inside of it or on the opening where they might have tied the bag closed," Ashe said.

"I'm on it. We'll start cutting into this as soon as we can." She took out her cell, cursed at it, then went to her car and drove back toward the entrance.

Bob came over after conferring with his team, looked for Rachel, then said to the sheriff, "Hey, I need a place locally to work. Some place big enough and private to work on this big block of concrete we'll be cutting up."

"Block?" Jacobs asked.

"Yeah, I think it's better for the forensic examination to cut out an entire block and take it indoors to slowly cut away at it and expose what is there. It'll get us out of the weather and allow us to do our jobs better."

"Ok, I'll find you a place." Jacobs went back to his cruiser and got on the radio.

Ashe walked away and climbed into the bed of his borrowed truck to see if he could get high enough for a cell signal. Hopping up and sitting on the top of the cab, he got a couple of bars.

"Pat…"

"Yeah, Chig, you find CJ?" Pat said.

"No. You still in Metro?"

"Yes, I have a job, you know. What'cha got?"

"The GPR team is pretty confident they've found something that could be her. I think they'll be cutting into the concrete here in a bit."

"Well, if it's her, we're in a whole new ball game."

"Anything up there?" Ashe asked.

"On CJ Portals? Haven't found him yet, but I've nailed down that security company. They're of course claiming client confidentiality, which doesn't exist for them, but I got our DA working on subpoenas and Metro is pulling their license. They'll have to tell us who the other BG is and where they took CJ."

"Breslin and I discussed this last night. They should have to reveal if they have any tracking devices on their guy or CJ, which a lot of security companies do now as kidnap prevention."

"Oh, you and Danny came up with that, eh? Who the hell do you think taught *him*?"

"Who the hell do *you* think taught *you*?" Ashe said.

"Bite my Irish ass, Chig. I'll stay in touch. And hey, you get her out of the concrete and find out it's Georgia or not, let me know," Pat said and hung up.

Ashe watched from his perch as they hauled out the GPR gear. Just finding a corpse wasn't going to incriminate anyone beyond Paul Milton, and then only for the unlawful disposal of a corpse. They already had Milton on much more serious charges.

They had to prove, first, that any corpse discovered was Georgia Murphy. That would close the mystery and take them from a missing person case into a homicide investigation. It would also solidify Milton's statement, because as of this moment, it was only his word that CJ was even involved.

But any physical evidence from CJ, DNA, anything, would remove all doubt he had been directly involved.

Screw racketeering. Murder.

Secondly, Ashe hoped they would be able to get a cause of death. It was an awful lot to hope for after two years encased in concrete.

But first, is it Georgia?

Ashe called a second number.

"Hello," Susan Marlin answered.

"Suze, it's Chig. I need a little information on Georgia."

"Oh lordy! I'm not supposed to talk to you, Chig! My lawyer will kill us both!"

"I'm not *talking*, talking, I'm just asking you something important. We may have found Georgia."

"Really? Oh God. You were right, she's dead, isn't she?"

"Yes, I need to know if there is anything personal you can tell me about her to help identify her. Like a ring or jewelry she never took off, or a tattoo…anything?"

"I don't know. Did CJ kill her? Oh crap! I don't think I'm up to identifying her body!"

I doubt anyone could.

"Suze, please. Focus. We have to go a step at a time. Can you think of anything?"

There was a silence on the phone, and for a few seconds Ashe thought maybe she'd hung up on him.

Finally, "She had a gold bracelet, like a solid wide bangle bracelet. It was gold plated, I'm sure because it was pretty wide and would have cost a fortune. She wore that almost every day."

"Anything else?"

"Her wedding band but she took that off a lot too. Oh, I don't know, Chig! My God, poor Georgia!"

"Thank you. Call down to the sheriff's office if you think of anything else. Also, please go through any pictures you have with her and find any that show the bracelet," he said and hung up.

In the pool, the workers being led by Bob had taken measurements based on the GPR data and were lining it out with spray paint. One of the techs with him was taking photographs, and another had a video camera recording their progress and keeping an evidentiary record. They'd moved the lights to flood their work site and were apparently discussing where to start.

Rachel returned and was sitting on the edge of the pool. She'd gone to call the DA and was watching everything intently. She was holding herself tightly and rocking back and forth.

She's got to be freezing in this wind. Everyone else was protected from it down in the depth of the pool.

"Sheriff!" Ashe shouted. Jacobs stepped out of his cruiser.

Ashe pointed at Rachel and pantomimed freezing by holding his own arms together and shaking. Jacobs stared at him a second then looked at Rachel. Then he got it and gave Ashe a thumbs-up. He got in his car and drove it around to where she was sitting and parked so that she could sit inside and still watch.

Again, Ashe saw in Rachel what Pat must see. *She's not only a trooper; she's a hunter.*

Ashe was about to climb down and get out of the wind himself when he had a thought. A bracelet was easy enough to get lost during a murder and he had no idea what would happen to a "plated" bracelet if it was covered in hot, fresh concrete. Then concrete cold for two years.

He took out his phone again and called a familiar number.

"Ashe," she said as she answered. "I'm at work. I'm being good and staying here with this creepy old guy downstairs."

"I know. Probably the same old guy that was 'watching' my house. Listen, I need to talk to you about…"

"Georgia?" Stevie asked. "It's all over town. Have you found her?"

That was fast. Maybe dangerous for Stevie.

"We found *something*. But when we get to it, I need your help with some personal insight. You knew her as well as anyone, so I need to know anything I should be looking for that proves it's her. She'll likely be unrecognizable."

Stevie was silent for a minute. "She had a cheap gold-colored bracelet she almost always had on," she said.

"Yeah, I know about that. Anything else?"

"God, I hate to ask, but will she even have skin? Eww!"

"I don't know. Maybe, why?"

"She had a tattoo of a dolphin on her left upper arm, surrounded by big water splashes."

"Okay."

"And, this is corny, but on her right shoulder blade, she had a tat of a cinder block and a shovel with, like, beams of light kind of coming off them. It was supposed to be for Tony and the Concrete Crew, but they didn't get it. Tony just said to her, 'Shit, babe, we don't do block work!' But, how would you tattoo concrete anyway?"

"That's good, thanks. I still need to talk with you later, so be careful today. If word is out about what's happening here, *he* might get desperate," Ashe said.

"I mean, it was a nice gesture but any way you try to draw

concrete, it'd look like a gray pile of crap or something."

"Stevie, stay at work. Don't go out."

Then he lost the connection. Ashe didn't know if she'd heard his warnings or not.

CHAPTER 28

It took all that day and well into the early morning of the next to cut out a block of concrete six feet wide by nine feet long and three feet deep. It wasn't only the cutting that took so long, it was ensuring they didn't destroy any evidence. All done while copiously recording their work in notes, drawings, measurements, photographs, and video.

Ashe, Rachel, and Jacobs all slept in two-hour shifts, driving back to use a couch in the sheriff's office. Around one a.m., the team at the site was done and was only waiting on daylight and a crane to arrive. Bob and the forensics team all had motel rooms over in McCormick City, a trooper took over security at the site, so Ashe went home and showered and changed before coming back to the sheriff's office. He found Rachel on the couch and woke her.

"Hey, here is the key to my house. Go help yourself to the guest bedroom and shower if you want."

"You wouldn't mind?" she said through a yawn. "I've been going since four thirty yesterday."

"Go. Take your time. Leave my Jameson's alone though."

Rachel smiled and rubbed her eyes. "If this all works out, I'm buying you, Sheriff Jacobs, and Pat a bottle of whatever you all want." She took the key and left.

Jacobs had received permission to use the old elementary school, slated for destruction. In it was a gymnasium, small but perfect for their use. That next morning about seven-thirty, Ashe, Rachel, and Jacobs arrived back out at the site about the same time as the crane. It lifted the block out of the pool onto a flatbed truck. Once at the school, a large forklift moved the block from the truck into the middle of the old gym.

The wood floors complained loudly and Ashe heard the forklift operator say the block must be two, to two and a quarter tons.

The school was a three-story brick building from the 1940's and stood empty for years waiting on the county to come up with enough money to tear it down. The walls and floors were covered in peeling paint, old wiring, and rotting insulation. Almost all the fixtures were gone. Some graffiti in the halls told Ashe that Hurrt County sucked and the Real Lake Kings had been there, whoever the hell they were.

The gym was built for elementary children and not the larger high school crowds, so only a small set of retractable wood bleachers lined one wall. Several college-aged-looking people were sitting there as a teacher or professor took roll call.

Bob was in charge with a senior crime lab technician to help. They introduced themselves to a South State University criminology professor who brought about a dozen forensic science students working on their post-graduate degrees. Another professor shook hands all around and introduced six or so archeology grad students to assist. All these adult students had volunteered to assist in any capacity in order to be a part of opening this concrete block and exposing what was inside.

Outside, a big satellite news truck pulled up with a van following it. More young people piled out and began setting up an awning and lights as the truck lifted its satellite dish into place.

Oh Lord. Better not be just a dog.

"Rachel," Ashe said. "I think we should set this up as a controlled area. Black out the windows to prevent on-lookers, news media with telescopic lenses, you know. And control the access to both the parking lot and this room."

"Uh-huh," she said. She'd noticed the news crew outside. "How can we black out the windows? Paint?"

Ashe shook his head. "Hey, Sheriff, you have an account at the hardware store, right?"

"Yeah, why?"

"We need to use it. We need five or six big boxes of fifty-gallon black leaf bags. Or maybe rolled plastic vapor barriers, whichever is cheapest. Also, a lot of duct tape." Ashe pointed at the rows of tall windows.

Jacobs nodded. "Good thinking, I'll get some of our young volunteers on that," he said.

"I'll handle the access control piece," Rachel said.

"Uh, actually, you need to be involved with whatever happens next right here. I'll get the security set up," Ashe said and went and looked for one of the deputies.

In a couple of hours, they were ready. There was no electricity, so they moved the generators from the site into place to power the high intensity lighting and big work fans. A big air compressor outside powered the air tools from handheld cutters to bigger jackhammers.

The windows were covered and they used crime scene tape to tape off the outside area for twenty yards in every direction with Deputy Minor stationed at the parking lot entrance.

The news crew didn't look happy when Ashe backed them up a few yards, but they eventually obliged when he promised Sheriff Jacobs would give them a statement in exchange for their cooperation.

"Sir, excuse me," a young woman Ashe recognized from TV asked. "What is your name please?"

"I'm, um, Pat, Patrick K. *Speakes*," he said, and turned and walked back inside.

Back in the gym, Ashe noticed everyone had some sort of official identification, so not having anything from Hurrt County yet except his badge, he used his old Metro Retired Police ID hung on his shirt pocket.

Evidence cameras rolling, everyone wearing the right protective gear, with big air-powered saws under the direction of Bob, they started in on the concrete block.

This time, Mark Portals didn't ignore the call from Ashad.

"Mark, what is all this I'm hearing from down there? Your nephew hired armed guards and confronted the ADA?"

"Rollin, I cannot get any straight answers from him. I believe the sheriff and your state police agent may have found a body out at the DBA site. That's what's on the news anyway. I think this is making him act, ah, a bit out of his head."

Ashad was silent on the phone for a minute or so then said, "Mark, your damned nephew has been out of his head for years.

News! I warned you about this, and we agreed to *lower* our damn profile! He was supposed to surrender himself by now."

"Yes, and he agreed, but...I'm sorry, Rollin, I don't seem to hold much sway over him anymore. He told me yesterday he'd give himself up, but, ah, I am not convinced."

"Then, my old friend, I feel our agreement is null and void. They catch him, they prosecute him, but you...*you* need to stay out of it."

Mark exhaled sharply. "I understand. Let the chips fall where they may, but I want you and the investors to know I'm rock solid and prepared to do whatever I need to in order to see this project through."

"Good," Ashad said. "I'll let them know. I'm going to send some help to the ADA there to get your nephew in custody. Do not interfere further."

"I'm sure he'll appreciate that. Listen, I mean it when I say I am thoroughly committed to this, no matter what," Mark said.

There was another pause from Ashad. "Good, Mark. I'm glad you said that."

The teams from both the crime lab and the university were cautiously but steadily cutting away everything on the concrete block that wasn't near the cavity. The forensics students had some new handheld radar scanner they were applying to the flat sides and then, like kids at Christmas, marveling at how much detail it could reveal.

"It's so clear!" Ashe heard one female student exclaim, so he walked over to look at her smartphone display that was linked to the handheld radar.

Ashe couldn't make anything out of it, but he was glad she was enthusiastic.

It was afternoon and the inside of the gym was hot from the lights and the tools despite the fans. He polished off his fourth cup of coffee and tossed the cup into a big box they'd set up for trash. He didn't sit down for fear of falling asleep.

He'd stripped off every layer he could and was down to just a T-shirt and jeans. He noticed almost everyone else had done the same, especially those working with tools right under the powerful lights. He made a special effort not to look at the female students who probably should have thought more about undergarments than they had when leaving the hotel this morning.

There were small groups of college "kids," as Ashe thought of them, sitting on the floor in circles looking over the scan printouts, some standing by to relieve those working on the block, and some others serving as "pit crew" members, rapidly changing out saw blades. Another couple of them found an old basketball and were playing horse at the other end of the gym.

Sitting on the floor with her back against a wall, Rachel wore a set of earbuds and was staring at her phone. Despite her being cold earlier, she had stripped down to a tank top and fanned herself with a manilla folder.

Jacobs left for a couple of hours to run to the sheriff's department then returned and was sitting in a lawn chair, looking at some paperwork.

"Oh, who the hell is Deputy Speakes? He told the damn press I'd give them a statement?" he shouted, looking at Ashe.

Ashe shrugged. Rachel shrugged.

Four more hours went by as the generators droned a steady beat and the air compressor outside added a staccato vibration. Ashe yawned and stretched. His next couple of blinks might lengthen out a bit.

"There!" someone yelled. All the tools stopped.

Ashe turned and looked at the senior crime lab technician who was on a short scaffold. Three of the university students were with her and pointed at something from the top of the block.

"No, wait," the lab tech said. She used a paintbrush to carefully wipe away some concrete dust and debris.

Ashe saw Jacobs and Rachel get to their feet.

"Yes!" one of the students yelled. "It is a body!"

In a second, it seemed every one of the university students and the forensics lab techs converged on the block. Ashe tried to get where he could see but gave it up as they crowded forward. Rachel had come over and stood close beside him.

"Make way, make way!" Bob said and had to pull at the shoulders of the students to get closer. He climbed the scaffold and examined what they'd uncovered.

"Give me that handheld," he said. The female with the smartphone climbed up and handed him the unit while holding her phone so he could see.

"Bob," Rachel said. "Anything?"

"A minute, Agent Hume," he replied and moved the handheld in tiny overlapping circles.

"That's it!" someone screamed and then the entire ensemble erupted into cheering.

"Okay, okay, everyone back off and let Agent Hume and the sheriff up here," Bob said.

The students and lab techs moved back, grabbing out their phones, and began taking photos.

"Hey, dammit! Nothing online, nothing on social media! You all signed NDAs to get to work here! I mean it!" one of the professors said.

"What do you see?" Jacobs said as he climbed up with Rachel.

"It's a corpse, all right. I can see a hand and parts of a black plastic bag," Bob said.

"Ashe, get up here!" Jacobs shouted. The lab tech hopped down to make room for him.

Exposed from a broken corner of concrete was unmistakably a crushed human hand, still mostly enclosed. It was reaching out and upward, based on the orientation of the block. The block had been set in the gym to match how it had been removed from the pool, so what was facing up out there, was up in here.

Ashe looked closely. Strips of decaying black plastic were between its fingers.

"That's...bizarre," Ashe said.

"What? What's bizarre?" Jacobs asked.

Rachel tilted her head sideways, as if trying to imagine the orientation of the body. "It's as if she is reaching up, meaning, her head and shoulders are...down...deeper," Rachel said, mimicking the hand and arm position.

"Where?" Jacobs said. He moved quickly back and forth on the scaffold trying to see what Ashe and Rachel saw. "Show me!"

"Sheriff, imagine her lying on her back, facing up, but her head is down deeper in the pool than her feet. Then her arm here is extended up, away from her body," Ashe said.

"Hey, is that 3D image compiled yet?" Bob shouted to the

senior tech.

"Yeah!" she yelled.

"Okay, everyone off the scaffold so we can get evidentiary video and photos," Bob said.

Over nearer the door, a table was set up that held a laptop computer and a big screen TV as a monitor. A pair of students had been working on the GPR scans.

"Check this out, Dr. Dufflin," one of them said to Bob and clicked open a file.

Bob came over with Ashe, Jacobs, and Rachel and stood and stared at the monitor. The display came up multicolored and sharp. The image showed the surrounding concrete as white on the display; the cavity showed up as gray.

The body was bright blue.

Rachel had been right. She lay on her back, facing the top of the pool. Her head, such as it was, was crushed to only a few inches thick, was leaned back and at the very deepest part of the pool. Her shoulders and down her back arched upward following the pool floor. Her legs were intertwined and bent, like she'd been forced down into the bag. The display didn't clearly show her feet.

But her upper body and arms were extended, *not* like in a bag. As the student rotated his computer mouse, the image moved around on the screen to show her from all sides.

She was bent over backward along the steep downward sloping angle of the pool. Her head bent back, and what put a chill into Ashe was what he saw next.

It looks like her mouth is open. Her arms out in front of her, he thought.

"Oh, God," Rachel said.

"Exactly," Ashe said. "The legs are collapsed, compacted, bent close together. I bet there will be plastic all around them.

"Her...arms," Rachel said. "It appears they are out of the bag and..."

"Reaching for something?" Jacobs said.

"Or trying desperately, futilely to stop the hundreds of pounds of concrete suddenly pouring over her," Ashe said.

"Shit," one of the students said. "You mean, she...was alive?"

"Bob," Rachel said, taking out her phone and dialing. "Get back to work and get me an ID on this body, and get me DNA."

Ashe left the gym after seeing it would still be hours before they would know any more. Rachel had called Price to update him and then called Pat. Ashe couldn't help but notice she had Pat on her phone's speed dial.

On his way up town, Ashe stopped near the courthouse and looked over at Harold Marsh's office. There was no one on the road behind him as he sat at a stop sign, looking at her window. He decided to risk it and pulled over and called her.

"Hey, I'm outside. Can you talk?"

"You bad boy, my attorney has advised against it," she said. "I'm not supposed to be talking to the prosecution."

"I want to discuss something, can you come go for a ride?"

"Okay, but, *Clyde*, you mustn't run me out of the state while I'm out on bond," Stevie said.

In another minute she appeared at the office door. The old reserve Deputy Franks stuck his head out of the front door and recognized Ashe, so he let Stevie go out.

She was dressed for work but as always, she had a slightly suggestive take on her business wear. Ashe admitted to himself it almost hurt to look at her, and what he wanted to say to her, he easily could have said over the phone.

But, he *wanted* to see her.

She wore a white puffy blouse over a mid-thigh black silk skirt. The ache in his throat returned when she smiled and trotted over to the truck. She was still tan enough she needed no hose and her bright-red pumps set off her red belt and a red flower lapel pin.

"Is this…yours?" she asked, looking at the truck.

"A loaner, hop in."

"I'll try, but this little skirt…" she said, and giggled and mock-groaned as she pulled herself up backward into the high truck seat with her legs together then swung them in. She fell over when she made it in and her head fell against his lap.

"You good?"

"I made it! And I didn't give anyone a panty shot either!" she said and laughed. She got herself upright and wiped her hair back from her smile.

Ashe started the truck and drove lazily down country roads away from town so they wouldn't be seen together.

"We're just… riding?" she asked. "My lawyer will be *so* pissed at me."

"Remember the last time we just had a nice time riding around?"

"No, when?"

"I rented the convertible. You played hooky from work," he said.

"No…wait, was I, um, *high*?"

"Several glasses of wine high."

"No, that wouldn't do it. I must have had more than that, or I'd…hey! You called me a litterbug!"

"That's it. That was a wonderful afternoon."

"It was. I mostly remember the afterward, but, Ashe, I was probably wasted."

"I liked you a little tipsy back then, I suppose. It was, I guess, sexy," he said, but she shot him a look.

"I know, I know," he said.

"Baby, there was nothing sexy about it. I had to figure that out myself."

They drove on, aimlessly for a few more minutes.

"Tell me about why you are texting with CJ," he said.

"I thought this was more personal, not business. I'm tired of all this." She leaned over and put her head on his shoulder.

"I'm tired too, Stevie. This is personal *and* business. I need to know."

She held up a finger and poked him in the forehead. "If it's business, I should have my lawyer with me."

"This is me and you. Why are you texting with CJ? Do you know where he is?"

She sighed and smiled, and Ashe knew she was about to say something vague and cute.

"Don't," he said. "I need you to know how much danger you are in. I need you to take this more seriously. Do you know where CJ is?"

"God, Ashe! Mood killer! I *am* serious and, no. I have no idea where he is!"

"Honey, when did you last see him? Is he still in town? If you withhold any information, anything at all about this, your immunity deal could be in jeopardy!"

"I haven't seen him since the night those men tried to get you but he keeps texting me, look," she said and pulled up his texts on her phone.

Ashe didn't stop to look at her phone but even glancing as he drove, he could see there were maybe a dozen texts from him, the most recent telling her he was going to give the DA a statement to clear his name.

She had responded to a few, warning him to be careful, asking that he give himself up. It was almost like she cared about him.

"Texting with him? Why?"

"He texts me. I don't respond much, if at all!"

"Looks to me like you are encouraging him," Ashe said.

"I am *trying* to get him to trust me and give up. Harold knows all about this."

"Give me his number, I can have his phone location pinged."

"I thought you guys would have tried that already. Besides it's always a new number."

"Do you get that he's toying with you? Using you to try and decoy us."

"Duh! I figured that one out myself, big-shot detective! Besides, I couldn't show the texts to you or even talk to you, remember? I have turned over all the text messages to my lawyer. You know, the judge? Harold Marsh? The guy you sent me to."

They drove for a bit more, then Ashe saw where they were. He hadn't noticed he'd even gone in this direction, but once he realized their location, he turned down a familiar road. They passed a sign that read, *No Trespassing.*

"I know this is serious. I'm sober now…mostly. I know CJ can be dangerous, but not to me. He'd never hurt me, so I am fine, Ashe."

"Honey, I have to tell you something you're not going to like hearing. You're right, I shouldn't even be talking to you. But…I …can't help myself."

She kicked off her shoes and curled her legs up onto the seat beside her then turned to face him, her back against the passenger door. "Mister Ashe, did you bring me all the way out here to try and seduce me?"

"No, I need to show you something about your CJ Portals," he said. "I think I brought you out here to show you…"

"There is a much more comfortable sofa in the office…"

"Stevie, *please*, this is serious. Listen to me!"

"Okay, shoot. Whoops! Poor choice of words!" she said and giggled to herself.

Ashe sighed. "Ah shit, you've been drinking!"

Stevie tried to keep looking at his eyes, but her eyes darted about for a beat before answering.

"No! Damn, Ashe."

But he didn't believe her. "We found a body out here at the Doorbella site. I don't know for sure yet, but it will be Georgia."

"I knew you guys were out here looking for…wait," she said as her smile and laughter shut off. Her face grew dark, her body tensed. She looked around and seemed to recognize where they had arrived.

"There is a …*was* a farm over there," she said. But it had been reduced to a part of the huge concrete pad being built.

Ashe pointed out her side of the truck. "See that big depression over there, where the broken concrete is?"

She nodded.

"Sinkhole, a big one."

"Sinkhole? Really?"

"Uh-huh. While you and CJ thought you were conning that farmer, he was conning you. That sinkhole collapsed under all the early work done out here. Maybe it will ruin the whole thing, especially if there are more."

"Why are you showing me that?" she asked, but Ashe could tell her bright mind was racing ahead. She knew why.

"Georgia Murphy. She must have found out about it when she worked at the L&T."

"Wow, I haven't seen this. They've done a shit-ton of work out here," she said.

"Georgia found out about the sinkhole and must have thought she and Tony could make something for themselves out of it with Mark or CJ," he said.

Stevie frowned and looked around more. "I hate to say it, but that was within her personality. Certainly within Tony's."

"That means Susan Marlin probably knows," he said.

"But, Ashe, that would mean she's at least superficially involved. She must have never said anything or..." Stevie didn't finish her sentence.

"Yeah, exactly. Rachel Hume has her under protection now."

Ashe drove farther down the road and onto the DBA site and over to where the pool was and parked.

"This is it? This is...where you were working yesterday," she said, not really a question. "I helped procure some of this land."

Ashe pulled up close to the pool site. "Yeah, you did. You and CJ."

She shot him a look then twisted around in the truck to look over it all.

"Now look. They cut a huge block of concrete from the deepest end there and transported it to town to work on. This afternoon the state crime lab uncovered a hand."

"Georgia?" she asked.

"Georgia. Not definitively yet, but...well, Georgia."

"Oh my God. We worked this area together. She and I drove out here after a sale and she had some...together we did a...right over there, I think. There was a farmhouse that was empty."

Ashe ignored her. "They used radar imaging and can see a face. They'll get teeth maybe. Bone marrow for sure. We'll have DNA soon."

All the brightness and playful sexiness drained away. Stevie looked shocked as if she never really expected anyone to find Georgia.

"She was in...this? Way down there? In concrete? I thought...*you said*...she was buried."

"Stevie, CJ did this. I don't know if we'll ever find out who exactly killed her, but it doesn't matter. CJ did *this* part. Your 'harmless' friend, CJ Portals! He and his Concrete Crew shoved her in a big trash bag and then poured a couple tons of concrete over her. And there's more."

She looked at him with a face taking in the horror of his words. She shook her head slowly, not being able to absorb it all at once.

"I'm telling you this, not to be cruel, I know you loved her, but I wanted you to see this for one important reason. CJ Portals did this. I need you to *feel* this, to *know it* in your bones! Yes, honey, you *are* in danger from him!"

"Ashe, I guess I…" she said and then just stopped.

"He's flirting with you, texting. Let me guess, he's asked you to meet him, right?"

She looked at him still in a bit of shock. "How would you know? But, yeah. He wants to surrender and give himself up, but to me. He asked me to help him," she said.

"Christ!" Ashe said. "He wants to meet you, alright. Him and his new 'Guys' want to get you alone."

"I don't know…I wasn't going to."

"Where? Where does he want to meet? C'mon, snap out of it. No more texting with him and telling us afterward. No more pretending he couldn't do this, or that he was just trying to save my life the night his men attacked me!"

She shrank back from Ashe as far as she could in the truck cab.

"Stevie, dammit! The same men who killed Billy Clark and tried to kill me *and would have killed you*, are the same ones who took Georgia Murphy down this road to this very spot. Look down there, where that missing section is!"

She rolled down her passenger door window and looked into the pool. It had grown dusky out, but construction lights gave off enough light to see. She opened her door and got out, this time not worrying about her skirt. She walked barefoot over to the edge of the pool and looked down into it.

Ashe joined her. "There, way down there. That's where they not only took her body to just *dump it* but where they killed her."

"They…killed her? Here?"

"Where and when has he asked to meet you?"

"Ashe, God as my…I wasn't going to meet him. I was going to try and talk him into surrendering to the sheriff or John Price."

Ashe just shook his head. "I think as they poured concrete over her, she tore through the plastic bag they'd stuffed her in and tried to get up, but she was head over backward and her legs were shoved into the bag. The concrete pouring onto her would be terribly heavy."

"My God, Ashe, my God!" Stevie ran back to the truck and climbed in, slamming the door behind her.

Ashe walked over to her open truck window.

"Where did he want to meet you?" he asked.

She just lowered her head.

"Stevie, please, honey. Where and when?"

She drew in a breath, her chest hitching as she did. "This Saturday night. Near the lake, near your dad's place, actually, where they are building a…"

She snapped her head up and looked wide-eyed at Ashe. "Where they are starting to build new condos."

"And CJ's company is doing that? Concrete work, I'll wager."

"I don't know," she said. "You think he was going to kill me too?"

"Or use you to get away, I don't know. But you're a powerful witness against him and his uncle and he didn't pick another construction site for no reason."

"Georgia," Stevie said to herself.

"She was fighting, right to the end. But the main point is this," he said.

She started to cry but looked into his eyes.

"She was alive when CJ buried her in concrete."

CHAPTER 29

"**A**she, can you hear me?" Rachel said over Ashe's cell.

"Yeah, I'm almost back out there," he said.

"It's her. We confirmed it's Georgia Murphy semiofficially. The techs and the students uncovered enough to see her tattoo. The one on her shoulder," she said in his ear.

Ashe looked over at Stevie as they drove the back way into town. She probably couldn't hear Rachel, but Ashe decided she would figure out their conversation from his part.

"The dolphin?" he asked.

"Oh, my poor Georgia," Stevie said.

"No, the cinder block and…hey is that Stephanie Collins there with you? Where are you?"

"Don't get on that, don't worry. But the body, DNA?"

"Dammit, you can't tell *me* what I'm to be concerned about, this is my case! You shouldn't be with her…ah shit."

There was a lengthy pause as Ashe drove into town, then Rachel came back on.

"Yeah. Bob and the lab techs got samples we should be able to collect DNA from. She's crushed and damaged of course, but also parts are remarkably well…preserved."

"What about the plastic bag? Any clothing? Anything we might be able to get any *other* person's DNA from?" Ashe asked.

"Can *she* hear me? Ashe, take me off speaker," Rachel said.

"No, you're not on speaker. Well?"

"Well…yes. We have large pieces of the plastic and some of her clothing. They've reduced the block now to just her and what concrete we need to keep her intact. Bob is taking it by van to the state crime lab here in a few minutes."

"Her."

"What?"

"*It* is a *her* now. And we'll need CJ Portals' DNA and Paul Milton's," he said.

"Yeah, okay, *her*. I get that," she said. "Pat is on it getting CJ's from his clothing they seized during the search of his place and the Concrete Crew office in Metro. The sheriff said they have Milton's. They did a mouth swab during his jail intake."

"I would get Tracy Davis's from Carson County as well, just to be thorough. I'll ask Jacobs about her fingerprints, too. You still at the gym?"

"Yes." Rachel paused again then said, "*You?*"

"Ten minutes."

Stevie stared at Ashe as he put his phone away. "So?" she finally said.

"So, I shouldn't discuss what we talked about. Bad enough you heard what you heard, *Bonnie*."

"Oh, kiss my ass! It's confirmed now, right? The tattoo I told you about?"

"Yeah, it's her. They have enough to get DNA like I said before."

They pulled up at the rear of Harold Marsh's office and Ashe parked beside her car. They sat there for several minutes and didn't talk, staring out the windshield.

He couldn't know for sure what Stevie was thinking, but by her face and the way she clinched her fists and then pulled at her skirt, she was both angry and afraid.

"Look, you can't tell anyone yet. We have to get the tests done and then be ready. You have things inside you need?" he said. "Go get them. I'll follow."

"I want to go home," she said softly.

"That can't happen. Word will get out, if it hasn't already. There were some college students helping so I'm assuming this is all over social media. If CJ is within a hundred miles or just ten, he'll be even more desperate now. I'm going to arrange protection."

"I don't want to be holed up in some motel with a cop."

"Just until we catch him," Ashe said. "Now let's go get your stuff."

Stevie sighed loudly then threw open her door and got out.

Inside the office, the old judge had apparently gone home. Ashe drew his pistol and a small flashlight and walked through every room; Stevie close behind him. Once he was sure it was safe, he followed her to the room she'd been using as an occasional bedroom and Stevie picked up some clothes and toiletries.

She started to grab her laptop and some papers, but Ashe put his hand on her arm.

"No, I don't know if he's phished your email and got some kind of malware tracker on your computer."

"You really think he would come after me, Ashe? Why wouldn't he just run?"

"He can't run. Oh, he'll run eventually, just not yet. His ego won't let him until he's finished with you and me. Maybe then."

Stevie started to argue but gave up, and they went back to his truck. He drove them to the old gym. Rachel was outside about to get into her car and when she saw Ashe and Stevie pull up beside her, she made a terrible face.

Ashe hopped out and walked over to Rachel.

"You are a bold piece of work, my friend," she said to him. She crossed her arms and shot Stevie a glare over Ashe's shoulder.

"She has information we need to catch CJ," he said.

"Oh, I'll just bet. And her lawyer?"

Ashe ignored that. "CJ wants to meet her Saturday. To surrender, he says. I know, it's bullshit, but we can maybe set a trap."

Rachel snapped out of her pissed-off mode and back to special agent mode.

"Wait, you think staking her out as bait would even work with him? It's probably against policy, not to mention neither Pat nor I trust her, Ashe!"

"You're right, it's a risk," he said. "I don't think he'd risk being caught for only her. But maybe he'd risk it for her *and* me."

Rachel thought for a minute. She looked over at Stevie, and the irritation returned to her face, then she turned and kicked at a rock.

She jabbed a thumb over her shoulder in Stevie's direction. "She's willing?"

"I haven't asked yet. We need to put her into protection first until we come up with a plan."

Rachel shook her head. "No."

Ashe blinked. "Uh, no?"

"No. Stop thinking like a moonstruck teenager. If she disappears from this small a town, CJ Portals will know it in five minutes. He probably knows she's been out with you now."

Ashe turned and looked at Stevie, sitting in the truck waiting. She looked somehow smaller to him as she stared back. She had to know they were talking about her, but she still gave him a faint smile.

She trusts me.

Ashe spoke to Rachel while still looking at Stevie. "You're right. We can loosely surveil her. Bug her office, put a tracker in her clothing, whatever Harold Marsh will allow. But she has to stay in sight somewhat until Saturday."

"I don't know, I want to talk this over with Price and my bosses," she said.

"She's seen where her friend died horribly, out at the site. It's real to her now," Ashe replied.

Rachel stepped over and looked Ashe directly in the eyes. "I think she's been playing for both teams for a while now and whatever you've told her, she tells CJ Portals."

"I don't think..."

"We...*you*, have to know for sure."

Ashe thought about that a second. Deep down, did he have any doubts about her left?

No. Yes. Dammit.

"You're right. We cannot risk this case only on her. But she's valuable to us and to the Portals'. This will work."

"Okay, buddy. I just want you clear on this. We need to work out the details and get her attorney's and the DA's chop before we do anything. No cowboy shit, Ashe."

"Right."

"Now go. Get her back to where she's supposed to be and stay the hell away from her. Everyone is gone here except a few of the students packing up their gear. I'll meet you at the jail in thirty," Rachel said.

Ashe nodded and started for the truck.

"Hey! Stay away from her until it's time, Ashe, I mean it. If there's a next time, I'll have to take official action."

"Yes, ma'am," he said and climbed into the truck.

"Okay, fine. Where am I going?" Stevie said without looking at Ashe. In the passenger side mirror, he could see that she was staring daggers at Rachel.

"Back to your office."

Stevie turned, surprised, and looked at Ashe with a furrowed brow.

"And…we need to talk," he said.

Mark Portals sat in his Metro office looking over the warrant the state police investigators had served on Phillip Crews for their Seacord office. They had hauled off dozens of boxes of files, thumb drives, disks, and almost every computer in the building according to his copy of the warrant's return.

He glanced over at the small service table at the decanter of expensive scotch, but decided against it.

Stay clear-headed. There's no reason to panic. They will not find anything against me.

About the time he had relaxed himself, the worst thing he could imagine opened his door and came in.

"Uncle," CJ said.

"Carl Jack," Mark said.

He motioned CJ in and as he rose to walk around his desk, he noticed a pair of men in ill-fitting suits in his outer office. Both wore earpieces doubtlessly wired to concealed radios and made no attempt to hide it. Their suits didn't fit over what Mark assumed were their guns.

"You've brought protection *here*?" Mark said.

"I'm a target of a corrupt legal system," he said and smiled.

Mark walked over and while glaring at the bodyguards, closed the door.

"They can get through that door if I yell the code word," CJ said, still smiling.

"Well, they won't," Mark said as calmly as he could muster. "Because you are going to dismiss them. Then you are going to sit there while I call the state police and you are going to surrender to them."

CJ kept his smile. "I'm thinking I need to renegotiate my deal. I need that cash up front, then I'm splitting for somewhere warm in a couple of days. You guys go ahead and blame everything on me; I won't be able to be extradited where I'm going."

Mark drew in another calming breath. "CJ, perhaps you haven't heard, but they found that woman from Hurrt County. According to our source at the lab, they identified her based on a tattoo and will get DNA to identify her further."

"So?" CJ said, but the smile had disappeared.

Mark walked over a little closer. "So, they found her clothes somewhat intact and...the plastic bag she was shoved into as well."

"That's...incredible, Uncle. I mean, I'm impressed. Cops these days."

Mark sat on the corner of his desk and leaned over CJ and said in a low tone, "I mean, they have a good chance of finding well-preserved DNA from *anyone* who touched her, her clothing, handled her body, or shoved her into that bag."

"She...they can't...I..." CJ tried to smile again, but it didn't stick.

"Yeah, so listen. If you want to avoid the gas chamber, you let me turn you in. As an officer of the court, if I fail to report this meeting, I can be disbarred. You need me to, well, *coordinate* your defense."

CJ sat and his eyes moved around, obviously reliving the night from two years ago.

Mark pressed his nephew harder. "You wore gloves, right? The entire time you were around her then? I mean, we can explain some incidental hair or tissue transfer, but when you...disposed of her body. You wore gloves, eh?"

"You know she was going to tell Tony Murphy about the sinkholes. She was going to blackmail us to get him out of jail, then *they* were going off somewhere warm!"

"I told you to keep her quiet, not kill her," Mark said. "That, you did on your own."

"You knew we were at your place in Seacord. Everitt got a little rough with her. She was supposed to get high, wake up in a compromising situation where we could control..."

Mark raised a hand to stop him. "I don't care about this; I care about keeping our situation solid with DBA."

"But she hit him and he hit her back...hard," CJ continued. "Too damn hard. And we took her to dispose of her there at the site."

"Oh, yes. Right in our backyard. DBA's backyard, Brilliant," Mark said.

"You," CJ said. "It was you who got the case moved to Metro, even after I told you what happened."

"The murder of Deputy Clark. Unnecessary. Given his children, cruel."

"You know, I don't think I did have gloves on," CJ said to himself. "Never figured they'd find her."

"Be calm. It will be over soon." Mark picked up his office phone. "I'll call the police."

"I cleaned up her apartment. Took care of the sheriff's department, at least I thought I did. I got this as far away from Hurrt County as I could. For...you. Did what you said."

"You got sloppy. Ashe and Sheriff Jacobs pieced together enough—"

"No!" CJ shouted. "That fucking Ashe and his little team of hicks! If he hadn't shoved his big fucking nose into our business, none of this would have happened!"

The door opened and one of the bodyguards came in. "You all right, sir?" he said to CJ.

Mark hung up the phone. "Get out of here!"

"No, get *me* out of here. I'm leaving, Uncle. Thanks for your *helpful* counsel, but if they are going to pin this on me, then I have nothing to lose by leaving!"

"CJ, dammit!" Mark reached for him, but he had walked too briskly out of the office. One of the bodyguards then stepped between them, blocking Mark.

"Get out of here before I have you drug out and charged!" Mark shouted at him. He smiled and then sprinted after CJ and his partner.

One of Mark's secretaries rushed over to him. "Are you all right, sir? Shall I call the police?"

"No, thank you, I will call them myself," he said.

She poured him some water and followed him to his desk chair. "Are you sure? Do you need your doctor?"

"I'm fine, please close the door behind you."

She left, and Mark drank a good deal of the water, then picked up the phone and pressed a speed-dial number.

"Mark?" Ashad said when he answered.

"Rollin, it's worse than we think."

Ashe pulled up to a different side of Harold Marsh's office. As before, he went in with her and checked every room up to the second floor where she'd been staying.

"It's all secure," Franks said. "Nobody's been here since you two left."

"We never left, *she* never left, *I* wasn't here," Ashe said to Franks.

Then to Stevie, he said, "Stay put. Lock the doors, pull the blinds. No texting CJ without us. No calls, no meetings, nothing. Tell Harold we met and what I'm thinking."

"He won't go for it."

"I'll speak with him or maybe Price will."

"I got this," Franks said.

Ashe sighed heavily and looked at her. "I know your damn stubborn streak. You have to listen to me and *please*...do as I say. I need you to remember what happened to Georgia."

"Ashe, be careful yourself. I think he wants you more than me. And...I think he still hears stuff through the sheriff's office somehow. Just a notion," she said.

"Okay, thanks."

Franks started to add something, but Ashe turned and walked out.

In five minutes, Ashe met Rachel and Price at the jail in the sheriff's office. When he walked in, Pat and Breslin were there waiting with Jacobs.

Price started. "Alright, to bring everyone up to speed, I notified AAG Ashad that we have presumptive confirmation that Georgia Murphy's body has been recovered. Final authentication will come from dental records or DNA we can match. Good work to Dr. Bob Dufflin and of course, to you, Rachel."

"Yeah, good job," Pat said, smiling. She looked at him and smiled back.

"I understand you have a theory, a theory she was still alive at the time she was…ah, buried," Price said.

Rachel nodded. "I think, and Dr. Dufflin may be able to confirm, that by the positioning of her hands up and out, and her having torn through the plastic bag she was in, we may be able to establish that. 'That' meaning, she was animate, alive, and that this position could not have happened with an inanimate corpse."

"Any other way of establishing she was alive?"

"If any of the concrete got into her lungs," Ashe said. "Her mouth and nose, sure, but they're crushed. So if any of it was swallowed or aspirated deeply, it'd be a sign of her struggling before being crushed."

Price didn't look at Ashe but stayed focused on Rachel.

"What do we have that connects CJ Portals to this crime scene, if anything?"

"Other than Paul Milton's statement, nothing yet," she said.

Price nodded as he thought about that for a moment. "Okay, thinking out loud, I think I can rebook Paul Milton for First-Degree Murder. Kills his immunity deal, especially if we posit to a jury, he was directly involved. I'd like more on this possibility that she was alive, at least a high percentage of it. I'll hold off on new charges until I talk with the pathologist and get a written opinion."

"So as of now, we can't prove CJ had any hand in this except by Milton," Jacobs said.

"We have the Racketeering and Felony Fraud warrants out, and we can hold him without bond for seventy-two hours while waiting on the lab results. Any progress arresting him, Sheriff?"

Jacobs shifted in his seat. "He's not been here in town. I'd have heard."

"Lieutenant Keagan? Any updates from Metro?"

"Well, yes a little," Pat said. "We got his security company nailed shut by having their license suspended and we served the subpoena for their records. Seems the two bodyguards we met here were ex-employees, at least according to the company lawyer. The one that got away is named Hacker, goes by Hack, of course. The fat guy Ashe caught was fired earlier that day. At least so they say."

"So, no tracking, no locations they might be hiding him?"

"No. The company gave us two safe houses they use and he's

not been to either."

Price exhaled and tipped his chair back, balancing on its hind legs.

"So, how is he paying for all this? His company is not working, no cash flow. Rachel?"

"Carl J. Portals has two banking accounts and three credit cards we can identify. We've got tracers on his cards, but his bank accounts don't show any withdrawals for over three weeks. I suspect he has an offshore account and I have the Financial Crimes desk on that."

Price looked at the table in front of him and drummed his fingers on it. "How does he move around, buy gas for his car, eat, hell, how does he pay for bodyguards?"

"Ex-armed bodyguards would want cash," Breslin said. "And a lot of it, given they have to know he's wanted."

Jacobs asked Breslin a question at the same time Pat and Rachel started talking about how to check on offshore fund transfers.

"Excuse me. Anybody ask Mark Portals?" Ashe said.

Everyone stopped and looked at him.

Finally Price looked at Ashe, but it was if he didn't want to. "He's only slightly more likely than his ex-girlfriend to be funding CJ," he said.

Ah, there it is. "Stevie? She's broke," Ashe said.

"I can confirm that," Rachel said. Both Ashe and Pat turned and looked at her. She shrugged. "I got a subpoena and ran her finances after she was arrested and have been tracking her money as well."

Damn. She's thorough.

"But, Mister Ashe, I think you may have a sideways kind of point. I think we need to get Mark Portals working our way. Rachel, you subpoenaed his Hurrt County law firm office records? Let's get in front of a Metro judge and go after his office there."

"Yes, sir, we've already laid out a case from what we have from here that would support that," she said.

"Okay, go get 'em. Let's start squeezing these people until someone coughs up CJ Portals. Rachel, work that and also let me know any updates on DNA from the lab."

"I'll assist in Metro," Pat offered.

And she called me a moonstruck teenager.

"Before we break up, I want to discuss something else," Ashe said.

"I know you do. Rachel, Lieutenant Keagan, Sergeant Breslin, take off. Let me know if you need any help with the Metro ADA's office. Sheriff, you and Mr. Ashe stand by."

Everyone filed out and as Pat left, he made a face at Ashe that said, *You're in trouble, boy!*

Price closed the door and flopped heavily back into his chair.

Here it comes.

"Mis-ter Ashe. I have asked, directed, shit, *begged* you to stay out of this. I heard from Rachel about your little stunt and your idea. By rights, and just damn GP's, I ought to arrest you."

"He is here because *I say so*, John. You wouldn't have jack-shit on a two-year-old murder without him," Jacobs said.

"I say..."

"You say? *I* am the one elected to protect the people of Hurrt County. Dammit, Ashe here led us to the motive through DBA, led us to the body because of his interview with Susan Marlin! He proved the case was here in *your* jurisdiction, not Metro, and even risked his damn life to tie in the suspects!"

Price just looked at the table in front of him. "Okay, Larry. I know all that. Please hear what I have to say. I am going to be giving all the credit to you and Rachel, though, and *not* Mister Ashe. He has to be a key witness and a victim in front of a grand jury and a trial, if any."

"You're right," Ashe said. Then to Jacobs, "He's right. I don't give a damn about any credit. But we want CJ for Georgia Murphy, not a bunch of land fraud. We need the evidence besides Paul Milton's word to get him."

"Which brings us to your idea," Price said.

"Look, Stevie is not at all involved in Georgia's death, but she helps you establish the motive. The Big Damn Deal of maybe a half a billion bucks is jeopardized by an overzealous woman who probably hatched a get-rich-quick scheme. Portals had to deal with her to keep everything rolling."

"Yeah, and?"

"We need to get CJ in custody. We drive a wedge between him and Uncle Mark. One of them will likely turn on the other when it's murder one."

Price smiled. "They said you were good. Tenacious. Yes, Ashe, that's why I sent Rachel and company after Portals' Metro office. To turn up the heat."

Ashe sat back in his chair and stayed quiet to hear Price out. *He has a plan. I like it.*

"As to your idea. I agree I want CJ arrested here, in Hurrt County, not Metro. Neither Rachel nor the state AAG's office nor Metro PD's leadership can be involved. I'll speak with old Judge Marsh about Ms. Collins' involvement."

"So we are on our own?" Jacobs said.

Price shrugged. "It has to be that way, Sheriff. See, I am…ah, I'll say *uncomfortable* with how our attorney general's office with the sudden cooperation by Captain Speakes have been *managing* this investigation."

Ashe smiled to himself. *He knows more than he's saying. I agree. Speakes spread the P.I. rumor and Ashad is too buddy-buddy with Mark Portals. Good man, Price.*

"As to the details of your tricking CJ Portals, I leave that to you two since, hell, you'd do it anyway. All I ask is in order to have a clean, unbiased investigator to put in front of a jury, leave Rachel out of it."

"I think we can manage that," Jacobs said. They got up and as Price started to leave, he paused at the office door.

"Ashe?"

"Yeah?"

"I need CJ Portals alive, please."

"I'll do my half of that," Ashe said.

Price left and Ashe closed the door and turned back to Jacobs, getting right up to his ear.

"Stevie seems to think that CJ is getting information from someone here, be careful."

Jacobs nodded and walked with Ashe back up to the front of the jail, but stayed behind as Ashe walked out.

Across the town square, Ashe saw a familiar face so he got in his truck and drove around the jail to an old broken-down car wash at the edge of town and parked in one of the stalls. In five minutes, a Ford Explorer he'd never seen before pulled into a different stall.

Ashe walked around the back past an old dumpster and slid into the back seat of the Ford.

"What do you need from us?" Pat asked, smiling.

"Aren't you supposed to be holding your girlfriend's hand on the way to the big city?"

"Up yours, you're the one getting sloppy over a chick in your old age!"

"Well, for what it's worth, Rachel's smart, aggressive, and too good for you."

"You two done?" Breslin said and openly sighed.

"I need bugs. For phones and the office where Stevie works. Her car too. Also, the smallest tags you can get to put on her person in case we get separated," Ashe said.

"Can do," Breslin said.

"And nothing to Speakes. Our boy DA has developed a mistrust for him *and* for Mr. Ashad."

"About time. You think you can bait CJ out of hiding?" Pat said.

"Oh, I'm going to make myself damned irresistible."

CHAPTER 30

Ashe watched as an electronics technician from Metro set up her equipment on a motel room table in McCormick City, twenty-eight miles from Hurrt County. In an adjoining room, Pat was on the phone while two other officers from Metro Police and a uniformed state trooper milled about.

Seems we have disregarded Mr. Price's desire to not involve outside agencies.

Outside, Breslin, another Metro officer, and a state trooper were posted to watch the parking lot. They had all arrived in vehicles that were older, unmarked, and not police-types. There were vans, pickups, and older SUVs; almost all were imports. They were taking no chances.

"She's here," Breslin said over the radio.

Ashe picked up his portable radio. "Watch for tails. Maybe go circle back the way she came," he said.

"On it. I'm sending Officer Novak in with her," he said.

The outer door to the adjoining room opened and Stevie stepped inside with the blonde Metro police officer who had posed as his orderly back when he'd left the hospital.

"Hello again," Ashe said to her. She smiled back and closed the door behind them.

"Hello, Lieutenant," she said. "I'm Jean Novak. We sort of met at the hospital."

"Hello, Lieutenant," Stevie said. "I'm Stephanie and we sort of met at a gunfight."

Novak looked curiously at Stevie who gave her a sarcastic fake smile in return.

"Stevie, in there. Give the tech your phone and they're going to scan you for bugs," Ashe said. He took her by the arm and led her through the adjoining door.

The room with the technician was getting crowded, so Pat and the others walked to the adjoining room. Pat was still on the phone and had it to his ear with his hand over his other ear. He nodded at Stevie as they passed each other.

Ashe sat in a chair and watched as the technician took Stevie's small clutch-type purse and checked it with a wand that had a circular loop antenna. She slowly pulled it through the loop back and forth several times while watching her laptop screen. Then she set the purse down.

"Phone," she said to Stevie.

Stevie produced her smartphone, and the tech checked that it was off per previous instructions. She moved the phone through the loop for several passes. A small light went off on the wand and a "beep" sounded on her laptop.

"Bug," she said.

"What?" Stevie said and started to reach for it.

The tech took it over to the table where her gear was laid out and opened it up expertly.

"Then someone knows I came here," Stevie said to Ashe. "They might know what's going on!"

Ashe shook his head and pointed to a small device plugged in near the outer door. "That's a signal jammer. It's like a hot spot but in reverse. We had one in the car that brought you as well."

The radio in the other room made a crackling sound then Breslin's voice came across.

"All clear, both ways, no trailers," he said. Ashe heard a trooper respond to him.

The tech examined the inside of the phone and found a tiny part that didn't match. Then she worked on her laptop a minute. "Got it," she said.

"You have the frequency?" Ashe asked.

"We don't even have to add ours. We can just hack this one." She looked up at Ashe and added, "Whatever they hear, we'll hear."

"Good, okay, now check Ms. Collins, herself. Novak, you get ready too. We leave in ten," Ashe said.

"Chig, Rachel says she's ready on her end. She wants to coordinate the time just right," Pat said after hanging up.

"Okay, Pat. You text her when we're sure the rat is in the trap. That way they can't warn each other."

"Got it. Hey, where is Sheriff Jacobs?"

"In Seacord doing Sheriffing stuff. And being very conspicuous about it."

Ashe saw the technician was ready for Stevie, so he stepped out of the room as she peeled out of her jeans, leaving only Novak and the tech as they had Stevie strip. He'd told her this was coming.

"Pat, your girlfriend, Rachel. She's a hell of a cop for a statey," Ashe said.

"Yours is a lousy informant," Pat said. "You sure she hasn't screwed the deal already?"

"Well, we'll know soon enough."

Ashe took Pat to one corner and spoke in a low tone. "Buddy, just do me one favor. If shit gets real, promise me you'll get her out. I'll take care of myself, just get Stevie to safety."

Pat started to say something, probably wise-ass in nature Ashe assumed, but then just said, "Sure. Your funeral."

"Let's hope not. Thank you, Pat. Seriously, for all of it. For all of this." Ashe gestured at the rooms and the people.

Pat leaned back in close to Ashe. "Now don't you get all squishy on me, or try to kiss me, I'll knee you in the jimmy. Besides, this is mostly compliments of Captain Speakes," he said.

Speakes?

"Why the heck would he provide all this assistance to Hurrt County?"

Pat shrugged. "He told me and Danny this morning to get whatever we thought would be needed to get CJ Portals. And yes, to your point, I too, found it a little odd."

"Huh. Gift horse, I guess. Let's oblige him and nail the bastard."

The tech stepped out and had her equipment packed into a case with wheels. "We're done. When we leave the room, it's burned. No radios, no phones. And I just killed their Wi-Fi."

"She's ready?" Ashe asked.

"They both are," the tech said and walked out toward an old van.

Ashe looked into the other room and caught a glimpse of Stevie stepping in front of a mirror to fix her hair, then another Stevie doing the same thing.

Novak had pulled her longish blonde hair up and donned a dark-brown wig. She was fixing it to look like Stevie wore her hair.

Looking them over carefully, it was obvious there were differences; Novak was an inch or so taller and more athletically built. But at any distance, wearing the same clothes, the disguise would work.

Stevie shot Ashe a sharp look through the mirror. "How come you didn't have to strip for Mrs. Spock?" she said.

"Well, for one thing, I *want* CJ to know *where I* am," he said.

The road that led to the cabin Ashe's father had owned was built of rough gravel and dirt. As recently as a month ago, Ashe had been up to it once it was his and worked on the boat the day Pat came down from Metro and he had met Danny Breslin.

Except it wasn't. As he and Stevie turned off the main county route onto it, it was hard packed and widened, ready to be paved. He drove the small used SUV they'd been given down to the lake and he saw what had happened only in a month.

There were a dozen or more concrete pads and footers poured for houses and probably larger condominiums. About a hundred yards away along the shoreline was the start of a marina.

"Hoy crap," Stevie said. "Skee-ah's been busy."

Ashe's cabin and the lake's main boat dock were to the right where the road split as it approached the lake, but he turned to the left.

"We're not going to your cabin? I did a lot of estate work so you could have it, *Clyde*," Stevie said.

Ashe just shook his head and drove for about two hundred more yards and parked out of sight under a tall carport next to another old cabin.

She made a curious face but followed him inside.

Once in, Ashe said, "Us" out loud, seemingly to no one.

"Us?" she repeated.

Ashe ignored her and went around closing blinds and curtains, so Stevie followed suit and helped. Once they were done, and the cabin was almost completely dark, Ashe switched on the small light above an old electric stove.

"Okay? Happy? Now, are you going to fill me in?" she asked.

"This is Cabin Two. It belongs to your lawyer and my dad's best friend, Judge Harold Marsh," he said as he walked into a dark bedroom where a hunting spotting telescope sat on a tripod just behind a window. Being careful not to disturb it, he slid back about three inches of curtain then peered through the scope and made a tiny adjustment.

"Take a look," he said.

Stevie bent down and looked. "Ah. That's your cabin, all lit up."

"Tonight, that is Cabin One."

"Hey, there's your new girlfriend pretending to be me."

"Uh-huh, probably a lot less dramatic too. Danny Breslin will soon come in my truck, pretending to be me."

"So to be more like you, he will act all asshole-y and use a walker?"

Ashe cut his eyes at her.

"Nut-uh," she said, wagging a finger at him. "You started that."

"Anyway…" he said.

"Oh!" she said and stood up straight. "You're trying to fake out CJ so he goes to their cabin," she said.

"Um, yeah. See, you said *he* wanted to meet *you* out here to surrender. He's lying of course. He also said he'd meet you here in…" Ashe looked at his watch. "About two hours. Second lie."

"You guys texted with him from my phone? Okay, then when he comes, you guys will trap him, right?"

"That's the idea. Except I don't think so."

"You don't? Then what the hell are we doing here? If you have Miss Pony-tail Tight-Butt to stand in for me, why am I here?"

Ashe just smiled at her and walked her back into the main room. He opened a cabinet in the den and took out a palm-sized handheld radio and a wireless speaker. "Ready?" he said into the radio.

"Ready," Novak said, her voice coming across the speaker.

"Ok, start," Ashe replied by radio.

"What is going on?" Stevie said and crossed her arms.

"We have my cabin bugged so she can just talk to us over this speaker. Now, we have some texting for me and you to do." Ashe took a burner phone out of his pocket and fished out his reading glasses.

Stevie moved around and got up on her toes to see over his shoulder. "Who's that texting?"

"You."

She looked at him then seem to get it all at once. "Ah, they took my phone to Cabin One so anyone tracking it would think I was there."

"That's half of it. We believe your phone got cloned, so to speak. You see, CJ has not only been texting you, he may have sent a kind of hidden program by text or email to clone, or copy your phone. Malware, it's called. Anyone with the ability and the access to install a tiny tracker could easily do that. I'm betting he's been reading your texts for quite a while."

"Then he knows I've told *you* everything *he's* told me."

"Uh-huh, I'd guess for months. I can't imagine they wouldn't want to keep tabs on you. Who you talked to, what you said. See, he's been one step ahead of us this whole case. I think this may be why."

"He knows where I've been and everyone I've called or texted. Yeesh!"

"And yet he nonetheless wanted to meet you *here*, tonight, near the concrete construction sites he manages. Still think he wouldn't hurt you?"

She crossed her eyes and made a face at Ashe, then said, "Okay, so that burner isn't yours. Anyone looking at my stuff won't recognize...wait, *hey*! You cloned your own phone."

"Bingo. This one will show us anything my number does, but you can't track it. Metro Narcotics uses this system all the time. My actual phone is in Breslin's pocket back in town."

"Oh, so since you think they are tracking you, they will believe you're still in town?"

"Yeah. If CJ hired someone who could do all this to you, I'm going to exercise extreme caution and assume they might somehow have got a track on my cell through your texts or email to me. Anyway, soon Breslin-as-me will text 'I've arrived' or some such. He'll act as me coming to see you in my truck, and to any one of his security guys that don't know us that well in the dark, they'll report we are in the cabin together. That should trigger CJ, if he takes the bait."

Ashe's burner beeped. A text from "Stevie" read, *@ your cabin. Can U drive up?*

"Hook is in the water," Novak said over the speaker.

On my way, Breslin-as-Ashe texted, then he pressed the mic button on the radio three times.

Ashe responded by two long clicks on the radio.

"He'll wait a few minutes then leave town. My truck is at the jail, so hopefully they're watching it. Better yet, maybe they've planted a tracker on it. And them that are here already and watching my cabin, will see it arrive."

"They're watching Cabin One," she said and looked through the scope.

"Hope so. They're supposed to be somewhat professional ex-military security dudes."

Stevie then walked around the darkened den in circles for a minute, obviously thinking about the setup.

"Ok, cool. They texted CJ from 'me' telling him to please give up. Like I've said before."

"Uh-huh, back at the motel. He replied he'd arrive in two hours."

"You guys just sent a text from 'me' to 'you' asking 'you' to come see me here at your cabin."

"Uh-huh."

"You're betting he's reading these."

"Hope so. Or at least following the tracker he put in your phone. We're just covering every base we can think of."

"So he sees me texting you and you say you're coming up…you're taunting him."

"Yeah, I believe he tipped his hand when he was at the courthouse. He kept using you and mentioning you to get a rise out of me. That told me what I needed to get him to come out here, maybe even suspecting a trap."

"*Me.* And *you,* us, together in Cabin One."

"Uh-huh."

Stevie smiled her sarcastic smile again. "So what am *I* doing here? I mean *me* as *me,* not *her* as me?"

Ashe held up a finger and went and checked on Novak through the spotting scope again. He clicked the radio once, then paused, then two fast clicks.

"All good," Novak said over the speaker.

"Well?" Stevie asked.

Ashe went into the kitchen and grabbed a bottle of water from a small cooler with Stevie following him.

"Such a nice night, eh?" he said.

"Dammit, Ashe! What is the reason?"

"Aggravating as hell when someone avoids your direct questions, ain't it?" Ashe said and smiled.

She balled her fists and fake punched in the air at him. "Oh...you! You...ass!"

"Sit down and hear me out."

She found a stool and flopped on it, staring angrily at him.

"See, I don't think this will work," he said.

She dropped her frustrated look and raised an eyebrow.

"In fact, I think CJ is very smart. He has to know this is a trap. The Metro guys and the sheriff think it will work. Me? I don't think so."

Stevie seemed to take this in then said, "Why?"

"Too easy. I think he will figure out my cabin, Cabin One, is a trap and then he and his guys will start looking around. They'll come here."

"Again, why me? Hell, for that matter, why *you*?"

"Because, Stevie. My *Bonnie*. If they go there to Cabin One first and pick up that it's a trap, well, then they'll search and find us here. We then need to show we're the real McCoy's. They'll have to come for us and then our friends still can still catch him."

"Okay," she said slowly. Still not getting his full meaning.

"But if they come here first, to Cabin Two, ignoring Cabin One? Then we'll know."

"Know? Who? Oh," she said. "You and your pals still think I might have somehow tipped CJ off."

"Like I said, just being over cautious. Covering every base we can think of. If it means anything, honey, *I'm* sure of you, really I am. But this way, the DA's office and the sheriff are sure."

She drew in a sharp breath and exhaled loudly. "They *still* doubt me? I gave them everything I had on the Portals'. I was booked into jail because you asked me to! Dammit, I should storm out that door! Damn them and damn you too!"

She started for the door and Ashe didn't try to stop her.

"Go ahead! Go right the hell ahead! Might prove their point though. Price and your lawyer worked this out as part of your continued cooperation."

"Shit," she shouted.

The radio made a static noise.

Ashe went and looked through the scope, saw everything was still good, then turned to her and said, "So, shut up."

"Uh…"

"I said, *shut up*. Don't you dare pitch a fit with me! *You* are in this mess because of *you*, not me, not them…*you*! You and CJ defrauded half a dozen people out of their land. Ok, you were kept drunk or high or whatever, but you did this to yourself!"

Stevie looked at him as if in shock. He was giving it to her hard and he felt his face get hot. This time he let it.

"Shit! I kept you out of this every chance I had and even smuggled you to your lawyer. Pat wanted to arrest you then and *he was right*!"

Stevie stared at him, frozen at the door.

"You want to fuck up the rest of your life, fine! I tried to help you when the lockdowns started and you spat at me. Your friends you used to party with tried to kill me and they did kill Billy Clark!"

Her mouth fell open.

"I don't mean to beat you up too bad. I know it's been tough for you these past two years, but everybody told me I fell in love with the wrong girl. Everyone said it! Me? I said *no*! I said, she's a good woman. They said I was an idiot. That I embarrassed myself in my old age by falling for a young, pretty-faced woman like you. A party girl, they called you."

Ashe threw his water bottle across the room. "I've heard the talk in town, they say 'no fool like an old fool' behind my back! Then, even still, here I am standing up for you tonight, even still. God! I really *am* an old fool."

"Ashe, please. I…I do…"

The radio clicked. "We got company," Pat said.

Ashe snapped out of his anger and snatched it up. "Where?"

"Two black Suburbans just parked up the road from the split a ways. Lights off since they left the main hardtop."

"I heard," Novak said by speaker.

Then the radio clicked four times. Breslin was in motion. *B there in 15,* he then texted to Stevie's phone.

"Notifying Team Two," Pat said.

"It's in motion. Someone has taken our bait," Ashe said softly. Then he turned back to Stevie. "You want to leave, looks like you have a ride."

"Please, Ashe," she said. "Sorry. I'm a brat."

"Men," Pat said. "Looks like five. Two with carbines. Three with pistols out. Moving to the split in the road."

Stevie suddenly looked frightened. "Which way? Can he tell? Us or the other cabin?"

"Be quiet, sit in the corner, stay away from windows."

She did as he said.

Ashe drew his Smith 9mm and went to the bedroom to look through the scope. In Cabin One, Novak held a wineglass in her hand.

She's really playing the part well.

"Are they coming?" Stevie whispered from the den.

"Yep."

"To…here?"

"We'll know in about thirty seconds," Ashe said, then press-checked his pistol.

CHAPTER 31

It was Mark's third attempt to call Rollin Ashad that evening with no answer when his Metro office doorbell rang. He was alone and angry at being ignored, so he went to the main entrance and forcefully threw the door open.

"What is it!" he yelled and then noticed the group of police officers assembled at the door.

"Mark Portals, we have a warrant to search these premises," Rachel Hume said as she displayed her badge.

"You're that state investigator working in Hurrt County, aren't you?" he said.

Portals took the warrant and started reading it as several men and women pushed past him wearing navy-blue windbreakers and ball caps that read *State Police* and *Special Agent*. They carried banker boxes and packing tape, and two of them held video cameras.

"Wait, now hold on!" Mark barked.

"Keep going," Rachel said.

"I need to read this before anyone touches anything!" Mark's cell buzzed in his pocket as he was trying to look at the warrant and keep track of who had swarmed into his office. When he pulled it out, he saw it was Ashad.

"Rollin! Dammit, I've been trying to call you!"

"Mark, now is the time for you to step up *like you said* you would."

"Excuse me, Mr. Portals, our warrant includes your phone," Rachel said.

"Well, Agent Hume, I just *happen* to be on the phone with the deputy attorney general!"

"Good, put him on speaker," she said.

"Huh?" Mark said but pressed the button.

"It's Hume, sir. We're here and the other team is at his residence," she said.

"My what?" Mark shouted. "Now hang on! Rollin…"

"Agent Hume," Ashad said over the speaker. "I am here with the Metro DA. Execute your warrants. All of them."

"Yes, sir," she said, then Ashad hung up.

"Wait, I need to get him back. What did he mean all of the warrants?" Mark said.

Hume donned vinyl gloves and plucked Mark's cell phone from his hand, dropping it into a bag and handing it to an evidence technician.

"Mark Portals, you are under arrest under the state RICO act," she said.

A trooper stepped in and placed handcuffs on Mark Portals and read him his rights as he was walked outside.

Mark was smart enough to stop talking.

Rachel pulled out her own phone and texted Pat. *TM 2 is a GO.*

"Ashe, that female officer playing me, she's alone over there!" Stevie said softly, still sitting in a dark corner. "They might hurt her."

"Oh no," Ashe said. "No, she's not alone."

"Ashe…you might have been right. Cabin One," Pat said over the radio. "Also, Team Two has The Big Turd under wraps."

"You see Little Turd?" Ashe asked.

"Not yet, but time to go," he said.

"Be ready!" Ashe said loudly, but not to Stevie.

"What?" she asked.

"Shh," he said.

He heard a tiny sound from the kitchen. It might have been the kitchen door lock. Ashe left the scope and walked softly through the den where Stevie sat, to check on it, his gun low and close to his chest.

He heard the sound again, slightly louder, so he bladed his body and tried to peel carefully around the corner to see into the kitchen, one small "slice of the pie" at a time.

It didn't work.

"Well hello, Mister Ashe!" CJ said, pointing a Glock straight at his face. "I guess your little ruse didn't work."

"Didn't it? You're here," Ashe said, lowering his pistol. CJ had the drop on him.

"CJ, please put down your gun and surrender," Stevie said and stepped toward the dim kitchen light.

"Hello, baby," he said. Ashe took benefit of the momentary distraction and holstered his gun before they took it.

"Come on in, Mister Hack," CJ said over his shoulder.

The other bodyguard, who Ashe had thought of as "Military Guy" before at the courthouse, stepped in and secured the kitchen door behind him. He held a short M4-looking carbine with a three-point sling across his chest and neck.

"Get on your knees, both of you!" Hack barked.

"Hold!" Ashe said loudly.

"Hold? My ass!" Hack said and hit Ashe in the face with a sharp left hook.

The punch dazed Ashe and he felt blood running from a cut on his face. The bastard was wearing a big ring.

"Get her in the car first," CJ said. "Ashe, your friends outside and across the way will be much too busy for a while to help you."

"You're not here to surrender?" Ashe said, holding his right jawline, trying to stop the blood. "I'm shocked."

"Go," CJ said to Hack. "I'll get his gun."

Hack lowered his carbine muzzle to walk toward Stevie, moving between Ashe and CJ in the cramped kitchen. Right as he passed, Ashe stepped forward and quickly with both hands slapped CJ's wrist, causing his Glock to clatter to the floor. Then as a continuation of the movement, he stepped forward with the other foot and drove a hard palm heel strike right to CJ's nose.

CJ fell over backward tripping over his own feet and down against the stove. But he recovered almost immediately.

"Not bad, old man. You still throw a…*medium* punch," CJ said, wiping blood from his nose off his face with his sleeve. "But I think…"

Ashe jerked out a kitchen drawer and hit CJ over the head with it, smashing it and the silverware inside all over his head.

Hack tried to turn around and raise the carbine in the tight quartered kitchen, but Ashe threw what was left of the drawer at him then grabbed his M4 sling and twisted it around Hack's arms and neck until he had to let go with one hand. Then Ashe shoved the gun receiver and optical sight straight into his face. He tried to foot sweep him at the same time but missed, so Hack threw out a quick punch that connected solidly into Ashe's face.

Then at almost the same second, CJ hit Ashe hard on the left side of the face from behind, maybe trying for his old wound, causing Ashe to stumble toward the den and backward.

Hack untangled himself enough to punch Ashe hard again in the jaw then roughly grabbed him and threw him all the way into the den and onto the floor. Hack took off his rifle sling then using the butt of the gun, hammered him in the gut twice.

"*Oh crap. Now,*" Ashe said, but having had the breath knocked out of him couldn't get any volume.

CJ found his Glock and said to Hack, "No shooting. Not here."

"Not anywhere, damn you!" Stevie yelled. She sprayed CJ in the face with the thick foam from a fire extinguisher she'd grabbed off the wall.

CJ screamed in pain and again dropped his gun and clawed at his face, pulling off large gobs of foam, his eyes tightly sealed shut from a direct hit. She fired the extinguisher again at CJ then sprayed it at Hack who ducked most of it until it was empty. She then swung the red metal can like a bat hitting CJ hard in the neck.

"Stop that! Drop it!" Hack yelled at Stevie and started to turn toward her.

Ashe hooked his left foot behind Hack's left ankle then drove his right heel into Hack's left knee, sending him to the floor hard, yelling and holding his knee.

"Ok, you're toast, pal," Hack yelled. He abandoned his carbine and started clawing for his pistol as he struggled to stand back up.

And that's when the Hurrt County SWAT team arrived.

Big Ed Bell kicked in the front door and, seeing Hack holding a gun on Ashe, lifted him by the belt and collar and threw him across the room. Ashe got to his feet much more slowly than he wanted and drew his own pistol to arrest CJ, but he was busy at the moment.

CJ was on his hands and knees as Stevie continued to clobber him over and over with the empty fire extinguisher can.

"You…you! Ooo! You!" she yelled each time she hit him, but she was beginning to breathe harder and was slowing down.

Sheriff Jacobs rushed in with Pat and Deputy Minor as Ashe scooped up CJ's pistol, tucked it in his belt, and Pat caught Stevie's arm to stop her.

"I…I think you got him, *slugger*," Pat said.

Ed Bell had Hack in cuffs and took him, limping badly, out the door. Ashe flopped onto a stool and leaned over heavily on the kitchen bar.

"Deputy Bell," Ashe said.

"Yes, sir?"

Ashe just nodded at the man and pointed at the door. Bell smiled and hauled Hack outside.

"What the hell, Chig?" Pat said, holstering his Colt 1911. "We waited longer than we should have. Why didn't you holler?"

"If I could've, I would've," he said.

"You all right?" Jacobs asked.

"Honey," Ashe said to Stevie, laying his head down on the counter. "You can drop the can now."

Stevie was wild-eyed, her face all flushed and sweaty, and was out of breath. She dropped the fire extinguisher.

Pat got her out of the kitchen and over to a chair in the den as Deputy Minor and Jacobs lifted CJ off the floor and radioed for an ambulance.

"Oh. One thing," Ashe said, without lifting his head up off his arms on the counter.

CJ could only open one eye, but he glared toward Ashe as they handcuffed him.

"Carl Jack Portals, you're under arrest."

They cleaned up Harold Marsh's cabin, did the best they could to repair the front door, then withdrew to Ashe's "Cabin One." Ashe was sitting on a sofa holding a bag of ice to the left side of his head again as Stevie kneeled beside him, dabbing at his right side with a cool washcloth.

Pat and Jacobs took turns on his landline as cell coverage was iffy inside, giving updates to Price and Rachel.

"Hey, what was all that 'hold' and 'now' stuff you kept saying in the other cabin," Stevie asked Ashe quietly.

"Our cabin was wired too. Deputy Bell and the sheriff were waiting outside listening for me to call them in. I had them wait, thinking maybe we could get CJ to talk some, but it went south pretty quick," Ashe said, also in a low manner.

"Wait, what?" she said in a louder tone.

Pat said, "We apprehended the men CJ brought without much of a fight once they saw all the badges. I don't think they figured they were being paid to shoot it out with cops."

"Huh," Jacobs said with a hand over the phone receiver. "They quit when they saw that damn big ol' forty-five of yours staring at them!"

"Any word on...ouch, damn, baby," Ashe said as Stevie kept dabbing at his cuts. "On DNA?"

"I just got off the phone with Price. Are you okay to go meet him?" Jacobs said.

"Yes. I'm fine, Sheriff."

"No, you are not," Stevie said. "But, uh, getting back to our cabin also being wired..."

Pat spoke over her. "Well, since all the arrests were made by either Hurrt County or state troopers, I'm taking this Metro gang back to the city," he said.

"Wait...Breslin? Dan Breslin didn't collar anybody?" Ashe asked.

Pat smiled. "Well...he may have pointed out a couple of CJ's men to the deputies. Them that were, ah, made eager to surrender."

Jacobs shook Pat's hand enthusiastically. "I cannot thank you enough, Pat. I'm glad I got to know you and Sergeant Breslin, uh, I mean *Danny* too."

Pat pointed at Ashe and said to Jacobs, "Keep him out of trouble," then to Stevie, "Both of you. Call me if you hear anything else with the pathology, okay?"

The phone rang and Jacobs answered it. Ashe stood, slowly, and walked Pat to the door.

"Pat, I want you to think on something," Ashe said quietly. "Speakes, so willingly offering you and this team to assist us. Ashad, pushing through all the warrants on Mark Portals."

"Yeah?"

"Yeah. I have the sinking feeling we have cut off only the tail of a much larger dragon."

"I, uh, was thinking something similar," Pat said. "You think Speakes and them?"

"I think a half a billion bucks is a big, damn, deal. So watch your back."

Pat nodded and patted Ashe on the shoulder. "Brother," he said.

"Brother," Ashe replied and grabbed Pat's large hand.

Pat turned and as he walked off said over his shoulder, "You know, you still suck. You let CJ Portals kick your ass."

"Hell there were *two* of them, Pat. So speaking of asses, you can jump up mine!" Ashe shouted.

"Your girlfriend fights better than you," he said, then quickly got in his car.

After he left, Ashe sank back in the sofa. He was exhausted and ached all over, and then in places he was still in real pain. Stevie meant well, but her dabbing at his head was accomplishing nothing.

"I'm getting too old for this shit, to coin a phrase," he said.

Stevie kissed him on top of the head. "You never looked better to me."

"I got my ass thoroughly kicked tonight." He turned and faced her. "Hell, you did great. You beat the tar out of Carl Jack, girl."

"So…" She motioned with her fingers toward Jacobs. "Am I okay?" she asked.

He leaned over and looped an arm between the sofa back and her waist. He held her tightly and with his thumb, he traced small circles across her back. "Yeah. You did good."

"We should go when you're ready, Price is waiting for us," Jacobs said after hanging up the phone.

"Just one minute though," Stevie said. "Sheriff, you and Pat, and everybody…you heard *everything* we said to each other in the cabin?"

"Uh, Sheriff, can you please have someone escort Miss Collins back to town," Ashe said.

"Yes. With pleasure," Jacobs said. Then he winked at Stevie.

"So…I can go home?" she asked.

"We'll keep an eye on you for a day or so, just to be careful. And we'll also need your statement on tonight's events and full cooperation for the prosecution," Jacobs said.

Stevie stood and, facing Ashe, pressed herself firmly against him. "I'm not done with this whole conversation about our cabin broadcasting what you said to me, *Clyde*."

Jacobs stepped outside leaving them alone.

"You did good. I told you I already believed in you. Now they do too."

"Yeah? I did, didn't I?" She smiled and kissed him on the non-cut side of his mouth.

Yeah, Stevie. You did damn good tonight.

At the courthouse, Price was reviewing a stack of documents and smiling to himself when Ashe and Jacobs arrived.

"First, Mister Ashe, congratulations on not killing every suspect and witness tonight. I see you two completely ignored my desire for you to stay out of this and to not involve Metro or the state police," Price said.

"Hey, I did not call them," Jacobs said. "And I had to use Ashe, I'm low on qualified help."

"I certainly didn't call them, but interestingly, Captain Speakes instructed Lieutenant Keagan to assist tonight with his blessings. And AAG Ashad personally got the stateys involved," Ashe said.

Price looked long and hard at Ashe directly in the eye. Ashe stared back. He hoped Price was on the same channel. Then without replying, Price turned to Jacobs and handed him a small collection of documents clipped together.

"Thank God they did come help, you know," Jacobs said. He read the first page in silence, then flipped to the second and started smiling.

"Yep," Price said. "Thought you'd like that."

"May I know what *that* is?" Ashe asked.

Jacobs offered the documents to Ashe who waved them off. "Glasses got broken, boss, just give me the short version."

"DNA results. First, it is Georgia Murphy for sure. Secondly, the pathologist gives high odds she was alive when they threw her in that pool and…buried her in concrete."

"Shit," Ashe said. "That's…"

"First-Degree Murder," Price said.

Jacobs read on. "Next, from her clothing and the plastic bag, they not only captured small DNA samples to compare, they actually got a fingerprint off a piece of the bag."

"Hot damn!" Ashe shouted and smiled. "Anybody we know?"

"The DNA samples collected as compared with …yada, yada, low percentage of the population…blah, blah…okay, here it is," Jacobs said, flipping to the last page.

"The partial print is 89 percent likely to be Paul Milton's left thumb."

"Mister Assistant District Attorney, I'd like a new warrant on Mister Milton," Ashe said.

"Already done," he said.

Jacobs continued. "And the DNA samples from the bag and her clothing are a statistical-enough match to…Lawrence Everitt, Gerald MacNeal…and Carl Jack, Mother Bitching, Cock Whore, Portals! Enough to be a…ah, hell, Ashe! We got him!"

"Mister Price, I'd also like to request a warrant for the First-Degree Murder of Georgia Murphy against Carl J. Portals, please," Ashe said.

Price pulled out a pair of signed arrest warrants and although Ashe reached for them, Price turned and gave them to Jacobs.

"Mister Sheriff, please serve these warrants. Then after you get your paperwork sorted out, join me for a drink."

Jacobs took the warrants, still smiling, then picked up Price's phone and dialed the jail.

"Place a hold on Paul Milton and Carl Portals. No bond until set by the circuit judge," he said. Then, "Let's go, Ashe."

As they started out, Price said to Ashe, "You too, Mister Ashe."

"Huh?"

"Join us for that drink."

"I'd like that," Ashe said and gestured at his own face. "But maybe the ER first."

At the jail, Ashe and Jacobs waited for the jailers to pull Paul Milton up to an interview room. The jail nurse had come and patched up Ashe's cuts some, but told him he'd need stitches soon.

After she left, Ashe said, "Sheriff, there's one thing. I know Tony Murphy at the state pen has refused to talk to us, but we have a lot of information now that he doesn't know. I think we should try again."

Jacobs shrugged. "You are free to try. I'll make the call."

In his office, Jacobs called the "LE Agency Only" assigned phone number for the state prison.

"This is the Hurrt County sheriff calling on official business for inmate Tony Murphy."

"Is it important? He's already in lockdown in the hospital," the prison official said.

"Hospital?"

"He has Covid," the official replied.

"Yes. It's important. If he doesn't want to talk to us, tell him it's about his wife and CJ Portals," Jacobs said.

They went to get a phone to Tony, so Jacobs turned on the speakerphone and left to charge Paul Milton with murder. Ashe waited alone several minutes.

Eventually a prison hospital technician came on the line and turned on a speaker at their end.

"What do you people want!" Murphy sounded like he was very sick.

"My name is Ashe. I worked for Metro when you were arrested and I'm deputized here in Hurrt County."

"Then in both places, you tried to railroad me!"

"I know you had nothing to do with Georgia. We found her."

"What? Bullshit."

"We discovered her body at a construction site here near Seacord. She was buried in concrete. We have arrested CJ Portals and Paul Milton for her murder. Everitt and MacNeal are already dead."

"Yeah, I see the news. You killed them."

There was a long pause. Ashe could hear him sniffing and clearing his nose.

"She...you found her body? CJ told me she was still missing but he was looking for her. He was supposed to be taking care of my mother."

"He lied. He and his Concrete Crew that you used to work with killed her then buried her at the site. I don't know about your mother, but I'll check."

Ashe hedged a little, not mentioning she was buried alive. *No reason to hurt him further.*

"You got him?"

"Here in jail. But I imagine he'll be up there soon enough."

Then for the next few moments, Ashe could hear Tony start to sob. The hospital tech came on and discontinued the call.

Ashe drew a breath. He'd done what he could and got up, slowly as everything was sore, and went to find Jacobs. A dispatcher showed him where the secure interview room was and buzzed him in.

Jacobs had obviously told Milton what was going on and after being rebooked for murder, he burst into tears. "I'm so sorry," he said between sobs.

"Horse shit," Jacobs said. "You're only sorry and all crying now for *yourself*!"

Ashe waited outside the room until Milton was led out by a jailer and placed back down in confinement.

"Bring me Carl Jack Portals next," the sheriff said.

His voice has a bit of a lilt to it. "You're enjoying this," he said to Jacobs.

"Damn straight. You know, I was partially elected because of Georgia Murphy. I was never sure I'd ever get a handle on it, either. I just wish Sheriff Laughton was alive to know this."

"You did fine, Larry. These people here are lucky to have you as sheriff."

Jacobs took a long breath. "No, I was lucky to have *you*, Ashe. This is all because of you."

Ashe started to protest. A lot of people were responsible. But before he could say that, Jacobs held up his calloused hand.

"In our line of work, you don't very often get to say this, but I'm saying it, Ashe. You weren't alone, I know, but every step of the way, you led us to tonight. You damn sure have *bled* more than anyone. Plus, hell, you almost bought it that night, but you never backed off."

"You don't have to…"

"Yeah I do. I know I ain't got the words, there's no way to really thank you, but I can think of one thing," Jacobs said. Then he handed Ashe CJ's warrant for murder.

"*You* can arrest him."

Ashe felt his own smile spread across his face, cuts and all. "A true pleasure, boss."

CJ was led into the interview cell, shackled and in a white jumpsuit. His face was mottled, swollen, and one eye was bright red from the fire extinguisher foam.

He looked at Ashe and the sheriff and realized they were looking at his face.

"*Women*," he said and shrugged. Then to Ashe said, "I'd be careful with that one."

"Carl Jack Portals…" Ashe started.

"Uh, rights first please. And I'd like to have my lawyer present," CJ said.

"Which lawyer would you like to contact?" Jacobs asked.

"Take a fat flipping guess."

"Sheriff? I think maybe he means Mark, his uncle. CJ, you want Mark Portals as your lawyer?"

"Yes, damn you," he said.

Jacobs nodded and took out his cell and dialed a number. Rachel Hume answered.

"Hey, Agent Hume. Sheriff Jacobs here. CJ Portals is in custody and wants us to put him in touch with his uncle Mark."

"Okay," she said. "He can hear you."

"Uncle, I…"

"You stupid piece of crap! You can go screw yourself! Stupid, stupid! I hope you rot in prison along with your stupid father!" Mark yelled. "I not only will *not* represent you; you are lucky in that I won't help them *hang your ass* from the damn courthouse roof!"

CJ sat back, apparently stunned.

"Now, last chance! You keep your stupid mouth shut!" Mark shouted.

Rachel came back on. "Mark Portals is being held against a two-hundred-thousand-dollar bond on our state RICO charges, but given the money transfers and what not, I think the Feds will have something to discuss with him by Monday."

"Thank you, Rachel," Ashe said. "For everything."

"We'll talk soon. You owe me a lot of paperwork, Ashe," she said and hung up.

CJ sank even farther in his seat. "I don't understand, my uncle is..."

"In Metro's custody. You're here with us until you see the circuit judge," Jacobs said. He then read CJ his rights, but he declined to give a statement.

"Okay. You are held without bond," Jacobs said.

"Wait, *no bond*?"

Ashe nodded. "You have been served warrants already for Fraud and Racketeering. I am adding Aggravated Assault with a Deadly Weapon on a Law Enforcement Officer, namely me tonight, oh, and one other warrant."

"Huh," CJ huffed.

"First Degree Murder of Georgia Murphy."

CJ's mouth dropped open for a second before he recovered. "That's not true! I did not lay a hand on her! I told you; I think Everitt killed her, and most likely by accident!"

"You waiving your right to remain silent?" Ashe said.

CJ shook his head, but said, "Just this one note. I had nothing whatsoever to do with Georgia's death, I liked her, *a lot*, such a sweet girl. But whatever you have is only because I helped Lawrence Everitt bury her body. I'm *that kind of friend*."

Ashe looked at Jacobs. "May I?"

"Go ahead, but just a little."

"CJ, you are a damn liar and a murderer. We have sufficient forensic evidence to not only tie you directly to her entombment in concrete out at the DBA site, but to prove that she was alive while you did it."

The blood ran from CJ's face. "Wait, no. Bullshit, Ashe. She was..."

"Georgia Murphy was still alive and trying to get out of the garbage bag you stuffed her in. The autopsy proves it. She was alive and fighting for her life when you poured a couple of tons of concrete onto her."

"She...couldn't have been... we..." CJ said.

"You buried her alive, CJ Portals. That's worse than murder. You sentenced her to death by *your* hand under a heavy, wet, gray blanket. To lay there, unknown for years under it. Waiting quietly to be found. In the cold and the dark."

CJ put his forehead down on the table in front of him.

Ashe put his head down close to CJ's and whispered in his ear.

"But she is telling us about it now, CJ. From the grave you built for her, Georgia Murphy will no longer be silent."

CHAPTER 32

Four months later

Ashe sat at an outdoor table with a big umbrella overhead outside Roger's Café sipping iced tea and watched the people moving around the town square.

The local businessmen had substituted pastel polos for their dress shirts and ties under their blazers, and the business women wore floral-print dresses without hose and open-toed shoes. The tourists wore as little as possible and sipped iced coffee or fruit slushes as they snapped photos of themselves in the historic old town of Seacord.

Ashe himself was in khaki shorts and a white cotton polo with a big pair of dark sunglasses. He also had his .38 Smith and Wesson revolver which the sheriff had returned to him in a suede pocket holster.

Tilly came out and refilled his tea. She had on lavender cotton shorts and a T-shirt under her apron and as always, still looked remarkably fit and pretty to Ashe.

"Where have you been, Chig? How do you like the new patio? You've been gone for months, I thought you'd run off or something!"

Ashe grinned at her. "Well, let's see if I can answer all that in order. You know about my taking the boat trip. I guess I had to just take off, kind of clear my head. The patio is a nice addition and, oh yeah. I've missed you too, Till."

"Did you go with…"

"No. I was alone. On my boat."

"You took your daddy's old boat out, huh?"

Ashe drew in a breath and released it slowly. "It's *my* boat, Till, or it was. I took it across the lake to the Hurrt River, then all the way down to where it meets the Stuart River. Then up river to Stuart itself. The city."

"Holy smokes, Chig, that's a long damn way," she said as she grabbed the umbrella that had come undone and was pitching about in the gusty late-morning breeze. She pushed it up and locked it back in place.

"A week and a half or so to get there, then I stayed awhile to fish the Stuart River. Then a little over two weeks back. The current, you know."

"I love that old boat," she said as if reminiscing to herself and sat down with Ashe.

"I always wanted to make that trip. Three hundred miles one way. My mom and dad did it the year between our junior and senior year in high school. Dad and I talked about doing it again after Mom passed but...I was always too damn busy and, well, he got old."

"Seems I remember that," she said.

Ashe closed one eye and cocked an eyebrow at her. "Ah...Miss Tilly, you *should*."

Tilly smiled suddenly and winked at Ashe. Her eyes got wide as she rubbed her legs together and leaned over the table toward him.

"Oh yeah, now I remember! We had your parent's place to ourselves."

Ashe saluted her with his tea glass. "It is one of the best times of my life, Till. We were so damn young."

She sat back and looked at her watch then cast a glace over her shoulder at her other tables. "You're having a turkey club and sweet potato fries today," she said and hopped up to go put in the order he didn't make.

Ashe sat there, in no hurry to move or progress through his day. He'd selected this exact date to have an early lunch outside on purpose, and he'd picked this exact table for two special reasons.

First, it allowed him to keep an eye on the sally port of the courthouse where a jail van was backed in. He wanted to see a certain someone's "perp walk" in shackles and leg irons out of court and into the van. Then, if he hopped over into the other seat at his table, he could see the same person be walked into the jail. So he waited patiently, sipping tea.

The second reason for this table was less cheery. It was all but the exact spot where Everitt, MacNeal, and Milton had ambushed and shot him.

It was his own subtle act of defiance in the face of all that had been planned and attempted against him.

"I'm still here, boys," he said out loud, and hoped somehow he was heard in the beyond.

Across the street, a different courthouse door opened and out walked Pat and Rachel in dress clothes. It was the nicest suit he'd ever seen Pat wear. He and Rachel walked close together and leaned toward each other as they spoke. She touched his arm or his back every now and then. They smiled at each other a lot.

Good for you, Patrick.

Behind them, Danny Breslin walked out also dressed for court. He noticed Ashe before Pat or Rachel and raised a hand. Ashe lifted his glass and gave him a two-fingered salute. Breslin smiled and saluted back, then he climbed into his Dodge Charger and pulled away.

Good man. Nice to have a new ally.

All this made Rachel notice Ashe, so she and Pat walked over to join him.

"Rachel, you still dragging this big-assed Irish galoot around?" Ashe said as they sat.

"Hey, watch who you call a galoot!" Pat said, feigning annoyance.

"But, you're not arguing the big-ass part?" Ashe said and shrugged at Rachel.

"Damn, boys! Behave!" she said and reached over and pinched Ashe on the arm.

"So, ah, you aren't exactly dressed for court?" Pat said.

"Wasn't going to be a hearing. CJ plead out to the murder, right?"

"Yes, but how did you know that?" Rachel asked.

"I just had the sense someone, or *someones*, would want to ensure this would be behind them as fast as possible."

Pat and Rachel looked at each other. Then Pat said, "What we discussed a few months ago. About only the tail of the dragon being cut off."

"Uh-huh."

"I haven't given up that thought either," she said. "And

coincidentally, Mark Portals has been given another continuance of his court date. Until late next year!"

"Meanwhile here in little ol' Hurrt County, construction of the Doorbella facility continues under new management," Ashe said.

"Phillip Crews?" Pat asked.

"Bingo."

"Hell of a thing," Pat said.

"Patrick, you know as well as I that the rich never really fail. They always find a way to stay rich," Ashe said.

Rachel said, "So, um. You and... have you seen..."

"Nope," Ashe interrupted her. "I'm sure I will, small town and all, but she had a lot of legal problems and had to get her own court dates behind her. Her assisting us helped some, but I heard she was disbarred."

"I guess I want to say I'm sorry about that," she said.

Ashe nodded but didn't look right at Rachel. "Yeah, well. I guess I knew all along we were not going to wind up together. Probably best...for her."

"Her? What about *you*?" Rachel asked and rubbed his arm. "Are you okay?"

"I just took a long boat trip then sold the boat. I'm also selling the cabin up at the lake. Too many neighbors now. Condos and rentals. Tourists. It's not the same. Dad would hate it."

"Damn, Chig, sorry to hear that. That cabin has been in your family since..." Pat said.

"Cabin? Since the fifties I guess," Ashe finished for him. "I'm making a killing off both of them though."

Rachel tapped his arm again. "I asked about *you*, not your damn boat."

Ashe just shrugged again. It was the only answer he had. They sat there quietly for a couple of minutes, enjoying the breeze and the sun.

"You're keeping the house though?" Pat asked suddenly.

"Yes. Forever. Dad, and I think Mom, are still there."

Pat nodded. Then a few more minutes passed until Rachel broke the spell. "Well, despite this scintillating conversation, I need to get back to the city. It's springtime and crime time!" she said.

They chuckled together at that as they stood, and as they started to walk off, Rachel suddenly turned and hugged Ashe firmly around the neck. "You take of yourself."

"I will. You two take care of each other."

"You going to say something smart-assed?" Pat asked.

"No, buddy. Not right now," Ashe answered.

As Pat and Rachel walked off toward the same car, Ashe watched and waited until they were across the town square. Then cupping his hands around his mouth, he suddenly shouted, "Pat, your big ass makes two of hers!"

Rachel started laughing and almost tripped. People on the square stopped and looked at Ashe as if he were nuts. Pat stared back hard at Ashe as he got into his SUV, a faint smile on his face. He mouthed a word toward Ashe.

Brother.

Ashe sat and waited on his lunch a few minutes more, then across the square at a new coffee and sandwich place, he saw her.

Stevie sat at an outdoor table with a man about her age talking and drinking from huge recyclable cups. She wore her hair shorter than before and had on a tiny sundress with her shoulders bare but for spaghetti-thin straps. She was smiling and laughing and staring right at her companion the whole time, fully involved in their conversation. Fully involved in *him.*

Although he couldn't hear, he could see as she laughed out loud in her boisterous and wide-open belly laugh. Ashe had heard that laugh often back in better times and watched as she threw herself against her chair back, head back and mouth wide open. One of her dress's tiny straps dropped off her shoulder and the top of her dress fell some, revealing a good deal of her cleavage. She didn't pull it up but leaned forward allowing her breasts to roll on the tabletop a little, leaning in so he could see.

And she let him.

My God. She really likes this guy.

He decided not to torture himself further and looked back toward the courthouse sally port and the jail van. He didn't want to miss his show.

"She was never right for you," Tilly said quietly from behind him. She must have been there long enough to see what he'd seen. She reached around and put his lunch in front of him, pressing her belly against the back of his head, then put a hand on his shoulder where it met his neck as she refilled his tea.

"I know, Till. I guess I must have really made a fool out of myself."

She stood there behind him, her hand rubbing him for a minute. "No. Not really. The heart wants what the heart wants," she said, then walked away.

Ashe ate and kept up the watch on the jail van, intentionally not looking across the square. He had a false alarm as a pair of court officers came out, but they just had a smoke and went back in. Several more minutes went by, but he sat vigilant. Ten minutes turned into twenty.

"Well hello, *Clyde*," Stevie said.

Ashe jumped a little. She must have walked all the way over while he was trying *not* to look at her.

"Hi there, *Bonnie*."

"You've been gone a long while. Did you make that boat trip?"

"I did. Then I sold it, like I said."

"I couldn't go, for reasons I'm sure you know," she said and sat down.

"You had your own troubles to get through. Did you make out okay with the state bar?"

"Disbarred a minimum of five years, court-monitored probation for five years. So I'm a clerk working for Tom Fischer now."

"You weren't in court today, either."

"I wasn't needed. And...I never want to see him ever again," she said.

Ashe nodded. He could understand that.

"Wait, you mean Mark Portals' Fischer?" Ashe furrowed his brow at her. "Seriously?"

"He was never involved in the...dealings here. He bought an old law office building in Carson County. He's going to restart the L&T with Susan Marlin, too. I'm going to stay out of it mostly, try and help more from behind the scenes."

Ashe was eating his fries with a fork and pointed one at the man across the square. "That's him, huh?"

Stevie turned and looked, her short hair swinging as she did. "Yeah, that's Tom."

"So what's Prince Valiant think of you coming over and talking to *me*?"

"Who?" she said, then looked at Fischer, then back at Ashe.

"Valiant, Prince…it was a cartoon strip."

"Oh, okay," she said. "Oh! I know, like in *Shrek*?"

Ashe shook his head. "No, but…oh, never mind. Is he a good guy?"

"He is very good to me. He's helped me get unsupervised visitation with Nora. Today! We're taking her over to Carson County to that water park where they have the paddle boats and the ducks and all!"

Ashe smiled. "That is fantastic, congratulations!"

"I know, he wants to meet her and I want her to get to know him."

That stung a bit. *I've never met Nora.*

"You and Tom should, um, you know, meet," she said.

Ashe speared another pair of fries with his fork. "Maybe some other day. You have a lot going on," he said.

"Hey, why are you out here today? And don't tell me it's the food."

"Well, *I* do want to see CJ one last time," he said and pointed at the courthouse.

"He's coming out of there? Now? Hell, I better go I guess."

"Hey, Stevie." He reached out and took her hand for a second or two. "You look really good. You look happy. I'm glad for you."

She stared into his eyes and hers began to get moist. Then she looked at his left ear and cocked her head to one side. "That's healed well, kind of. Still, that left ear is cut off flat on top."

Ashe shrugged. "I was thinking of having the other one shaved off to match."

She burst out laughing. "Oh my God, Ashe!"

"It'd be more *feng shui*. Plus, my hat would fit better."

She smiled and stared at him for a moment then her face became more serious. "You are a…you know, I loved you. It took a while for me to really understand it, much less figure it out myself. I know I've always been a mess to you but…why wouldn't we have had a chance? I mean before?"

"I don't know. Why pick at it? You have a new life. Go for it."

"It was my drinking, I know."

"I think that…" Ashe started, then changed his mind. He had really loved her so he had to be a man, *the* man she needed him to be once more.

"Um, for one thing, your music is shit," he said.

That made her laugh out loud again. *That* laugh, the one he loved.

"I think your boyfriend's waiting, Stevie."

"Ashe?"

"Yeah?"

"I want babies. I have to go with someone I think I can build a family with. You know?"

"Yeah." He swallowed hard. "And you should. I...can't be there for you for that. I can't...give you that."

She got up from the table so he did too, then she wrapped herself around him in a powerful embrace. He held her full-on for almost a minute, longer than he should have, but half as long as he wanted. He had no idea what to say, so he let her go.

She stepped back, pulled her dress strap up, and smiled through a few tears.

"I know one thing now, one thing I've learned from you, Mister Ashe. I was loved. You were my first *real* man. You didn't just tell me you loved me, you *showed* me at every turn, every chance, how deeply you cared."

Ashe felt his throat ache and his hands tremble.

Like no other woman.

"You're a good man and even when I was a mess, you never deserted me. I did not deserve you."

"Yeah. I really loved you, too, Stevie."

"I wish...I wish I had first met you today," she said and turned to walk back toward her future.

Ashe didn't feel like he could watch her, but he did anyway. She and Fischer got in his car and left right away, so he sat back in his chair and looked at his watch. It was getting warm out. He wasn't sure how he felt exactly, but he hadn't prepared for the emotions surging through him. He almost didn't give a shit about seeing CJ Portals paraded out of the courthouse anymore, a convicted murderer.

The boat trip gave him a chance to heal inside and out, but today was probably the real last piece of closure he needed. Now, he could move forward with his life.

But to where? That's the question.

He admitted to himself that he was almost a year older and

given the injuries of the last year, he was tired. Slower, less eager to leap out of bed.

A boating term came to mind. *Rudderless.*

Summer was coming and he had absolutely no plans and no one to do them with. So he sat at his post and decided not to plan anything past an afternoon nap. But first, he would go ahead and watch the CJ show about to happen any minute.

"Ashe!" Jacobs hollered from behind him. "Glad you're back. Your trip go okay?"

"Sheriff. Figured I'd see you leading CJ out of the courthouse."

"I couldn't wait for that, I had a lot more on my plate this morning," he said and sat down. He waved down Tilly from another table and made a drinking gesture. She nodded and went inside.

Just then it happened. Two court officers and a uniformed deputy walked Carl Jack Portals out of the courthouse in leg irons and shackles, then into the jail van.

"Hot damn," Ashe said. Jacobs turned around and watched as well.

The van pulled off, CJ was their only customer, and rolled right past Ashe's table. He stood, took off his glasses, and watched to see if CJ would look at him. He didn't, but Ashe smiled just the same.

"Change seats, Sheriff. Quick!" Ashe said. Jacobs jumped up and let Ashe have his chair.

The van pulled into the jail and once again, the officers removed CJ to walk him in. Ashe waved and maybe, just maybe, CJ saw him and knew who he was.

They both laughed a little then Jacobs said, "You've been staked out right here all morning...for that?"

"Yeah, buddy."

Jacobs smiled and then fidgeted with a big legal-sized envelope he was carrying.

"Oh, I should have done this a while ago, I guess," Ashe said. He took out his deputy sheriff's badge and slid it across the table toward Jacobs.

Jacobs furrowed his brow and frowned but didn't take the badge.

"Uh, Ashe. I need you to take a look at this," he said. He laid the brown manilla envelope on the table.

Ashe opened it and a couple of black-and-white 8x10 photos spilled out onto the table. He picked up the first one. It showed a well-dressed man lying on his stomach at a shoreline, half out and half in the water. The clothes looked wet and had sand all over them.

There was a bullet wound in the back of his head. There looked to be a pair of entry wounds in the center of his back.

The body appeared to have been there, or possibly deeper in the water, for quite a while. Even in black and white, the hands and the back of the neck looked extremely pale and bloodless. There were no signs of blood on his head even around the entry wound, which supported his idea the body had been in water for a while.

Meaning, this body wasn't killed where it lay.

The second photo was of the same body but turned over face up. He had no face left. There was only a giant gaping exit wound that had ripped away the entire front of his head just below the eyes.

Large caliber. Likely a rifle.

His chest had two equally big exit wounds close together. The man was in a suit. He had a lapel pen. Then Ashe noticed something else. Something that shocked him.

"Uh, Sheriff, is that an earpiece? Like to a radio?" The photo showed a coiled clear wire running from the body's left ear into his suit jacket.

"Yeah. I've been out *there* all morning."

There? "Where was this?" Ashe said, scanning every detail he could.

"At the lake. *Our* lake, and not too far from your cabin."

"Holy hell," was all Ashe could think of to say.

Then Sheriff Jacobs slowly pushed the badge back across the table toward Ashe.

ABOUT THE AUTHOR

David C. Reed is a retired criminal investigator with extensive experience in major crimes cases, including homicide, fraud, and missing persons.
As a veteran, writer, analyst, and division chief for the DoD, he wrote and conducted courses in special tactics and policing management worldwide.

www.amazon.com/author/david-c-reed
WriteDCReed@gmail.com

If you enjoyed Cold, Dark, and Silent, please leave a review on Amazon!

www.ingramcontent.com/pod-product-compliance
Lightning Source LLC
Chambersburg PA
CBHW021436240626
47153CB00001B/182